### Praise for *On Secret Service*

"*On Secret Service* draws you back into the Civil War and the wrenching days preceding Abraham Lincoln's assassination. The factual details are simply astonishing: You walk the muddy streets, smell the acrid smoke of battlefields, and experience firsthand the inner workings of a vast conspiracy." —Patricia Cornwell

"The author saves the best for last in dealing with Lincoln's assassination, bringing the drama to life by giving each of his protagonists a crucial role as the conspiracy unfolds with expert pacing and suspense. Jakes uncovers the little-known history of espionage and counter-espionage during the War Between the States with his signature combination of meticulous research and epic narrative." —*Publishers Weekly*

"Gripping, exciting, and historically accurate . . . a very good book." —*Library Journal*

"An absorbing study of how human affairs stubbornly fall outside the simplistic categories of 'right' and 'wrong.' " —*Kirkus Reviews*

*continued . . .*

**Praise for the *Crown Family Saga***

*American Dreams*

"Jakes has a grand old time spinning his yarns. . . .
He mixes his fictional offspring with the likes
of Charlie Chaplin and Mary Pickford, making us
feel as if we too have brushed our shoulders with
celebrity." —*Toledo Blade*

"Realistic detail and period color galore keep this
swift-moving story grounded . . . as the
automobile and WWI arrive to shake the republic
out of its golden idyll." —*Kirkus Reviews*

"Historical fiction at its finest, as only John Jakes
can tell it." —*Wheaton Gazette*

"A worthy successor to *Homeland*."
—*The Columbia State* (SC)

*Homeland*

"First-rate . . . chock-full of fascinating period detail . . . brings to life the sounds, smells, and tastes of turn-of-the-century America in a manner comparable to Michener's *Hawaii* and Doctorow's *Ragtime*. An absolute must."
—*Publishers Weekly*

"This intelligently written novel, full of colorful characters, moves swiftly along, vividly resurrecting the America of the 1890s. Quite simply, *Homeland* is John Jakes's best work."
—*The Philadelphia Inquirer*

"A powerful tour de force, a rich, sweeping story of America as only Jakes can tell it. . . . *Homeland*, interspersed with real characters such as Teddy Roosevelt, Black Jack Pershing, and Jane Addams, is a marvelous blend of fact and fiction, the stuff of great historical novels. Another winner from an old pro."—Nelson DeMille

# By John Jakes

*On Secret Service
*American Dreams
*Homeland
*California Gold

## THE NORTH AND SOUTH TRILOGY

*North and South
*Love and War
*Heaven and Hell

## THE KENT FAMILY CHRONICLES

The Bastard
The Rebels
The Seekers
The Furies
The Titans
The Warriors
The Lawless
The Americans

*Published by Signet

# THE
# BOLD
# FRONTIER

## John Jakes

Previously published as
*In the Big Country*

A SIGNET BOOK

SIGNET
Published by New American Library, a division of
Penguin Group (USA) Inc., 375 Hudson Street,
New York, New York 10014, USA
Penguin Group (Canada), 90 Eglinton Avenue East, Suite 700, Toronto,
Ontario M4P 2Y3, Canada (a division of Pearson Penguin Canada Inc.)
Penguin Books Ltd., 80 Strand, London WC2R 0RL, England
Penguin Ireland, 25 St. Stephen's Green, Dublin 2,
Ireland (a division of Penguin Books Ltd.)
Penguin Group (Australia), 250 Camberwell Road, Camberwell, Victoria
3124,
Australia (a division of Pearson Australia Group Pty. Ltd.)
Penguin Books India Pvt. Ltd., 11 Community Centre, Panchsheel Park,
New Delhi - 110 017, India
Penguin Group (NZ), cnr Airborne and Rosedale Roads, Albany,
Auckland 1310, New Zealand (a division of Pearson New Zealand Ltd.)
Penguin Books (South Africa) (Pty.) Ltd., 24 Sturdee Avenue,
Rosebank, Johannesburg 2196, South Africa

Penguin Books Ltd., Registered Offices:
80 Strand, London WC2R 0RL, England

Published by Signet, an imprint of New American Library, a division of
Penguin Group (USA) Inc. Previously published in different formats
under the titles *In the Big Country* and *Best Western Stories of John Jakes*.

First Signet Printing, September 2001
10  9  8  7  6  5  4

Copyright © John Jakes, 2001
Introduction copyright © Dale Walker, 1993
All rights reserved

*Author permissions appear on pages 371–72.*

Ⓡ REGISTERED TRADEMARK—MARCA REGISTRADA

Printed in the United States of America

PUBLISHER'S NOTE
These are works of fiction. Names, characters, places, and incidents either
are the product of the author's imagination or are used fictitiously, and
any resemblance to actual persons, living or dead, business establishments, events, or locales is entirely coincidental.

The publisher does not have any control over and does not assume
any responsibility for author or third-party Web sites or their content.

*Dedicated to the memory of*
*some of the great ones*

*Cooper*
*Wister*
*Grey*
*Brand*
*Henry*
*Schaefer*
*L'Amour*

# CONTENTS

# Preface

## My Love Affair with the Western

It began in 1939 when I saw my first Western movie—*Dodge City* starring Errol Flynn—at the Indiana Theater in Terre Haute. I was seven years old. I crawled under the seat when the guns blazed in one particularly noisy scene (*blazed* is a verb I learned from the pulp magazines).

Flynn turned out to be a moral leper. The history dished up by the script writers turned out to be doctored, if not altogether phony. Still, the picture inspired me to attend all the pseudo-historical epics Flynn made thereafter. The pounding musical scores of Max Steiner and others were always part of the thrilling experience. As I've written elsewhere, it astounds me that musicians with classical European training could so marvelously capture the spirit of the American West.

In the '40s I saw almost every Western picture that came along: big-studio features, serials, and the one-hour Saturday afternoon programmers. I drew the line at "modern" Westerns with singing cowboys in sequined shirts.

I bought and devoured Western pulps such as *The Rio Kid Western*, *Frontier Stories*, *Texas Rangers*, and

*Masked Rider Western*, a blatant rip-off of the Lone Ranger. By the '50s I was established as a writer, selling Western short stories and novelettes, principally to Popular Publications.

In 1952 on my first visit to my then-agent, Scott Meredith, in New York, Scott chewed one of the Life Savers he was using to curb his smoking and said, "I was going to send you over to see Mike Tilden"— the editor who bought my stories at Popular—"but he thinks you're this middle-aged Western guy. If he sees you're just a kid, there goes that market." So I never met the editor responsible for publishing much of my Western output.

By the end of the 1950s the pulps were gone and the market for Westerns was vastly diminished, if not almost nonexistent. Nevertheless, in the years that followed, I would occasionally write a Western and Scott would find some obscure market for it—a resuscitated *Short Stories*, for instance.

I never lost my love of the locales, the history— the genre itself—and so continued to incorporate Western sequences into my historical novels. There is material about the frontier in *The Kent Family Chronicles*—the old Ohio Territory, the Alamo, the gold rush, the building of the trans-continental railroad. *California Gold* is nothing short of a Western, though hardly a conventional one, since it begins in the 1890s and ends in the twentieth century. My good friend Dale Walker said it deserved a Spur Award but unfortunately only made this suggestion after the nomination deadline passed. Western Writers of America requires that the author nominate his own work. I have never liked to hustle my writing that way. I still belong to WWA, but with a marked lack of enthusiasm.

My only definitive novel in the Western genre, *Wear*

*a Fast Gun*, was published in 1956 by one of those small companies that churned out titles for rental library racks found in drugstores. It has been reprinted once or twice. Technically, I also published a Western in 1952. *The Texans Ride North* was a young adult title of about thirty thousand words, dealing with the post–Civil War cattle drives. It was my first book, and I remain proud of it because in addition to having a good story (albeit with no cussing and no romance), it had historical background.

I'm delighted to see this collection in print, with the addition of stories that have not appeared in it before. I don't recall the origin of every story in the book, but some are worth highlighting.

"The Woman at Apache Wells." This is by far the most popular Western I've written, if I'm to judge from the number of times it has been anthologized. I recall very little about the creation of the piece, except that the title came first. Titles were always key elements of my pulp Westerns, although my original ones were often changed by the publisher.

A writer with an impressive list of screen credits maintains that the story deserves to be a movie. Perhaps one day it will be. I've never been sure why it appears so frequently in collections, but I'm happy that it does.

"Hell on the High Iron." One of my novelettes for Popular. Mike Tilden changed my original, equally purple title, "High Iron—Hot Guns."

"A Duel of Magicians." A Western sequence from a novel, the final volume of *The North and South Trilogy*. The Cheyenne magic performed by Whistling Snake is authentic, and the tricks of Magic Magee reflect my own lifelong fascination with illusions and close-up magic.

Often I base the appearance of a character on a

real person. Magee with his wonderful smile was created in the image of the late Flip Wilson, who unfortunately did not get the opportunity to play the role in the 1994 *Heaven and Hell* miniseries. Due to time constraints, Magic's tricks were shown only fleetingly in the picture. The duel with Whistling Snake was omitted entirely.

"To the Last Bullet." My title for this opus was "Outcasts of the Big Snow," which I preferred. But I also liked cashing Popular's check, so I remained mute.

"Little Phil and the Daughter of Joy." This is a story I wrote for my friends Martin Greenberg and Bill Pronzini, who edited an excellent but short-lived anthology series called *New Frontiers* (I came up with the title for them).

I wrote the story under a new pseudonym, John Lee Gray. It was 1989, and I wanted to see whether I'd learned anything about my craft since my pulp days. Also, I hoped John Lee would have a slightly different voice, and was pleased to find that he did.

"The Tinhorn Fills His Hand." My title: "Last Deal for the Blackwater Tinhorn." Just as purple but not necessarily better.

"Dutchman." This story is based in part on incidents in the life of my maternal grandfather. Although he lived as a naturalized citizen in the Midwest, not California, and there was no physical violence connected with his story, at the time of World War I he experienced some of the same anti-German hostility and sad sense of rejection as the character Willi.

My grandfather, Wilhelm Karl Rätz, was born at Neuenstadt-am-Kocher, Germany, in 1849. Around 1870, he emigrated from Aalen, a small town forty kilometers east of Stuttgart. My only living relatives reside there today.

Grandfather died in Terre Haute in 1936 at age 87. He had Anglicized his name to William Carl Retz. I was never able to learn whether this was a matter of pride or protection. It makes no difference, I would have loved him as much either way. But a certain curiosity lingers.

My grandfather's immigrant story was the inspiration for the first novel about the Crown family of Chicago, *Homeland*.

"Carolina Warpath." Three South Carolina historians inspired this 1993 novelette, though none is in any way responsible for the content.

In 1989 my wife Rachel and I took a course in the history of our adopted state from the beginnings to the Civil War. It was one of the most stimulating and exciting academic experiences of my life. The professor, Dr. Lawrence Rowland of the History Department at the University of South Carolina at Beaufort, introduced me to the rousing action of the Carolina frontier in prerevolutionary times. Here we had a veritable Old West in the East of the eighteenth century. Have you ever heard of "cattle-minders"— cowboys of the Sea Islands of the South Atlantic coast? I hadn't. I vowed that I'd write something about the period someday.

Two other University of South Carolina historians who were helpful with sources and advice were my good friend, the late Dr. George C. Rogers, Jr., author of a wonderful little book called *Charleston in the Age of the Pinckneys*, and Dr. Robert Weir, now retired.

Since original publication of the story, two editors, friends, and many readers have asked for more adventures of Nick and Noggins. If only there were more time . . .

My fascination with the state where I've lived for 22-plus years has never waned. Aspects of South Carolina's colorful and dramatic past form the background of a new historical novel I'm writing at this moment.

"Snakehead." This is the second story by the pseudonymous Mr. Gray. Following it, he seemed to return to hibernation.

"Manitow and Ironhand." This one originated in an anthology of new Western short stories I edited with Martin Greenberg. It sprang from my first visit to my grandfather's home town, Aalen, mentioned before.

In the Aalen bookstore where I signed copies of German editions of *The North and South Trilogy*, I saw for the first time the enormous amount of shelf space given to the German-language Westerns of Karl May. He gets the same treatment over there as Louis L'Amour receives in bookstores here.

I'd heard vaguely of May because his characters appeared in German-language Western movies, a couple of which showed briefly in America. One starred Lex Barker. Research into May's books and biography produced "Manitow and Ironhand." More information about May is found in the story's afterword.

I was thrilled when "Manitow and Ironhand" won the 1994 Western Heritage Award as the year's best short story. I didn't have to nominate myself, or hustle shamelessly to win. The award came as a complete surprise.

"Mercy at Gettysburg." Marcia Bullard, editor of Gannett's *USA Weekend*, commissioned this fifteen-hundred-word story for one of the magazine's summer fiction issues. Appropriately, it ran on the weekend of July 4, 1994, and has gained in popularity ever since. For public readings, it's the story I choose. It takes less than ten minutes to perform, and usually produces some tears in the audience. Admittedly it isn't a Western, but to me it has something of the open-air Western feel about it. Hence I wanted to include it.

I'm grateful to New American Library, to my friend and publisher Louise Burke, and to my editor, Dan Slater, for seeing this collection through the editorial process. You can see that I love Westerns. I hope you enjoy what has resulted from that love affair of more than sixty years.

—*John Jakes*
Hilton Head Island
January 15, 2001

# Introduction
# by Dale L. Walker

*"The American West still shines with a timeless fascination. The literature of the West, both fiction and nonfiction, still fires the imaginations of millions around the world."*

—JOHN JAKES

John Jakes's spectacular writing career is bracketed, literally, by Western stories. He began selling them in the early 1950s to such pulp magazines as *Ranch Romances, Max Brand's Western, .44 Western, Complete Western Book, 10-Story Western,* and *Big-Book Western.* His editors thought so highly of these early stories that Jakes found himself featured on the cover of a Western pulp and proclaimed a "top-hand author"— high praise for so young a storyteller.

And:

Jakes's first published book was a Western juvenile, *The Texans Ride North,* published in 1952.

His first adult novel, published by Ace Books in 1956, was *Wear a Fast Gun,* an excellent tale of a new lawman in a mythical Western town that opens with these two reader-snatching lines: "Eli Fallon, commonly called Reb, did not know a solitary soul in

Longhorn when he first arrived there. But in less than sixty minutes, he had shot a man to death."

One of his best science fiction novels, *Six-Gun Planet*, is as much Western as fantasy.

Five of the eight novels of his *Kent Family Chronicles* contain substantial frontier and western material: *The Seekers* includes the stories of "Mad Anthony" Wayne and the 1794 Battle of Fallen Timbers and homesteading on the Ohio frontier; *The Furies* has the 1836 Alamo battle and the discovery of gold in northern California in 1849; *The Warriors* has the construction of the Union Pacific Railroad; *The Lawless* has the western cattle towns; *The Americans* has Theodore Roosevelt's ranching venture in the Badlands in the 1880s.

In *Heaven and Hell*, the third and final volume of his *North and South* trilogy, Jakes writes of life among the Plains Indians, of the 10th (Negro) Cavalry in Kansas, of Indian treaty problems and the betrayal of the tribes by the U.S. government, and of George Armstrong Custer and the Battle of the Washita.

His *California Gold* (1989), a 658-page historical Western in locale and spirit, opens thirty years after the great California gold rush and takes its protagonist, the young Pennsylvania wanderer James Macklin Chance, through all the great events of California history, including the Los Angeles real estate boom of the 1880s, the San Francisco earthquake and fire of 1906, the era of railroad monopolies, labor wars, the citrus and oil industries, the birth of the film business, and even the environmental movement.

Before publication of *The Bastard* in 1974, before that string of eight books, the *Kent Family Chronicles*, that made him a household name and one of the most recognizable, beloved, and frequently read American authors, John Jakes had published forty-three novels and hundreds of short stories in a writing career that began in his sophomore year at DePauw University in Indiana.

John William Jakes was born in Chicago in 1932, the son of an executive with the Railway Express Agency. A voracious reader during the years he was growing up in the Midwest, Jakes enrolled in the creative writing program at DePauw in 1950 and in his second year there sold his first story, a tale of a man pitted against a diabolical device—an electric toaster—to Anthony Boucher of the prestigious *Magazine of Fantasy & Science Fiction*. More amazing for even the most promising of undergraduate writers, he sold his first novel, a juvenile Western titled *The Texans Ride North*, to John C. Winston Publishers in Philadelphia in 1952.

Jakes graduated from DePauw in 1953, earned a master's degree in American literature at Ohio State in 1954, and entered the Ph.D. program there. By now he was married (in 1951, to Rachel Ann Payne, his zoology lab instructor at DePauw), had a growing family and all the attendant responsibilities, and the academic life that a doctorate in literature would have provided seemed less alluring than more immediate gainful employment.

From 1954 to 1971, Jakes worked in advertising as a copywriter, as a product promotions manager for Abbott Laboratories in North Chicago, for ad agencies in New York and Ohio, and as a writing freelancer. By 1971, when he became a full-time fiction writer, he had risen to an agency vice presidency in Dayton.

In those advertising years he wrote fiction at home, in stints sometimes limited to two or three hours a night after a full day's work, but any full-time writer would envy the product of those sixteen years. Under his own name and the pen names Jay Scotland and Alan Payne, Jakes produced forty books and two hundred stories.

He wrote mystery and suspense thrillers, detective novels, fantasy, science fiction, and historicals; he wrote movie novelizations, nonfiction books, juveniles, plays, and stories. He gained a substantial fan following for his Brak the Barbarian novels (which he calls "straight-faced clones of the R. E. Howard 'Conan' series"); his *Six-Gun Planet* (1970), set on the mythical planet of Missouri in which the Old West is replicated, preceded the 1973 film *Westworld* with Yul Brynner, which employed the same essential idea; he wrote the libretto and lyrics for a musical version of Kenneth Grahame's *Wind in the Willows*; and he wrote other plays and musicals that were performed by stock companies.

The year before the debut of the *Kent Family Chronicles*, Jakes's *On Wheels* appeared, a science fiction novel about a future time in which overpopulation forces people to live in their automobiles in a sort of perpetual motion on the interstate highway system. One critic called this novel "a minor masterpiece of social speculation."

Then, in 1974, Pyramid Books got a two-year jump on the 200th anniversary of the American Revolution by issuing Jakes's extraordinary 630-page novel, *The Bastard*, the first title in the *American Bicentennial Series*, also known as the *Kent Family Chronicles*. The series ran through 1980, covering seven generations of the Kent family in eight fat novels (*The Rebels, The Seekers, The Furies, The Titans, The Warriors, The Lawless,* and *The Americans* followed *The Bastard*), which sold an estimated 40 million-plus copies and which became a legend in the book industry. Not only did the series become one of the most successful paper-back publishing enterprises in history, but the Kent saga also marked the virtual birth of a new and sustaining form of popular fiction—the paperback original, multivolumed, continuing-character, generation-spanning, romantic-historical family saga.

Jakes followed the dazzling success of the Kent saga with another series that took up what seemed permanent residence on the bestseller lists, the *North and South Trilogy*. These novels (*North and South*, 1982; *Love and War*, 1984; *Heaven and Hell*, 1987) covered the antebellum period, the Civil War, and the Reconstruction era in two families, one Southern, the other Northern. The first two novels were adapted for a pair of highly successful television miniseries.

The stories in this collection, covering as they do all of John Jakes's writing career, from the 1950s to the present day, form an excellent representation not only of the author's devotion to the timeless American West but of his unpretentious description of himself as a writer-craftsman aiming for the mass market with a singleness of purpose: to entertain.

During the early years of his career, when his primary markets were the pulps, Jakes wrote what has become known as the "traditional" Western story. His more recent Western fiction tends toward the nontraditional, offbeat, historical tale.

In "Carolina Warpath," written especially for this collection, Jakes not only transports the reader to a wholly different "western" frontier—the British Carolina colony a half-century before the American Revolution—but introduces a hero as memorable as Natty Bumppo: Nick Bray. Bray's up-country expedition, with his bulldog Worthless and his sidekick Huger Noggins, to rescue the woman he loves in the midst of hostile Yamassee country, is a tale reminiscent of James Fenimore Cooper.

In "Dutchman" the time is 1917, when America has gone to war against Germany, and the story is a melancholy reminder of how blind hatred can transform ordinary people into something quite unordinary. In "Shootout at White Pass" Jakes takes us to the California Sierras and introduces us to a sheriff who dreams of retiring to Florida—if he survives a confrontation with a notorious outlaw who has come to town. The title, situation, and characters of this story all seem quite traditional, lacking only a *High Noon*–type shootout at the end. There is in fact a shootout, but it is nontraditional and pure John Jakes.

Also nontraditional and Jakesian are "A Duel of Magicians" and "Little Phil and the Daughter of Joy." The former, a self-contained excerpt from *Heaven and Hell*, tells of a search across the great southwestern plains for the abducted son of a white man and of a confrontation between a Cheyenne medicine man and a black "saloon magician." The latter story, which appeared under Jakes's pseudonym John Lee Gray in the first volume of an anthology of original Western stories, *New Frontiers*, is a wry and good-humored tale of a "soiled dove" named Jimmy, her determined plan to do away with Major General Philip Sheridan, and the heroic efforts of a cavalry scout to deter her.

Even in his traditional stories Jakes gives his readers something more than stock characters and plots. A rare locale, for instance, such as the Sierra Nevada, also the scene of "To the Last Bullet" (*New Western*, May 1953). Note the similarities in plot as well as locale between this story and "Shootout at White Pass": both are about lawmen of a rather unheroic sort doing their duty in little mountain mining towns. Written forty years apart, these two stories demonstrate the maturation of Jakes as a writer and how the same basic fictional material can be turned to traditional and nontraditional ends.

Clever little surprises and imaginative situations distinguish all the other stories in this book.

In "The Woman at Apache Wells" (*Max Brand's Western Magazine*, September 1952), a woman named Lola saves Tracy, an ex-Confederate soldier, from a bitter life of outlawry.

In "Hell on the High Iron" (*Big-Book Western*, March 1953), troubleshooter Mark Rome employs some unusual methods to overcome local opposition to the building of a railroad across frontier Kansas.

In "Death Rides Here!" (*10-Story Western*, October 1953), freighter Jeff Croydon fights to obtain a contract to ship barrels of Oklahoma crude oil.

"The Winning of Poker Alice" (*Complete Western Book*, February 1953), one of three short fillers based on fact and written by Jakes on assignment, poses a question about who is courting whom in the case of gentleman gambler W. G. Tubbs and Poker Alice Duffield.

In "The Tinhorn Fills His Hand" (*10-Story Western*, June 1953), gambler Graham Coldfield finds himself in a brace of deadly struggles against illness and a "disease of greed" on the steamboat *River Queen*.

And in "The Naked Gun" (*Short Stories*, January 1957), a little girl named Emma puts an end to the career of mankiller George Bodie.

"I have always had a great love of the Western experience in America," John Jakes has written, "and I have researched and written about it all my writing life. That love for the West and the Western story has not diminished in the forty years I have been writing professionally. The West and the spirit of the

West will always haunt me and I will always write about it."

This collection provides the best introduction to that Western haunting of John Jakes.

# The Western;
# and How We Got It

*But westward, look, the land is bright.*
>                                    —ARTHUR HUGH CLOUGH

The word *west* is central to American reality and myth. But *west* is a chameleon. Sometimes it means a geographic region, sometimes a direction, or then again, a period of time in our national experience.

But however it's used, it brings with it a whole trove of secondary meanings. They speak an alluring language of hope; adventure; riches; escape; beginning again.

The sense of renewal and rebirth contained in *west* goes far back, to Europe and beyond. Thoreau speculated that "the island of Atlantis, and the islands and gardens of the Hesperides, a sort of terrestrial paradise, appear to have been the Great West of the ancients, enveloped in mystery and poetry." Even when the wealth of the Orient, imaginary and real, drew European explorers in that direction, the better, faster route was imagined to lie the other way, and for years, mariners tried to find this fabled western passage.

But it was a series of events on the North American

continent in the nineteenth century that gave the word its final form and densely interlocked meanings:

- West—the way you go to reach the unpopulated country. The gold. Free land. Breathing room.
- West—where the buffalo roam. A vast space beyond the Mississippi.
- And West—a period of time, of roughly thirty-five to forty years' duration—say, from the strike at Sutter's Mill to the massacre at Wounded Knee. Often, this time frame is called the "Old West," a common shorthand for the years encompassing the final explosive thrust of the United States population, native and foreign-born alike, into and through all the empty lands from the Old Northwest to the Pacific.

Some would argue that the "Old West" is better defined by fixing its limits at either end of the heyday of the cowboy—a span much shorter than the first one; only a decade or so. There is something to that argument since, in large parts of the world, the American West is definitely not the sodbuster or the railroader, the owner of the Blue Hotel or the young reporter on the *Territorial Enterprise*. The West is the cowboy, and vice versa, period.

No matter what time period you choose for your definition, one thing's clear. America took *west* and put its own brand on it. Frederick Jackson Turner saw that. In Europe, he observed, the "frontier" was traditionally the boundary, clearly defined and often fortified, between countries; there could be hundreds of thousands of people living settled lives along this kind of frontier.

Eighteenth- and nineteenth-century Americans, on the other hand, transformed the meaning of *frontier* to the edge of settlement, which was sparsely populated and slowly but steadily moving as more people approached.

And if you wanted to know where to find this moving border of civilization, you generally looked west.

The popularity of literature about the West isn't hard to explain. From the earliest European voyages of exploration, accounts of the beauties and perils of remote, exotic lands have exerted a strong appeal on readers. Although some men and women always go out to the unexplored places, wherever those happen to be, a lot more stay safely at home, preferring to do their traveling vicariously.

There you have the reason for the success of *The principall Navigations, Voiages and Discoveries of the English Nation*, as chronicled in three volumes by Richard Hakluyt, the geographer. You understand why people savored the journals and diaries of the epochal Lewis and Clark expedition. Or rushed to buy all the guidebooks to the California gold fields (frequently written by men who had never seen them).

But we're dealing here not with advice to the goldseeker, or descriptions of the flora of what would turn into the states of the Pacific Northwest. We're talking fiction. "The Western," to use a familiar name. Europeans and others have written them, but as a genre, Americans invented them.

The Western was, in its first life, an Eastern. Although part of our frontier almost always lay to the west—the far reaches of Virginia; the more remote and legendary Kentucky—for a while other parts lay down in the Carolinas, or up in the forests of New

York. Western authors owe an immense debt to the authors of "Easterns"—Fenimore Cooper and all his literary kin, including his now largely forgotten colleague from the South, William Gilmore Simms. During the antebellum period, Simms's historical frontier novels were nearly as popular as Cooper's had been. But he was a South Carolinian, and bullheaded in his defense of slavery. That and the Civil War eroded his popularity and thrust him into obscurity.

Neither Cooper nor Simms wrote the kind of fiction this book contains. They are its grandfathers, certainly. But who are the parents? And how did the offspring get to be so universally beloved?

Some of the reasons have already been suggested. The materials and background of the Western have an instantaneous appeal. They are colorful; exciting. And, as noted, nineteenth-century stay-at-homes were wildly curious about the country's far reaches, to which increasing numbers of their fellow citizens were rushing in search of precious metal, farmland or freedom from pursuit by law officers, wives or cuckolded husbands. People who didn't go wanted to know what it was really like out there where the sirens sang the song of manifest destiny.

So the moment was ripe for the appearance of a new kind of fiction. I would argue that three forces in nineteenth-century popular culture propelled the Western to national, then global acclaim:

The debut of the dime novel.
The fiction of Ned Buntline.
And the life of Buffalo Bill Cody.

The earliest dime novels were created in the tradition of Cooper, Simms and Sir Walter Scott. Their authors wrote of the frontier, all right, but in a manner that made at least some pretense of literary quality.

The very first of them was one of those "Easterns." *Malaeska: The Indian Wife of the White Hunter* was published in June, 1860, by the firm of Beadle and Company of William Street, New York. The work carried impeccable credentials. It had already appeared as a prize story in a magazine called *The Ladies' Companion*.

Edmund Pearson's entertaining study of dime novels gives us this description of the first offering from Beadle: ". . . a thin little book, of one hundred and twenty-eight pages . . . about six-inches-high and four-inches-broad . . . the covers were of saffron paper—the book was a 'yellow-backed Beadle.' "

The term quickly became pejorative, which Mr. Beadle resented; he also insisted his covers were orange. Whatever the hue, Beadle books went to war in many a military haversack. The soldiers couldn't get enough of them. So it wasn't long before a picture of a ten-cent piece was printed on every cover to foil Army sutlers, notorious price-gougers.

The all but unpronounceable *Malaeska* is a Cooperish frontier romance set in the Hudson River Valley in the 1700s. It opens gently—a stylistic refinement which other Beadle authors would soon demolish:

> The traveller who has stopped at Catskill, on his way up the Hudson, will remember that a creek of no insignificant breadth washes one side of the village . . .

The reader must wait until the second chapter to encounter the woodsman-hero, Danforth, and a fight featuring feverish dangers as well as feverish prose:

Sternly arose the white man's shout amid the blazing of guns and the whizzing of tomahawks, as they flashed through the air on their message of blood . . . Oh, it was fearful, that scene of slaughter. Heart to heart, and muzzle to muzzle, the white man and the red man battled in horrid strife.

The author of this stirring stuff was no obscure hack, but an accomplished and well-regarded magazine editor (*Graham's, The Ladies' World,* etc.) and the creator of some eminently respectable novels (". . . published at the conventional price of one dollar and fifty cents, and bound, decorously, in boards"). She ran a fashionable New York salon, and received "marked attentions" from the likes of Thackeray and Dickens during an 1850 world tour. Her name was Mrs. Ann Sophia Winterbotham Stephens. She was deemed, correctly, a pillar of propriety.

Yet she did create the first work presented in a new and lusty fiction format; one which would serve as the earliest popular vehicle for Western stories.

Relatively soon, the dime novel would become—to busybody clerics, narrow-minded parents and other spoilsports—what Pearson delightfully terms "a literary pestilence." The objection was usually moralistic. Lack of quality would have been a better target. As the dime novel grew, expanding its scope to deal with all sorts of subjects and introducing series characters who solved mysteries, invented fabulous electric boats or lettered in every sport ever conceived by God or man at Yale, the writing became a lot more punchy. A typical opening instantly removed any doubt as to whether this was, or was not, a tale of derring-do:

> Bang!
> Bang!
> Bang!
> Three shots rang out on the midnight air!

I guess we can agree that it isn't your average literary prize-winning diction. But it surely gets the blood going (!!!).

The dignity and talent which a few writers such as Mrs. Stephens brought to the form were cake-icing that rapidly disappeared. But the stage was set; a means was at hand to make exciting fiction, including tales of the West, affordable and widely available.

Enter the bizarre Edward Zane Carroll Judson, alias Ned Buntline.

No author would dare invent Ned Buntline; his manuscript would be rejected as too outrageous.

"Colonel" E. Z. C. Judson was a short, stocky, slightly lame man of quick wit and tongue. He was a propagandist without peer, in print or in front of a mob. He instigated the bloody Astor Place Riot in 1849 to protest the presence on a New York stage of a famous Shakespearean actor from Britain (it robbed America's premier thespian, Forrest, of the chance to work, Judson claimed).

In the same generous vein, Judson helped organize the American Political Party, or "Know-Nothings," who stood foursquare against anything and anyone not white, Protestant and native-born.

Judson served two-and-a-half years with the First New York Mounted Rifles during the Civil War. He saw no battle action, but he did see the interior of a cell in which he was placed for deserting. Over the years he had up to half a dozen wives (the records of his marriages and divorce settlements are confused), and was a bigamist at least once.

Using the Buntline pseudonym, he became an author of sensational fiction: sea stories, and adventures set in the Seminole and Mexican Wars. The firms of Beadle and Street and Smith published his material. One biographer unequivocally calls him "America's best-paid writer" during his prime years (the annual income cited in support of this claim is twenty thousand dollars).

In the summer of 1860, Buntline/Judson heard or read of a hot skirmish between Indians and cavalry at Summit Springs, Nebraska. Sioux and Cheyenne under Chief Tall Bull had been pursued by General Eugene Carr's 5th Cavalry, aided by the irregulars in Major Frank North's Pawnee scout battalion. Buntline boarded the westbound cars to see whether there might be fresh story material in it.

He hoped to interview North, the man who had reportedly killed Tall Bull. He tracked the scout to a military post, but North apparently had no wish to become grist for the fiction mill: "If you want a man to fill that bill, he's over there under the wagon."

The man snoozing in the shade was a frontier-wise young fellow, born in Iowa and revealed as tall when he stood up. One source characterizes him as "handsome as Apollo." William Frederick Cody was a veteran of the Union army, a hunter and a supplier of buffalo meat to railroad construction crews.

Although not actually present at the battle of Summit Springs—he had been on a scouting assignment for General Carr—he arrived at the Indian village soon after the engagement. He was sufficiently charmed by Mr. Buntline so that he was willing to discuss the experience.

Cody, already nicknamed Buffalo Bill by his friends, suggested they go out looking for Indians. Buntline abandoned his previously announced plan to give a temperance address (it was another way he made money; he also had a stock lecture on the subject of "Woman As Angel and Fiend," a topic he seems to have researched in some depth). Off they rode, the scout and the fiction writer, talking a blue streak. Buntline described his heroic exploits in the Seminole, Mexican and Civil Wars. Presumably the young and likable Cody was more truthful.

At the end of the research trip, Buntline went back to New York City and to work. He had seen no Indians except maybe a few hanging around the post. But he'd heard enough stories from Cody and other scouts and soldiers to send the kettle of his imagination to full boil. In December of that year, Street and Smith proudly announced a new Buntline story: *Buffalo Bill—The King of Border Men.*

The archetype of the Western hero was about to burst on the world. A young plainsman with a sense of humor, a liking for spirits (he often said that when he volunteered for the war, he was so drunk he didn't know what he was doing) and a God-given gift for showmanship, he was about to begin his journey to fame. As he went, he would carry and spread the legend of the West far beyond the shores of his own country.

The Buntline story portrayed Bill Cody not only as the greatest scout in the West, but as a staunch cold water army man, a teetotaler. Well, no law requires that the truth be told by, or about, living people, as numerous memoirs of movie stars and ex-presidents demonstrate.

Don Russell's life of Cody disputes many claims of Buntline's chief biographer, as well as subsequent exaggerations of Buffalo Bill's early career. (One has the scout simultaneously shooting Tall Bull, tipping his sombrero respectfully to the chief's white female captive, and holding the reins—"presumably with his third hand.") Russell also questions the extent and value of Cody's contribution to the Street and Smith story; he claims most of it was actually based on the adventures of another frontiersman, James Butler Hickok, and that all Buntline really got out of his meeting with the young Iowan was "the alliterative magic of the name Buffalo Bill."

Whatever the truth, the magic was more potent. The serial was a hit. Buntline churned out a few more while shuttling between a wife in Manhattan and another up in Westchester. The stories featured not only Bill and his horse Powder Face, but Bill's real-life wife Louisa, her invented sisters Lillie and Lottie and various frontier pals including "Wild Bill Hitchock" (sic). Later dime novels about the famous Westerner were authored by Prentiss Ingraham.

While Buntline was still the one writing about him, Cody continued to work as a scout and guide, although the quality of his clientele improved rapidly as his fame spread. He was chosen to take General Phil Sheridan and powerful newspaper publisher James Gordon Bennett on a hunting expedition. Then came an even bigger plum. Sheridan recommended that Cody be the guide for the Grand Duke Alexis of Russia, age 19, who was making a triumphant tour of America and hankered to go on a buffalo hunt— the 1871 equivalent of a visit to Disneyland.

Cody soon succumbed to the lure of the big cities,

where his name was being heard with greater and greater frequency. He went to New York, where Gordon Bennett's editors and writers treated him as a media star. He was sighed over, fussed over, fought over as a guest. He was asked to dine with the Belmonts. And from Ned Buntline's personal box at the Bowery Theatre, he watched the dramatization of his own adventures, which playwright Fred Meader had created from the half-truths and plain lies of the first Buntline story.

Something in Cody must have stirred then. He must have glimpsed El Dorado—a way to earn far more than he ever could as a cavalry scout or supplier of buffalo meat. Somewhere in the two or three years that culminated in the Bowery Theatre premiere, Buffalo Bill the showman came to life.

He was off the army payroll by late 1872 and on his way to Chicago to star personally in a new Buntline venture—a stage extravaganza in which Ned filled the multiple roles of producer, director and actor. He also wrote the show, *The Scouts of the Plains*, which was nothing more than Meader's play slightly refurbished.

On stage, Cody didn't fool around with memorized dialogue. He just extemporized a narrative of some of his experiences. He was no actor, but he received an ovation anyway. (Buntline portrayed a white renegade; he managed to slip a temperance lecture into one of the character's long monologues.) From time to time, thrilling action broke up the talk. The scouts bravely slew a lot of Indians portrayed by "supers in cambric pants."

The reviews weren't good. The Chicago *Times* called the production "a combination of incongruous drama, execrable acting, renowned performers, intolerable stench, scalping, blood and thunder." When the show eventually arrived at Niblo's in New York, the local critics were even more unfriendly (some things never change). Said one: "As a drama it is very poor slop."

It made no difference. Buffalo Bill was an American original, and the public fell in love with him. The love affair would last a long time.

Cody was a genuinely brave man. He fought in at least sixteen battles with Indians during his lifetime, the most famous being that with the Cheyenne, Yellow Hair (not Yellow Hand), in 1876. Contemporary accounts indicate that he realized he was spoofing himself and the West, just a little, when he organized his first arena show in 1883.

It became known as Buffalo Bill's Wild West and Congress of Rough Riders of the World—and eventually brought to amphitheatres all over America, and then Europe, such sights as simulated stage robberies and personalities such as Annie Oakley and Chief Sitting Bull.

And if the show was still not exactly the truth any more than the dime novels had been, it was *enough* of the truth so that it can honestly be said that no other entertainment, and no other man, did more to implant the myth and magic of the American west in the minds of his countrymen and millions of others besides. The working cowboy did part of the job of course. But he was anonymous. (And until recent years, we've seldom seen him written about or depicted as he really was—often still in his teens, or barely out of them; frequently black.) Cody remains *the* Westerner.

Bad management cost him the fortune he made in show business. His death in 1917 was messy and unheroic; the cause was uremic poisoning. But he was a showman to the end, making his last appearance two months before he was buried.

Personal problems linked to flaws in his character vexed most of his later life. But he has a just claim to immortality, because he bequeathed the West to the whole world. The rest—from Zane Grey and Max Brand to John Ford and Sergio Leone—is history.

I've always loved the Western in all of its permutations.

Well, not *every* one. As a kid, I went faithfully, not to say eagerly, to the Saturday matinees. I couldn't see too many of those one-hour programmers from Republic and Columbia, Monogram and PRC—with one exception: the pictures featuring singing cowboys in embroidered shirts who hopped on their too-pretty horses to chase crooks driving vintage convertibles back and forth across strange hermaphroditic landscapes, half old, half new. There is a lot of never-was in Western fiction and film, but that sort of thing was too ridiculous even for a true believer.

Still, a believer I remained, thanks to pulp novels about Texas Ranger Jim Hatfield, richly detailed *Saturday Evening Post* serials by Luke Short, and Errol Flynn pictures scored in epic style by Max Steiner, a Viennese who seemed to understand the West better than most Americans.

When I broke into writing, I divided my time between science fiction and Western stories, and wrote a couple of dozen of the latter, novelettes mostly, published by the great old Popular pulps. I can still remember haunting Indiana drugstores whenever a new shipment of magazines arrived; I knew the delivery schedules by heart.

There is one thrilling moment in my memory in which, for the first time, I discovered my story, and my byline, among those featured on the cover (bright yellow, incidentally) of a magazine which proclaimed above its name:

*Frontier Fiction by Tophand Authors*

I didn't really believe I was a "tophand author"—I was twenty-one or twenty-two at the time. But it was heady to find someone else saying it, even as hyperbole; and saying it about one of my Westerns to boot.

So I'm proud to have a small place in this company of men and women who, no matter how diverse their literary approaches, share belief in the verity set down by a Victorian poet and printed as the epigraph to this piece:

Westward, the land is indeed a little brighter.

# Shootout at White Pass

He came suddenly, wrenchingly out of the dream.
*Oh God it's cold.*

His bare feet stuck from under the comforter,
which had pulled out while he slept. Two woolen
blankets on top of the comforter, and his nightshirt
on top of his union suit with its whiff of mothballs,
and he still woke with rattling teeth and shivering
shanks. *God God it's cold.* But then it was always cold
in White Pass, except in high summer.

*Why do I stay here?*

Because he was sheriff. Because he didn't have any
other place to go.

No, wrong. There was a place. But not, somehow,
the energy to reach it. He always blamed it on his
age. He'd be 46, next birthday.

He put his bare feet on the old crocheted rug beside the bed. His tin-plated clock showed half past
six. He shuddered going to the window, where he
lifted the blind and gazed with despair on the frozen
mud and dirty snow piles along the main street.
Above the false fronts and shoddy cottages of the
town, the Sierra ramparts looked down, heartless as
gravestones, and just as cold.

Downstairs, he heard loud, excited voices. An ore
wagon creaked past in the street, traces jingling in

15

the frosty air. It had snowed night before last. A
howler of a storm, a foot or more dumped on the
trails and high passes. He stood scratching his
paunch, which had lately grown till it was impossible
to ignore, and wondered about the hurrah below.
Sure didn't sound like the normal conversation of the
snatch-and-grab breakfast table . . .

The drab furnished room depressed him unbearably. He sat on the edge of the bed, arms crossed,
hands tucked in his armpits, and hung his head.
He'd been having a dream, all about home.

In the dream, the sky was cloudless and hot. The
sea grape and palmetto stirred gently in the noon
breeze. Little nervous sandpipers scurried up and
down the sand, and hungry gray pelicans soared and
dove for prey, splashing the bright smooth water of
the Gulf into the air like flung sapphires. Sitting here,
growing old in White Pass, he could feel the blessed
heat of the Florida sun . . .

He thought about his boyhood and young man-
hood as he pulled on his worn pants and plaid shirt.
He thought of picking up great clattery handfuls of
shells on the beaches, and putting them in jars just
because they were pretty. He thought of crabbing
from an old skiff in Red Fish Pass, between two of
the long narrow coastal keys. He'd had a decent
enough business, clerking in the mercantile with the
prospect of buying it when the owner gave it up.
Why had he left? Why had he left the sunshine and
slogged all the way out here to this?

With a curious look of contempt on his face, he
touched the reason. A clipping from an Atlanta
newspaper, years old, crackly and yellow. It was part
of an article about Mr. Horace Greeley of the *New
York Tribune*. He had underlined the famous charge

of the journalist. *Go west, young man, and grow up with the country.*

He was over 30 when he married. He'd courted Marthe Schiller, the teacher at a one-room schoolhouse in Hillsborough County, south of Tampa. Marthe was a sturdy, square-jawed woman of German descent, with eyes as blue as the Florida heavens; they relieved the severity of her face. He first admired Marthe because of her book-learning; he was poorly educated, leaving school eagerly at age 10. When love came, it came quickly, completely, generously: he wanted to find a much better existence for them. Although Florida was home, life there was a hardscrabble existence, in a beautiful but poor place to which man had added exactly nothing except towns that seemed to consist mostly of windowless shanties, impoverished farms populated by scrawny red cows, and the sad-eyed black folks who seemed all but abandoned by the world in the hovels you found at the end of nearly every sandy track into the scrub; abandoned, that is, until there was a need for bending the back in the pitiless sun doing work even the dirtiest, most ignorant white cracker wouldn't touch. That was the real Florida if you looked at it with clear vision.

Greeley's charge inspired him. It was inspiring a lot of Americans, single and married. He and his wife of one year set out for California. Eleven months later, marooned in White Pass by another snowstorm, Marthe died of influenza.

That was nine years ago. He was still here. Longing for Florida and somehow incapable of going back.

Maybe it was the responsibility. The job. Which he cared for as little as he cared for the town. He picked up the yellow metal star with the word Sheriff stamped in, and pinned it on his plaid shirt with a little puff of his lips, as though he'd just tasted something bad.

He walked downstairs and turned into the dining room, where the Widow Thorne's three other boarders of the moment were already ravaging the plates of eggs, thick tough sowbelly slabs, fresh baking powder biscuits. "Morning, Lou," said Bill Toombs, the recent widower who ran the hardware. "Morning, sheriff," said a man who stopped for a night every month or so; a drummer with a handlebar mustache and showy Burnside whiskers. Lou Hand greeted both of them, then the 13-year-old boy, Will Pertwee, who sat at the end of the table, watching him with a peculiar intensity.

"Sheriff, did you hear?" Will asked. He was a shock-haired kid; an orphan. Jesse gave him room and board in exchange for his work around the place.

The door to the kitchen opened. Jesse Thorne looked in, rosy-faced in the heat rolling out in blessed waves from the unseen stove.

"More coffee here? Why, good morning, Lou. Sleep well?"

"No, I nearly froze. I'm getting old, Jesse. Blood's too thin."

"If you got thin blood, a place at this altitude ain't no good," announced the drummer. Lou shot him a look as if to say, Tell me something I've not heard before.

Will Pertwee was practically jumping out of his chair. "Sheriff, did you hear, or didn't you?"

"Hear what?"

"About the gent who came to town last night. Walked in 'cause he had to shoot his horse up at Five Mile Wash. It's Bob Siringo."

Bill Toombs was watching him, resting his fork in the gooey yellow residue of his eggs. The Widow Thorne looked stricken, noticeably pale; even women knew the name of the notorious gunman who had been through trials for murder at least four times, had done a stretch in Nevada Territorial Prison, and was said to have done away with up to a dozen enemies.

"How do you know it's Bob Siringo?" Lou Hand said with a deadly heaviness filling his belly, where only a moment before there had been the first pleasurable and diffuse warmth produced by Jesse's strong coffee.

"Well, I don't," Will said with a grin, as if he knew very well what the whole conversation implied for Lou. "But he sure *looks* like Bob Siringo. I mean, he's a ringer for that drawing on the dodger hanging in your office."

Lou swallowed. "And where is the man?"

"Staying at the Congress Hotel." Will Pertwee leaned so far forward, his chin nearly upset his glass of buttermilk. "Guess you'll have to look him up and see he behaves, huh?"

"Not necessarily," Lou said. "Not if he is behaving."

It came to him that, in his customary fashion, he'd left his .44-40 Frontier Model Colt and gunbelt hanging on the bedpost, where he always kept them. That was his morning routine, to walk downstairs for breakfast without the gun. Other times, it was of no importance. This morning the absence of the familiar pressure against his thigh seemed of keen, even dangerous significance.

Jesse Thorne gave him a long, quizzical look. She was a heavy, handsome woman, ten years younger, with red-gold hair and large slightly tilted gray eyes.

She had a soft, billowy breast; Lou had always fancied the buxom kind.

Jesse was self-educated, and religious in a quiet way. She read the Bible every evening before she retired, but he hadn't learned this until they'd been acquainted for over a year. She wasn't prudish, though. She loved to dance, and play cards, and mix up a rum toddy on cold nights. She didn't belong to a regular church, no doubt because they'd have scorned her, and her habits, as un-Christian.

Lou and Jesse often shared cups of hot tea of an evening, when White Pass was quiet—as it usually was—and they enjoyed playing hands of rummy once or twice a week. In the all too short season of warmth, they walked in the high meadows and occasionally had a picnic supper on a Sunday evening. Now Jesse gave him that long, level look full of anxious concern. "Lou, could I see you privately a moment?"

With a nervous, unconscious brush at the lock of oiled hair carefully curled over his forehead in the fashionable mode, Lou exchanged the table for the hot haven of the kitchen. There he was warm, actually warm, for the first time since arising. The kitchen, old but spacious, smelled of flour, and skillet grease, and all the good odors of the best part of a home.

"Do you think it's really Bob Siringo?"

"I don't know, Jesse."

"If it is, will he cause trouble?"

"Don't see why he should. Maybe he's simply passing through."

"Won't you have to find out? Talk to him?"

"Not unless he causes a ruckus. The morning will tell, I imagine."

"Well, I just wanted to say—" She cleared her

throat while avoiding his eye. "You're my dear friend, and a good sheriff. I wouldn't want anything to happen to you."

"Oh, I don't think it will." It was a hope, not a certainty. He was frightened. After Marthe died, his ambition for heading on down to California had died too, and in those first dull-headed, glaze-eyed weeks after his wife's burial, he'd accepted the offer of old Sheriff Jeffords, who needed a deputy because his previous one, Neddy Wattle, had died. In bed. Of old age.

"Little or no crime in White Pass. Never has been," old Jeffords assured him. Truthfully. After Jeffords died of a stroke three years ago, Lou Hand didn't think very long about town council's offer of a promotion.

Over and above his experience, one work-related incident of heroism made Lou Hand the logical candidate. While Lou was a deputy, a jobless man named Jocko Brust had held up the now-defunct Merchants and Miners Bank of White Pass. Chancing to walk by at the precise moment, Lou Hand heard screams inside, then saw the culprit come backing out the door wearing a bandanna up to the bridge of his nose, as if that would possibly conceal his identity from anyone who knew him.

It was a sunny spring day, full of hope and the gurgle of melting snow; the time of year when some men left their wives or hung themselves. Lou was in fine spirits, however, and he jumped Jocko without thought. Jocko shot him, a grazing shoulder wound. The bank manager ran out with a heavy cuspidor and nearly beat out Jocko's brains, leaving him bleeding and washed with tobacco-colored water.

People hailed Deputy Hand as a hero. Pastor Humphreys lauded him from the pulpit of the Methodist chapel (he was told). Lou Hand had nightmares for months after, realizing what could have happened if the bullet had traveled a little more to the left.

Still, he didn't deliberate long before he accepted council's offer and put on the sheriff's star. The incident of Jocko Brust (he went to prison) was unusual, not to say unique, for White Pass. Never once in all his years as deputy had Lou Hand fired his pistol in anger, and he'd only drawn it half a dozen times, to cow noisy but harmless Saturday-night drunks. The same proved the case during his tenure as sheriff.

But now someone purporting to be the notorious Bob Siringo was staying at the Congress . . .

"You'll be careful," Jesse said. "I wouldn't want to lose my boarder and card-playing companion . . ." The words trailed off, and Jesse impulsively touched his sleeve. Lou rested his hand on hers and gazed into her eyes, realizing again how much he cared for her. That affection had grown almost unconsciously over the months and years he'd lived under her roof. He wanted to say something to her . . . something meaningful and important. The desire had come on him several times before, usually in the evening, by lamplight. But he was a shy man. Told himself there was always another time. Plenty of time . . .

The kitchen door banged open and Will Pertwee jumped through. "Say, that drummer's hollering for more flapjack syrup, Mrs. Thorne."

"All right, tell him to keep his britches on." She reached for the crockery pitcher while Will danced past her, fairly jigging on the old linoleum in front of Lou Hand.

"You going after Bob Siringo, sheriff?"

"Not unless he gives me cause."

"But outlaws, gunfighters, they always do, don't they? That's why they're outlaws."

He couldn't refute Will's bloodthirsty logic. It angered him. He grabbed Will's shoulder and shoved him aside so hard, the boy exclaimed, "Ow!" Jesse gave him a startled, alarmed look as she prepared to take the full pitcher of syrup to the dining room. Lou tramped through the dining room and up the stairs, strange leaden pains deviling his belly all of a sudden. Though fully dressed, he was freezing.

On the stair landing he paused by the lace-curtained window and stared at the vista of the Sierras with the sun above their icy peaks. The sun was a pale yellow-white disk, clearly visible in blowing misty clouds. Wish I could shoot down that sun, he thought. Shoot it down here for some warmth.

Or go back to Florida. Why didn't I have the gumption? There were so many mornings I could have turned in the star and said, "That's it, I resign." Any morning up till this one . . .

He trudged on up the stairs. He hauled his gunbelt off the bedpost and cinched it around his expanding middle. He re-settled the Frontier Colt in the holster, and as he did so his eye grazed the yellowed news clip with the admonition from Mr. Greeley. Lou Hand made a face.

"You damn fool," he said.

He walked past the Congress Hotel, but on the opposite side of Sierra Street. He saw nothing more alarming than Regis, the colored porter, emptying last night's slopjars in the street.

White Pass smelled of woodsmoke this morning, and horse turds in the street, and the cold-metal stink of deep winter through your half-stuffed nose. Lou Hand shivered and stuck his gloved hands deep in the pockets of his sheep-lined coat. Under the slanted brim of his flat hat, he saw the main drag of White

Pass for what it was: a pitiful excuse for a town. It was a way-station on the California stage route—one through coach a day, each day, when the passes were open—but the mines in the neighborhood didn't produce much ore any more, and the White Pass Reduction Mill filled the morning with a slow *chump-chunk* that had a lugubrious rhythm of failure about it.

Reaching his one-story office on the corner opposite Levering's Apothecary (*CLOSED PERMANENTLY* said the crude paper sign in the window), Lou Hand drew the door key from his pocket. When he put it in the lock, the door swung in. Lou felt his heartbeat skip.

"Come on in, it's me," said a voice he recognized. Then Lou Hand smelled the vile stink of his caller's green-wrapped nickel cigars. The visitor was installed behind Lou Hand's desk, his tooled boots resting up on the blotter. "I let myself in with the council's key."

"Perfectly all right, Mr. Mayor," Lou Hand said, shutting the door and shucking out of coat and hat.

Marshall Marsden ran the livery, one of the few businesses in White Pass that wasn't failing or up for sale. He was a slight, bald man with eight children, all of whom were named Marshall Junior or Marcella or Marceline or some other M-variant of his own, apparently-revered name. The mayor loved off-color stories. This morning, however, there was no trace of humor in his small brown eyes.

"Did you hear about Bob Siringo?"

Lou Hand pulled the dodger off its tack on the bulletin board. The illustration was one of those pen-and-ink sketches of infinite vagueness: the bland features, staring eyes, and mandarin mustaches of the desperado could have belonged to any number of innocent-looking young men.

"I heard about some guest at the hotel who *looks* like Bob Siringo."

Marsden jerked his boots off the desk and landed them on the floor with a bang. "Well, it's him, he's making no secret of it."

"Is that right." Lou Hand had dreaded some such confirmation. He began tossing kindling into the stove. His hand wasn't steady as he lit the match.

"That's right," Marsden said, and Lou Hand noticed a glint of perspiration on his brow despite the chill of the tiny office. "And what I've got to say to you, sheriff, is short and sweet. Get him out of town."

Lou Hand lit a third match and finally got the kindling started. The warmth was small, of no use against the mortal chill that had invaded his heart and soul after he woke from the frequently repeated dream.

"Why?" Lou Hand said to the mayor.

"We don't want his ilk here. He was down at the livery first thing this morning, talking to Marcy. Trying to find a new horse. She said he made—lewd suggestions."

Lou frowned. "Is she positive he meant—?"

"You calling my own daughter a liar? I want him out, Lou. As elected mayor of White Pass, I'm officially telling you to get him out of town."

"I surely hate to push something like that if there's no . . ."

"I'm *ordering* you to push it, in the name of town council. Why do you think we pay you? Hell, this is the first time you've ever faced something this serious."

*And the last?* he thought, with a strained, almost wistful look at the dodger tossed onto the desk.

"Time you earned your wages," Mayor Marsden

exclaimed as he grabbed his derby and put it on with a snap of his wrist.

"If he hasn't got a horse . . ." Lou began.

"No, and Marcy refused to sell him one. She was scared to death, but she stood up to the little slug. If a woman can do that—"

"I hear you," Lou Hand interrupted, beet-faced and furious all of a sudden. "But you hear me for a minute. If it's Bob Siringo, and he doesn't have a horse, he can't get out of here until six P.M., earliest, when the Sacramento stage comes through." The eastbound presumably had cleared the way station at half past five, while Lou Hand was still enmeshed in his dreams of Red Fish Pass at high noon. The place he never should have left.

Mayor Marsden sneered. "It's a convenient excuse for stalling all day. But all right, six p.m.'s your limit. See that he's gone."

Marsden slammed the door and Lou Hand listened to his boots tap-tap quickly away on the plank sidewalk. The sheriff felt heavy and old and doomed as he walked to the potbelly stove, yanked the door open and swore. For the kindling had gone out, and what wafted against his upraised palms from the black ashy interior was cold; just more cold; a brush of air that seemed, to his worried imagination, cold as the breath from a grave.

Lou Hand fooled around the office all morning. It was his custom to stroll back to Jesse Thorne's for his big meal at noon, and he started in that direction but gave up the idea after walking one block. His stomach hurt, too severely for him to eat so much as a mouthful of Jesse's usual: pot roast with horserad-ish on the side; boiled or mashed potatoes and a gravy boat almost big enough to float a Vanderbilt yacht.

He leaned his hip against a hitchrack and squinted over the swayed back of an old gray looking half dead from the weight of its saddle. Diagonally in the middle of the next block, opposite, Lou Hand had a fine view of the portico of the Congress Hotel. As he studied the hotel and chewed on his lower lip, a recognizable figure walked out jauntily, almost colliding with an old woman in a bonnet and faded cloth coat.

Lou dodged back, into the shadows of the entrance alcove of Weinbaum's Hardware, boarded up and plastered with *To Let* notices. The man outside the hotel wore a stained tan duster and boots with very high heels. When he bumped the old woman, knocking a parcel out of the crook of her arm, he immediately snatched it from the dirty snowbank into which it fell, presented it to her, then swept off his tall loaf-crowned hat with a deep bow. In a sorry place like White Pass, that kind of bow should have brought a snicker, but somehow, the man made it look not only graceful but proper.

Mollified, the old woman patted the man's stained sleeve and went on. The man watched her go, then started walking, cutting left into an alley beside the hotel and there disappearing.

But not before Lou Hand had a clear look at the pale cheeks and mandarin mustaches under the tall hat. No mistaking the features from the dodger. It was Bob Siringo, or his twin.

Where was he going? In search of a horse? He wouldn't find any but plugs in White Pass, that was probably the problem, Lou thought. He glanced at the icy disk of the sun, still mist-shrouded, and noticed his own faint shadow fading in and out as he walked slowly back to his office. There he shut the door and sat bundled in his coat in the chill silence, wondering—asking himself—how long he could wait before he carried out Mayor Marsden's charge.

The sun vanished behind threatening clouds of dark gray that rolled over the mountains from the northwest about four o'clock. Hungry and bone-chilled, Lou Hand stared at the ticking wall clock and realized he couldn't procrastinate any longer—principally because he could no longer bear the nervous pain torturing his gut. He checked his Colt once again, and set out on what he fancied might be his last walk anywhere.

Sid Thalheimer, the hotel clerk, was scratching a pen across some old bills at the counter of the Congress. Lou pushed back his hat.

"Sid, I hear you had a Mr. Bob Siringo registered. Is he still here?"

Sid caught the hopeful note and gave Lou Hand a sad, even pitying look. "He was upstairs taking a nap. Came down ten minutes ago. He's in there." Sid's thumb hooked at the connecting door to the hotel's saloon bar.

"Say anything about checking out today, did he?"

"No, he's staying one more night."

Lou swallowed back a large lump in his throat. "No he isn't, you can have the room."

Without waiting for a reaction, Lou Hand pivoted on the scuffed heel of his boot and walked across the old Oriental carpet to the batwings in the archway, and the incredible pregnant silence that seemed to be waiting in the dim room beyond. Lou's boots sounded loud as the trampling of a mastodon; at least they sounded that way to his inner ear.

He unbuttoned his coat before he pushed the doors

open. Clarence, the day barkeep, flashed him a look
from behind the long mahogany, then quickly found
some glassware to polish at the far end. The Congress saloon bar held but one customer, standing up
in front of an almost untouched schooner of beer that
had lost its head. Like everything else in White Pass,
the saloon bar looked dark; grimy; cold.

"Bob Siringo?" Lou Hand said from the entrance,
hoping his wild inner tension didn't show.

"I am, sir," said the young man, taking off his loaf-
crown hat and smoothing his thinning oiled dark
hair with his palm. The desperado's smile was polite
but wary.

"I'm the sheriff."

"Yes, sir, so I figured," Bob Siringo said, in a tone
that revealed nothing.

"Lou Hand's my name."

"Pleased to meet you. May I invite you for a
drink?"

Lou Hand's cold nose itched. Was this some trap?
He took three steps forward, between the flimsy
stained tables, and paused by the upright piano
whose keyboard resembled a mouth of yellow teeth
with several missing. From there he had a better look
at Siringo's eyes. Pale and keen in their awareness
not only of the sheriff but all the surroundings of the
room—even, somehow, the barkeep behind Siringo's
back, furiously polishing glassware near the hall
leading to the rear door.

"Yes, that'd be all right."

"Over there?" Bob Siringo said, picking up his
schooner and gesturing. He didn't leave any room
for Lou to answer one way or another. He'd chosen
the round table in the corner at the front of the bar.

He dropped a coin, *ka-plink,* on the mahogany, and
said to Clarence, "Give Mr. Hand anything he wants,

please." Then Siringo walked quickly to the table and slid around to the corner chair, dropping his hat in front of him. Where he sat, his back was fully protected, and he could observe not only the room but, on his immediate right, a good portion of Sierra Street beyond the streaked and dirty front window.

Lou Hand picked up his shot of whiskey with a short nod to Clarence, who was still staying out of range. He sat down opposite Bob Siringo, who had a pleasant, watchful expression on his face. The sheriff sipped from the shot of redeye, wanting the Dutch courage, every last drop of it. But he held back because he was fearful of losing whatever advantage a clear head might give him.

Noting again the alertness of Bob Siringo's pale eyes, he realized that was exactly none.

"Mr. Siringo . . ." Lou Hand cleared his throat. "What are you doing hanging around this town?"

"Well, sir, I didn't know a man had to explain himself that way in the free United States . . ."

"A man like you always has to explain himself."

Siringo didn't like that. He started to reply, then checked as a shabby man Lou Hand didn't recognize rubbed some dirt from the outside of the window and peered in at the drinkers.

The man's jaw dropped; he knew who was sitting there in the corner. He rushed away. The winter twilight was closing fast on the sad, nearly deserted street. A few snowflakes flurried suddenly, and Lou Hand wished he were lying buck naked and frying on a sandy beach back home . . .

Bob Siringo sighed. "Day before yesterday, up the trail a piece, when the snowstorm hit, my mount foundered and snapped a leg in a drift. I had to shoot Rex. Then I had to come the rest of the way on foot. That was a pisser of a storm, sheriff. For a long time

I didn't know whether I'd find a town. Whether I'd make it. I did, and here I am, resting up." He smiled and lifted one shoulder in a shrug, then drank a good swallow of beer.

Lou Hand helped himself to another sip of courage. "Well, I'm not on the prod, Mr. Siringo, because you haven't caused any trouble. But the town fathers want you to leave White Pass."

"Shit," Bob Siringo said, losing his smile and thumping his stein on the table so hard some of the golden beer slopped out. The smell was strong; sweet; melancholy, somehow.

"It's that girl, I'll bet. The one at the livery—?"

"You're a quick study, Mr. Siringo. Yes, exactly right. You see—ah—unfortunately, she's the daughter of the mayor."

"Just my God-damn luck," Bob Siringo said with another sigh. "I've had two bad, bad weaknesses, sheriff. One is for young females with a lot of stuff up here." He patted the bosom of his duster. Now, instead of smiling, he smirked.

"Every man's got a weakness, sheriff. What's yours?"

*Mine? I hate this place. This job. I don't want to die here . . . for the sake of a godforsaken, frozen, no-account town full of people with no hope left . . .*

"Never mind. May I ask you to move on, Mr. Siringo?"

"Well, you can ask. But I can't find myself a decent horse. I've looked."

"There's a coach through here at six P.M. every evening. Going the way you want to go—down toward Sacramento."

"Oh, no, I don't take that kind of transportation," Bob Siringo said. "Too many strangers. Too many windows for people to get at you."

Lou Hand swallowed again.

"I'm afraid you haven't got any say in it. I'm ordering you."

Bob Siringo's pale eyes showed a moment's murderous malice. Then he covered it by leaning back; relaxing; letting the tension visibly leave his shoulders.

"Oh, come on. You do that, sheriff, you'll probably draw to back it up—I'll kill you—what's accomplished? I came to this burg by accident. I'll leave when I can."

"No, not good enough . . ."

"I'm not getting on any fucking stage, do you understand?"

Lou Hand just stared at him, terrified. Bob Siringo turned in his chair. "Barkeep? What's the time?"

"Quarter past five, sir," Clarence sang out.

Bob Siringo put on another smile, though Lou Hand thought this one was false; intended to lull him. "Then we've got at least forty-five minutes to be friendly. Don't go wild when I unbutton my duster and reach, sheriff. I'm going to put my hogleg on the table as a gesture of my good will. You can take hold of yours if you want, just in case. But don't shoot me by mistake, all right?"

"All right," Lou Hand whispered.

He lowered his hand down to his Colt while Bob Siringo pulled his. It was a .45-caliber Colt, U.S. Army model, with the intimidating 7.5-inch barrel. A real show-off piece. Well cared for, too. It gleamed faintly with oil, showing not a spot of rust, as Clarence illuminated the room by lighting three of the kerosene chimney lamps in the fixture hanging from the ceiling.

"There," Bob Siringo said. "That's my one and

only weapon. So relax." He rubbed his upper arms. "Jesus, it's cold in here."

"It's always cold in White Pass." Outside, Lou Hand saw someone dart along the far side of the street, pointing toward the window. A second dimly-glimpsed figure rushed away. Youngsters, he realized as he watched the first one tie a muffler tighter under his chin and over his ears. Will Pertwee.

"Sheriff," Bob Siringo said with apparent sincerity. "I want to show you that I don't have any bad intentions. Barkeep? Bring us a bottle. A good bottle. On my tab." Clarence delivered a bottle of expensive Kentucky whiskey. Siringo uncorked it and sniffed. "Very fine. Put a good tip down for yourself, barkeep." Clarence swallowed his answer and hurried away. Siringo shoved his stein to one side and gestured for Lou Hand to finish his shot, which he did. Then Siringo poured.

"Have a good drink, sheriff. Warm up. Think it over. Do you really want to push this issue of my leaving town?"

Lou sipped the smooth warming whiskey.

"No, but it's my job."

"Wouldn't you rather be doing something else?" Siringo asked, and Lou Hand had the feeling that the young gunman was mocking him somehow, but he was not clever enough to figure out how he could be sure. Siringo leaned back and smoothed his long shiny pointed mustaches with his index fingers. "Wouldn't you rather be sleeping, or reading a fine novel, or eating a plate of stew, instead of sitting here wondering if, and how soon, I'm going to blow you to kingdom come because I can't take your orders?"

Just a little fuzzy from the whiskey, and knowing he was probably in even more desperate trouble be-

cause of it, Lou Hand answered. "You're right, I'd
rather be doing something else. Rather be sitting in
the sunshine in a rowboat in the middle of Red
Fish Pass."

"Where's that?"

"Back home. West coast of Florida."

"Why'd you leave?"

"Why did everybody leave the East? To start over.
To make a fortune. I listened to Mr. Greeley."

"Who?"

"Horace Greeley. 'Go west, young man, and grow
up with the country.'"

"Oh, him." It was clear Bob Siringo didn't know
who the devil Mr. Greeley might be.

"Tell me about Florida," the younger man said affably. "I've never been down there. I'm from Hoope-
ston, Illinois, originally."

"Well," Lou Hand said as the darkness settled
faster outside the dirty window, "first thing is, it's
warm there. Warm, and bright. The light's almost
unbearable when the noon sun hits the sand and the
water on a hot day. A man could go blind, and fry
his hide red as a lobster, too. But it isn't a bad way
to d . . ."

He cut it off, realizing what he'd almost said. All
of a sudden his mouth was dry as sand above the
tide line. The liquid he'd drunk was exerting a ferocious pressure in his bladder. He wanted to run.
Jump up, and run. He just sat there.

"Why don't you go back to Florida?"

"I don't know. I've sure thought about it. Maybe
one day I will. Meantime . . ." He stared. "I'm responsible for doing this job the best I can."

Bob Siringo stared right back for what seemed forever. Then:

"Barkeep? What time is it now?"

"Twenty-five to six."

Lou Hand coughed. "The coach is almost never late. We've got to get back to the main discussion."

In a flat, mean voice, Siringo said, "Subject's closed, sheriff."

"No. You're going."

"That's it?"

Hoping he wasn't shaking, Lou Hand looked him in the eye and said, "That's it."

"Well, shit." Flurried motion outside the window caught his eye; whipped him around in his chair. "Get away. Get away, you little fuckers," he shouted, gesturing at the shadows lurking on the other side of the steamed-up glass. Two of the boys ran. The other, Will Pertwee, simply darted back to the edge of the walk and hovered there, captured by the spectacle of the adversaries facing each other across the table.

Slowly, carefully, Lou Hand pushed aside his coat. Freed the butt of his gun. His heart pounded like surf in his ear. Bob Siringo eyed his Army Colt gleaming there, then suddenly wriggled in his chair.

"Damn, some kind of vermin in this place. Bit me."

Angry, he reached under the table. Alarms rang in Lou Hand's head. "Siringo, keep your hand up where . . ." Then, the small popping shot. Lou Hand felt the bullet hit his foot and stiffened with a cry. He tried to draw, but there was sudden pain, and a feeling of warm blood in his boot, to distract him. Before he could act, Bob Siringo had a small two-barrel hideout pistol above the table, aimed right at Lou Hand's brain.

"You draw on me, sheriff, you're guaranteed dead. Hands flat on the table. Flat!"

Lou Hand obeyed. He was sweating despite the cold. Cringing behind the bar, Clarence looked em-

balmed; he gestured wildly toward the lobby door,
where, apparently, the clerk had rushed. "Stay out,
Sid, stay out!"

Bob Siringo blew a whiff of smoke off his little
pistol. Then he managed a tense smile.

"One of my bad faults is a weakness for big-busted
females, but the other one is lying, sheriff. I lie right,
left, and Sundays. I lied about my hogleg. This is
true, though. If I placed that bullet right, your left
foot won't be much good any more. A gimpy sheriff,
a sheriff who isn't agile, who can't run, that kind of
sheriff's not much use to anybody. I'd say it's time
for you to go back home."

He jumped up suddenly, overturning his chair,
sweeping his hat onto his head, then switching the
hideout pistol to his left hand and snatching up the
fearsome long Army Colt with his right.

"You bastard, you really fucked things up for me,"
he said, spitting it like a little boy robbed of his
candy and the privacy to enjoy it. "By God I'm not
too sure why I didn't kill you, so you damn well
better speak some good about Bob Siringo after this.
Don't say he never did anything but bad to folks."

And he ran, straight back past the bar, brandishing
his weapons and screaming venomously at Clarence,
"What are you looking at, shit-face?"

Clarence dropped to his knees, out of sight. Bob
Siringo ran through the penumbra of lamplight and
down the hall and out into the wintry dark with a
slam of the back door, and was never seen again.

Still seated, with his boot full of blood, Lou Hand
was gripping the table's edge while trying to keep
from fainting.

He failed.

*       *       *

Four mornings later, Jesse Thorne called on Lou Hand in his room at 11 A.M. She brought him a mug of hot beef broth, which she'd been doing ever since the shootout at the Congress saloon bar.

"Here's the weekly," she said, showing him the four-page single-sheet tabloid paper. "The editorial calls you the town's hero."

"Oh, yes, sure," he said, turning his face away, toward the lace curtain and the familiar sad spectacle of Sierra Street all churny with mud and dirty water from the snow-melt. And no sunshine; just winter gray.

"Well, it was very heroic . . ."

"Just to sit there? I don't think so."

"You're wrong. Maybe it wasn't dime-novel heroics, but it was brave. You knew he was a killer. But we won't argue," she said, coming closer. "Time for you to drink this nice hot . . ." Through the steam from the mug, she sniffed something. "Lou Hand, have you been imbibing?"

"Definitely. Bottle in the drawer over there."

"Why?" she said, with mystification and some outrage.

"To work up courage."

"For what?"

Almost as terrified as he had been at the Congress Hotel, he couldn't reply for a minute. Inside the heavy bandage on his left foot, which was resting on an old footstool, he hurt, badly. Doc Floyd had confirmed that the vanished Bob Siringo was an artful shot, or at least a lucky one, because Lou might indeed be permanently crippled, since some muscle or other had been severed.

"For what, Lou?"

"For asking—Jesse—would you consent to become my wife?"

* * *

When she got over the surprise, he asked her politely whether she would bring from the bureau the little news clipping from the Atlanta paper. She knew what it was; she saw it when she cleaned the rooms of her boarders once a week. He uttered a soft thank-you and immediately tore the clipping in half, then in quarters, which he dropped on his lap robe.

"Why on earth did you do that?"

"Because, Jesse, I realized the last day or so that the same dream won't work for everybody. And it's nobody's fault that it doesn't." He clasped her big, work-rough hand. "I've got my own dream, Jess. Come with me back East. We'll make out somehow. Let me show you Florida while there's still time. Sitting there with Siringo, I realized there isn't as much as I always pretended. Will you go?"

She crouched down beside him, eyes tear-filled, which was something quite unusual for a woman of her independence and strength.

"Of course I will, Lou. I've always wondered why you couldn't work up nerve to ask."

She smiled and put her right arm around the shoulder of his nightshirt. He was, as usual, dreadfully, resentfully cold.

But that wouldn't be the case much longer.

# The Woman
# at Apache Wells

Tracy rode down from the rimrock with the seed of the plan already in mind. It was four days since they had blown up the safe in the bank at Wagon Bow and ridden off with almost fifty thousand dollars in Pawker's brown leather satchel. They had split up, taking three different directions, with Jacknife, the most trustworthy of the lot, carrying the satchel. Now, after four days of riding and sleeping out, Tracy saw no reason why he should split the money with the other two men.

His horse moved slowly along the valley floor beneath the sheet of blue sky. Rags of clouds scudded before the wind, disappearing past the craggy tops of the mountains to the west. Beyond those mountains lay California. Fifty thousand dollars in California would go a long way toward setting a man up for the rest of his life.

Tracy was a big man, with heavy capable hands and peaceful blue eyes looking out at the world from under a shock of sandy hair. He was by nature a man of the earth, and if the war hadn't come along, culminating in the frantic breakup at Petersburg, he knew he would still be working the rich Georgia soil.

But his farm, like many others, had been put to the torch by Sherman, and the old way of life had been wiped out. The restless postwar tide had caught him and pushed him westward to a meeting with Pawker and Jacknife, also ex-Confederates, and the robbery of the bank filled with Yankee money.

Tracy approached the huddle of rundown wooden buildings. The valley was deserted now that the stage had been rerouted, and the Apache Wells Station was slowly sagging into ruin. Tracy pushed his hat down over his eyes, shielding his face from the sun.

Jacknife stood in the door of the main building, hand close to his holster. The old man's eyes were poor, and when he finally recognized Tracy, he let out a loud whoop and ran toward him. Tracy kicked his mount and clattered to a stop before the long ramshackle building. He climbed down, grinning. He didn't want Jacknife to become suspicious.

"By jingoes," Jacknife crowed, "it sure as hell is good to see you, boy. This's been four days of pure murder, with all that cash just waitin' for us." He scratched his incredibly tangled beard, unmindful of the dirt on his face or the stink on his clothes.

Tracy looked toward the open door. The interior of the building was in shadows. "Pawker here yet?" he asked.

"Nope. He's due in by sundown, though. Least, that's what he said."

"You got the money?" Tracy spoke sharply.

"Sure, boy, I got it," Jacknife laughed. "Don't get so worried. It's inside, safe as can be."

Tracy thought about shoving a gun into Jacknife's ribs and taking off with the bag right away. But he rejected the idea. He didn't have any grudge against the oldster. It was Pawker he disliked, with his boyish yellow beard and somehow nasty smile. He wanted the satisfaction of taking the money away from Pawker himself. He would wait.

Then Tracy noticed Jacknife's face was clouded with anxiety. He stared hard at the old man. "What's the trouble? You look like you got kicked in the teeth by a Yankee."

"Almost," Jacknife admitted. "We're right smack in the middle of a sitcheation which just ain't healthy. A woman rode in here this morning."

Tracy nearly fell over. "A woman! What the hell you trying to pull?"

"Nothin', Tracy. She said she's Pawker's woman and he told her to meet him here. You know what a killer he is with the ladies."

"Of all the damn fool things," Tracy growled. "With cash to split up and every lawman around here just itching to catch us, Pawker's got to bring a woman along. Where is she?"

"Right inside," Jacknife repeated, jerking a thumb at the doorway.

"I got to see this."

He strode through the door into the cool shadowy interior. The only light in the room came from a window in the west wall. The mountains and the broken panes made a double line of ragged teeth against the cloud-dotted sky.

She sat on top of an old wooden table, whittling a piece of wood. Her clothes were rough, denim pants and a work shirt. Her body, Tracy could see, was womanly all over, and her lips were full. The eyes that looked up at him were large and gray, filled with a strange light that seemed, at succeeding moments, girlishly innocent and fiercely hungry for excitement. Just Pawker's type, he decided. A fast word, and they came tagging along. The baby-faced Confederate angered him more than ever.

"I hear you joined the party," Tracy said, a bit nastily.

"That's right." She didn't flinch from his stare. The knife hovered over the whittled stick. "My name's Lola."

"Tracy's mine. That doesn't change the fact that I don't like a woman hanging around on a deal like this."

"Pawker told me to come," she said defiantly. From her accent he could tell she was a Yankee.

"Pawker tells a lot of them to come. I been riding with him for a couple of months. That's long enough to see how he operates. Only a few of them are sucker enough to fall."

Her face wore a puzzled expression for a minute, as if she were not quite certain she believed what she said next. "He told me we were going to California with the money he stole from the bank."

"That's right," Tracy said. "Did he tell you there were two more of us?"

"No."

Tracy laughed, seating himself on a bench. "I thought so." Inwardly he felt even more justified at taking the money for himself. Pawker was probably planning to do the same thing. He wouldn't be expecting Tracy to try it.

"If I were you, miss, I'd ride back to where I came from and forget about Pawker. I worked with him at Wagon Bow, but I don't like him. He's a thief and a killer."

Her eyes flared with contempt. She cut a slice from the stick. "You're a fine one to talk, Mister Tracy. You were there too. You just said so. I suppose you've never robbed anybody in your life before."

"No, I haven't."

"Or killed anybody?"

"No. I didn't do any shooting at Wagon Bow. Pawker killed the teller. Jacknife outside didn't use his gun either. Pawker likes to use his gun. You ought to know that. Anybody can tell what kind of man he is after about ten minutes."

Lola threw down the knife and the stick and stormed to the window. "I don't see what call you've got to be so righteous. You took the money, just like Pawker."

"Pawker's done it before. I figured this was payment for my farm in Georgia. Your soldiers burned me out. I figured I could collect this way and get a new start in California."

She turned suddenly, staring. "You were in the war?"

"I was. But that's not important. The important thing is for you to get home to your people before Pawker gets here. Believe me, he isn't worth it."

"I haven't got any people," she said. Her eyes suddenly closed a bit. "And I don't have a nice clean town to go back to. They don't want me back there. I had a baby, about a month ago. It died when it was born. The baby's father never came home from the war—" She looked away for a moment. "Anyway—Pawker came into the restaurant where I was working and offered to take me west."

"Somebody in the town ought to be willing to help you."

Lola shook her head, staring at the blue morning sky. Jacknife's whistle sounded busily from the broken-down corral. "No," she said. "The baby's father and I were never married."

Tracy walked over to her and stood behind her, looking down at her hair. He suddenly felt very sorry for this girl, for the life lying behind her. He had never felt particularly attached to any woman, except perhaps Elaine, dead and burned now, a victim of Sherman's bummers back in Georgia. He could justify the Wagon Bow robbery to himself. Not completely, but enough. But he couldn't justify Pawker or Pawker's love of killing or the taking of the girl.

"Look, Lola," he said. "You don't know me very well, but I'm willing to make you an offer. If you help me get the money, I'll take you with me. It'd be better than going with Pawker."

She didn't answer him immediately. "How do I know you're not just like him?"

"You don't. You'll have to trust me."

She studied him a minute. Then she said, "All right."

She stood very close to Tracy, her face uplifted, her breasts pushing out against the cloth of her shirt. A kind of resigned expectancy lay on her face. Tracy took her shoulders in his hands, pulled her to him and kissed her cheek lightly. When she moved away, the expectancy had changed to amazement.

"You don't need to think that's any part of the bargain," he said.

She looked into his eyes. "Thanks."

Tracy walked back to the table and sat down on the edge. He couldn't understand her, or know her motives, and yet he felt a respect for her and for the clear, steady expression of her eyes. Something in them almost made him ashamed of his part in the Wagon Bow holdup.

Jacknife stuck his head in the door, his watery eyes excited. A big glob of tobacco distended one cheek. "Hey, Tracy. Pawker's coming in."

Tracy headed outside without looking at Lola. A big roan stallion with Pawker bobbing in the saddle was pounding toward the buildings over the valley floor from the north, sending a cloud of tan dust into the sky. Tracy climbed the rail fence at a spot where it wasn't collapsing and from there watched Pawker ride into the yard.

Pawker climbed down. He was a slender man, but his chest was large and muscled under the torn Union cavalry coat. He wore two pistols, butts forward, and cartridge belts across his shirtfront under the coat. Large silver Spanish spurs jingled loudly when he moved. His flat-crowned black hat was tilted at a rakish angle over his boyish blond-whiskered face. Tracy had always disliked the effect Pawker tried to create, the effect of the careless guerrilla still fighting the war, the romantic desperado laughing and crinkling his childish blue eyes when his guns exploded. Right now, the careless guerrilla was drunk.

He swayed in the middle of the yard, blinking. He tilted his head back to look at the sun, then groaned. He peered around the yard. His hand moved aimlessly. "Hello, ol' Jacknife, hello, ol' Tracy. Damned four days, too damned long."

"You better sober up," Jacknife said, worried. "I want to split the money and light out of here."

"Nobody comes to Apache Wells any more," Pawker said. "Tracy, fetch the bottles out o' my saddle, huh?"

"I don't want a drink," Tracy said. Lola stood in the doorway now, watching, but Pawker did not see her. If he had, he would have seen the disillusionment taking root. Tracy smiled a little. Grabbing the money would be a pleasure.

"Listen, Pawker," Jacknife said, approaching him, "let's divvy the cash and forget the drink—"

Suddenly Pawker snarled and pushed the old man. Jacknife stumbled backward and fell in the dust. Pawker spat incoherent words and his right arm flashed across his body. The pistol came out and exploded loudly in the bright air. A whiff of smoke went swirling away across the old wooden roofs.

Jacknife screamed and clutched his hip. Tracy jumped off the fence and came on Pawker from behind, ripping the gun out of his hand and tossing it away. He spun Pawker around and hit him on the chin. The blond man skidded in the dust and scrabbled onto his knees, some of the drunkenness gone. Glaring, he slid his left hand across his body and down.

Tracy pointed his gun straight at Pawker's belly. "I'd like you to do that," he said. "Go ahead and draw."

Cunning edged across the other man's face. His hand moved half an inch further and he smiled. Then he giggled. "I'm going to throw my gun away, Tracy boy. I don't want trouble. Can I throw my gun away and show you I'm a peaceable man?"

Tracy took three fast steps forward and pulled the gun from its holster before Pawker could seize it. Then he turned his head and said, "Lola, find the satchel and get horses."

Pawker screamed the girl's name unbelievingly, turning on his belly in the dust to stare at her. He began to curse, shaking his fist at her, until Tracy planted a hand on his shoulder, pulled him to his feet and jammed him against the wall of the building with the gun pressing his ribs.

"Now listen," Tracy said, "I'm taking the satchel and I don't want a big muss."

"Stole my money, stole my woman," Pawker mumbled. "I'll get you, Tracy, I'll hunt you up and kill you slow. I'll make you pay, by God." His eyes rolled crazily, drunkenly.

Jacknife was trying to hobble to his feet. "Tracy," he wheezed, "Tracy, help me."

"I'm taking the money," Tracy said.

"That's all right, that's fine, I don't care," Jacknife breathed. "Put me on my horse and slap it good. I just want to get away from him. He's a crazy man."

Tracy shoved Pawker to the ground again and waved his gun at him. "You stay right there. I've got my eye on you." Pawker snarled something else but he didn't move. Tracy helped Jacknife onto his horse. The old man bent forward and lay across the animal's neck.

"So long, Tracy. Hit him good. I want to get away—"

"You need a doctor," Tracy said.

"I can head for some town," Jacknife breathed. "Come on, hit him!"

Tracy slapped the horse's flank and watched him go galloping out of the station yard and across the valley floor. Lola came around the corner of the building leading two horses. The satchel was tied over one of the saddlebags.

Tracy turned his head for an instant and when he turned back again, Pawker was scrabbling in the dust toward his gun which lay on the far side of the yard. Tracy fired a shot. It kicked up a spurt of dust a foot in front of Pawker's face. He jerked back, rolling over on his side and screaming, "I swear to God, Tracy, I'll come after you."

Lola was already in the saddle. The horses moved skittishly. Tracy swung up and said, "Let's get out of here." He dug in his heels and the horses bolted. They headed west across the floor of the valley.

They rode in silence. Tracy looked back once, to see Pawker staggering away from the building with his gun, firing at them over the widening distance. Until they made camp in the early evening at a small grove, with the mountains still looming to the west, Tracy said almost nothing.

Finally, when the meal with its few necessary remarks was over, he said, "Pawker will follow us. We'll have to keep moving."

She answered absently, "I guess you're right." A frown creased her forehead.

"What's the trouble?" He was beginning to sense the growth of a new feeling for this woman beside him. She was as silent and able as the hardened men with whom he had ridden in the last few years. Yet she was different, too, and not merely because she was female.

"I don't know how to tell you this right, Tracy." She spoke slowly. The firelight made faint red gold webs in her hair and the night air stirred it. "But— well—I think you're an honest man. I think you're decent and that's what I need." She stuck her finger out for emphasis. "Mind you, I don't mean that I care anything about you, but I think I could."

Tracy smiled. The statement was businesslike, and it pleased him. He knew that there was the possibility of a relationship that might be good for a man to have.

"I understand," he said. "I sort of feel the same. There's a lot of territory in California. A man could make a good start."

She nodded. "A good start, that's important. I made a mistake, I guess. So did you. But now there's a chance for both of us to make up for that. I'm not asking you if you want to. I'm just telling you the chance is there, and I'd like to see if what I think of you is right."

"I've been thinking the same," he said.

They sat in silence the rest of the evening, but it was a silence filled with a good sense of companionship that Tracy had seldom known. For the first time in several years, he felt things might work out right

after all. Right according to the way it had been before the war, not since.

The next morning, they doubled back.

It was a five-day ride to Wagon Bow. The job was
carried off at around four in the morning. Tracy rode
through the darkened main street at a breakneck gallop and flung the satchel of money on the plank walk
in front of the bank. By the time the sun rose he and
Lola were miles from Wagon Bow. The only trou-
bling factor was Pawker, somewhere behind them.

He caught up with them when they were high in
the mountains, heavily bundled, driving their horses
through the lowering twilight while the snow fell
from a gray sky. Actually, they were the ones who
caught up with Pawker. They saw him lying behind
a boulder where he had been waiting. A rime of ice
covered his rifle and his yellow boy's beard. His
mouth was open. He was frozen to death.

Tracy felt a great relief. Pawker had evidently followed them, knowing the route they would probably
take, and circling ahead to wait in ambush. It would
have fitted him, rearing up from behind the boulder
with his mouth open in a laugh and his avenging
rifle spitting at them in the snow.

They stood for a time in the piercing cold, staring
down at the body. Then Tracy looked at Lola through
the veil of snow between them. He smiled, not
broadly, because he wasn't a man to smile at death,
but with a smile of peace. Neither one spoke.

Tracy made the first overt gesture. He put his thickly
clad arm around her and held her for a minute, their
cold raw cheeks touching. Then they returned to
the horses.

Two days later, they rode down out of the mountains on the trail that led to California.

# Hell on the
# High Iron

The land had a familiar rolling quality about it. Rome rode westward in the early dawn, a big, stocky man in his early thirties. He followed the movements of his horse easily, his clear gray eyes sweeping over the vast prairies. Those eyes suggested a quick mind, and his whole bearing said that he knew his mind could often help him just as much as the pistol strapped to his right hip.

It was a sort of homecoming. He followed the tracks, two bands of iron stretching ahead of him. The business was well taken care of, the morning air had a cool crispness, and he was in high spirits. The sun glinting from the rails seemed to symbolize the future, alive with pleasant prospects.

His mood changed abruptly around noon when he rode into the end-of-track of the Kansas & Western. The place had an air of idleness. Here and there, groups of section hands sat near piles of ties, drinking coffee and playing cards. He heard no clang of hammers on spikes, no curses of men sweating under the sun. Work had stopped. The rails no longer crept inevitably toward the Rockies.

As troubleshooter it would be his job to iron out

whatever was slowing up the work. His mind moved rapidly over the possible causes as he dismounted and tied his horse to the platform rail of the office car. He took the steps two at a time and slammed the door behind him.

Ben Hamilton, the wiry, white-haired head of the Kansas & Western, sat behind his desk, staring at Rome over the top of a coffeepot. His eyes were red with sleeplessness. Rome waited for him to speak, sensing defeat in the slump of Hamilton's shoulders.

At last the older man sighed. He switched his gaze to the coffeepot and poured himself another cup. "Hello, Mark. You want some coffee? It's cold . . ."

"No, thanks," Rome answered. He swung his leg across a chair before the desk, resting his arms on the back.

"You don't look very good, Ben."

Hamilton laughed in a cracked tone and gulped some of the coffee. "I guess not, Mark. How's things in Saint Louis?"

Rome gestured. "All cleared up. The hitch was coming from back East. We'll be getting rails and spikes to spare in a couple of days."

"Don't know as it'll do us much good," Hamilton commented sourly.

"Ben, you might as well spill it. It's my job."

The older man sighed again. "All right, dammit. It's simple enough. We're stopped. Turns out we don't have the right of way we need through three of the spreads. The owners refuse to sell. So we can't meet our contract. It'll mean an extra week if it turns out that we have to bypass Warknife."

Rome sat up abruptly. "Warknife!" He hadn't realized they were that close.

"Yeah. You know the town?"

Rome nodded. "I was born there. Lived there until I was eighteen, before I went East."

"Fine." Hamilton's tone was sarcastic. "You must have a lot of friends there. One hell of a lot of good that'll do us."

Friends. The word stung Rome. More than friends. Cathy Thompson. He remembered her, painfully. Remembered how much he'd been in love with her, how many times they had ridden together, hunted together—and laughed at the antics of the young calves together.

Rome knew then it wouldn't work. The cattle were in her blood. They were her life and her heritage. She could only see cattlemen, and no one else. For him there had been another call, from the East, from the world where the iron horse was beginning to move and bellow as it cut the continent in half. Since that morning, years ago, when he saw locomotives standing on the wharf of Saint Louis, the railroad had captured him.

Sitting before Hamilton in the shadowy car as the older man stared at him, Rome thought about each of the two dreams. The iron horse. He had caught that excitement as a small boy and never lost it. Then came Cathy, when he was older. The two couldn't live side by side, not then. The smokestack, the churning pistons, the wheels westward, the whistle-scream . . . the railroad won. He left Warknife and Cathy and went East.

Now he was here again. One dream had been fulfilled, but the other still left its empty ache within him.

"Why all the trouble?" he asked at last. "I thought our buyers had the land contracts sewn up a year ago."

"So did we," Hamilton exclaimed. "Why, dammit,

we were set to lay track all the way to the mountains, picking up the contracts as we went along!"

"Didn't our buyers get anything on paper?"

Hamilton shook his head. "They should have. That was where we slipped."

"Everybody slips once in a while," Rome told him. "We've got to correct the slip, that's all."

"Look!" Hamilton exclaimed. Rome realized that the man's nerves were frayed. "We've been trying for the last four days. Somebody's stirred up the three ranchers—most of the town, in fact—and they're dead set against the railroad coming through. Or at least that's the way it stacks up."

"Any particular reason?"

"God knows. A lot of hogwash about too much too quick. I've got a pretty good idea who's behind it. An hombre named Bruce Gashlin. He's got his main office in Warknife." Hamilton paused. "Central Kansas Overland Company."

"Stages, eh?"

"Yeah, and we can't fight 'em, not legally at least. It's all in folks' minds, the way it appears to me. Progress is comin' too fast. The coaches have worked for them well enough for a long time, so why change? A little fast talking here and there, and we're blocked."

"You had any trouble?"

"Not much. Couple of boys got in an argument at the Emporia and got cut up a little, but that's all. But I think this Gashlin has it in him to make serious trouble for us if he wants. He has one boy working for him named Yancey who looks like a real killer."

Rome picked a cigar out of the inlaid box on the top of the desk. He struck a match to it and inhaled the strong smoke. "I've got a pretty good idea of what you want me to do."

"Thought you would."

"I'd like to know the names of the ranchers with the land we need for the right-of-way."

Hamilton pulled out one of the desk drawers, shuffled through a sheaf of papers, and drew one out, laying it on the desk before him. He scanned it a moment. "Harry Drew, Giles McMaster, and Job Thompson."

Once again the knife of memory and regret twisted. Job Thompson . . . Cathy's father, big and powerful and rock-faced, with his voice like velvet thunder. When the children of the Warknife Congregational Sunday School had thought of God, they thought of Job Thompson's voice.

And Cathy . . . The prospect of seeing her again worried Rome. By now she must be married. Any number of younger ranchers with small spreads near Warknife would have found her a fine wife. And a beautiful one at that.

Rome eased himself to his feet and looked straight at Hamilton, trying not to show his tangled emotions. "I'll ride in and see what I can do."

"You're a good talker, a damned good talker. Maybe you can get 'em to change their minds."

"I'll try."

Hamilton jabbed a warning finger at him. "Let me tell you something, Mark. I know you're never anxious to use that gun of yours, but I've met this Gashlin, and, believe me, he's somebody to watch out for. He hates us. And Yancey's nothing but a paid killer. Gashlin's got a bunch of them working for him, but this Yancey's the worst. He hung around Dodge City for a long time, I hear."

"I'll watch out," Rome promised. With a brief farewell wave, he left the office car and swung up into his saddle, moving at a brisk trot out through the end-of-track camp. It still lay quiet under the burning yellow of the noon sun. The sound of a harmonica lifted mournfully from somewhere beyond the cook car.

Outside the camp, Rome kicked his mount to a gallop. Warknife lay less than a half mile away. He felt ashamed that he had forgotten so much of the territory in the years he'd been gone.

Warknife itself hadn't changed greatly. The board fronts were still there, some with new coats of paint, some worn even more from the weather than he remembered. He rode slowly through the main street, noticing the new druggist's shop, the new name posted over the livery stable. A hundred boyhood incidents flooded back: memories of warm summer evenings near the stable, of the excitement of the first rolled cigarette, the first church meeting. His father, his mother . . . They were vague figures; sad-faced people broken by years of work in the general-store business. Someone named Hopeman now owned the store, he saw.

No one recognized him. He rode slowly through the main street. People bustled on the sidewalks doing after-dinner shopping. Cattlemen were in the saddle on various errands. The loungers on the front porch of the Emporia Saloon paid no attention to him. He spied the Reverend Paxton, who peered at him from the sidewalk for a minute. Rome stared back impassively. Paxton's eyes took in the gun on his hip, the rawboned body, the determined face. No expression of recognition appeared. Rome felt a little lonely then.

The Circle JT lay three miles on the other side of Warknife to the northwest. Rome caught his breath angrily as he saw that the land would make a perfect right-of-way. Except for a deep cut in the midst of a stretch of uncleared timber that would have to be bridged, construction would be relatively easy.

The yard of the ranch house was empty. Most of the hands, including Thompson himself, would be out on the range. Rome tied his horse and walked across the porch, conscious of the loud sound of his boots. He knocked.

Mrs. Thompson, a stout woman with a retiring manner, came to the door. She stared at him with the gaze she must have reserved for strangers, Rome thought. She made no attempt to recognize him. They had all forgotten. . . .

"Yes, sir, good afternoon," she said, "what can—?" She caught her breath abruptly. "Why, my goodness! Is it . . . Mark Rome? Is it?"

Rome grinned. "Yes, ma'am, it is."

Mrs. Thompson opened the front screen quickly. "My heavens, boy, come in!" She ushered him into the parlor, a musky place smelling of handmade lavender sachets and adorned with the customary motto, *God Bless Our Home*, on the wall. "Sit down, Mark," she said affably. "I'll call Cathy." She raised her voice. "Cathy? Cathy, come see who's here."

Rome turned his hat in his hands. In a moment Cathy appeared from the kitchen. She stared at him, a slender woman with brown hair, frank brown eyes, and a faintly sensual mouth set in an oval face. She was still very good to look at, he thought.

"Mark Rome!" she said, smiling, and Rome felt the inner glow of warmth that always came from seeing that smile. She shook his hand with just a hint of pressure. He saw that she wore no wedding ring.

"When did you come back to Warknife?" she asked.

"Only today. I've been in Saint Louis doing some work for the railroad."

"Railroad?" Mrs. Thompson stiffened perceptibly.

"Yes, ma'am, the Kansas & Western."

Cathy laughed in a forced way. "It always was the railroad, wasn't it, Mark?"

"Yes, I guess it was. I came to see about the trouble over the right-of-way." The moment was broken. The wall had been erected; they were strangers again.

"Dad isn't going to sell," Cathy said evenly. "Bruce Gashlin's stages work well enough. You know that."

"I'd like to talk with Job, if I could," Mark said.

"You'll have to wait for him," Mrs. Thompson told him. "He'll be in about the middle of the afternoon. If you'll excuse me, I'm putting up pickles in the kitchen. Sure was nice to see you again." Her smile carried no feeling.

He and Cathy talked for an hour or so, exchanging news of what they had both been doing in the intervening years. Cathy didn't mention anything of marriage, and Rome avoided the subject. Then they talked of the East, where Cathy had never been.

"Everything's too fast there," she declared. "Always trying something crazy before it's proven."

"There are plenty of railroads in operation," Rome said with a trace of sharpness.

"Plenty of stage lines left, too, I'll bet. They'll never be wiped out, no matter what happens. Dad doesn't like the East. He's been there." The wall between them was growing by the minute.

At about three, Job Thompson rode in, older of course, but his voice still had the quality of majesty. Rome exchanged a brief hello and stated his business.

Thompson thought for a moment. "All right, son. We'll see. We'll call a meeting at the church, and you and Bruce Gashlin can talk it out in front of everybody. I'll make sure Drew and McMaster are there.

You haven't got a chance, but we'll give you an opportunity to tell folks in town what you think—so you can see how damned wrong you are. How's tonight?" he finished curtly.

"Tonight'll be fine."

He found himself disliking Job Thompson and respecting him at the same time.

"Make it eight o'clock," the rancher told him.

With an even briefer good-bye than he gave to Thompson, Rome left Cathy and the house and rode out of the Circle JT. Lead-colored clouds were lowering in the north. Even the sky acted unfriendly.

Well, he might be able to get something across at the meeting. He hoped so.

But he did realize that he and Ben Hamilton were entirely alone, strangers in a strange land. The iron horse had become an enemy to a way of life. People were slow to change. Sometimes they never did. And he was losing his contact with the one woman he had ever cared about. Not that there had been much chance of starting things over, though . . .

As he rode slowly back toward Warknife, his eyes roamed the grasslands. The stalks were dry and brown, sun-parched and tinder-brittle. The gray clouds might bring rain, but until they did the grass was dangerous, like the situation in Warknife. Explosive. There was potential trouble in a man called Gashlin, and another called Yancey from Dodge City. . . .

For once he was thankful for the pistol on his hip.

He tied his horse in front of the Emporia, walked across the porch and in, conscious of the indifference of the loungers. It wouldn't be long, though. Job Thompson had ridden out of the Circle JT behind him. Rome had watched from a distant rise. The word would spread fast.

Feeling the hunger in his belly, he made his way

through the gaming tables, past the bar and up the stairs to the mezzanine. It wouldn't look good to be seen downing straight whiskeys when he was to present his point of view at the church that evening.

A tired waiter with a pasted-down mustache sauntered over and took his order for a steak, fried potatoes, and beer. Tired, Rome leaned elbows on the table and fixed himself a cigarette. He was just putting a match to it when someone at his elbow said, "May I sit down, Mr. Rome?"

Rome glanced up, blowing out the match. The stranger was tall, of medium build, and finely dressed with a checked waistcoat. He was about Rome's age, hard-faced and ruddy, with sharp, cold blue eyes. He smiled at Rome, his lips curling faintly as if the whole world was a freakish spectacle that he could control at will. Rome catalogued him as an opportunist.

"Sure, sit down. You seem to know my name. I can't say the same."

"Gashlin, Bruce Gashlin."

News had traveled faster than he'd expected. His eyes moved briefly to the head of the mezzanine stairs. A young kid in dirty denims and sweat-stained shirt was watching him, grinning idiotically. Above the grin were eyes like stone chips. A youngster, Rome thought, taking in the well-worn holsters and pistol butts. That would be Yancey.

Gashlin fixed himself a cigarette with careless precision. "Guess you and I are going to be on opposite sides of the fence tonight," he said as if it didn't really matter.

"I'm going to tell them I think the railroad should come through, and why, if that's what you mean."

"Your buyers didn't have much luck pushing that story."

"That's when I go to work, Mr. Gashlin, when the buyers don't have much luck."

Gashlin nodded. "You know what my business is."

Rome laughed. "Yes, I know."

"I'm not going to give you any line about too much progress. That's for the people I deal with." He waved a hand at the crowded, noisy bar below with its lush nude mural, its row of bottles. "Frankly, I've got a business to run. My business is essentially the same as that of the Kansas & Western—passengers and freight. It's a good business, and I've worked hard to build it—cutting corners sometimes, I'll admit. I don't want to lose it."

Before Rome could reply, the waiter appeared with the food. When he left, Rome stuck his fork into the steak. "I could figure most of that for myself."

Gashlin shrugged. "Just wanted to let you know what you're up against. I'm not planning to lose the Central Kansas Overland."

Rome stared at him. Gashlin kept his eyes narrowed, not avoiding the scrutiny. "If you can't keep it honestly," Rome asked quietly, "then you'll do it some other way?"

Gashlin nodded. "I reckon so."

"I guess we don't have much more to say." Rome ate a piece of steak and swallowed some cold beer.

Gashlin made no attempt to move. "Now that the formalities are over, I can get down to business. When I heard what Job Thompson planned for tonight, naturally I didn't like it. I'm willing to offer you a thousand dollars to stay away from the church."

"You're wasting your time."

"Twelve hundred is my top offer. It's a lot, but it's worth it to me."

Rome pushed his plate away from him in irritation.

"Look, Mr. Gashlin, get something straight. I want to see the railroad come through. It isn't a matter of my business succeeding or failing. I think the railroad will be an improvement. I don't own any stock in the company, and I wouldn't be more than ordinarily sore if they fired me next week, so long as they laid their track when and where they're supposed to. You understand?"

Gashlin stood up abruptly, gesturing with one hand. "Afraid I do, Rome." The youngster sauntered up to the table and stood behind his employer, pushing at the brim of the hat sitting crookedly on his head. "Mr. Yancey, this is Mr. Rome. You might be seeing a lot of each other."

Yancey said nothing. He merely looked at Rome, grinning his foolish smile. But his eyes were angry and hard. Rome shivered inwardly. Yancey was the kind of gun-crazy kid who killed for the sport of it. He would be a good helper for a man like Gashlin.

Anger at Gashlin, the proposed bribe, the whole situation stacked up against the railroad in Warknife suddenly burst to the surface. He jerked a thumb at Yancey.

"Does your hired gunslinger say anything?"

"Once in a while," Gashlin replied. "He's quiet most of the time, except when he's sore."

"Then tell him I'll be watching for him. When he thinks he's old enough to face men, I'll be ready."

Yancey's grin widened even more. Rome knew that the youngster wanted to jerk out his gun and kill him right there. His stomach went cold. He kept his hands rigid on the knife and fork, watching Yancey's fingers moving nervously.

Yancey spoke abruptly, his voice a whine. "It'll be soon, Mr. Rome. Real soon."

"Get the hell out of here, both of you," Rome said.

Gashlin didn't say anything. He moved among the tables, down into the bar and outside, Yancey following behind.

Rome ate the rest of his meal hastily and pushed back his chair. The clock over the bar said twenty to six.

He bought some cigars and sat on the front porch of the Emporia for two hours, listening to the talk around him. There were three main topics of discussion. The first two were almost tied in importance. One was what would be said at the debate at the church, the other was the prospect of rain for the already tinder-dry grasslands. The clouds still hovered, ominously darker as night came on. But they gave no rain.

Rome couldn't tell whether the opinions of the loungers were meaningful since they didn't represent the town's influential element. But the saloon crowd knew what others were talking about.

The third subject was the railroad in general. Most of the loungers thought it might be a pretty good thing. Maybe most of the people would be on his side after all, except McMaster and Drew and, of course, Job Thompson.

At quarter to eight, when the lamps were beginning to glow butter-yellow against the twilight dark, Rome made his way to the church. It was already packed to overflowing. He walked stiffly down the center aisle, looking straight ahead, conscious of the eyes on his back.

Gashlin and Yancey sat in the first pew. Rome sat in the one opposite them. Exactly on the hour, Job Thompson walked up to the platform and told the people why the meeting had been called. He and Drew and McMaster controlled the unsold portion of the right-of-way, and he wanted opinions on the subject of the railroad. His voice rolled out, sonorously rich and powerful, capable of swaying them. But his presentation was fair.

"Our first speaker, representing the railroad, will be one of Warknife's former residents, Mark Rome."

Mark made his way forward amid the whispers of the audience. Many of them, when he turned to face them, peered like bright-eyed birds. Job Thompson, his wife, and Cathy sat stern-faced in the second pew behind Gashlin and Yancey. Behind them in turn were two more families. The Drews and the McMasters, Rome supposed.

He didn't like being first. Gashlin had a better chance for an effective climax. But he would do the best he could. He cleared his throat and began to speak, clearly and with all the sincerity of his convictions.

He told them of the railroad providing faster travel in more comfortable circumstances. He told them of the reduced fares possible on the Kansas & Western because of the larger turnover of freight and passengers. He told them the railroads would eventually link the oceans, whether Warknife liked it or not. That part had to be worked carefully, politely.

And then he told them of the direct shipping of cattle. No more drives to railheads. No more hiring extra hands to make the long and dangerous cross-country journey. Direct shipping. *Direct shipping.* He hammered it home with quiet, forceful tones, then sat down as a ripple of enthusiasm stirred the audience. One rough-garbed cowman started to clap but stopped with a nervous cough.

Thompson showed his partisanship when he introduced Bruce Gashlin more favorably, more glowingly. As the stage-line owner rose to speak, he smiled in an innocently boyish manner, working for audience support. Rome thought, He'll get it, too. He's a showman.

Gashlin's speech was brief. "Friends, you know me, Bruce Gashlin. I run the Central Kansas Overland Company. I don't like the railroads, and you know that, too. They won't last. Things like this, fly-by-night schemes, don't last long. The Central Kansas Overland has done all right working for you, transporting your goods, and I think you appreciate the fact. As for direct cattle shipping, it would mean the ruin of the industry. The drives are one of the most important parts of that industry, and, without them, men who make their living from the range, ordinary hands like many of you once were, would be out of work a good part of the time."

He cleared his throat and smiled at them again. Then he made a pretense of pondering, and frowned. "I don't like to say things like I'm going to say now, but I must. It may help you think this thing through. I can't tell you about the operating methods of the Kansas & Western, but I do know they're afraid of us. A couple of hours ago, Mr. Rome down there talked to me in the Emporia Saloon."

His voice rose. "Mr. Rome offered me five hundred dollars of Kansas & Western money not to appear here tonight. If you want proof, Mr. Yancey was with me."

Rome jumped up, forgetting where he was and started angrily for the platform. "You're a liar!" Hands grabbed at him. "You're a damn liar, Gashlin, and you know—"

The meeting exploded. People pushed out of the pews, milling, shouting. Gashlin moved easily toward a side door, with Yancey following. The youngster's eyes watched the crowd, his hand hovering over his gun.

Job Thompson grabbed Rome's shoulder, thundering accusations. Rome tried to argue back, unsuccessfully. Angry talk, punctuated by denunciations of
Rome's language, filled the church. Rome glimpsed
a frantic Reverend Paxton standing by the far wall,
bewildered by the sacrilege breaking loose.

Rome jerked away from Thompson. He wanted to
find Bruce Gashlin, make him admit the lie. He had
been warned: every trick available, and a few more
Gashlin was probably inventing. He shouldered his
way through the crowd. Some of the women struck
at him.

He bumped into Cathy Thompson near the door.
She stared as if he were a mortal enemy. He took
hold of her arm. "Listen a minute, Cathy, I don't
want you to think—"

The crowd pushed him away from her, outward,
down the steps of the church and onto the plank
sidewalk. Job Thompson was following close behind,
still shouting questions. The crowd had turned, become a mob manipulated by Gashlin's strategy.

The stage-line owner and his gunman stood at the
edge of the crowd. Rome pushed toward them,
fighting his way through. Once he dropped his hand
to his hip, making sure his pistol was free.

Job Thompson caught up with him just as Rome
reached the other two men. From then on, it happened very quickly, and no one but Rome and
Gashlin and Yancey saw what went on. The crowd
milled blindly, paying little attention. The four men
at the edge of the crowd formed a tight, closed-in
band with their gun hands shielded from obser-
vation.

Gashlin's eyes widened. Rome felt a quick, terrible
sense of the opportunity being instantly seized.

Gashlin elbowed Yancey. The youngster reached for his holster.

Rome twisted aside, dodging low and pulling his own gun. He aimed at Yancey's belly as the youngster drew. Just as Rome fired, Gashlin slapped his gun barrel down so that the bullet would plow into the dirt of the street. Yancey's gun roared at the same instant.

The tight group of men stood bunched together. A woman screamed, a high, shrill sound. The noise of the crowd dropped away to silence.

Yancey had already disappeared. Rome whirled, his gun still smoking. Job Thompson was reeling unsteadily, half a foot behind Rome, his eyes closed in pain, his hands clutching the red hole in his belly. Mrs. Thompson and Cathy were pushing through the crowd while Mrs. Thompson screamed hysterically.

Like a great tree, Job Thompson fell forward and smashed face first in the street. A halo of dust rose around his head.

Rome turned to Gashlin, bringing the gun up again, cursing. Gashlin's finger whipped out accusingly.

"Here's your man! I saw him do it. They were arguing—Job didn't even draw. I saw it all."

Rome aimed the gun at Gashlin. A hand jerked it from his fingers. An angry growling rose from him as Gashlin backed cautiously away. The crowd closed in.

Rome whirled once more, realizing what had happened. There was no place to run. They were all around him. The lamp-lit street echoed with their cries for vengeance.

He knew that fighting them was useless. They swarmed around him, raining blows on his face and shoulders. He dodged, to no avail. The angry talk grew louder. Finally one hoarse voice grated above the rest, and Rome knew what was coming.

"Lynch him! *Lynch him!*"

Others repeated the cry. Almost miraculously, the rope appeared. Eager hands darted over it, twisting, coiling, fashioning the death noose. The women crowded on the church steps, watching coldly. Rome had seen two hangings in his time, but now he was caught up in the blood-crazy spell of one. Outside God's house, this mob had become drunk with hatred.

Cathy stood in the middle of the women, stiff and haughty. Rome caught a glimpse of her avenging look. Someone clubbed him on the back of his neck. His knees buckled. Next thing he knew, he was being lifted and set in the saddle. His head spun, full of garish colors and ringing sounds. Then a steady, throbbing pain wiped even his fear away.

Another voice shouted something about the livery stable. Hands seized the reins of the horse. The mob began to move, sluggishly at first, then faster, racing down the street. The horse jerked beneath him; Rome held on tightly to keep from falling. Lamp-lit windows blurred by. Rome couldn't see Gashlin anywhere.

A couple of torches were lit. Rome wondered dully how all this could have happened so fast. But the fury had burned, caught, and spread. Job Thompson had been a respected man.

The trees around the livery stable moved with soft whispers in the shadows. A pungent smell of animals and straw filled the air. A circle of glaring white faces surrounded Rome. The women had stayed behind— no, he was wrong. Cathy watched from the fringe of the crowd.

Hands pulled him down from the saddle, started

to slip the rope around his neck. One of the men with the rope wore a deputy's badge. He wondered what the sheriff was doing. . . .

The thunder of the shotgun roared through the darkness. The leaves stirred with faint hissing as the lead passed through.

The mob stopped.

Like a single organism, its voice died. Frightened eyes peered toward the shadows. The rope fell to the ground. Rome gazed at the figures in the darkness vaguely outlined in the torchlight. He heard a familiar voice.

"Get away from him, all of you."

Ben Hamilton. My God, it *was* Ben! Rome wanted to shout his name aloud.

Hamilton was mounted, a shotgun leveled at the mob. Behind him were other riders, men from the camp, similarly armed. Their gun barrels shone dull blue in the starlight.

"The next blast," Hamilton said, "may get some of you."

The mob stirred, whispering. No one reached for his gun.

"Open a way there," Hamilton ordered. "Mark, are you all right?"

"Yes," Rome called.

"Can you ride out by yourself? Do you need help?"

"I can ride," Rome said quickly.

The men didn't move. Hamilton's face, craggy and determined, was dimly visible in the orange glare of the torches. *"Let him through!"*

The shotgun roared again, scattering shot skyward. A pinched-faced puncher squealed in fear. The crowd parted.

Rome kicked his horse through the aisle. Hamilton

and the railroad men wheeled their mounts and pounded down the dark alley behind the stable. The angry voices lifted again, but they soon faded under the drumming of the hoofs.

The men rode from Warknife to the end-of-track without a word being said. Rome hung on tightly, letting the horse have its head to follow the others. He felt strength slowly returning; he began to think clearly again.

At the camp, Hamilton posted guards all around, then he and Rome went into the office car. Hamilton lit the lamp and pulled the green blinds. His eyes bored into Rome. "This is pretty damned serious, Mark."

"Goddammit, you don't have to tell me that! What I want to know is how you got there. I was almost stretched out. I had the feeling I was going to die. I've never felt like that, so damned sure. It isn't pleasant."

"Two of the boys bought supplies in town this afternoon. They had a drink at the Emporia and heard about the meeting. I was afraid there might be trouble. We rode in just as the meeting was breaking up. We heard the shooting, and it was damned clear that a necktie party was being organized, with you as the guest. I'd like to hear about it."

"There's quite a bit," Rome said shortly.

"Well, make it quick. They'll be out here before long. I've got the men standing by to signal. They won't touch us—they'll be afraid to, because lynchings are illegal. But with you it may be a different story. They're liable to take you anyway."

Rome laughed, sharp and hard. "A price on my head." Rapidly he outlined what had happened since their discussion at noon. When he finished, Hamilton looked even more dismayed.

"God, this looks bad. You didn't try to buy off Gashlin, did you?"

"Ben, don't you know me better?"

"All right, don't get sore. We've got to figure out what to do next. And, on top of that, we still have a contract to meet." He shoved a hand through his white hair, his eyes reflecting the yellow glow of the lamps.

To Rome, the interior of the car with its green blinds and shadowed corners seemed secure and untroubled. The feeling was shattered by the blast of a rifle. Hamilton leaped to his feet, knocking over the chair.

"They're coming, Mark. Get out of here, fast! Ride back when it looks safe, and we'll see what's happened by then."

Rome already had the door open. He jumped off the steps, swung up onto his horse, and booted it hard. From the opposite side of the camp came the noise of a large party of riders. The sound of his horse's hoofs would be muffled by the arrival of the men from Warknife.

He headed away from the camp, to the north, and circled back wide, riding across the dark prairie toward the town. The wind fanning his face was cool and invigorating. He began to organize his thoughts.

He figured Gashlin would be with the Warknife men. Yancey would be undercover, probably holed up in a room at one of the town's boardinghouses. That gave Rome an opportunity.

He didn't exactly know what he was looking for, but he held a hope that he might find something to untangle the web of treachery and death gathering around him. Hamilton and the other railroaders were helpless. He was the free agent—with a price on his head.

The realization struck home with biting force. He rode on beneath the cloud-filled sky, suddenly feeling cut off and alone. The moon came out from under a black veil of cloud, shining down like a bloated pale face. The air had grown very cold.

Warknife lay quiet now, its streets deserted. Rome kept to the back alleys. Most of the lamps in the houses were out, the people in bed. The hoofs of his horse made soft, thudding sounds in the dirt.

He dismounted in back of the main yard of the Central Kansas Overland Company. Coaches loomed against the moon as Rome crept silently among them toward the office building. He saw no guard posted anywhere.

He eased out his pistol, slipping into a patch of shadow. He tried the door. It was locked. Moving to the right, he began a systematic check of the windows. Finally he found one open in the rear.

He crawled over the sill, finding a small storeroom piled with boxes of invoices, shipping forms, and company letterheads. The door to this room was locked. Conscious of the creak of the floorboards, he smashed twice at the lock with his gun butt. Then he listened. He heard nothing but a few faint shouts from the street. Drunks, probably. The lock hung broken. He stepped into the main office.

Across it, behind a gold-lettered door, lay Bruce Gashlin's office. In there, Rome reasoned, might be something to help him expose the man for what he was. Cautiously, he eased the door open and started a methodical rifling of the desk.

One of the bottom drawers was locked. He tugged at the handle, then noticed something and felt a burst of satisfaction. There was no safe in the office. Gashlin was evidently too sure of himself for that; a locked drawer would suffice.

Rome took a letter opener from the desk and thrust it into the slit at the top of the drawer. He worked the opener back and forth a few moments; cursed when it snapped in two. He found a second one with a heavy ivory handle and finally managed to break the latch and open the drawer.

Three papers lay inside. Rome hesitated, listening again. The drunken shouts again, closer. He crouched under the desk and struck a match, reading the first paper.

> *Received of Bruce Gashlin*
> *1500 dollars for services.*
> *Signed,*
> *Job Thompson*

The other two, for seven and nine hundred dollars respectively, were signed by Harry Drew and Giles McMaster. Rome blew out the match, working on the significance of what he'd read.

Gashlin had plenty of money. Enough money to pay the ranchers not to sell the right-of-way. Pay them, in effect, to maintain his business. It was more money than the railroad could offer for the small parcels of land. The Kansas & Western was not yet that big a firm; it ran on a tight budget.

Gashlin was the one with capital. Thompson, McMaster, and Drew certainly knew what kind of a man he was. Knew, for instance, that he would buy people off to get what he wanted; that it wasn't strictly a matter of being opposed to progress. The three of them were in on the scheme, while the rest of the townspeople were unaware of it.

"Damn," Rome said under his breath. The church meeting had been a farce, a show staged to keep the townspeople quiet. They could have thrown a lot of weight, but now they were against the railroad. Thompson's wrath at Gashlin's lie concerning the attempt to bribe him must have been an act, and that same anger provided the setting for his murder. Thompson evidently was expendable from Gashlin's point of view. But there was one man who might be able to blow things open, if Rome could get to him.

Stuffing the papers into his pocket, he straightened suddenly. One of the drunken voices was coming from the front porch of the office building. A key rattled in the lock. The door swung open.

Rome crouched in the shadows. The watchman's lantern swayed in one hand; a bottle hung slackly from the other. The watchman stumbled against the outer office rail, swearing. Rome started to move toward the storeroom through the open door of Gashlin's office.

The watchman turned, setting down his lantern. "Who in hell . . . Who is it?" he shouted. He reached for his gun.

Rome moved faster than he thought possible. He clubbed the man's gun away and kicked him backward with his knee. He had learned the lessons of running outside the law very quickly.

The watchman staggered, his eyes wild in the smoky light from the lantern. He jerked a knife from his pocket and lumbered at Rome, mumbling, "What the hell are you doing in here?" Rome tensed himself and swung out, striking the drunken man across the temple with his gun barrel.

The knife clattered to the wooden floor, blade first. A faint whine filled the air as it stuck and quivered. Then the watchman dropped, a splotchy bruise widening on his skin.

He wasn't dead. Rome made sure of that, then blew out the lantern. As he stood in the darkness listening to the watchman's irregular breathing, a new thought twisted the pit of his stomach.

He was now bound to the railroad more closely than ever, though in another way he remained cut off. He was bound to it not merely because he worked for the Kansas & Western—it wasn't that simple. If the railroad went through, Gashlin would be out of business and there was a good chance Rome would be cleared. If the railroad *didn't* go through, he would eventually be a dead man, swinging in a noose.

The thought was ironic. He laughed softly. He had to put the Kansas & Western through. Not with actual rails and ties, not by sweating in the sun, but as an outlaw, with his gun and his mind. It was surely a new way to drive the iron west. . . .

He stopped laughing then. A noose wasn't funny. He remembered how close he had come, how he'd felt death near.

He went out through the storeroom window to the back of the yard, the papers in his coat. His horse waited in the shadow thrown by the coaches, whose angular shapes rose against the swollen white moon.

Yancey. The answer lay with the grinning, death-crazed youngster. At least, Rome thought, the first step lay there. He had to clear himself and thereby clear the railroad. With the moon out and night lying on the town, he had the opportunity. He knew very little about Yancey and yet he knew a great deal. Enough, perhaps, to give him the edge he needed.

He rode slowly through the shadowed streets. They wouldn't be searching for him at this hour. His horse moved quietly between the rows of houses while he looked to the right and left till he found the object of his search.

The first boardinghouse, run by an Irishman named Harrigan, revealed nothing. The irate and sleepy landlord told him nobody named Yancey lived there. The door slammed in Rome's face. He moved back to the street, mounted, and rode on.

The second boardinghouse stood on a large lot on a dusty street directly to the rear of the Emporia. Rome heard the rhythms of the player piano still dinning into the night along with occasional laughter. He tied his horse at the sagging gate and stepped as quietly as he could onto the squeaking boards of the run-down porch.

He knocked three times before a landlady appeared, carrying a tall lamp. Her hair was put up in papers, her thick face mottled. Her breath reeked of alcohol. Rome felt safe. She was too full of rotgut to recognize him, even if she had been at the church. Judging from her appearance, chances were she hadn't.

"What the hell's the idea of waking a lady at this time of night?" she growled, pulling her wrapper close. The liquor fumes clouded around Rome's head as she spoke.

"I'm looking for a man named Yancey. Does he live here?"

"Sure he does. Cole Yancey. Second floor. First door to the left of the landing."

He moved by, into the hall. She slammed the door and continued to babble drunkenly about being awakened, standing in a pool of lamplight by the newel post. She was still complaining when he turned the corner at the head of the stairs.

He halted at the first door, standing in the gloom, listening. Beyond the thin panel he heard loud snoring. He eased his gun from its holster and shoved the barrel near the lock. Then he rapped on the door.

He kept knocking till the snoring stopped. Yancey mumbled incoherently; footsteps padded to the door. Rome heard the noise of a hammer going back. Even if Yancey was still groggy from sleep, he couldn't get out of the habit. But his reaction would be slow . . . or so Rome hoped.

"Yeah?" Yancey called. "Who is it?"

"Gashlin sent me over," Rome whispered.

"What about?"

"About you and Job Thompson. Now open up." He tried to sound angry and harried at the same time.

Rome's heart slugged out a beat within his chest. The key rattled in the lock. A tiny bit of light appeared as Yancey pulled the door open.

Rome shoved the barrel of his gun against the man's stomach. "Let go of your gun. *Now!*"

Yancey's face lost its look of sleepy idiocy. His eyes flared with the sudden awareness that he was caught. He tried to step back, but Rome jammed the barrel deeper into his flesh, gouging. "Drop it on the floor!"

Yancey choked and coughed, still not totally awake. He eased the hammer carefully into place. The gun thudded on the carpet, and Rome stepped quickly into the room, shutting the door. Yancey, barefoot, in his underwear, looked like a helpless and frightened boy. He didn't have a gun anymore.

That was what Rome counted on. Without his gun he was nothing; a harmless youngster. Rome scooped up the weapon and thrust it into his belt. Yancey waited submissively, terror in his eyes as he stared at the glinting blue metal in Rome's hand.

"What do you want from me, Rome?" he croaked. "Listen, I only work for Gashlin . . ."

Rome moved to the bed and sat down. A smell of rotting garbage filtered into the bedroom through the open window. The Emporia piano clattered its mechanical melodies.

"I know you work for him, Yancey. That's why I want to know a few other things. You'd better answer my questions. If you don't, I'll kill you. Do you understand?"

Yancey trembled. Rome felt a surge of triumph. He had been right. Yancey was like so many of them, master of a situation only when armed. The youngster was scared of the cold muzzle eye looking at him. He was seeing the fire of the explosion, seeing the smoke rising before the bullet slammed him. He said, "Ask your questions."

"Did you know you were going to shoot Thompson before the meeting tonight? Was it planned?"

Yancey shook his head doggedly. "No, Mr. Rome." He emphasized the *mister*. "Gashlin give me the nod, and I knew what he meant. I always understand when he gives me the nod. People were packed so tight, nobody could see much. It was easy. I had a few drinks afterward and came back here."

Suddenly a new thought wrote itself across his face. "Say, they were supposed to hang you. I saw 'em start . . ."

Anger filled Rome. He rose, staring. His voice grew loud. "You cheap punk, I'm good and alive, and I've got half a mind to kill you right now. Remember in the Emporia? You said you'd accommodate me soon. Well, here I am."

"Yeah," Yancey mumbled faintly.

"No good without a gun, are you?" Rome couldn't resist the remark.

"No, sir, I ain't."

"You're damned quick with the answers, too." Rome felt angrier by the moment. This crazy kid had put the murder brand on him as casually as he'd

taken a drink afterward. Finally, Rome got control
of himself.

"All right, Yancey. I want you to do something."

"Sure, anything."

"You got some paper and a pen?"

Yancey pointed to the dresser. "In there. Belongs
to the landlady."

Rome moved to the bureau and pulled open the
drawer. Beneath two soiled work shirts were a few
yellowed sheets of writing paper. He also found a
metal-tipped pen and a bottle a third full of ink. He
set the items on top of the table in the center of the
room. Then he caught the chair with his boot tip and
jerked it forward. "Sit down."

Yancey sat, fidgeting with his underwear.

"You're going to write what I say. Pick up the pen.
You can write, can't you?"

"Yeah, I went to school in Indiana when I was
a kid."

"Don't waste my time. Write this. *I, Cole Yancey . . .*"

The pen scratched laboriously. Yancey hunched
over the table, peering at each word.

"*. . . killed Job Thompson outside of church tonight on
orders from my boss, Bruce . . .*"

"Not so fast, will you?" Yancey whined.

"Shut up and keep writing. *Bruce Gashlin.* Got
that?"

Yancey nodded.

"Date it and sign your name."

Yancey obeyed, then pushed the paper away from
him. Rome picked it up, scanned it briefly, and put
it down again. "Not just the initials. I want your
whole name."

"I always use my—" Yancey stopped, looking
again at the gun. He wrote out his full name.

Rome was reaching for the paper, feeling satisfied,

when the door opened abruptly. Bruce Gashlin stood there, his clothes dirty and sweat-stained from hard riding. His fingers curled around the doorknob. His husky face remained calm, but his blue eyes narrowed just a bit.

"Well!" He laughed gently. "Mr. Rome, I didn't expect you." He noticed the gun immediately, closing the door and stepping into the room. Rome's backbone tingled. A new factor had entered the situation. It was now no longer just Rome against Yancey.

Rome indicated the paper on the table. "I've got a nice confession from Mr. Yancey about Job Thompson's murder. It implicates you."

A tiny superior smile edged Gashlin's mouth. His fingers dipped into the pocket of his checked waistcoat, and he pulled out a cigar. "Unfortunately, we couldn't do a thing at the railroad camp since you'd already gone. Anyway, your boss Hamilton had plenty of men with guns. I just wanted to have a talk with Cole here. I didn't think you'd be on the scene."

"I'm leaving," Rome told him. "But I think the sheriff will be looking for you in a little while. I'll be with him. I want it to be legal."

Gashlin shook his head. "The paper won't stand up in court." His fingers dipped down into the waistcoat again. Rome observed him carefully. Controlled as it was, Gashlin's tone still revealed more than a trace of anxiety. The paper could finish him, and he knew it.

"I'll take my chances," Rome said. "And get your hands up where they belong."

Gashlin shrugged. "I only want to light my cigar."

The fingers reappeared, holding a pepper-pot derringer.

Rome tried to move fast. He swung the pistol toward Gashlin, but the other man slid the tiny gun across the table. "All right, Yancey." The youngster's eyes flared wildly as the derringer fell into his lap. He fumbled for it.

Rome swung his gun back again, the finger whitening on the trigger. He had no time, and Yancey was back in power, his young eyes full of kill-lust as he brought the derringer up from beneath the table. Gashlin was smiling; Yancey's face broke into its idiot grin. *He had no time. . . .*

A ragged burst of piano music came through the window, cut off abruptly by the thunder of Rome's gun exploding three times. Yancey dropped the derringer on the table with a loud thump, then sat back, his eyes bulging. Blood poured out of the hole Rome had blown in his neck. Slowly, he toppled to the floor.

Rome whirled. The last fragments of the confession were curling into black ash. Gashlin tossed the match onto the table. He kept smiling. "Do you want to kill me, too, Mr. Rome?"

From the first floor, the drunken landlady began to shout. Rome cursed and ran to the door. He did want to kill Gashlin, kill him where he stood, but he had to get away. The foundation had fallen, the bottom had tumbled out, and the hole had grown death-deep. He was caught now, more than ever.

He crashed against the landlady coming up the stairs, knocking the lamp out of her hand. There was a rattle of glass, then a leaping of flame as she screamed again. He bolted through the door and vaulted onto his mount, digging his heels in savagely. He thundered away through the darkened streets, out toward the end-of-track. Behind him, hoarse shouting filled the night. The moon had vanished; the world lay dark as he rode.

*The gun, the law of the gun,* he thought. You couldn't

outwit it, you couldn't beat it. In the end, it trapped you; you returned to it, and it destroyed you.

He had actually killed a man. The hoofbeats echoed it. *Killed a man, killed a man, killed a man . . .* The wind screaming in his ears sang it to him. Nothing remained but force, animal force. He knew it was wrong, but the other way had failed.

The end-of-track camp lay in darkness. The guards challenged him and he called out to identify himself as he rode past. He ran up the steps of the office car, pushed the door open, and faced Ben Hamilton, his heart beating furiously, his mind whirling.

"I killed Yancey, Ben. I shot him, I killed him, I couldn't help it. . . ."

His nerve broke, and he sank onto the chair before Hamilton's desk. He cradled his head on his arms, letting the dry sobs shake him, letting the strained emotions break loose.

He was no gunslinger. He was no fast-draw man. He worked for the railroad. He had a job. But they were killers. Ruthless . . .

*He worked for the railroad . . . my God . . . the railroad . . . the wheels . . . round and round . . . killed a man . . . and round . . . killed a man and round and round . . . killed, killed, killed . . .*

It took Ben Hamilton nearly an hour to quiet him down.

When Rome began to talk coherently once more, Hamilton drew the story from him.

Rome felt a sense of calm slowly returning. The familiar interior of the old car with its closed-in atmosphere of protection soothed his nerves. "I'm just not the man to handle a gun like that," he said wearily. "I thought times were changing. I thought you could work out differences in other ways."

"Back East, maybe. The country out here's slow to change. You ought to know that."

"I'm a killer," Rome said, as if he hadn't heard the other man.

Hamilton jabbed a finger at him. "The important thing is to get out of sight. We'll fix a place for you to hide in one of the boxcars. Then we've got to get the Kansas & Western rolling through Warknife."

Rome nodded. "Maybe these'll help." He fished the three papers from Gashlin's office out of his pocket, shoved them across the desk, and explained briefly what they were and how he had gotten them.

Hamilton read them, then laughed.

"By God, this may be our break." He got to his feet quickly. "Come on, let's get you under cover. They may be looking for you soon."

It was cold in the boxcar, cold and dark. He slept huddled among some old blankets Hamilton had collected in the camp. The first night he rested fitfully, lying awake for hours listening for the drum of hoofs in the distance. The night air remained still.

When dawn gashed the east with gray streaks, he realized they wouldn't be coming. The Thompson killing still stood; they would be hunting for him on that count. But Gashlin probably figured Yancey could be forgotten. There were a hundred others like him to be bought anywhere in the West.

Toward noon, while Rome hunched in the boxcar playing solitaire with a worn-out deck furnished by one of the Irish section hands, he heard the sound of horses. He slid the door open a fraction of an inch, peered out and saw a big man, evidently the sheriff, with a party of horsemen from Warknife drawn up in front of the office car. They were conferring with

Hamilton. Presently, they rode out again, back toward the town.

Hamilton made his way across the sprawling camp to the boxcar. "Looking for you," he reported. "About Thompson. Told them you'd gone—lit out of here last night after we saved you from stretching the rope. They don't seem to feel too bad about it. They've quieted down, and the sheriff doesn't like lynchings. They figure somebody else will catch up with you."

"What now?" Rome asked quietly. He gestured at the boxcar's interior. "Do I have to stay cooped up in this damn place when I should be out clearing myself?"

Hamilton's eyes bored into him. "Can you do that?"

There was silence for a moment. Then Rome shook his head. "Gashlin's free and I've got nothing on him."

"Nothing but those papers. They aren't incriminating, but they may help."

"You got an idea?"

"Yeah," Hamilton said. "Right now, you wait." Without another word, he stalked back across the camp. After Cookie brought Rome his noon meal, he saw Hamilton ride out in the direction of Warknife.

*Wait. . . .*

The hours stretched on, dull, colorless, relieved only by an unwanted nagging fear about which he could do nothing. He was trapped. He had no alternative but to wait, as Hamilton had said. Even then he didn't have an idea in the world of how to clear himself. Maybe he would have to ride out permanently. With a sick feeling, he realized that he might always be a hunted man. Something had to break . . .

Ben Hamilton returned right at sundown, riding

directly to Rome's car. He was grinning as he swung up, passing Rome a cigar. "This is it, boy! I think we'll be laying track within two days."

"What happened?"

"I took the papers to the sheriff."

"What for? They won't put anybody in jail."

"That's true. The sheriff himself told me he can't touch any of the ranchers, or Gashlin. The papers are strictly legal. But he didn't like the idea of the ranchers double-dealing Warknife like that. A lot of people really do want the railroad. Now the word's going to spread."

It spread rapidly; Rome heard it secondhand from the men who came back after an evening in Warknife. The town was reacting; rising on its haunches; wondering, voicing questions, even hurling accusations. As individual citizens had once fused into a single mass of hatred directed at Rome, now they were uniting against the trickery of a few. They began to wonder about Gashlin's statement of Rome's attempted bribery.

"Everybody, and I mean everybody, knows about them papers," one of the men reported. " 'Course, with Job Thompson dead, there ain't much said against him. But the others are getting laid low. The small ranchers didn't have any idea those three and Gashlin was sinking their chances of shipping beef by rail."

The voices rose, became angrier. The news carried back to the dim, lonely boxcar where Rome waited.

"Gashlin's about five hundred percent more unpopular than before. People don't like being shoved around because of him . . . they're starting to cuss the stink—and him."

Rome felt small satisfaction. Maybe the rails would stretch out. Maybe the Kansas & Western would roll.

But Job Thompson's killing remained bloody on his hands.

Three mornings after Hamilton took the papers into Warknife, more riders came to the camp. After they left, Hamilton didn't appear so Rome made his way to the office car. Hamilton was busy at the desk when he entered.

"Dammit, Mark, you're not supposed to be roaming around. Somebody might ride in here any time and spot you—"

"I just wanted to find out what those men were doing here."

Hamilton grinned. "The whole town's busted wide open. Drew and McMaster gave back the money Gashlin paid them and tore up the papers. Cathy Thompson plans to do the same. It appears she didn't have any idea that old Job was part of a deal involving bribery."

"That means something—"

"You're right it means something. Gashlin's sore as hell." Hamilton fingered the green metal cash box on top of the desk. "But I bought the right-of-way through all three spreads. Public opinion just got too strong. I heard those three families were almost social outcasts. Like they had leprosy or something. We're going through, starting now."

That made Rome feel better. The wheels were turning again. New life was being pumped into the Kansas & Western. He glanced out the window and saw it. Men bustled about busily. Track foremen were assembling their crews; flatcars were being loaded.

"I think maybe we've got this thing licked," Hamilton said at last.

"I wouldn't count on it a hundred percent."

"Why not?"

"Gashlin will still try to stop us. And this time it

won't be with paper deals. He'll use guns and dirty tactics. We ought to expect it and get ready."

Hamilton studied him. "We will. Maybe it'll be a good thing. In one way it scares the hell out of me— we're cutting our time pretty thin as it is. But maybe we can draw Gashlin into the open and get rid of him once and for all." He paused. "The situation's backwards now. Gashlin's out, we're in. He'll fight for sure. But we're in."

"All except me," Rome said quietly. "I swear to you, Ben—somehow I'll get that Thompson thing cleared up."

"Your chance'll come."

Rome nodded. "Right now I want to work."

"All right. We're going to hit this thing hard. Day and night. I'll put you on nights."

"I want to be out on the track. I want to help put those rails down myself, Ben."

"Good enough. Only don't expect to do that all the time. We may need extras in everything, foremen, engineers. We'll be working on a rough schedule."

"Suits me."

Hamilton slapped him on the shoulder. "Get back to your damned boxcar and wait till dark. Then you can get busy."

Rome thought of Gashlin all afternoon, wondering how and when the strike would come. When he got hold of him . . . well . . . He thought about that a lot. The bitterness feeding in him, gnawing at his mind, changed him. All he wanted was Gashlin before him and a gun in his hand. Rome wondered if he would be strong enough to keep from murdering the man the first time he laid eyes on him, the first time he was unprotected.

Noise filled the camp. Whistles shrilled and flatcars began to move up the line about a quarter of a mile, pulled by the small switch engines. Hoarse shouting echoed everywhere. Smoke wisped in the sky, and soon from the west came the clang of hammers.

At four o'clock a storm came smashing down from bloated gray clouds. At six, in the rain, Rome was swinging a hammer, driving in spikes. Behind him the switch engine bored a yellow tunnel of light through the downpour, wreathing the working men in a ghostly aura.

The rain kept coming down, soaking into the parched ground. Hamilton drove the men, working them twenty-four hours a day. Rome's muscles ached almost unendurably when the dawn came, but he went back to his duties after a two-hour rest. His clothes didn't dry out. His head swam, and when he slept again, he swung a hammer in his dreams. He knew he was getting sick, but he didn't care.

*The Kansas & Western was going through. . . .*

They drove the rails across Drew's spread, then McMaster's, then through Warknife. Rome stayed completely hidden the night they laid track through the town. The next day they were beyond the eastern outskirts and he was eager to work again. He argued with Hamilton and finally won, working through the day, too, stopping only about seven hours for sleep when he got too feverish.

They cut timber and built the trestle over the cut on Thompson's spread. Once at night, working under the eye of the locomotive behind them, Rome saw Cathy Thompson watching on horseback, Hamilton beside her. He kept his head down as he slammed another spike home. She didn't matter. Even Gashlin had been wiped from his mind. The world consisted of the rails and the ties, the spikes and the watching yellow eye marking progress through the rainy darkness.

Men began to drop. The ones remaining worked harder than ever. The dispensary in the rear of the office car never closed, and the supplies of medicine dwindled. The men were sick, but a restless energy drove them on. Hamilton was often among them, swinging a hammer, cursing, as wet and as sick and as tired as they were. But, like them, he was proud of what they were doing, and it showed. It kept them going.

Nine days after they started work they were back on schedule and almost to the far boundary of Job Thompson's ranch. Rome went back to the main camp east of the recently constructed trestle, trying to find some warmer clothes. The air had grown cooler, turning the wet ground into thick mud.

Rome was in the mess tent, downing a cup of hot, acidic coffee when one of the foremen came in and spotted him. "Hey, Mark—they're short of iron up ahead. We're loading a couple of flatcars. Can you take them up?"

Rome nodded and finished his coffee. He tramped through the drizzle toward the snorting switch engine. "Steam's up," the foreman called as Rome climbed into the cab.

He edged the throttle back, his hands moving with skill over the controls. The railroad man's sense of precision, his sensitivity to the massive iron locomotive born of instinct as well as practice, took hold. Smiling, Rome leaned out and watched the track ahead.

The wheels turned, hissing, clacking, rattling off their song of triumph. They weren't beaten. They were rolling west again. They were going through. He felt elated, even with the residue of fever and sickness to dull his senses.

He wasn't making over eight miles an hour. But

that was all right. The trestle would be coming up soon, and he hadn't far to go after that. Just being in the cab, feeling the engine under his hands, made him feel immeasurably better. He thought suddenly of Cathy and wished that she were with him.

The seemingly endless rain slanted down through the headlight, cold and dreary. Rome didn't care about the rain anymore. He jerked the cord, listened to the whistle scream its cry of conquest. He wiped his forehead and smiled again.

A quarter of a mile east of the trestle, Gashlin struck.

The riders came out of the murk, half a dozen of them. They followed the train at a fast gallop. Rome whirled, jerking out his gun. He could make out the figure of Gashlin, leading the riders.

The locomotive rolled past a small gang of workers who dodged to avoid the oncoming horses. One of the riders shot at the railroadmen; Rome saw two of them go down. Then the locomotive swung around a bend. Rome hoped fervently that the men would summon help.

The train was rolling through the uncleared timber, the trestle coming up soon. Rome crouched in the cab with the pistons making a thundering sound beneath him. The wheels clacked as the riders swung onto the last flatcar one by one. Their guns were out as they advanced toward the cab through the rain. Gashlin carried a large dark parcel.

"Stop the engine," he shouted to Rome over the roar. "Stop it on the trestle!" Rome triggered a shot and the attackers ducked. Rome spied a couple of rough, unfamiliar faces in the gloom. Gashlin had evidently added a few professional guns to his force. By the hellish glow of the firebox, Rome could see that Gashlin's face was anxious. His back was to the wall. . . .

Rome debated the situation for an instant. They were not firing now but stalking cautiously because they wanted the locomotive halted on the trestle. Rome guessed what the parcel contained. Dynamite.

It would be a crippling loss; a valuable switch engine, and, more important, a key trestle that would take time to rebuild. They might never finish on time, and Gashlin would keep his business. . . .

*"Stop this thing!"* Gashlin roared, his voice ragged with desperation.

Carefully, Rome took aim and began firing. He slipped along the side of the tender, triggering his shots over the top. He had to time it carefully now, very carefully. Gashlin must be realizing that he couldn't stop the train; he shouted orders to his men and they began firing from the flatcar nearest the tender.

One by one, Rome shot them down, all except Gashlin. It was a new sensation, feeling the power of the weapon in his hand. He took his time with four, only wounding them. The fifth clutched his stomach and screamed, his body arching backward and pitching from the flatcar, lost in the darkness and the rain.

Gashlin remained. He was crawling down the opposite side of the tender, hidden from view. Rome edged his way back into the cab, his nerves strained. Fear gnawed the pit of his stomach. He pulled the throttle all the way out and felt the locomotive shiver. Imperceptibly, it picked up speed.

He waited.

Gashlin appeared at the far corner of the tender and hurled the package toward the boiler opening. Rome stepped out of the shadows, grabbing for it.

His fingers strained for it, and he wanted to scream with rage when he missed it; he felt the thing brush past his fingertips as the locomotive rocketed onto the trestle.

Gashlin was struggling to get a pistol out of his coat. The dynamite went spiraling into the maw of the firebox. Acting more by instinct than from thought, Rome ran forward, smashing into Gashlin and pushing him backward off the train. Rome tumbled with him for seemingly endless seconds, down and down, through rain and blackness.

Rome thought, My God, we may be falling into the cut, we may . . .

He hit the ground and felt his body vibrate with the jarring pain. The locomotive rolled a thousand feet beyond the trestle, the last flatcar careening wildly, before it blew to pieces.

Rome flattened himself on the sodden ground, hiding his face. Heat and steam and tiny shards of metal stung his back. He lay there, his heart thumping rapidly while the reverberations died away. Then he staggered to his feet and surveyed the situation.

The trestle remained intact with only a few lengths of rail ruined. The switch engine had disintegrated. The flatcars lay on their sides, rails and ties spilled onto the shoulders of the roadbed. Rome peered at them in the murk and then he thought of Gashlin.

Gashlin lay half a dozen yards away, face up, unconscious. Rome knelt near him, taking a match from his pants pocket. Then he realized that he still held his gun in his left hand. He shifted it to the right, then stuck it in his belt, laughing at his own clumsiness. He finally got the match lit and cupped his hands around it, shielding it from the rain.

He stared at Gashlin. The man's face was bearded and weary-looking. The strain must have worn him to nothing. His business sliding out from under him, making this one attempt to save it . . .

Suddenly Rome thought of Job Thompson. Anger flooding over him, he pulled his gun. Standing up, he pointed the barrel at Gashlin's head, his finger tightening on the trigger.

He stood that way for a long moment, the rain whispering down through the timber surrounding him. Then he scowled. Slowly he pushed the gun back into his belt. Bending down, he hoisted Gashlin's unconscious form onto his shoulder and began to trudge westward.

Ten minutes later he met a handcar coming toward him from the end-of-track. Thankfully he dumped Gashlin's body onto the car and huddled down beside it. One of the railroadmen pumped the car back west while the other workers trudged to look over the wreckage.

In the lighted work area, where men labored in the flaring glow of lanterns hung on poles beside the track, Rome met a tired Ben Hamilton. Quickly he explained what had happened. As he was finishing the story, the sheriff rode in.

"This here's Mark Rome," Hamilton said.

The sheriff reached for his gun. Rome, faster, already had him under his sights.

"Easy, sheriff," Rome said. "I want to get this cleared up as much as you do. That's Bruce Gashlin on the ground. He just blew up one of our switch engines and tried to dynamite our trestle on top of it. He killed Job Thompson—that is, Cole Yancey did, on his orders."

"I don't figure it," the sheriff said. "Not any of it."

"Wait till he wakes up," Rome said. "Things'll straighten out then."

At least he hoped they would. He was counting on Gashlin being the opportunist in any situation.

In the rain, Rome shivered. A ring of men had gathered, watching intently. Hamilton ordered them back to work and they tramped away through the mud. Slowly, Gashlin stirred on the ground, opened his eyes. The first thing he saw was Rome's gun.

Next his gaze fastened on the sheriff. He tried to get to his feet, slipped in the mud, and sank to one knee.

"Get up, Gashlin," Rome said.

He tried again, swaying until he made it.

Rome weighed his words with care, hoping he had judged the man correctly. "We've got you dead to rights for dynamiting the engine and for having Job Thompson killed. You can take your chances and keep quiet, or you can spill the whole thing and maybe you'll get off easier. Prison's better than a rope."

Gashlin didn't wait five seconds; he told his story. Rome noticed that his eyes moved continually as he did so. Stalling for time?

At the end, the sheriff fumbled to pull manacles from his pocket.

Rome was watching for the play. It came as the sheriff stepped between him and Gashlin. There was a flurry of movement. Hamilton shouted, and the sheriff jerked aside, howling in pain, clutching his hip. Teeth bared, Gashlin faced them, the knife shining for a moment until the rain washed the blood off. The sheath under his arm had a broken lace and dangled loosely by his belt.

Gashlin's arm started back, his eyes filling with hate for Rome. The arm lashed upward; Rome pulled the trigger once; the knife dropped.

Gashlin toppled forward. His arms moved out feebly in an effort to stop the fall. The last chance, Rome thought sourly. Gashlin fell facedown in the mud, quivered, and flopped over onto his back. His face hardened into a mud-daubed mask.

Hamilton was helping the sheriff. Rome tossed his gun away, feeling incredibly tired.

"Go to bed, Mark," Hamilton said over his shoulder. Rome nodded dumbly, rubbing his eyes. The collective exhaustion of the last few days hit him all at once, but he made it to one of the tents. Somehow he managed to find blankets and a dry spot on top of some pine boards.

When he woke up nearly twenty hours later, the railroad had moved on.

It continued to move, after time for the men to rest. During that interval, Rome saw the sheriff, answered a few last questions, and rode out of Warknife, a free man.

He stopped at the Circle JT. Mrs. Thompson welcomed him quietly, then left him and Cathy alone in the parlor.

"Well, you'll be moving on, won't you?" she said.

He nodded. "Guess I will."

She touched his arm. "To say I'm sorry isn't enough."

"You don't have to say anything, Cathy."

"Do you think"—she hesitated—"you'll ever get railroading out of your blood?"

"Someday, maybe. A man has got to settle sometime. The railroad will need an agent here to handle all the cattle shipments."

"It would be a good place," she agreed, and he smiled inwardly. Intuitively, silently, an understanding had sprung up between them. The old affection could be rekindled. . . .

"But I've got to do this job first," he told her. "I've got to see the Kansas & Western finished."

"I know. I'll still be here."

"Then I'll be back. It's a promise."

He kissed her in the doorway of the ranch house. She clung to him for a moment, then gently pushed him away.

"Go on, Mark," she said quietly. "The railroad's waiting."

He squeezed her hand and walked to his horse. He waved as he rode out of the yard.

The country was tinted with the light of early evening, and somewhere to the west men labored and cursed to meet the deadline. Slowly, inevitably, the bands were joining the oceans, and he was part of that conquest of immense distance. The iron horse. The eternal pioneers moving forward, sometimes clumsily, haltingly, but still forward.

Spurring his mount, he rode toward the burning ball of the sun, to where the end-of-track lay waiting.

# A Duel of Magicians

April brought the crows and the redbirds. Any shower brought a profusion of hoptoads afterward. The sweet blooming fecundity of the spring embittered Charles Main unreasonably. He slept deeply at night, and had many dreams. He had never felt so tired or hopeless. Conversation among the three men had long ago diminished to the minimum necessary to convey a question or the day's plan.

One morning, early, they spied the distant mass of the southern buffalo herd, returning north with the warm weather. They rode hard and reached the herd in two hours. They killed one cow, gorged themselves on fresh roasted meat, and packed all they would be able to eat before spoilage. Buzzards kept them company, awaiting their departure.

The ride to the buffalo reminded Charles again of the vastness of the Territory. A whole army corps could be maneuvering and they might miss it. He'd convinced himself that he could search the Territory as you'd search a room. He was desperate; he had to think that way. Now he saw the foolishness of it. He was thinking more realistically. That befitted a man who'd partnered with the Jackson Trading Company, but it whittled away his hope.

The mood of his companions didn't help. Magee

was morose because of the Delaware woman, and Gray Owl because he couldn't guide them with any success. He was failing in his life's purpose.

They rode for hours without speaking, each man sunk into himself. The Wichitas rose in the south like monuments in a flat field. Wending across the lower slopes of the western side, they found abundant sign. A large number of Indians had pitched their tipis about a week ago. So many Indians—several hundred by Charles's estimate—that time and weather had not yet been able to erase all the traces.

After they camped that night, Charles went searching on foot in the sparkling dewy morning. He discovered a rusted trade kettle which he picked up and pressed with his thumb, immediately making a hole in the thin rust. It was an impoverished village that had camped here.

Gray Owl trudged up. "Come see this," he said.

Charles followed him down to the base of the peak to a set of travois pole tracks that had survived. He knelt to study them. Between the pole tracks he saw the prints of wide moccasined feet. He brushed his fingers lightly over one print, half obliterating it. The print belonged to a woman, and a heavy one; no man would pull a travois.

Charles pushed his black hat back and said what Gray Owl already knew. "There are no more dogs. They've eaten them. They're starving. They didn't move because they wanted to; they're in flight. From here they could logically go south. Or west, to Texas. Maybe all the way into the *llano*."

Gray Owl knew the *llano*—the staked plains; a scrubby, inhospitable wilderness. "West," he said, nodding.

* * *

They rode with a little more energy. Here at last was a large group of people, one or more of whom might have seen a white man and a boy. Charles knew the odds against it but at least it was a crumb. Until now, they'd been starving.

The sign of so large a migration was easy to follow. They tracked the village to the North Fork of the Red, then northwestward along it for a day and a half. Suddenly there was confusing sign. The remains of another encampment and, across the river, trampled hoof-marked earth, which showed that a second large body of Indians had joined the first.

Gray Owl left for a day, scouting north and east. He returned at a gallop. "All moved east from here," he said. His skin was free of sweat despite his blanket and the hot spring day.

Magee used his nail to scratch bird droppings from his derby. "Don't make sense. The forts are east."

"Nevertheless, that is the way."

Charles had a hunch. "Let's go up the river a while. Let's see if all of them rode east."

Next morning they found a campsite where perhaps thirty lodges had stood. The day after that, they found the grandfather.

He was resting in cottonwoods with a few possessions from his medicine bundle—feathers, a claw, a pipe—spread around him. The malevolent odor of a chancred leg seeped from under his buffalo robe. He was old, his skin like wrinkled brown wrapping paper. He knew his death was imminent and showed no fear of the oddly assorted trio. Gray Owl questioned him.

His name was Strong Bird. He told them the reason for the great migration eastward. Some six hundred Cheyennes under chiefs Red Bear, Gray Eyes, and Little Robe had decided to surrender to the soldiers

at Camp Wichita rather than die of starvation or face
the bullets of the soldiers of General Creeping Pan-
ther, who was roaming the Territory sweeping up
bands of resisters. The grandfather was part of a
group that had bolted with Red Bear after he
changed his mind about surrendering.

"Thirty lodges," he said, his eyes fluttering shut,
his voice reedy. "They are eating their horses now."

"Where, Grandfather?" Gray Owl asked.

"They meant to push up the Sweet Water. Whether
they did I don't know. I know your face, don't I?
You belong to the People."

Gray Owl seemed heavily burdened. "Once long
ago."

"Age has rotted my flesh. I could not keep up. I
asked them to leave me, whether or not the soldiers
found me. Will you help me die?"

They hewed down branches and fashioned a burial
platform in one of the strongest cottonwoods. Charles
carried the old man up to it, with Magee bracing him
below. He could barely stand the stench but he got
the grandfather settled with his few possessions and
left him with warm sun shining on his old face, which
was composed and even showed a drowsy smile.

As they rode out, Gray Owl said, "It was a generous thing to help him to the Hanging Road. It was
not the deed of the man they named Cheyenne Charlie. The man who wanted to kill many."

"There's only one I want now," Charles said. "I
think our luck's changed. I think we're going to
find him."

That was his blind hope speaking again. But the
sunshine and the springtime buoyed him, and so did
the possibility that Red Bear's band of holdouts
might have seen a white man. Gray Owl warned

Charles and Magee that Red Bear, now a village chief, was formerly a fierce Red Shield Society chief, which no doubt explained why he'd balked at giving up along with the others.

They found the village far up the Sweet Water's right bank. The Cheyennes made no effort to hide themselves. Cooking fires smoked the sky at midday and from a rise, through his spyglass, Charles saw several men with raggy animal pelts on their heads shuffling in a great circle around the edge of the encampment. The wind brought the trackers the faint thumping of hand drums.

Magee used the spyglass. Uncharacteristically sharp, he said, "What the hell have they got to dance about? Aren't they starving to death?"

"Massaum," Gray Owl said.

"Talk English," Magee said.

"That's the name of the ceremony," Charles said. "They put a painted buffalo skull in a trench to represent the day the buffalo came to earth, and the dancers pretend to be deer and elk and wolves and foxes. The ceremony is a plea for food. The old man said they're starving."

Magee rolled his tongue over his upper teeth. "Damn mad about it, too, I guess."

"You don't have to go in with me."

"Oh, sure. I came this far to be a yellow dog, huh? That isn't the kind of soldier somebody trained me to be." Staring at Charles's haggard eyes, at the long pointed beard nearly down to his stomach, Magee suddenly winced. "I'm sorry I sound sore. I just think all this is hopeless. Your boy's gone, Charles."

"No he isn't," Charles said. "Gray Owl? Go in or stay?"

"Go." The tracker eyed the village, but not in a comfortable way. "First, load all the guns."

\* \* \*

It was a splendid balmy day. The wrong sort of day for the tragedy of a lost son or a starving belly. The wind floated fluffy clouds overhead and the clouds cast majestic slow-sailing shadows. In and out of the shadows, in single file, the three rode in the Z pattern Jackson had taught Charles.

One of the pelt-clad dancers was first to spy them. He pointed and raised a cry. The drumming stopped. Men and women and children surged toward the side of the camp nearest the strangers. The men were middle-aged or elderly; the warriors were undoubtedly off somewhere searching for food. Well before Charles was within hailing distance, he saw the sun flashing from the metal heads of lances and the blades of knives. He also saw that no dogs frolicked anywhere. The tipis were weathered and torn. There was an air of despair about the village beside the Sweet Water.

The wind still blew in their faces. Charles smelled offal, smoke, and sour bodies. He didn't like all the gaunt angry faces lining up behind the dancers, or the truculent expression of the stout old warrior who strode out to meet them with his eight-foot red lance and his round red buffalo-hide shield. The horns of his headdress were red but faded; he had distinguished himself in war many winters past.

Charles held his hand palm outward and spoke in their language.

"We are peaceful."

"You are hunters?"

"No. We are searching for a small boy, my son." That touched off whispers among some of the grandmothers. Magee caught it too, raising an eyebrow. Those starved old women with their watering eyes acted as if they knew who Charles was talking about. "May we come into the village a while?"

Chief Red Bear thrust his shield out. "No. I know
that man beside you. He turned his face from the
People to go and help the white devils of the forts.
I know you, Gray Owl," he exclaimed, shaking his
shield and lance. One of the dancers with a scrap of
pelt on his head sank to a half-crouch, his knife moving in a small provocative circle.

"You are soldiers," the chief said.

"We are not, Red Bear—" Gray Owl began.

The chief pointed his lance at the trackers and
shouted: "Soldiers. Call Whistling Snake from the
Massaum lodge."

Magee brought up his Spencer from the saddle
where he'd been resting. "Don't," Charles said in English. "One shot and they'll tear us up."

" 'Pears they'll do it anyway." There was a slight
quaver in Magee's voice; Charles feared that what he
said was so. More than a hundred people confronted
them. In terms of physical strength each of the Cheyennes was no match. Hunger had shrunk them and
age enfeebled them. Numerically, however, they had
the fight won before it started.

"Do you know this Whistling Snake?" Charles
asked Gray Owl.

"Priest," Gray Owl replied, almost inaudibly.
"Ugly face. As a young man he scarred his own flesh
with fire to show his magical powers. Even chiefs
like Red Bear fear him. This is very bad."

Small boys darted forward to pat the horses. The
animals sidestepped nervously, hard to control. Indian mothers chuckled and nudged one another, eye-
ing the trackers as if they were so much contract
beef. Charles didn't know what to do. He had bet on
having an ace facedown and turned over a trey.

One last try. "Chief Red Bear, I repeat, we only

wish to ask if anyone in your village has seen a white man traveling with a small—"

The crowd parted like a cloven sea. There was a great communal sigh of awe and dread. The old camp chief's gaze was curiously taunting. Along the dirt lane fouled with human waste came the priest, Whistling Snake.

Though Whistling Snake was at least seventy winters, he walked with the vigor of a young man. His neck and forearms had a taut, sinewy look. His pure white hair was simply parted and braided without adornment. He wore a hide smock that long use had buffed to the color of dull gold. A plain rawhide belt gathered the smock at his waist. In his right hand, chest high, he held a fan of matched golden eagle feathers two feet wide from tip to tip.

Charles couldn't remember seeing another old man with such an aura of strength. Or human eyes quite so arrogant and unpleasant. The right iris was only partly visible, hidden by a lip of puckered flesh. Scar's face was smooth by comparison with that of Whistling Snake's, which looked as though his flesh had melted from temple to jaw, then been pushed and twisted into ridges as it hardened. Indentations like large healed nail wounds stippled the ridges of flesh. The man was hideous, which only made him seem stronger.

"They say they search for his son," Red Bear told the priest, with a nod at Charles.

Whistling Snake regarded them, fanning himself with a small rotation of his bony wrist. A toddler, a plump bare girl, started toward him, reaching out. Her mother snatched her back and clutched her, dread in her eyes.

The priest shook the fan at Magee. "Buffalo soldier. Kill them."

"Damn you," Charles said, "there are other black men on the Plains besides buffalo soldiers. This is my friend. He is peaceful. So am I. We are looking for my little boy. He was stolen by another white man. A tall man. He may be wearing a woman's bauble, here."

He pulled his earlobe. An elderly Cheyenne covered his mouth and popped his eyes. Charles heard the excited buzz of the women before Red Bear's glare silenced them. Charles's stomach tightened. They'd seen Bent.

The priest fanned himself. "Kill them." The brown iris shifted in its trench of hard scar tissue. "First that one, the betrayer of the People."

Gray Owl's pony began to prance, as if some invisible power flowed from the priest to unnerve and befuddle his enemies. The pony neighed. Gray Owl kneed him hard to control him. His face showed uncharacteristic emotion. Fear.

Magee spoke from the side of his mouth, in English. "What's that old bastard saying?"

"He told them to kill us."

Magee swallowed, visibly affected. "They better not. I want to get out of here with my wool on my head. I want to see Pretty Eyes again." The squaw, Charles assumed. "I'm not going to cash in here. I been trounced by nigger-hating saloon trash—"

The priest pointed his fan, exclaiming in Cheyenne, "Stop his tongue."

"I been cussed by white soldiers not fit to shine a real man's boots. I won't let some old fan-waving Indian just wave me off this earth, whisssh!" There was a strange, fear-born anger prodding Magee. He shook his derby the way Whistling Snake had shaken his fan. "You tell him he doesn't touch a wizard."

"A—?" Startled, Charles couldn't get the rest out.

"The biggest, the meanest of all the black wizards of the planetary universe. Me!" Magee flung his hands in the air like a preacher; he was back in Chicago, encircled, with only his wits to forestall a beating.

Red Bear retreated from him. A fat grandfather protected his wife with his arm. Magee looked baleful sitting there on his horse, arms upraised, shouting. "I will level this village with wind, hail, and fire if they touch us or don't tell us what we want to know." A moment's silence. Then he yelled at Charles like a top-kick. "Tell 'em, Charlie!"

Charles translated. Where he faltered, as with the word for hail, Gray Owl supplied it. Whistling Snake's fanning grew rapid. Red Bear watched the priest for a reaction; Whistling Snake was temporarily in control of things. "He is a great worker of magic?" Whistling Snake asked.

"The greatest I know," Charles said, wondering if he was insane. Well, what was the alternative to this? Probably immediate annihilation.

"I am the greatest of the spell-workers," the priest said. Charles translated. Magee, calmer now, sniffed.

"Cocky old dude."

"No," Charles said, pointing to Magee. "He is the greatest."

For the first time, Whistling Snake smiled. He had but four teeth, widely spaced in his upper gum. They were fanglike, as if he'd filed them that way. "Bring them in," he said to Red Bear. "Feed them. After the sun falls, we will test who is the greatest wizard. Then we will kill them."

He studied Magee over the tips of the fan feathers.

His laugh floated out, a dry chuckle. He turned and walked majestically into the village.

Magee looked numb. "My God, I never figured he'd take me up on it."

"Can you show him anything?" Charles whispered.

"I brought a few things, always do. But it's only small stuff. That old Indian, he's got a power about him. Like the devil was singing in his ear."

"He's only a man," Charles said.

Gray Owl shook his head. "He is more than that. He is connected to the mighty spirits."

"Lord," Magee said. "All I got is saloon tricks."

The prairie sunshine had a precious glow then; this morning might be the last they'd be privileged to see.

The Cheyennes put the three of them in a stinking tipi with old men guarding the entrance. A woman brought bowls of cold stew too gamy to eat. Before dark, the villagers lit a huge fire and began their music of flute and hand drum.

An hour of chants and shuffling dances went by. Charles chewed on his only remaining cigar, nursing a superstitious certainty that they wouldn't get out of this if he smoked it. Gray Owl sat in his blanket as if asleep. Magee opened his saddlebags, rummaged in them to take inventory, closed them, then did it all over again ten minutes later. The shadows of dancing, shuffling, stomping men passed over the side of the tipi like magic lantern projections. The drumming grew very loud. Charles reckoned two hours had passed when Magee jumped up and kicked his bags. "How long they going to string us out?"

Gray Owl raised his head. His eyes blinked open.

"The priest wants you to feel that way. He can then show a different, calm face."

Magee puffed his cheeks and blew like a fish, twice. Charles said, "I wish I hadn't got us into—"

"I did it," Magee said, almost snarling. "I got us here. I'll get us out. Even if I am just a nigger saloon magician."

A few minutes later, guards escorted them outside. A hush came over the ring of people around the fire. The men were seated. The women and children stood behind them.

The evening was windless. The flames pillared straight up, shooting sparks at the stars. Whistling Snake sat beside Chief Red Bear. The latter had a bleary smile, as though he'd been drinking. Whistling Snake was composed, as Gray Owl had predicted. His fan lay in his lap.

A place was made for Charles to sit. Red Bear signed him to it. Gray Owl was roughly hauled back with the women, further punishment for his betrayal. The grandfather on Charles's left drew a trade knife from his belt and tested the edge while looking straight into Charles's eyes. Charles chewed the cold cigar.

Red Bear said, "Begin."

Magee spread his saddlebags flat on the ground. Charles thought of the campfire circle as a dial. Magee was at twelve o'clock, Whistling Snake sat fanning himself at nine o'clock, and he was seated at three, with Gray Owl behind him at four or five.

Magee cleared his throat, blew on his hands, reached up for his derby, and tumbled it brim over crown all the way down his arm to his hand. An old grandfather laughed and clapped. Whistling Snake's slitted eye darted to him. He stopped clapping.

His face already glistening with sweat, Magee pulled his blue silk from a saddlebag and stuffed it into his closed fist. He chanted, "Column left, column right, by the numbers, hocus-pocus."

Red Bear showed a slight frown of curiosity. Whistling Snake regarded the distant constellations, fanning himself. Charles's belly weighed twenty pounds. They were doomed.

Magee pulled a black silk from his fist and popped the fist open to show it empty. He waved the silk like a bullfighter's cape, displaying both sides, and sat down. Whistling Snake deigned to glance at Charles. The four filed teeth showed, in supreme contempt.

Whistling Snake handed his fan ceremoniously to Red Bear. He rose. From his robe he produced a wide-mouth bag made of red flannel. He crushed the bag, turned it inside out, displayed both sides, balled it again. Then suddenly he began a singsong chant and started a hopping sidestep dance around the circle. As he danced and chanted, he held the top corners of the bag by the thumb and index finger of each hand.

The heads of two snakes with gleaming eyes suddenly rose from the mouth of the bag, as if the snakes were crawling straight up to the stars. People gasped. Charles was momentarily mystified. Then, as the snakes dropped back into the bag, he noticed their lack of flexibility. Magee, cross-legged by his saddle-bags, glanced at him with a disgusted look. He too had identified the snakes as snakeskin glued over wood.

The Cheyennes thought it an impressive trick, however. Chanting and dancing, Whistling Snake went all the way around the fire, revealing the climbing snakes at each quarter. He finished the circuit and crumpled the bag a last time before he sat. He fanned himself with evident satisfaction.

The Cheyenne faces shone in the glow of the fire. The atmosphere of lighthearted sport was gone. Whistling Snake watched the black soldier as if he were game to be cooked and devoured.

Magee produced a quilled bag. From the bag he took three white chicken feathers. He put two in his leather belt and changed the third to a white stone. He held the stone in his mouth as he changed the next two feathers. He took the three stones from his mouth one at a time and with one hand passing over and under the other he changed the stones back to feathers. When he had three feathers in his belt, he concealed them all in one fist and waved over it. He opened his mouth and lifted out three feathers. He showed his empty hands, reached behind the head of a seated man, and produced three white stones.

He eyed the crowd, awaiting some sign of wonder or approval. He saw hard glaring eyes. Charles realized Magee had not offered a word of patter during this trick. The black soldier sat down with a defeated look.

Whistling Snake drew himself up with supreme hauteur. Again he handed the village chief his fan. He showed his palms to the crowd; Charles saw the heavy muscles on his forearms. Tilting his head back and chanting, the priest stepped forward close to the fire and laid his right palm directly into the flame.

He kept it there while slowly lowering his left till they were parallel. His face showed no sign of pain. No stutter or falter interrupted his singsong chant. Magee sat stiff as a post, his eyes brimming with curiosity and admiration. He had momentarily forgotten that the Cheyenne wanted to kill him and take his wool and hang it up in his lodge. He was won-derstruck by the magic.

A great rippling sigh—"*Ah! Ah!*"—ran around the circle, and there were smiles, grunts, scornful looks at the three interlopers. Slowly, Whistling Snake lifted his left hand from the fire. Then his right. White hairs on his forearms above his wrists curled and gave off tiny spurts of smoke. His palms were unblistered; not even discolored.

Charles looked at Gray Owl, who exhibited as much expression as the granite of the Wichitas. Try-ing to hide what they all knew, no doubt. Magee flung Charles another look that was almost apolo-getic. Charles smiled as if to urge him not to worry. With a defeated air, Magee climbed to his feet. Charles snatched a faggot from the fire and with the hot end lit his last cigar.

From a saddlebag Magee pulled a leather pouch which he carefully laid on the ground. He next took out a small hand-carved wood box which he opened and displayed. The box held four lead-colored balls of a kind Charles hadn't seen for years. Magee plucked one out and carefully placed it between his teeth. Then he closed the box and put it away. With a sudden flourish, he yanked a pistol from the saddlebag.

Several Cheyennes jumped up, readying their knives or lances. Magee quickly gave them the peace sign. He balanced the pistol on his palm and slowly turned in a complete circle, so all could see it. Where had he found an old flintlock? Charles wondered. The barrel showed no rust. Magee had cleaned it well.

With slow, ceremonious motions, Magee opened the leather pouch and inverted it, letting powder trickle into the barrel. Suddenly he stamped his right foot twice, as if bitten by an insect. Along with most of the others, Charles looked down and didn't see anything.

Magee pinched off the flow of powder and tossed the pouch aside. He found a patch in his pocket and wrapped it around the ball he took from his teeth. He slipped ball and patch into the barrel, unsnapped the ramrod underneath, and with careful twisting motions seated the ball. He replaced the ramrod and primed the pan.

Fat sweat drops rolled down Magee's cheeks. He wiped his hands on his jeans pants. He signed for Charles to stand up.

Astonished, Charles did. Magee glanced at Red Bear. The chief's attention was fixed on him. Whistling Snake saw that and frowned. His fan moved rapidly, stirring the hair at the ends of his white braids.

"What I did before was just play," Magee said. "I am going to kill King Death before their eyes. Tell them."

"Magic, I don't understand what—"

"Tell them, Charlie."

He translated. Hands covered mouths. The fire popped and smoked. If silence had weight, this was crushing.

Magee faced about in precise military fashion. He used his hands to make a parting motion. Those in front of him jumped up and shoved one another until a yard-wide lane was cleared. Magee summoned Charles to him with a bent finger. He gave Charles the old flintlock pistol and looked hard and earnestly into his eyes.

"When I say the word, I want you to shoot me."

"What?"

Magee leaned up on tiptoe, his mouth next to Charles's ear. "You want to get out of here? Do it." He made a puckering sound, as if kissing the white man. Several Cheyennes giggled over the strange ways of the interlopers.

Magee snapped the brim of his derby down to snug it; the shadow bisected his nose. In the shadow, his eyes gleamed like discs of ivory. He took ten long strides, rapidly, along the cleared lane, his posture soldier-perfect. He stopped, knocking his heels together, at attention. He about-faced. He was standing a foot from a tipi with a great ragged hole in its side.

"Aim the pistol, Charlie."

Christ, how could he?

"Charlie! Aim for the chest. Dead center."

Charles felt the sweat crawling down into his beard. Whistling Snake leaped up, his fan flicking very fast. Red Bear rose too. Charles drew the hammer back. Magee's shirt was taut over his ribs and belly. Charles's arm trembled as he extended it. He couldn't—he wouldn't—

Magic Magee said, "Now."

He said it loudly, a command. Charles responded to the tone as much as to the word. He fired. Sparks glittered, the priming pan ignited, the pistol banged and kicked upward.

Charles saw a puff of dust, as if something had struck Magee's chest three inches below the breastbone. Magee stepped back one long pace, staggering, closing his eyes, snapping his hands open, fingers shaking as if stiffened by a lightning charge. Then his arms fell to his sides. He opened his eyes. Whistling Snake's fan hung at his side.

"Where is the bullet?" Whistling Snake cried. "Where did it strike?"

In a drill-ground voice, Magee said, "King Death

is dead. You will answer our questions and release us without harm or I will bring back King Death, riding the winds of hail and fire, and this village will be finished." He shouted, "Tell them."

Charles translated quickly. Gray Owl's guards had drifted away from him as awed as he was. While Charles spit the words out, trying to make them as fierce as Magee's, he scanned the trooper's shirt. He saw no sign of a tear. Magee brushed his shirt off as if something had tickled him.

Red Bear listened to the threats and instantly said, "It shall be so."

Whistling Snake screamed in protest. The sound broke the moment. The Cheyennes rushed forward to swarm around Magee, touch him, pat him, feel his black curls. Charles stared at the old flintlock pistol, felt the warm barrel. King Death was dead, and there through rifts in the surging, laughing crowd was the banner of his conqueror. The familiar huge white smile of Magee, the wizard.

Red Bear prepared a pipe while Gray Owl attended to the horses. Charles didn't want the forgiving mood to fade, didn't want to linger and possibly lose their advantage and their lives. Ceremony required that he sit at the fire with Red Bear, however. Magee sat on his right. The village chief and several of the tribal elders passed the pipe.

Red Bear had forced Whistling Snake to join the group. When his turn came he passed the pipe without smoking. He snatched a handful of ashes from the edge of the fire and flung them at Charles's crossed legs. They covered his pants and the toes of his boots with gray powder. Red Bear exclaimed and berated the priest, who merely dusted his hands and folded his arms. Red Bear looked embarrassed, Gray Owl upset.

Since the ashes did no real damage, Charles forgot about it. Having finished his cigar, he was grateful for a deep lungful of pipe smoke, though as always, the unknown mixture of grasses the Cheyennes smoked left him light-headed and euphoric, not a good thing at a time like this.

Red Bear was not only polite but respectful. After asking Charles to describe again the white man he sought, he said, "Yes, we have seen that man, with a boy. At the whiskey ranch of Glyn the trader, on Vermilion Creek. Glyn is gone and they are staying there. I will tell you the way."

He pointed south. Charles was so dizzy with relief, his eyes watered.

Silently, the People formed a long lane through which the three trotted out. Looking back, believing their luck would break any moment, Charles heard Gray Owl laugh deep in his chest. A single figure remained by the campfire, apart from the others. Charles saw Whistling Snake raise his golden feather fan and disdainfully walk away.

They put miles and all of the rest of the night behind them before Charles permitted a stop. Spent men and spent horses rested on the prairie in the cool dawn. Charles knelt beside his black friend.

"All right, I know you don't tell your secrets, but this is one time you will. How did you do it?"

Magee chuckled and produced the hand-carved wooden box. He removed one of the round gray balls and displayed it sportively, just out of Charles's reach. "An old traveling magician taught me the trick back in Chicago. Always wanted to do it for an audience, but till this winter I couldn't afford the right pistol. Saved my pay for it. First thing I did was to short the powder. You never saw it because everybody looked down for a few seconds when I pretended a bug bit me. A little misdirection. But that's only half of it. The trick won't work without this."

"That's a solid ball of lead."

Magee dug his thumbnail with its great cream-colored half-moon into the pistol ball. The nail easily cracked the surface of the ball. "No, it isn't solid, it's melted lead brushed all over something else."

He caught the ball between his palms and rubbed them hard back and forth. He showed the crushed remains, tawny dust. "The rest is just good Kansas mud. Hard enough to build a house, but not hardly hard enough to kill a man."

He blew on his palm. The dust scattered against the sun and pattered on the ground. He laughed.

"What d'you say we ride and find your boy?"

# Death Rides Here!

When the wagon blew, Jeff Croydon had no time for thinking. His dozen high-sided wagons were pulling up, one after another, to the boxcars on the siding in the town of Sooner. Number four wagon had just pulled away, the skinner bawling lusty obscenities at the mules, and number five was swinging in toward the car. Jeff Croydon stood near the wagons, the hot dust clouding around him, sweat dripping down his plain, serious face. Several of the handlers, stripped to the waist and shining with perspiration, stood in the open door of the freight car in which the barrels of crude were transported east, adequately if not safely.

The skinner pulled number five wagon up beside the door. Someone in the crowd of town loungers standing by the freight train whistled shrilly. Croydon's head whipped around as he heard the nervous bray of the mules and the curses of the skinner trying to frighten them into line once more.

Croydon saw no one in the crowd whom he recognized. At the moment the thing had the quality of an idle prank, but Croydon knew and respected the hellish power lying dormant in the gummy crude. As he turned back to the wagon, something bright flickered in a downward arc across his line of vision.

A short stick, with a flaming rag attached to the end. With a curse he turned instinctively back to the crowd. They were brawling now, slugging senselessly at each other, their voices a roaring babel. He still couldn't spot a familiar face, nor a guilty one. Right then his thinking processes stopped.

From down the line he heard the wild shout of Dunc Limerty, the oldster who helped run his freight line. *"Holy God, get that stick outa. . . ."* The wagon exploded. The skinner howled and jumped to the ground. The sweating workers backed into the car, shouting like everyone else. Croydon saw flames licking at the flimsy boxcar walls. Then heat fanned his cheeks like the air from hell's own ovens. The deadly fire so frightening to men here in the oil fields danced out like whirling human figures, extending sudden gouting arms into the car door. Another minute and the whole train might blow. . . .

Croydon had no thought of heroism. He thought only of the flames as a danger. He shoved the frightened skinner out of the way, yelling at the spooked mules as he vaulted onto the wagon seat. In the seconds following the explosion, the mules had begun to move, so the flaming wagon was actually rolling when Croydon hit the seat and gathered up the reins. Banners of flame streaming behind him, he swung the wagon over rows of tracks, cut down a side street and headed past a few last shacks into open country. The rush of wind kept the flames away from him, but the great heat flayed his back. Croydon held his balance, standing wide-legged. He spotted a patch of arid ground ahead. He used all his strength to halt the frantic mules, swing them to the left and brake the wagon.

The mules brayed and threw themselves back and forth in the traces. Croydon dropped to the ground, jerked the pin and let them break free. Then he backed off and watched the wagon burn itself out. He stood there, empty-eyed, counting the loss. Each barrel of crude delivered to eastern oil companies was paid for with monies transferred directly to the well owner, who then paid Croydon a percentage based similarly on barrels delivered to the railroad.

Croydon stared bleakly at the forest of derricks thrusting up all across the face of the land. He freighted crude for none of the big outfits, like that of the wealthy midwesterner, Senator Lucas Bryant. He handled only the shoestring outfits, and barely kept his nose out of debt. This calamity, the first in his three years of management of the small outfit, had come at a time when success had seemed forthcoming at last. Now, he didn't know.

A wagon rattled toward him, and he came back to reality. He squinted against the sun and saw Dunc Limerty driving. Dunc's weary eyes took in the charred ruin of the wagon as he braked. He scratched his beard and shook his head. "T'warn't no accident, Jeff."

"I know," Croydon said, climbing up beside him. "Let's get back to Sooner."

Limerty swung the mules, and they jogged along back toward the boomtown. The older man reported that the rest of the shipment had been safely loaded on the train. Croydon said, "That still doesn't cancel the loss. Dunc, somebody tossed that burning stick from the crowd. It wasn't just some fool's idea of a prank. Somebody's out to get us."

Limerty grunted agreement. The clapboards of Sooner rose ahead of them. The freight train was chugging slowly away from the yards. "Think it's Hunter?" Limerty asked.

"If it is, I sure as hell don't see why," Croydon

answered. Tom Hunter ran the big freighting outfit in Sooner, handling shipments for the larger wells including Senator Bryant's holdings, largest of all in this field. Hunter was the established business man, Croydon the johnny-come-lately trying to compete. Croydon pointed out that Hunter was making as much money as any man would want.

"And besides, Hunter's not that stupid. He's got all he needs. I don't think he'd risk putting us out of business when we don't even make a dent in his contracts."

"Well," Limerty declared, "you o' course may be right. But I saw an hombre named Flinch in the crowd. Flinch did the whistlin' that spooked the mules, and though I didn't see him toss the stick, he sure as hell got out of there right after the fire started."

"I don't know this Flinch," Croydon told his partner. "Skinner?"

Limerty spat contemptuously over the wagon side. "Naw. Six-gun artist. Dirty work boy. But he works for Tom Hunter."

"Still," Croydon said, "I can't figure Hunter to make a play like that. It just isn't like him."

No more was said of the matter until they had unhitched the wagons in the freight yard and Croydon lay on his belly on the cot in the cubby-hole office while Limerty slapped liniment onto his back. Driving the flaming wagon had scorched his shirt. "Things can change fast in the oil fields, Jeff," Limerty observed. "I'd sure ask around and see if you can figure out what's going on. You can't get the law to investigate when it looks like Hunter had no reason for jinxing us, even if I did see Flinch. Somebody else would swear he was in the Sooner House having a beer."

Croydon nodded. He pulled on his rough shirt,

feeling it prickle against his singed hide. He strapped on his six-gun, more for appearances than anything else, since he was a business man and not inclined to settle matters with lead.

He started on a tour of saloons. He drank beer with drillers, listened to their woes, their laments, their sudden dreams of glory waiting under a new patch of earth, bubbling and black and worth a fortune in the country of quick gains and quicker losses. Slowly he pieced a story together, a story that had come out in the two days he had been out in the field getting this shipment together. When he joined Limerty for dinner at the Sooner House, his mind seethed with anger.

"Wal," Limerty drawled, brushing away foam flecks from his beard, "what did you do, carouse all afternoon? I thought you'd never show."

Croydon ordered a steak and beer. "Hunter's got a damned good reason for wanting us out of the way, Dunc. Senator Lucas Bryant died over a month ago, and nobody knew it until yesterday."

"I can't understand why," Limerty said dryly. "Men forget they's got a Christian name when they smell oil. Nobody in town's interested in anything that can't be put in barrels and sold." He frowned. "But what's the connection?"

"Senator Bryant's widow is arriving here tonight on the train. They say she's a hell of an independent woman. Smart. She's going to look over Bryant's holdings, and the word is she's tossing the freighting contract up for grabs."

"Hell's bells," Limerty exclaimed. He set down his schooner. "That means we can underbid Hunter and cut ourselves in on the Bryant holdings."

Croydon nodded. "Tom Hunter had that contract

when I started up here. Now he could stand to lose it. That's reason enough."

Limerty indicated Croydon's six-gun. "You better practice up with that thing, and get real good. You may need it."

He and Dunc Limerty went down to the depot to watch the evening train come in. Croydon felt like a ragged urchin in his grimy clothes. He spotted Tom Hunter sitting in his buggy, heavy-faced, confident, a cheroot tilted in the corner of his mouth. Hunter's clothes were Eastern, expensively tailored.

The funnel-stacked locomotive chuffed its way through the twilight, sparks flying up like red insects. In the smoky glow of the passenger coach lanterns, Croydon saw a woman standing on the platform, obviously impatient to get off. She wore a brown traveling dress, a feathered hat tilted gaily on her head. Her eyes were dark like her hair, and . . . my Lord . . . she was *young*.

Briskly the woman ordered two older women following her to bring her bags. She stepped quickly down the steps when the train halted, and Tom Hunter moved forward, sweeping his hat off and taking her hand. The woman smiled.

"They ain't strangers," Limerty muttered sourly. "He's probably been slickin' his way in by mail . . ."

Croydon watched Hunter help the woman into the carriage. The maids followed with the baggage, and, amid the awed stares of the depot loungers, the carriage clattered away through the dusk toward the Sooner House. Croydon felt an angry wrath building again. He caught the woman's name. Elizabeth Bryant.

"Come on," he said somberly. "Let's get a drink."

He drank a good deal that evening. Next day he turned up before Mrs. Bryant had awakened, dressed

in his best clothes. The maid ushered him into the
parlor of the suite at the Sooner House and left the
room. He fidgeted, taking in the expensive lamps,
the thick, rich carpet, the Eastern furniture. He rolled
himself a smoke to calm his nerves.

The bedroom door opened and Elizabeth Bryant
swept into the room, skirts belling behind her. She
was a damned pretty woman, Croydon reflected.
And the way she held her head indicated a strong
will and perhaps a temper.

"Well, Mr. Croydon," she said briskly, seating herself, "what can I do for you? I take it this isn't a
social call."

"No, it isn't. I run a freighting line, Mrs. Bryant."
He hesitated, then decided to show her his hand all
at once. "I can haul your crude from the wells to the
railroad here in town for one dollar per barrel less
than Tom Hunter charges. I came because I heard
the contract was open for bid."

"You heard correctly." She gazed at him. Her eyes
*were* dark, almost black. "Do you have a cigarette,
Mr. Croydon?"

Astounded, he rolled one for her. Here was a
woman of a kind he'd never known before; a frank,
bold woman from the East. He handed her the cigarette. She smiled her thanks. She inhaled slowly. The
smoke drifted through the bars of sunlight streaming
in the windows.

"Mr. Croydon, Tom Hunter has the contract for
two more weeks. At that time I'll decide whether to
keep him on, or hire another company."

"Hunter and I are the only freighters in the
territory."

"I know that." Her coolness amazed him. "I base
my decision upon a tally that's to be made for me.

Men from my wells will check the total number of barrels of crude delivered here in Sooner during the next two weeks. The man who delivers the most oil gets the contract."

Croydon felt a surge of triumph. He could cancel off yesterday's loss now; he felt sure he could beat Hunter.

He'd hire more skinners, rent wagons . . . it would be two weeks of hellishly hard work, but he could do it.

"I feel I must tell you one thing," Elizabeth Bryant added. "Safety factors also enter into my consideration. Any accidents such as that which occurred yesterday will influence my choice."

Croydon's eyes blazed. "Who told you about that? Tom Hunter?"

"Mr. Hunter. . . ." she began.

"One of Mr. Hunter's men caused the explosion."

"That's a rather strong accusation."

"I can back it up if I have to."

Elizabeth Bryant came to her feet. Anger shone in her eyes too. "Mr. Croydon, I have no personal quarrel with you. You have no reason to shout at me, and I won't stand for it. You've heard my terms. Now please leave."

Croydon stood there dumbfounded. On one hand the Senator's widow was a lovely, desirable woman. On the other, she was willful and he decided to press the matter no further. He would fight for the contract by delivering the most oil to Sooner.

He put on his hat and said a curt, "Good day, Mrs. Bryant." He slammed the door loudly behind him.

Going down the stairs he met Tom Hunter. The big man started to brush by him, but Croydon caught his sleeve. Hunter whirled, his gray eyes narrowed. "If you're going to see Mrs. Bryant," Croydon said, "you can tell her how your boy Flinch caused the explosion yesterday. One of my men saw him."

Hunter laughed, but it was mirthless. "Croydon, you're a liar. What's more, you're annoying. Stay out of my way."

"You're going to lose that contract," Croydon said.

Hunter dropped his gaze to Croydon's hand on his arm. "Let go of my arm, Croydon."

Croydon hesitated. Hunter wore a gun, and knew how to use it. What's more, winning the contract was the most important thing in the world at this moment. He let go.

Hunter grinned. "My boy Flinch, as you call him, will blow a hole in your stomach if you keep on telling stories about him. Remember that, Croydon."

Hunter disappeared up the stairs.

Dunc Limerty was shouting hoarse orders when Croydon returned to the yard. "Hey, Dunc," he called, "what's the matter?"

Limerty scowled. "Guess you didn't notice when you left." Limerty pointed. "Some polecat got in here last night and sawed through every axle on every wagon we got."

Croydon took in the damage with a bitter gaze. Already the skinners were at work dismantling the wheels. "That's just fine," Croydon said. He described his interview with Elizabeth Bryant.

"She sounds like a real fire-eater," Limerty said when he had finished. "But that don't help the fact that we're due out at noon for the next trip, and we'll never make it. If we don't get our licks in first, we'll fall so far behind we never will catch up with Hunter."

"You don't need to tell me that," Croydon said. "Let's get to work." He tore off his shirt and tossed it on the office steps.

The sun boiled down as the morning wore on, sending salty sweat coursing down his back to make his scorched skin sting even more hellishly. He and Limerty and the others worked tirelessly, repairing axles and cutting and mounting new ones.

Toward the middle of the morning, Elizabeth Bryant appeared. She was driving Hunter's carriage, but she was alone. Croydon put down a hammer and walked out toward her. She kept moving, slowly. He grabbed the horse's headstall. The woman glared at him.

She was dressed differently, he noticed. Rough shirt and denim trousers. A damned desirable female. But on her hip rested a holstered pistol.

"What do you want, Mr. Croydon?"

"I just thought you might like to know somebody sawed through the axles on our wagons last night. I thought you might have a fair idea of who did it." He couldn't resist a note of bitterness.

"Release the horse," Elizabeth Bryant said.

He stood his ground, staring her down.

Suddenly she had the pistol in her hand, aimed between his eyes. "Move out of the way, Mr. Croydon."

Still he did not move. Her lower lip trembled. She shifted the pistol to her left hand with a lightning movement and pulled the long buggy whip from its socket. She lashed the whip across Croydon's face. The horses reared, throwing him to the ground. The carriage rattled away up the street.

Croydon got up, wiping blood off his cheek. No one looked at him when he came back into the yard. *Looks like she's setting her mind against me*, he thought. *The only way to do it is to beat Hunter's record, with no accidents. She won't be able to refuse the contract then.*

Work went on. Limerty cursed the men endlessly,

spurring them on. Croydon dressed after his noon meal and went to the bank. When he returned, he had rented a dozen more wagons and hired additional skinners. They rolled out of Sooner at dusk, toward the oil fields, half a day late. Hunter's outfit had left that morning. Every cent Jeff Croydon had had in the bank was gone now, sunk desperately into the extra gear.

## 2

## *The Stolen Tally*

The days of the following week blended imperceptibly into one another. Croydon's outfit worked day and night. In a haze of weariness, Croydon drove himself and his men, grabbing a wink of sleep when he could, a cup of coffee or a plate of beans. In their first two days they covered the Big Blow Wells, numbers one through five, and the Oh, Nellie! rig, one through four. They wheeled the mules back toward Sooner, rolling through the darkness, and Croydon imagined that his world would forever be one of darkness and eerie fire on the horizon, thundering wheels and braying mules, rattling barrels and loud curses.

They rolled into Sooner at dawn of the third day. Hunter's outfit had gone out again the night before. But Croydon consulted the begrimed tally sheet in the hands of Matheson, a Bryant man, and noticed with pleasure that they were fifteen barrels ahead of Hunter's freighters. The men had one hour off in which to grab breakfast, a shave, or a few jolts of whiskey, and then Croydon had them moving again, popping the buckskin over the heads of the animals as they clattered out of town under a lowering sky.

They covered the Oklahoma Enterprise wells that day, the Golden Garter wells the day after that, and finished with the Illinois Settlement wells at the end of the fifth day. The twenty-three wagons were jammed with tied-down barrels, tier upon tier, until the wagon beds fairly sagged. Limerty begged for a rest, for the other skinners as much as for himself. Croydon listened to the ominous rumbling, his eyes on the black sky beyond the forest of derricks.

"Storm's been brewing for two days, Dunc," he said. "This load has got to go back to Sooner tonight. We've got enough men, and they've been taking turns sleeping and driving all this week. They can keep it up one more night."

Limerty sighed. "But they won't keep it up much longer. We ain't paying them enough . . ." But despite much grumbling, the freight wagons rolled within the hour.

The storm broke about midnight, filling the world with a black roar of rain. The wheels bogged down, the mules spooked easily, and one of the wagon straps broke, toppling a tier of barrels into the mud.

Lanterns made eerie splotches of light in the gloom as Croydon labored, getting the barrels reloaded. The men grumbled louder now. He yelled at them, every angry word an outward sign of his own inward fear that they'd lose the race.

The storm abated before morning, and dawn found them again in Sooner. This time, the tally showed them twenty-five barrels behind Hunter. Croydon was not pleased. On top of that, the extra skinners and even a couple of the regulars confronted him and said that they didn't like his kind of hard work. Too hard, too little pay.

When Croydon returned from the bank this time, a heavy mortgage lay on his outfit. He doled out salaries, plus a bonus to each man, and promised them a double bonus if they lasted until the end of the two weeks. All of them said they'd stay.

Once more they rolled out, splitting up now, working the smaller outfits, two and three wagons at a time. They returned to Sooner on the evening of the seventh day, around meal time. As they swung past Hunter's yard, Croydon saw that the wagons stood idle. When they had unloaded he told the men that they had the night off. A few feeble cheers greeted his words. Croydon smiled grimly at the tally Matheson had made. Two barrels ahead of Tom Hunter. . . .

He and Limerty decided to eat in the Sooner House dining room. As soon as they entered, Croydon regretted it. For there at a secluded table, Elizabeth Bryant sat with Tom Hunter. The big man wouldn't trouble himself to go into the field. He had enough skinners to do the work. He stayed in town and kept Mrs. Bryant busy.

"Ain't that something," Limerty muttered, jabbing his fork into his fried potatoes. Croydon paid no attention. He watched the woman, the high tilt of her chin, the lush sweep of breast under the severe gown. Her cheeks were slightly flushed, perhaps from the bottle of wine Tom Hunter had furnished. She laughed a great deal.

Slowly the dining room cleared, until Croydon, Limerty, Mrs. Bryant and Hunter were the only ones left, separated by half a dozen tables. Hunter was leaning forward speaking to Mrs. Bryant when suddenly his head snapped around and he fixed Croydon with his gaze. Elizabeth Bryant turned too, smiling frostily.

Croydon nodded in a pleasant way, blowing smoke

from his cigar and noting Hunter's obvious displeasure in being watched. It was only a matter of moments then before Hunter piloted Mrs. Bryant out
the door, hand on her arm, brow knotted in a frown
of irritation.

Croydon laughed. "Hunter's getting rattled. But I
swear that Bryant woman is beyond me."

Despite the fact that he didn't understand her, he
still felt an attraction. It was almost with surprise
that he found himself knocking on her hotel room
door at half past nine that same evening.

The maid ushered him in with protests that Mrs.
Bryant had retired. But Mrs. Bryant greeted him, a
quilted robe wrapped around her and her dark hair
falling across her shoulders, lustrous in the glow of
the lamps. Croydon realized that she was truly
beautiful.

The maid bustled around for a few minutes,
straightening things uselessly, until Elizabeth Bryant
dismissed her.

"Well, Mr. Croydon. What is it this time?" Her
tone was faintly defensive. She stood close to him,
and he caught the fresh-scrubbed smell of her skin,
mingling with the scent of her hair. Her features
seemed softer in the lamplight.

He juggled his hat in his hands. "I just wanted to
inquire if you'd paid heed to the tally. We're keeping
up with Hunter."

She laughed. "That's a very lame excuse for calling
on me at this hour."

"I know." Their eyes met, held. Croydon's hat
dropped from his hands. He seized her shoulders,
kissed her hard. She responded for a long moment.
And then pulled backwards hastily, anger rekindled
in her eyes. "Damn you," she breathed. "Damn you,
Croydon, get out and don't come back."

And then he understood. Senator Lucas Bryant had been a much older man. How she'd married such a man, God alone knew. Family pressure, perhaps. Stranger things happened. But here was no woman born for a cold, passionless marriage. Here was a woman warm and alive and filled with a wild kind of desire. She saw that he knew her secret. Hence the anger.

"You didn't come out here just because of the Senator's wells, did you?" He said it without malice, but she didn't take it that way. Her hand swung up, smacking loudly on his flesh. He wanted to be angry, but he couldn't find it in him.

Croydon turned to go. He didn't look at her. And as he made his way back to the cot in the office, he realized that he might have ruined any chance of ever winning her over. Her pride would have been severely wounded. You're a fool, he told himself. He fell into a troubled sleep that night, rolling restlessly on the cot, but knowing he would double his efforts to win the contract now. He had a second stake. The chance it would bring him to be near Elizabeth Bryant.

They headed out early next morning. Before the sun had crawled up the sky to high noon, the raiders struck.

They came pounding down a rise, a dozen of them, dust rolling in gritty clouds behind them, their guns making strangely small flat popping noises in the vast land. Croydon, handling the first wagon, reined the mules, and seized the rifle on the seat beside him. He flung it to his shoulder and fired, jacking it a moment later for another, equally ineffective shot. Croydon had never been a marksman.

The raiders pulled half way between a low hill and the wagons. They all wore stained bandannas across their faces. Croydon leaped down and started forward in a crouch. All along the line of wagons, the skinners were doing the same thing. Dunc Limerty bawled orders. Croydon's stomach tightened as he flattened himself in the dirt, pumping a shot. If another wagon blew, they'd fall far, far behind. Perhaps they'd never catch up at all.

But fortunately the raiding party was a weak one. Croydon had nearly thirty men, and they were stretched out along the wagon line so that their fire could cut into the owlhoots from many points. Croydon let go a shot and saw one of the raiders spin out of his saddle and collide with the rider next to him. The attackers stayed less than two minutes. One of them, a man in a loud purple shirt, raised his arm and yelled something Croydon couldn't hear. They turned and spurred back up the rise. Limerty came racing toward Croydon.

"Shall we go after them, Jeff?"

Croydon shook his head. "But let's take a look at that dead one."

He and Limerty went over and knelt beside the fallen owlhoot. They pulled down his soiled bandanna. Croydon didn't recognize him, and neither did Limerty. But the breed was familiar enough. He had the vulturish look of a professional killer, even in death.

Croydon stood up slowly. "Dunc," he said, his voice barely a whisper, "this is getting pretty tight. These men couldn't have come from anybody but Tom Hunter."

"Hell, I recognized Flinch, in the purple shirt," Limerty exclaimed.

"Then if it's killing he wants, it's killing he'll get. Tell every one of the men to stay ready. Hunter's getting scared."

The men were nervous and obviously displeased about having to fight as a part of their job. Most of them had no personal acquaintance with Croydon, no loyalty other than the fact that he paid them. And none of them had a particular inclination to get a bellyful of lead in his behalf.

The next two days brought a number of serious foulups. Men reacted slowly to orders, surly glints in their eyes. One of the skinners scared his mules so badly that they snapped the traces and ran off. Another time, a man let a barrel tip out of his wagon out of pure carelessness. Croydon watched the crude bubble thickly into the earth. He spoke sharply to the man, who faced him with dull enraged eyes. Croydon saw that it would not take much to provoke a fight, so he let him off with a tongue lashing. It was a bad situation, and Croydon knew it couldn't last much longer. He was fighting uphill, and slipping down two inches for every one he gained. Each day reduced the efficiency of the outfit. The breaking point came on the tenth day.

They arrived in Sooner at noon, with full wagons, and proceeded to unload on the waiting boxcars. The tally showed they were thirty-six barrels behind Hunter.

Reluctantly Croydon gave the men the afternoon off. If he didn't, they would quit, and he would lose out then and there.

He was in the office in the middle of the afternoon when Tom Hunter stormed in, followed by portly Sheriff Hink Peters. Hink knew Croydon, and the freighter liked the law's representative in Sooner. But Peters was scowling. Croydon knew Peters wasn't linked up with Hunter, so this was something bad.

"Afternoon, Hink," he said, affably ignoring Hunter. "Have a seat."

"No time to sit down, Jeff. Miz Bryant's man Matheson just turned up in an alley with his skull bashed in. The tally sheet is gone. Plumb disappeared."

"Why would anyone grab the tally?" Croydon asked.

"Maybe you can answer that one, Croydon," Hunter said.

"Now wait a minute . . ."

"Hold off, Jeff." Peters put up one hand, palm outward. "I got to check up on everything. Somebody might want to alter them tallies so's to swing the contract. It's no secret you're fighting for Miz Bryant's business."

"Hunter here is fighting just as hard."

But he saw his own position. In the minds of the citizens of Sooner, he was the johnny-come-lately. He, and not Hunter, would be the obvious and likely one to make such a back-to-the-wall play.

"Just where were you about an hour ago, Jeff?" Peters asked.

"I was sitting right here. I've got a mortgage on the outfit, sheriff, and I was just sitting here stewing about how I could pay it off."

Hunter laughed. "Sheriff, there's one more motive for you. Croydon's whipped, and he'll pull any kind of stupid trick to save himself."

"Just try to slap me in jail on the strength of that, Hunter. It can't be done."

"I know it can't," Peters parried. He headed for the door, sad disappointment in his eyes. "Guess I'll have to do some checking anyways, Jeff. I'll get in touch with you." Hunter followed him out and slammed the door loudly.

Croydon stared silently after the two departing men. Any fool could see it was Hunter's trick. Any fool, that is, who didn't have the town's perspective. Everybody would automatically swing over, comparatively speaking, to Tom Hunter's point of view because he had seniority in the matter of reputation. Hunter was tightening the noose around Croydon's neck. And there was not a great deal he could do about it.

The freight yard lay deserted. A hot wind stirred powdery dust. The sun slanting in prickled Croydon's back and he couldn't concentrate. The gun on his hip weighed against his flesh. His palms tingled. He wanted to kill Tom Hunter. But that would only nail the coffin shut completely.

Dunc Limerty returned around five, in high spirits, heavily fortified with alcohol. Croydon explained the situation over dinner, and the older man's eyes darkened.

"Lord," Limerty said sourly, "they was even dumb enough to do it in an alley. Nothin' smart about that Hunter. I'm beginning to think he must be going off his head."

"He's in the position all of Sooner thinks I'm in," Croydon said. "But I can't prove that Hunter's the kind of man who'd pull such a stunt, while I sit by under my halo, ready to go down in honest but pure defeat." Deep cynicism edged his words.

"Look out, my friend." Limerty's voice became a hoarse whisper. "Peters just came in, along with Hunter and that Flinch."

Croydon turned toward the three men. Flinch, bringing up the rear, was a short toad-like man with sunken eyes and sagging cheeks. A witless smile hung on his pendulous lips.

Peters put his arm on Croydon's shoulder. "Jeff, I got some bad news for you." Croydon's eyes flashed to Hunter. The big man's hard gaze was self-satisfied.

"Rip Flinch here went nosing around your office a few minutes ago and found these." Peters extended a sheaf of papers. The tally, smudged with ink and grime.

Croydon rocketed to his feet. "Did you happen to ask Hunter whether he had Flinch plant those things in my office? My God, sheriff, don't be a fool . . ."

Peters shook his head. "I know there's always that possibility. Thing is, I've got to lock you up until I can do some more investigating. Right now you're guilty. Later on . . ." It was hellishly clear. In the delay, Hunter would be assured of the Bryant contract. Whether they ever really found him guilty or not didn't matter.

Croydon didn't wait. He rammed a fist into the sheriff's gut, then shoved Flinch out of the way. Flinch grunted and a bright flash of metal crossed Croydon's line of vision. He tried to dodge out of the way, but Hunter's pistol barrel slammed into his temple. Then Hunter struck him again. He went down and out with frightening suddenness. Next thing he knew, he was lying on his back, staring up at a clay ceiling. He rolled his aching head to the right. Cell bars. Beyond them a deputy lounged, playing solitaire in the glow of a lamp.

Croydon's mind whirled. He was beaten for sure. But something within him wouldn't let him stay beaten. This thing had been business, but now it had taken on a new aspect. Personal between him and Tom Hunter. Elizabeth Bryant's face danced in his mind. Then he forgot about her as the jail door opened. Dunc Limerty made his way past the deputy to the cell. Croydon got up to meet him.

"What's wrong?" Croydon asked.

"Hell, Jeff . . ." He scratched his beard. "It looks like we're through for sure. You know our skinners got pretty stirred up over working so hard these past few days. After Hink Peters locked you up here, well . . ." The oldster shook his grizzled head, unwilling to go on.

"Let's have it, Dunc," Croydon said softly.

Limerty's gaze settled on the floor. "Hunter moved fast. He sent Flinch around with a promise of triple the bonus we paid. I tried to stop them, but they wouldn't listen. Most of 'em said they wanted on the winning side."

"They quit?"

"That's about it, Jeff. We've got three men left, and God knows why they stayed. We've got all them wagons, and nobody to drive them. It wouldn't do us no good even if you was to get out of jail. I hate to say it, but it looks like we're licked in this game."

Croydon stared through the bars, gripping them, white-knuckled.

### 3

### *The Thirteenth Day*

Croydon languished in jail on the eleventh and twelfth days. In his mind he saw Tom Hunter, slowed down in his pace now, yet still hauling enough crude into Sooner to give him an unbeatable margin, and the contract.

Almost from the moment that Croydon had heard Limerty's announcement of their defeat, he had made up his mind as to the course he had to follow. Escape, that was the only way. And since he could no longer win the contest on the basis of barrels delivered, he had to do it another way. Expose Hunter, thereby putting him out of the running and leaving Elizabeth's only choice his own outfit, which he could rebuild quickly on the strength of her contract.

But for two maddening days no opportunity for escape presented itself. The only escape route was the cell door. That was opened three times a day when the two deputies brought him a tray of food. One deputy held a six-gun on Croydon while the other ducked and set the tray inside. They always made Croydon retreat to the far wall and stand. Hink Peters was a thoughtful, methodical man who allowed no carelessness.

When noon of the thirteenth day arrived, Croydon decided he had to make a desperate try. So far as he knew, Peters had unearthed no evidence either to clear him or to point conclusively to his guilt. He *had* to get out . . . do something to fight the sense of defeat rising within him.

Instead of waiting until the deputies decided to come into the cell, he placed himself in position beforehand. He stood on the cell bunk, which was fastened to the rear wall. He leaned his elbows on the sill and stared out the small barred window into the dusty alley. He was standing that way when the jail door opened and the second deputy arrived with the food, brought from the Sooner House.

The key rattled in the lock, and Croydon turned around, desperately trying to conceal his breathlessness. The first deputy pushed the door open, and Croydon noted that he still held his gun level. The other man put down his tray.

"Well," Croydon said, "guess I'll eat long as you brought it. The view isn't the prettiest I've seen." He waved over his shoulder to the window. The second deputy allowed himself a grin. Croydon shifted his weight as if to step down off the bunk. His height gave him a slight advantage as he leaped.

The deputies let out hoarse yells as he bowled into them, knocking them backwards through the cell door. The three men fell in a heap of thrashing limbs, but Croydon kept his head, seizing both their guns and leaping to his feet, each fist full of a heavy weapon.

"All right, boys. Get inside the cell."

They obeyed him without hesitation. He relocked the door and tossed the keys in the corner, far away from them. Thrusting one gun into his belt and holding the other at ready, he slipped out the side door into an alley that opened to the main street.

He slid along in the shadows of the wall, thinking rapidly. He knew where Sheriff Peters lived. That was his destination. The house lay on a quiet back street, shaded by big trees. He walked up the lawn and in through the front door without knocking.

He went into the parlor. Mrs. Peters, a ruddy buxom woman with graying hair, saw him first. Then she saw the gun. "Why, Jeff, what are you . . ."

Peters, seated with his back to Croydon, spluttered loudly. He leaped to his feet, his hand dropping toward his holster.

"Easy, Hink," Croydon said. "I don't want trouble."

"What in hell is this?" Peters thundered. "I'll throw the book at you for breaking out of jail."

"I've got to have a chance to prove I didn't take those tallies. You open to a bargain?"

"I sure as blazes am not," Peters shot back.

Croydon had to smile. "Here it is anyway. You know where this Rip Flinch lives?" Peters nodded. "Well, let's stroll over there. If you walk in on him, holding your gun, and ask him point-blank whether or not he stole the tallies and planted them in my office, I think you'll have what you really want to know."

"Got this Flinch all figgered, eh?" Peters said. His eyes narrowed thoughtfully. His wife had long since relaxed. She knew Croydon well enough to know that no harm would come to her husband. "I think if you act like you already know he did it, say you got some evidence—he'll spook. He's that kind."

Croydon softened his tone. "But if he doesn't scare, then I'm willing to hand over my gun to you and go back to jail peaceably."

He watched the lawman for reactions. "Hink, I'm betting everything I've got on the hunch that you can scare him into admitting the truth."

Peters hesitated only a moment longer. Then he extended his hand. "All right, Jeff. Hand over your iron right now, and I'll go along with the game. I never did like that Flinch's looks much."

Croydon handed his gun over, followed it with the one at his belt. Peters led him out through the kitchen, picked up his hat, and the two men moved across the back lawn. From the door Mrs. Peters wished Jeff good luck.

Peters had Croydon ride slightly ahead of him, on one of Peters' own mounts. "So folks don't think I let you run around loose," Peters explained.

Rip Flinch lived in a seedy rooming house near the yards. The landlady informed them that Flinch hadn't yet appeared for the morning. She goggled at the sight of the sheriff herding his prisoner upstairs with his gun.

Croydon flattened himself outside the door while Peters knocked loudly.

When Flinch opened the door sleepily, Peters said gruffly, "Flinch, you're in trouble."

"What?" Flinch grunted. "What's that you're saying, sheriff? I just got outa bed."

"The stolen tallies," Peters said. "The ones you took from Matheson and planted in Croydon's office." *God,* Croydon thought, *he's really taking a chance for me.* "Come on, Flinch. You took those tallies, and now I can prove . . ."

"Damn you!" Flinch yelped. Croydon was filled with a sense of victory. Flinch tried to slam the door shut, but Peters rammed his shoulder against it and heaved. It spanged open, throwing Flinch to the floor. Peters ran into the room, Croydon on his heels.

Flinch seized his gun from a chair and began a wild volley of shots that blasted the woodwork into splinters but missed Croydon and Peters. They retreated quickly into the hall again. Peters tossed Croydon a six-gun. Croydon poked his head around the door in time to see Flinch, clad only in trousers and undershirt, heave himself feet first through the window. "Jumped out," Croydon shouted, racing toward the stairs. "Let's go after him."

Flinch evidently moved fast. They spent twenty minutes prowling the neighborhood around the boarding house, but he had eluded them. So they mounted up and rode all the way across town to Hunter's office. The yard man informed them that Flinch and Hunter had ridden out perhaps ten minutes ahead of them, looking excited.

"Ah swear," the yard man drawled, "the fiends o' hell was after them, sheriff."

Croydon vaulted up the office steps, looked in quickly.

"They've skipped all right. The safe's cleaned out."

Peters mounted up. "I'll see if I can get some men. Maybe we can still catch them. You go on about your business. There's no need for you to stay in jail any longer."

Exultantly Croydon headed for the Sooner House. He slammed into Elizabeth Bryant's suite despite the protests of the maid, demanding to see the widow. Elizabeth Bryant appeared in the sitting room abruptly, surprise showing in her dark eyes.

"What's the meaning of all this, Croydon? I thought you were in jail."

"I was. But Flinch spilled his mouth to the sheriff. He stole the tallies, on Hunter's orders. Both of them have cleared out. Hunter's out of business, and I'm the only freighting company owner left in Sooner. So how about the contract?"

"Not on your life. Unless you're ahead in the tally. I'll hire someone to run Hunter's rig. You have till dawn tomorrow to beat his score."

It was stupid, prideful . . . but then Croydon remembered what he had done to her; how he had carelessly exposed her secret. This was her way of retaliating. He jammed his hat on his head and stalked out.

Croydon raced back to the freight yard. There, Limerty greeted him with an expression of amazement. "Jeff! What happened to you? Come on inside, boy, before somebody sees you. If you broke out they'll be after you . . ."

"I did break out," Croydon told him. "But things are all straightened around now." Rapidly he summarized the events of the previous hours.

"Then we got Miz Bryant's contract after all," Limerty said, pleased.

"No we don't. She's a stubborn woman. We've still got to beat Hunter's tally. Which won't be easy, seeing as we only have till dawn. Now, have we still got those three men?"

Limerty nodded.

"Then with you and me, that will have to do it. I hope to God it does. I'll go down to the yards and check the tally. Just say a long prayer that Hunter's slacked off since I landed in jail." He left Limerty wide-eyed as he leaped up into the saddle and went galloping out of the yard.

Matheson, head swathed in bandages, greeted him with apologies. He'd already heard of Hunter's treachery from Sheriff Hink Peters. "But the sheriff and his posse come back about half an hour ago," Matheson concluded. "No sign of Hunter and Rip Flinch anywhere."

Croydon looked eagerly at the tallies. "How far ahead is Hunter?"

Matheson consulted the grimy sheets. "Well, he ain't been pushing near as hard since they salted you away. Let's see . . ." He frowned, figuring laboriously. "A hundred and three barrels. He ain't done much at all."

Croydon clapped him on the shoulder. "Thanks. He won't be doing anything after tomorrow."

And before Matheson could shoot another question, Croydon was into the saddle and away up the street.

He reported the total to Dunc Limerty, who let out a yip of pleasure.

"Round up those three men," Croydon said. "We'll need five wagons. We're going to do some mighty fast hauling . . ."

Before sundown, the five wagons careened out of Sooner. Croydon had the lead, howling like a fiend at the mules, cracking the buckskin popper over their ears.

Croydon had already formed a plan of action. Each skinner would take one of the Oh, Nellie! wells, the ones closest to Sooner, and load their wagons with crude. The margin would be close, but Croydon felt they could work it. At a fork, he swung his wagon off and went roaring down a rutted road. The others split up in various directions, having their orders to load up and race hell-for-leather back to Sooner.

Croydon pulled up at Oh, Nellie! Number three about ten that evening. He started yelling questions to the drill boss, who informed him they had plenty of crude waiting to be freighted. Croydon sweated in the light of the lanterns, heaving the big barrels up to the wagon bed. The sound of the well, *pump*, *pump, pump*, echoed in his ears, inexorable as the ticking of a clock.

By midnight the wagon was loaded. Croydon hoped the others would be doing as well. He gigged up the mules, turning their heads back toward Sooner. Driving at a breakneck clip, the wheels flying over the tops of the wagon ruts, he reached Sooner by two. Matheson greeted him by lantern light and chalked up the load on the tally. Croydon rolled himself a cigarette and tried to relax. It was no good. As long as the other men weren't back he couldn't rest.

All the others except Limerty arrived by four o'clock. Croydon scanned the sky anxiously. It would be dawn soon, and without that extra wagon load, they would lose.

Horse's hooves clopped in the street. Croydon turned expectantly, then realized it was a single rider. Elizabeth Bryant, in shirt and denims, rode into the circle of lamplight.

She climbed down, nodded to Croydon and leaned over Matheson's shoulder to glance at the tally. Croydon saw pearly streaks in the east. Nowhere in the silent town did he hear the clatter of Limerty's wagon.

Elizabeth Bryant faced him. "You're still under Hunter's total."

"I've got one more wagon due in."

Elizabeth Bryant smiled a chilly smile, openly defensive against any more attacks. "But Mr. Croydon—it's dawn now."

"Then the contract goes to Hunter's outfit, whether he's around or not?"

"I'm afraid it . . ." she began.

Shots racketed in the night and the lantern exploded in a hail of glass. Instinctively Croydon swept his arm around Elizabeth Bryant and bore her to the ground.

He snaked his gun free, listening. The whole freight yard was dark. Croydon crept forward along the ground, trying to keep from making noise. Hunter had come back. Defeated, whipped and exposed, the man nevertheless had the will to revenge himself. He wanted Croydon's life.

Croydon scooped up a handful of gravel and tossed it to his right. Nothing happened. He picked up a larger rock and threw it in the same direction. A second later, a gun bucketed, aimed toward the right.

Croydon emptied his gun from where he lay. The powder-flame showed him Rip Flinch, jiggling in the door of a boxcar, his chest bleeding.

He teetered forward slowly, and Croydon dodged backward as Flinch fell.

Croydon turned around. Hunter was somewhere around. But where? He took a step backward, and a gun exploded. Fire ripped into his shoulder. He reeled from the pain. Somebody struck a match and touched it to a piece of wood and got a glowing torch.

It was Matheson, standing behind Hunter. Hunter stood clearly outlined, his head turned slightly so that his eyes glowed. His gun rose slowly.

Croydon knew his own gun was empty; it had clicked empty after he had downed Rip Flinch. He had no other.

The pain dizzied him. Another instant and Hunter would kill him. He had to move. He had to *fight*. He took a step forward, trying to lunge at Hunter, but he only succeeded in falling on his face. He heard an explosion, and then something jolted down on his back and didn't move.

A moment later, Hunter's lifeless body was lifted away.

Dunc Limerty stood there, pistol in hand.

*"Dunc!"* Croydon lunged to his feet, staggering.

"Hunter was about to finish you. I couldn't do much else."

Croydon blinked, realization sinking in. "You made it back. You got here! The contract . . ."

Limerty shook his head slowly. "I . . . I came in on one of the mules . . ."

"W—what?" Through the numbing pain, Croydon didn't understand.

"One of them repaired axles gave out, about ten miles out of town. I tried to fix it but I couldn't do it by myself. So I rode in on one of the mules. I seen the tally, Jeff. I'm sorry." The oldster averted his gaze.

Croydon swung bleary eyes to Elizabeth Bryant, standing beside a re-lit lantern. Her face had a dazed bleached quality about it. *Damn her*, Croydon thought, *she isn't going to stop us like that. I won't let her.* He started to walk toward the woman. Limerty put out a hand to restrain him but Croydon shoved it away. He kept walking.

He faced Elizabeth Bryant across the circle of lamplight. She averted her eyes suddenly, and he saw that her cheeks had turned a deep scarlet.

"You heard what Limerty said," Croydon told her.

"You know that our last wagon load is stuck outside of town. But for that we'd have won the contract. On your terms."

"I'm sorry," she said, weakly this time. "I set up the rules whereby . . . the . . . the . . ."

Silence.

He moved closer to her so that Matheson, Limerty, and the other three men could not hear.

"What's wrong? Are you ashamed of my finding out that you're a woman and not a machine? I don't think it's anything to be ashamed of."

She looked at him then, the flush deepening. He could see the battle being fought within her, wounded pride against womanly desire. Twice she almost spoke . . . twice she closed her lips again. She shook her head, still unable to speak.

Croydon turned away, disgusted. "Well, I guess I had you figured wrong, Mrs. Bryant. And I guess you can find someone to take over Hunter's outfit—"

"Wait." Her voice was barely a whisper.

Croydon turned and stared. "I'll . . . I'm moving the time up. The final tally will be made at eight A.M. this morning." She spun away, then, finding her horse, remounting and plunging into the darkness as if all the fiends of hell were pursuing her. *No, not fiends,* Croydon thought, *only emotions, pride against desire.* And desire had won. He'd found a chink in her armor.

Dunc Limerty raced up to him. "We've got until eight this morning to bring that wagon in. Get some of the boys and use one of their wagons. We'll have that contract."

"You're damned right we will," Limerty exclaimed. He slapped Croydon on the back. The impact was enough to send the weakened Croydon toppling. He stretched out on the ground, dimly aware that the astounded Limerty was bending over him. The darkness closed. . . .

Limerty brought the extra wagon in by seventhirty. On the spot, Elizabeth Bryant awarded them the contract to freight crude for the holdings of the late Senator. When Croydon awoke, he had his arm bandaged. He sat in his office all day, doing paper work, thinking of just how long it would take to pay off the mortgage, what kind of new equipment he could afford and a hundred other similar details. Now and then he took a little whiskey for the pain.

That evening he dressed in his best suit and called on Elizabeth Bryant in her hotel suite. They sat opposite each other on the sofa, a polite distance between them.

"What are your plans now?" Croydon asked.

"I don't know. I could go back east, but there isn't much to look forward to there, unless . . ."

"Why not stay here and manage the Senator's business? You could learn in a year's time, and you could probably step up production and profit if you took the trouble."

"I'm afraid I made a botch of things, Jeff." She used his first name casually, as if she were accustomed to it. "This is no place for me."

"I think it is," he said. He moved close, tilted her chin with his hand, and kissed her, long and hard.

She flushed again, but she didn't grow angry. Instead, she smiled. Croydon knew then that with time, they could have something rich and fine together.

"Would you like to go have dinner?" he asked.

Embarrassed, she smiled. "I think we'd better," she said.

# The Winning of Poker Alice

W. G. (for George) Tubbs belonged to the tradition of the gentleman gambler. He realized that here, as everywhere else, social levels existed. At the lowest rung came the card sharps, the professional cheats who used every trick in the book to fleece the wary Westerner of his cash. Higher up the ladder were the semi-honest gamblers; they cheated only when absolutely necessary. And at the very top stood the gentlemen of the trade, and such a one was Tubbs.

Not only were professional ethics important to him but also the matter of one's attire. The more ragtag was a man's dress, the less he belonged to the finest tradition; poor clothes stamped him as nothing but a shady tinhorn. Since the gentleman gambler enjoyed a spotless reputation for honesty and straight dealing in all the raw frontier towns, Tubbs felt that it was up to him to look the part.

Tubbs was large and red-faced, with friendly blue eyes and well-manicured fingernails. It was in the 1870's, when he was forty or thereabouts, that he thrived in the roaring Black Hills. He was regarded as one of the cleverest gamblers in Deadwood.

That is, until Poker Alice came along.

No one knew exactly how she arrived in town. One evening she was there, that's all. She walked into the Poker Chip Saloon, a big woman, dressed in an inexpensive but tasteful gown with her slightly grayed blonde hair piled fashionably high on her head. There was a determined, rugged cast to her jaw, and her eyes were shrewd. But they were also clear, straightforward and honest.

Nobody paid much attention to her at first. She strode up to the bar, with only a few of the local honkytonkers giving her haughty glances and being secretly envious of the fine-looking woman who no doubt would be equally at home in a luxurious drawing room. She waited for the bartender, Sherm Clagfield, who also owned the Poker Chip, to come to her.

"What'll it be, ma'am?" Sherm asked, his eyes glinting humorously.

The woman did not smile. "Rye."

Sherm almost hollered his head off with laughter. He wanted to, that is. But something about the woman—her air of determination, perhaps—kept him from it. Trying to keep a serious expression on his face, he set the glass of liquor down before her. She tossed it off with one gulp. Sherm felt a pang of admiration.

The woman seemed to hesitate a moment. "Anything I can do for you, ma'am?"

She surveyed the room. "Yes. I'm a gambler. I want to set up shop here. My name is Alice Duffield."

Sherm couldn't contain himself this time. He let out a loud *Haw!* He doubled over with mirth, but when his eyes came to rest on Alice Duffield again, he stopped laughing. A pistol muzzle, held in her steady hand, poked at him. A wicked-looking .38 on a .45 frame.

"Are you going to stand there and laugh like a

jackass?'' Alice said softly, ''or are you going to shut your mouth and give me a chance?''

Clagfield saw that she meant it. From the way she held the gun, she was no greenhorn. ''Sure, ma'am, you go on over to table six and tell Whitey I said for you to take over. What are you good at?''

''Stud or faro,'' she said briskly. ''I prefer faro, however.''

''Well, number six is stud.''

''That'll do nicely.''

She thrust the pistol back into her carpetbag which she had beside her, and walked over to table number six. Whitey didn't believe what she said. He too got a look down the business end of the gun, and saw Sherm's amazed nod. Whitey got up fast and Alice Duffield sat down. A crowd of curious, eager men thronged around the table. Alice faced them coolly. ''Gents,'' she said, ''sit down and play some cards. You'll get treated fair.''

A few men slid reluctantly into place, pushed by their comrades who haw-hawed at the idea of a woman being a good card player. The game got under way. ''The sky,'' announced Alice, ''is the limit.''

It was a fair, even game. One of the men lost a hundred and eight dollars, another won a hundred and forty. The crowd grew larger. The other saloons in town drained of their customers. Business boomed at the Poker Chip as the night wore on. Players left their chairs and new players sat down. But always, Alice sat there, watching the faces of the men, her own face unmoving as stone. By dawn they knew that she was square. A real gentleman gambler, if you could call a woman that. And in spite of her expressed preference for faro, they had already coined a name. Poker Alice.

Shortly after sunrise Alice approached Sherm Clag-field again. "Are you satisfied?"

Sherm nodded rapidly. "You want a job here?"

"That's why I came."

"Well, you're hired." So began the career of Poker Alice in Deadwood.

And now W. G. Tubbs re-enters the picture.

For you see, he had been on a trip, all the way down to St. Louis, when Alice arrived in Deadwood and made her sensational entrance. He rode confidently into town on his moderately well-cared-for mare just before noon one day, put on fresh clothes—light trousers, a colorful vest, broadcloth coat, white shirt with flowing black tie and tall beaver hat (for the dress of the true gentleman of the tables was highly conventional)—ate lunch at Mame's Cafe, and wandered over to the Poker Chip to let Sherm know he had returned.

A game was already in progress. Faro this time, with Alice handling the box. As usual, she had a large crowd of spectators around her, for the novelty of a woman gambler had not yet worn off.

Mildly surprised, Tubbs approached Sherm who stood at the bar. There was none of the pleasant foolish conversation about, How was the trip? And It was fine. Instead, Tubbs jerked a thumb at Alice. "Who's that lady?"

"Poker Alice," Sherm said. "Our new dealer."

Immediately a frown creased the broad forehead of Tubbs. He saw a problem. Several of the other dealers—Johnny Red Dog, Louisiana Irwin, The Count, among them—sat idle at a corner table, playing a listless game of twenty-one. Apparently Poker Alice was a threat to his livelihood. As if he had sensed what Tubbs was thinking, Sherm said, "Yep, nobody wants to gamble with anybody but Alice."

"Oh, is that right," Tubbs said, irritated. Well, the fad wouldn't last. The boys would come back to George Tubbs for a fast, honest game when they got tired of this female.

But the boys didn't come back. The weeks dragged on and Alice kept raking in the money. Tubbs played on a salary, but his self-respect grew battered and worn. Besides, the boys didn't care two hoops about him any more. If Tubbs had two men playing with him on a Saturday night (the liveliest time of the week of course) he was lucky. Whereas Alice could never be seen, there were so many men crowded around her table.

Tubbs realized that something had to be done. He found out more about Alice, and the more he found out, the greater grew his envy. She had learned to play cards, it was rumored, down in New Mexico. In fact, a bawdy story stated that instead of spending her wedding night with her husband, Frank Duffield, a mining engineer, she spent it in the Silver City, New Mexico, saloon, fascinated by the card playing. The wide-eyed bride had evidently learned fast and well, studying the expressions of men's eyes when they played, the uncontrollable nervous tics that showed when they bluffed, all those mannerisms that might betray them to the wary dealer. Alice herself stated that she took up gambling as a career after Frank Duffield got blown up in a mine accident in Lake City, Colorado.

Tubbs contemplated violence. He sat there at his generally empty table, glaring at the crowd of laughing rowdy men around Poker Alice. But violence, he decided, was out. One night a young punk of a kid got smart with Alice. That lady drilled him neatly in the shoulder with her .38 on the .45 frame before he could bring his own shoulder gun clear of the harness. And besides, Tubbs was not a violent man by nature. He made his way by the code of the gentleman.

One afternoon Alice approached him. She had often spoken to him, but he had snubbed her. "Mr. Tubbs," she said, sitting down across from him and pouring herself a drink. "I'd like to know why you don't take to me."

Tubbs stared gloomily at the table. "How do you expect me to? You're wrecking my business."

Alice nodded. "I heard you were a good man. Popular, too."

"I was. Before you came along."

Alice extended her hand. "I'd like to call a truce."

"No thank you," Tubbs said politely, and turned away from her, fuming. She shrugged and left the table. He couldn't help following her with his eyes, though. She had a certain mature, rugged attractiveness. For a moment he almost regretted not having accepted her offer.

Gradually, the novelty wore off and Alice assumed her place as just another of the dealers. Tubbs got business again, though he grudgingly told himself that Alice was just a *little* more popular than any of the men. But as the days passed and he watched her work the faro and stud games, his envy changed slowly. Now that the threat to his job had removed itself, he began seeing her in a more favorable light. As downright attractive, in fact. But he didn't exactly have the courage to approach her, after having rebuffed her once. After all, he was a gentleman, cool and calm, unused to rash impulses and actions.

But she grew more and more attractive in his eyes. None of the men of the town seemed romantically interested in her, for they were always moving on and new ones took their place. At last Tubbs determined something had to be done. He spoke to Alice now, a casual "Hello" and "Fine day" now and again, but nothing more. With the natural guilty feeling of a rather shy man, he followed her home one evening, at a safe distance, to learn that she roomed at Kate Colby's Boarding House.

If anyone had seen him ride out of Deadwood the next day, and had followed him, his reputation would have been ruined for good. He rode out across the countryside, always turning around for signs of pursuers, but there were none. He chose one spot, decided it was too public, and rode back up into the hills a little further until he came upon just the place. Quiet, secluded, and he could hear any horses coming that might happen to ride his way. He climbed down off his mare, clutching the section of newspaper. He still felt highly embarrassed, but something bigger than himself made him go ahead with his plan.

Carefully, he picked a bouquet of wild flowers and wrapped them up in the newspaper.

He rode back into Deadwood soon after that with the bundle clutched tightly under his arm. He was in a state of high nervous tension all afternoon, and did not go near the Poker Chip. Poker Alice had the habit of returning to Kate Colby's Boarding House at around six in the evening, eating dinner and resting in her room for a while, and then going back to the saloon about eight for an all-night session with the cards. So when his expensively-fobbed watch showed just seven-thirty, Tubbs dismounted before the boarding house, still clutching the flowers. He'd had them in a vase of water in his room all afternoon, with the shades pulled down, to keep them fresh.

He stole past the dining room unobserved by the few late eaters. He already knew which room Alice kept. He had, in fact, worked out an elaborate spy system among his town cronies so that he knew her movements almost exactly. He walked determinedly down the hall and stopped at the door of Alice's room. He fumbled self-consciously with his string tie for a moment and then knocked.

"Come in," said a wary voice.

Tubbs opened the door and his jaw dropped.

Alice was crouched down behind the bed as if expecting an attack. Her gun was leveled at Tubbs' ample stomach, and to add to the strange scene, a large black cigar stuck out of one corner of her mouth, curling up smoke that wreathed her blonde-gray head.

"What do you want, Tubbs?" she said sharply.

He held out the flowers awkwardly. "Just . . . just wanted to pay my respects." He felt his face getting hot and, presumably, red.

Poker Alice rose to her feet, seemed to debate with herself for a moment, and then put her gun away. She flicked an inch of cigar ash neatly into a brass spittoon by the bed.

"Well, close the door, it's drafty," she said.

Tubbs fumbled for words. He stared at her cigar with a peculiar expression.

"Well, what's wrong with it?" Alice exclaimed. "Other women smoke cigarettes. I like something stronger." She blew out a large puff of smoke. Tubbs was getting hold of himself now. He extended the flowers again and Alice took them. She unwrapped the package and a smile spread across her face.

"Why, Mr. Tubbs, they're very nice. Thank you." She began putting them into a vase. "I'm sorry I jumped at you like that, but I was looking out the window and I saw you ride up and you looked so

odd that I thought maybe you had something bad
on your mind. A woman can't be too careful."

"No," Tubbs murmured, sinking down into a
chair. He sprang up again immediately. "Well, I
guess I'd better get down to the saloon."

"Sit still," Alice said. There was a hint of authority
under the friendliness of her voice. Tubbs sat. "I'm
glad to see we've called off the feud, Mr. Tubbs."
She offered him a cigar and he lit up. "A woman
gets lonely in a town like this, and you always appeared to be such a gentleman, though I did get
angry when you refused to shake my hand."

Tubbs felt a little more at ease now. The cool demeanor of the gentleman that had left him so rapidly
a few minutes earlier was returning. "Yes'm," he
said, smiling. "I just thought we could be friends and
maybe go for a drive now and then . . . I've got a
buggy . . . and the front porch of this place seems
like it would be mighty pleasant and breezy in hot
weather . . ."

And so they talked on, the gentleman gambler and
the cigar-smoking woman who handled cards and a
gun like a professional. Their relationship made its
way forward from that night on a very friendly basis.
They took their drives and ate Sunday dinners together (for Alice refused to play cards on the Lord's
Day) and sat on the front porch of Kate Colby's
Boarding House. But the situation had not yet
smoothed itself out completely.

For W. G. Tubbs was by nature a cautious man.
The gentleman gambler, he could never forget, did
not let himself be guided by rash impulses. Tubbs
often considered matrimony, but even then he would
put himself off, saying mentally, *I'd best think about it.*

Nearly a year passed that way. Tubbs and Poker
Alice had accepted each other, and their rivalry over

the gambling tables was now an amicable one, and Tubbs did not mind kind of taking a back seat, for the woman was always just a *little* more popular than any of the men.

Tubbs was relaxing in his room one Sunday morning, thinking of the dinner he and Poker Alice would eat together in an hour or so, when the door opened quickly. Alice stood there in her best gown. A humorous light shone in her eyes but the .38 on the .45 frame pointed at Tubbs' stomach with unmistakable authority.

"Get your shirt on, Tubbs. I've been thinking for a long time that it'd be a good thing if we were married. We'd double our income and we wouldn't have to eat that boarding house food all the time. I know you were too frightened to ask me, so I thought I'd better do the asking." She waved the gun. "Now hurry up."

The Rev. Billy Watters married them in the Poker Chip Saloon, with Sherm Clagfield standing up for them. Sherm had a cabin back in the hills, so they got into Tubbs' buggy and drove off for a little holiday. Tubbs didn't seem at all unhappy about the shotgun, or rather six-gun, aspect of the marriage. And so they rolled out of Deadwood, Poker Alice Duffield Tubbs, queen of the gambling halls from Colorado to the Dakotas, and W. G. (for George) Tubbs. The gentleman gambler and the lady who smoked cigars.

# To the Last Bullet

In the small mining community of Sierra that day, the talk ran mostly to the weather. The ominous keening of the wind as it swept down out of the gray sky from the looming mountains seemed to lift the level of talk to a plane of high excitement. The first signs of winter, dead, isolating, bone-chilling winter, came blowing down the mountain with the wind. The old timers who sat perched on barrels in the Mercantile, greasy wads of chawin' tabac rotating in their cheeks, predicted the first big storm of the season. And in the Sierra, the first storm meant excitement, even if it was excitement of a familiar kind.

Marshal Trow Huston had passed the cool mountain summer and the sharper, more exhilarating autumn in relative peace. A drunken brawl now and then offered little disturbance to the taciturn, thirtyish-looking marshal's peace of mind. The crazy miner who had started shooting up the girls in one of the town's leading service establishments had folded up as soon as the marshal put in an appearance, heavy Colt in fist, blue eyes reproachful.

Perhaps, Huston reflected, finishing his evening meal in the hotel dining room, I'm getting old and set in my ways. Thirty-one, calendar-wise, was not old. But thirty-one, after the black days of Yankee slaughtering Reb with sabre and pitchfork and whatever else happened to be lying around the embattled meadows and farm towns, was ancient. War had soured him, he realized.

After the war, Sierra had seemed like a quiet and ideal place to settle. He'd worked on the mountain, mining his living from the rich lode, and taken the marshal's job under pressure from the handful of civic-minded citizens after the other marshal, an old man, died of a heart attack one Christmas Eve.

That was four years ago. He'd been growing less conscientious every day since, hoping more and more that the town would remain peaceful. A quiet hatred of violence had festered in him all the long years since the war. Perhaps one day, a younger man, with memories unscarred, would come along and take his place. When the former marshal died no one else had been available, and no one seemed available now. So he was stuck in the job for a while.

Huston pushed back his chair. He lit a cigar as he strolled through the lobby into the adjoining saloon. He watched with a feeling of satisfaction as the bartender scraped the foam off a schooner of beer with his stick and handed it over. Huston took a sip.

"The big snow's on the way, appears like," the bartender said amiably.

Shots racketed out in the street. Huston put down the schooner and whirled around, his body going tense. Eyes swiveled toward him. He walked quickly to the doors, pushed through and glanced up and down the street.

Three horsemen came pounding toward him. A gun exploded behind them on the Mercantile's front steps. Huston dragged out his Colt as the men galloped past. All three wore heavy coats and had their hats pulled down over shadowed faces.

"Hey there!" one of them shouted as they rode by. "There's the saloon!" The rider's gun exploded and the other two men fired after him. Huston ducked instinctively, realizing a moment later when he heard the plate glass window smash that they had been aiming for him. He fired one useless shot after them, but they had disappeared in the darkness at the end of the street . . . the darkness on the trail that led up the mountain.

The batwings flapped open behind him. A crowd of men, babbling excitedly, poured out. "Who was it?" one of them exclaimed. "See 'em, Trow?"

"Couldn't make them out," Huston replied. "But Amos is making a lot of noise up at the Mercantile. I'll go have a look." He shoved his Colt back into the holster and started to walk, followed by several of the men who conjectured loudly over the identity of the riders.

Amos Dean, owner of the Mercantile, stood on the broad front stoop of his store, pistol in hand. He stood in the cold night air without a coat, mindless of the chill his thin shirt and flowered vest couldn't keep out. In the light of the lantern in his other hand, his blue eyes snapped excitedly.

"Hello, Trow. Glad you got here."

"Who were they?" Huston noticed that the Mercantile's front door hung crookedly on its hinges, minus glass, as if it had been smashed open.

"Dogged if I know," Amos Dean said. "But they stole three suits of clothes, and three of my best sheep-lined coats, and six-guns and a whole bucket-ful of lead to fill 'em up with. And that ain't all." He jerked his head inside. "Come see."

Huston and the curious onlookers followed the short storekeeper into the darkened interior. Dean held his lantern high so that light fell on a pile of rough clothes lying in the center aisle. Dean put down his pistol and lifted a pair of trousers with broad black and white stripes. "Get an eyeful of these, marshal."

"Convict suits," Huston said. A warning bell went ringing in his brain.

"I swear if I'd made trouble, they'd of shot me down," Dean said with a shake of his head. "Mean looking, all of them. And they were about froze, wearing only these duds." His blue eyes narrowed. "You're going after them, ain't you, marshal?"

"Why sure, I suppose so."

"They can't get very far, if they don't know the trail over the mountain," one of the men in the crowd said. " 'Sides, it's dark, and there's a snow coming."

"I'll get a posse together," Huston said. "Round up a dozen men and—"

"Posse!" Dean snorted. "By the time you try to find enough guns around here, they'll be half way back to Kansas. You got to get after them right away, marshal. Hell, they're owlhoots from some prison, that's plain enough. And it's your job to catch 'em. Besides," he added in a grumble, "I want those duds and my guns back. I can't afford to lose merchandise like that." He glowered at the marshal.

"I don't know," Huston said, shaking his head. "I don't like to start up the mountain by myself—"

Dean's lips curled. "What's the matter, Trow? You goin' yellow of a sudden?"

Huston's eyes flared wide. "You've got no call to say that."

"No? It seems to me, Trow, these last months you've been mighty careful to keep your nose clean. You act like you're gettin' right scared of any jasper with a hogleg in his hand. If that's the kind of marshal you are, you aren't doing anybody in this town any good."

A murmur of assent followed his words. Huston whirled around to the other men. Eyelids lowered. Mouths clamped shut like traps. Somebody chewed a plug loudly.

In that instant, Dean's words lanced into Huston's brain. The very thing he'd been thinking while he ate. More and more he was coming to want security—safety for himself—when it was his job to guarantee safety to the other residents of the town, even if it meant personal risk. What a damned fool I am, he thought now. I've just become aware of it and they've seen it for—how many weeks, and months? Still, it didn't lessen the fact that the men who had robbed Dean were escaped prisoners, probably killers with nothing to lose in killing one man more. He was still afraid, with the terrible fear of death, a black unknown void, born in him when cannon thundered on the battlefields.

"All right," Huston said softly. "I'll go after them."

He shouldered his way through the silent crowd and walked down the front steps. He turned right, walking quickly until he reached the rude wooden building that served as his office and Sierra's jail. Lamps glowed yellow through the windows. Pink Fisher, his black-haired twenty-year-old deputy, was waiting for him. Pink usually laughed a lot. Tonight he was frowning.

"Howdy, Trow," he said, his voice quiet. Immediately he walked back toward the first of the jail's three cells. "Come take a took at what we got."

Huston followed him. Pink pointed. A boy hardly more than fifteen or sixteen lay on the cell bunk, his pale face turned to the light, looking delicate and thin as fine china. Beneath the thrown-back coat, an irregular stain of blood had dried on his shirt front.

"Deader than anything," Pink said. "Jake Robards found him on the trail less than ten minutes ago. This was inside his shirt pocket." He handed Huston a slip of yellow paper.

One edge of the paper bore a brownish stain. Huston recognized the handwriting of Lem Swope, a justice of the peace in a town down the mountain. *Three escaped criminals headed your way*, the note ran. *Gall, Cody, Elwood. Watch out for them, Trow. They are dangerous. Lem.*

Huston crumpled the paper. He'd had a poster on Bart Gall a few months before. Wanted for stage holdups, and two murders in Sacramento. Evidently prison couldn't hold him. Huston remembered the mean, pinch-eyed face in the poster sketch and shuddered.

"These are the same gents who did the shooting a little while ago," Huston said. "Robbed the Mercantile of some clothes and extra guns."

"I heard the shooting, but they brought the boy in just then. Sorry I couldn't make it down."

Huston didn't answer. He was thinking of this boy, sent to warn Sierra and being ambushed with what had perhaps been Bart Gall's last shot. Maybe the boy'd spotted them; or made too much noise following them. Whatever happened, he'd wound up dead on a cell bunk with the mountain wind singing his funeral dirge outside.

Huston pulled his heavy sheep-lined coat off the wall, put it on. He rummaged through his desk for more ammunition and put the surplus in his coat.

Yes, Dean was right. He had yellowed. He was yellow now; scared because up in the mountains Bart Gall was riding toward an escape through the pass.

There was no other way he could go. And Huston knew he had to go after him. His job was to protect the people of Sierra, not himself.

There was nothing wrong in being afraid, he knew that. The wrong part was letting the fear rule you. Being alone too much, no wife, no family, he thought of the war a great deal. And it had soured him. But now he knew he had to ride up the mountain and try to stop Bart Gall and the two other killers before they reached the pass. He *had* to, because now that he knew, something in him grew sick at the idea of being ruled by fear. A man couldn't live that way.

Pink shoved his arms into his coat. "I'm coming along, Trow." It was a statement, not a question. He strapped his guns across his lean hips.

Huston faced him. "Pink, let me ask you something. Have I gone yellow?"

Pink didn't answer for a minute. Then: "Why, Trow, I don't see why you ask something like that."

"Have I, Pink?" Huston's eyes burned fiercely.

Pink turned his back on him, shrugging. "People talk, Trow. I don't give it much heed— "

"What about you? How do you feel about it?"

Pink turned around again, a touch of sadness in his eyes. "Trow, I don't like to say it, but if you ask me, I guess I'll tell you. You act like you're scared to make a move any more. Almost scared to raise your voice to a drunk." He looked down at the rough plank floor. "I'm sorry, Trow."

The wind made a mad whining around the corners of the jail. "That's all right, Pink." Huston clapped the younger man on the shoulder. "We'll go out and bring those three back and maybe I won't be yellow any more." A note of self-inflicted bitterness edged Huston's voice.

"Sure, Trow." Pink smiled wanly. "We'll bring them back."

Huston jerked the door open. The wind lashed his face with new fury, stronger now, bitter with the bone-cold feel of winter. They bent against the wind as they made their way around the jail to the stable at the rear. Each man saddled his own horse by lantern light. Neither one spoke. The animals blew out their breath in long streams of vapor and stamped frequently. At last Huston extinguished the lantern and swung up into the saddle. He made sure his rifle rested tightly in the boot and gave a tug on the reins. Silently the two men headed up the main street toward the mountain trail.

Huston figured the outlaws might make camp for the night in Moon Hollow, an old ghost town half way up the mountain to the pass. Pink agreed with this estimate. They rode rapidly, hoofs rattling with sharp sounds on the rocky soil, their only light the pale glow of the stars outlining the shadow-forms of the great trees. They had been on the trail perhaps twenty minutes when a few snowflakes began to drift down, big and soft and wet. Huston licked one from his upper lip.

*How in God's name can we find them?* he wondered dismally. Up here there was nothing but a barren waste of lonely trees and hard earth. The cold pierced to the very heart of him, lulling him in the saddle, filling him with a sense of helplessness. When the rifle cracked, he was a moment late in reacting.

He jerked the reins wildly, pulling his horse off the trail. More shots racketed from up ahead, dim orange smudges behind the thickening wall of white snow. Huston dropped from the saddle and fired a futile shot in answer.

He listened. Somewhere up ahead he heard muffled voices. *Damn*, he thought, *a moment longer and they'd have gotten us, just like they got that kid. We came too fast, too loudly.*

Another shot boomed. He heard the slug bite a tree two feet above him. Then silence, and the soft whisper of the snow, coming faster now, driven by the rising wind.

Hoofs clattered in the darkness ahead. Then there was a rapid volley of three shots. Pink's horse went bucketing down the trail toward Sierra, flinging noisy echoes behind it. Huston saw that the saddle was empty. His stomach went hollow.

The outlaws moved further away up the trail. Huston fumbled in the darkness until his hands came into contact with an arm, stretched out rigidly. Shifting around on his heels so that his back was to the pass, he struck a match and cupped it in his stiff fingers.

Pink lay hatless on the snow. Mouth wide open, he stared upward with a grotesque kind of smile. A flake drifted down into his mouth. The match burned Huston's fingers and he turned away.

After a long minute he rose to his feet and climbed back up on his horse. His eyes searched the darkness ahead. Now he had to go on. More than ever, he had to go on. He kneed his mount, vengeful hatred filling him, seeming to burn the cold out of his bones. Laughing Pink Fisher, remembering Huston as a coward at the end . . .

That had to be proven wrong.

Approximately where the gunmen had lain in wait for them, he came upon an overturned coach. His horse shied away skittishly, letting out a whinny.

Huston leaned over and rubbed away the snow on the side panel.

SIERRA OVERLAND.

Puzzling at the deserted coach, Huston then remembered that it had passed through Sierra early that same morning, on its run across the mountain through the pass. Cautiously Huston urged his mount forward again.

He covered about a quarter mile more before the ground levelled off somewhat and he saw the ramshackle buildings of the ghost town of Moon Hollow. Directly at the opposite end of the deserted main street, the mountains sloped down to a jagged V, through which the moon had risen.

Something tightened in Huston's stomach. In the window of what had once been the Moon Hollow Hotel, a light glowed.

Huston scanned the street for horses. He saw none. Warily he dismounted and tied his horse to the low branch of a stunted pine. He drew his Colt and transferred it to his left hand, flexing the fingers of his right to get rid of the stiffness. Then, Colt held properly, he started walking through the curtain of snow toward the hotel.

He kept to the side of the street, moving rapidly. He slipped into an alley alongside the rotting walls of the hotel and sidled up to a window. Stretching, he looked in. A soft gasp came from his lips. He drew back, then ventured another look.

The first person he recognized was little graybearded Andy McNulty, the stage driver. He was stretched out on a sagging divan, one leg encased in what looked like a crude splint. Two other people were with him. An elderly man in a black suit, flowered vest and high black beaver hat, and a young woman with a hard, brittle face and rich red lips.

From her gown, he thought it was not hard to determine her profession.

Two lamps, evidently stripped from the coach, glowed feebly on an ancient table. The older man was gesturing drunkenly as he weaved on his feet and talked to McNulty. Huston looked for Gall and the other two. He didn't see them.

After a moment of debate, he rounded the corner of the hotel and walked toward the door, his gun ready. Perhaps they could tell him if Gall had ridden on. He put his hand on the door and pushed it open, stepping quickly inside. The woman gasped and the man in the beaver turned to peer at him with reddened eyes.

McNulty made an effort to rise, then groaned. "Trow Huston. What in hell are you doing up here?"

Huston closed the door behind him. "I might ask the same, Andy."

McNulty shook his head. "The horses stumbled on the way up and the coach went over on her side and I got a broken leg in the bargain. These here are my passengers, Miss Lil Carney and her father, Mr. Elihu Carney." McNulty glanced sourly at Carney. "Don't mind him, he's out on his feet." The girl's expression didn't change; it was stiff, bitter, defensive.

"She carried me up here and fixed up my leg," McNulty explained. "By then it was too dark to send her down to Sierra alone, what with the horses run off and Carney there too drunk to stagger. So we holed up here. Maybe Carney'll sober up enough by mornin' to go down for some horses. That is, if the snow lets up."

Huston glanced to the black squares of the windows. The flakes were larger now, striking hard.

"I'm looking for three men," he said.

McNulty looked grim. "They was here, just a few minutes ago."

"They're killers. Escaped prisoners. They just shot Pink Fisher."

McNulty let out a curse.

"Where are they, Andy? Did they leave?"

"Naw," McNulty spat. "Didn't want to hang around here, though. They're down the street in the saloon. They're holin' up for the night, too, so they said."

"And they stole my bottle," Elihu Carney said.

He was almost crying.

## 2

## *The Devil Wears Red*

Huston turned to go. If Gall and the other two were up at the saloon, the quickest way to accomplish his task would be to walk up there, surprise them and drill them down where they sat. Working on the old man's liquor bottle, their responses might slow a good deal. That coupled with the fact that the element of surprise favored him was enough to take the biting edge off his fear. But as he brought his hand down on the door knob, the woman's voice stopped him.

"Who is he, McNulty?" Lil Carney asked. Huston turned around. "The law in Sierra?"

McNulty nodded. The lamplight heightened the blaze in the girl's eyes, a blaze of animosity near to hatred. She kicked the hem of her scarlet gown around from in front of her with a flick of her foot. Then she planted her fists on her hips.

"Mister, I've a good mind to go down to the saloon and warn those men that you're coming."

Elihu Carney hopped from one foot to the other, "Lil! Don't talk like that to the marshal. Them jaspers stole my one and only bottle. You know how that just plain ruins me. Let him go."

"Let him go?" the woman said contemptuously. "Sure I'll let him go—after I tell him what I think of him and his fancy town."

Huston let out a long sigh. The woman had a rough kind of prettiness, a certain charm covered over now by the hard mask of bitterness. Huston felt nervous. He wanted to get the job over with, and yet it had suddenly become plain that he couldn't antagonize Lil Carney if he wanted to surprise Gall and his companions.

"I'm afraid I've never seen you before, ma'am," he said.

Lil Carney stepped forward, mouth twisting. "Pop and I were going to get off the stage in Sierra. But a whipper-snapper deputy, a young bobcat wearing a tin star, took one look at me and told me to get right back on the coach. But our tickets ran out there and we don't have any more money, so right now we're in debt to the company for all the cash it takes to cross the mountains."

"We've got a town ordinance," Huston explained, "against any new—uh—dance hall ladies setting up shop there. What ones we already have, we can't do much about. But we can keep others out, keep them from making trouble. I'm sorry if it inconvenienced you."

She snorted. "We've been run out of more towns than we can count, mister. If folks would just give us a chance, we'd show them that we wouldn't cause any trouble. Pop deals a fair game of draw or stud.

We might even go to work in some regular jobs if people didn't take one look at us and tell us to move on." She indicated the scarlet dress covering her shapely body. "But these are all the clothes I own."

Huston's mind worked quickly. "Tell you what I'll do, Miss Carney. If I get these men rounded up, you can come back to Sierra with your father and look for a job. And there won't be any extra coach fare." He glanced at McNulty for support, received it in a nod.

Elihu Carney did a ridiculous dance caper. "Marshal, I won't touch another drop again, I swear to God." He raised his right hand and stood straight, blinking his reddened eyes. Huston noticed, however, that the woman still wore a look of suspicion.

"Fine," he said quietly. His breath clouded before him as he spoke. "Suppose you also promise me not to go warn Gall and the others."

The woman looked away. "All right, we promise. Only you can't blame me for feeling the way I do. The kid with the star, if I'd had a gun, I'd have shot him."

Huston jerked the door open. "That was Pink Fisher, my deputy. He was killed not a half hour ago."

Lil Carney's mouth formed into a small sudden *O*. The closing door cut her off from Huston's sight.

The snow came down faster now, a white curtain ripped to tatters by the wind. Fear hammered at Huston as he walked down the main street of Moon Hollow. Bart Gall and his cronies wouldn't be able to hear his boots crunching in the fast-packing snow; not above the howl of the wind.

Huston pulled his woolen mittens from his pocket, stuck his hands into them for warmth. Soon he came to the alley just this side of the saloon. To the left in the alley's black mouth he heard a stir of movement. Crouching low, he ducked past the window and into the lean-to where three horses were blowing out their breath.

Huston stroked each one of the horses in turn, quieting them. The restless stamping diminished and he stole back to a window, squatting on his haunches and peering up over the sill.

The three men seemed small, over there on the far side of the deserted saloon. Huston recognized Bart Gall, hatless, a thin smile on his lips, his pinched-together eyes shining like shoe buttons in the dim light. On the bar sat another lantern from the coach. Beside it Huston could see Carney's bottle, almost empty now. Of the other two men, one was thick-chested, built like a bull through the shoulders. The second was scrawny and underfed-looking. Bart Gall reached out for the bottle, poured himself a shot. Their mouths moved in conversation but all Huston could hear was the wind.

He pulled off his right mitten, dug some bullets out of his pocket and fed them one after another into the cylinder. Cautiously he rose to his feet. His heart thudded. He held on against the fear, beating it down, refusing to be taken over. Wild random thoughts darted through his mind. Run back to his horse. Head for Sierra . . . *They rode fast, I lost them.* Nobody would ever know.

Very slowly, Huston tightened his hold on the Colt grip. Hesitating only an instant more, he dove forward at the window, rolling his shoulder to smash the glass. He fired a round as he fell through.

He scrambled to his feet, Colt barrel swinging up on the three men who stood open-mouthed at the bar. "Don't go for the irons," Huston said. "I'll shoot the first one who moves."

"And who might you be, pilgrim?" Bart Gall asked, tipping his hat back on his head in defiance of Huston's words.

"The name's Huston. Sierra marshal. Throw your guns over here to me."

Not one of them moved. Even with the wind outside Huston could hear the tense rapid breathing of the bull-shouldered man.

"Throw them down," Huston repeated.

Gall smiled. But behind his smile lay desperation, the same kind that had caused him to break out of prison. Huston marked him as one of those men who couldn't stand to have the will of another imposed on him. Gall's lips thinned out bitterly.

"You heard what he said, Cody. Throw in the hog-legs." These words to the bull-shouldered man, who grumbled something. "You too, Elwood," Gall said to the other. Then he turned his back on Huston.

Words growled up into the marshal's throat and his finger tightened before he realized that it was a trick. In the split instant it took his eyes to flick back to Cody, the huge man had whipped out his gun and swung it sideways. The barrel crashed into the lantern, sent it spinning to the floor. Darkness closed in.

Huston dodged to the right, away from the window, blasting out a shot. A voice shrilled in the dark. "Bart! I'm—" Then came a wild thumping of booted feet, the sound of a chair overturning and the flat thud of human flesh hitting the floor. The voice had been high and piping. Huston crossed off the man named Elwood.

A fusillade of shots ripped toward Huston. Something tugged at his sleeve as he fired back at the flashes of red. But the killers were moving. Another volley slammed into the wall where he had stood a moment before. Huston turned and hurled himself out through the window, hearing more shots as he fell.

He struck the snow and rolled. One of the horses bellowed in fright. Huston slapped a rump and pumped a shot at the sky to start them running.

The horses bolted out of the alley, milling a moment at the sidewalk. Then a sharp whistle turned them to the left. Huston felt a raging frustration. Gall and Cody had evidently come out of the front door of the saloon and picked up their mounts.

"All right," Gall shouted from around the corner. The horses' hoofs rattled, sweeping toward the alley mouth. Huston dodged around the lean-to and down the alley to the rear of the line of buildings, then cut left. He leaped into the intersecting alley just as a shot splintered the wood near his shoulder.

He reloaded as he ran. The hoofs pounded after him in the snow-swept dark, relentless and ghostly. Once back on the main street he made a desperate run for the hotel, found the door and got inside just as Gall and Cody galloped out of the last alley in pursuit.

It took him only an instant to get to the bar and blow out the brace of lanterns. The excited eyes of McNulty, the reddened ones of the woman Lil, all vanished as blackness claimed the room. "Get down!" Huston ordered. He heard them scramble, responding to the urgency of his tone.

Hoofs thudded outside; guns exploded. More windows smashed and Lil Carney let out a startled cry. Huston rose to his feet and crossed to a street window, flattening himself against the wall, then peering out. The riders circled around and came galloping back.

Huston made out four horses. They had his mount

from the tree where he had left it tied. He snapped two shots through the broken pane, useless shots that found no target in the deceiving snow. More shots answered him. Within the room someone groaned hoarsely.

"*Pop!*"

Gall and Cody retreated to the far end of the street and didn't return.

Huston waited a couple of minutes. The snow fell like a white shroud over the street. Finally he put his gun away and turned toward the groaning man.

Stumbling twice in the darkness, he found a small windowless room off the lobby. He carried Elihu Carney in there and set him in a chair. Then he helped Andy McNulty hobble in, found him a second chair and closed the door. On his orders, Lil Carney had brought one of the lanterns. Huston took a match in his numbed fingers and touched fire to the wick. A dim yellow glow threw their shadows on the walls.

Elihu Carney sat slumped in the chair, face drained of color. A reddish stain was spreading on his soiled gray shirt front. He bit his lower lip. "Looks—looks like I'm cashed in for this game, don't it?" He tried to smile; succeeded in wincing instead.

Andy McNulty searched Huston's face. "He's hurt awful bad, Trow."

Lil Carney knelt down and pulled the old man's shirt away. She gasped when she saw the gory wound. "Pop . . ." She buried her head on his chest for an instant.

Then she rose, lifted her skirt and tore off a length of her petticoat. She pressed the cloth against the wound and held it there. Carney's eyes closed and opened. Lil faced Huston.

"What are you going to do about him, marshal?"

"Do?" The question startled Huston. He'd been

concentrating on the problem of Bart Gall and Cody, how to kill them. For he knew that it was no longer a question of taking them prisoner; he wouldn't have a chance for that. He or they would die. "Do?" he repeated. "What do you mean?"

"Damn," she said softly. One hand swept out to indicate her father. "I'm not just going to stand by and see Pop die. I'm going to get him to a doctor."

Huston shook his head slowly. "We can't do it, Miss Carney. Not right now. Those men are desperate. They'd as soon shoot us as look at us. They've got my horse now, and you can't make it to Sierra on foot. You'd freeze before you got half way there."

McNulty nodded, his injured leg stretched out stiffly before him. "Trow's right. Nothin' we can do but set a spell, and maybe do some tall hopin'."

"Then do something yourself!" Lil Carney exclaimed. "Get rid of them! By God, marshal, if you're not man enough—"

Hot anger washed over Huston. Before he knew it, his hand had whipped upward, ready to strike her. His hand trembled in the air a moment. Then, shaken, he lowered it.

She swayed. He cursed himself for a fool; a fool who was letting the fear saddle him again, break him under its power.

"I'm sorry, ma'am," he said. But it was a wasted effort and he knew it. If only the damned wind would stop howling. If only the storm would break . . . But it was many hours until dawn.

Lil Carney didn't seem angry. Mostly she seemed hurt, as if a faint glimmer of faith, born in the promise he had given her, had suddenly been extinguished. She turned away from him and bent down over her father.

He fiddled with his hat. "I'll go out and see what I can do about getting a horse."

"Watch yourself, Trow," McNulty murmured as he closed the door.

Huston walked rapidly across the darkened lobby. He honestly didn't know where to turn. The odds had piled up against him with frightening swiftness.

He slid up beside the front door. The wind whistled through the shot-out panes, carrying puffs of snow with it. Huston eased his gun out, then risked a look.

He saw no sign of the two men or the horses. Silence lay over the street, and a white blanket of snow. Carefully he pulled the door open and stepped out. There was an orange flash from the building directly across the street.

He threw himself to the sidewalk as the slug smacked the wall over his head. He lay there, cheek pressed in the snow. He used his foot to feel around in back of him until he was able to hook his toe on the door frame. With effort he began to wriggle backwards along the sidewalk.

When he had wormed his way inside so that only his shoulders and head stuck out, he folded his legs under him and came to his feet, firing a shot. Glass smashed across the street. Answering bullets whispered around him. He dodged back, the breath coming heavily in his chest.

"Marshal!" Bart Gall's voice—not exactly hateful, yet filled with the doggedness of a man fighting for his life. "Marshal, you hear me?"

"I hear you," Huston shouted back. "What do you want?"

"I'm not moving from here until I get you, marshal. You can't stay there forever. You'll get tired and go to sleep in the cold. Cody's around back, so don't try that way." The last word was muffled by an explosion as Gall fired another shot. Huston hesitated, then drew away from the door.

He made his way back to the windowless office. Andy McNulty glanced up eagerly when he entered. "Any luck?"

Huston shook his head. "We're boxed in. Cody's got us sewed up in back—Gall's right across the street."

"Then there's no way out, is there?" McNulty said glumly.

Lil Carney glared at Huston. Her father's eyes were closed again. His breathing had shallowed and the red stain on his clothes had grown larger. "He'll die if we stay here much longer, marshal. I'm not going to let him die. You've *got* to do something—"

"I'll do what I can!" Huston exploded. "Just leave me alone and let me work it out." He jerked his hat down over his eyes, and left the room.

His thoughts churned. The icy chill on his skin was matched by the chill that gnawed his gut. Gall would starve them, wait until drowsiness claimed them, and then it would be no trouble at all to put a bullet in each one's brain as they lay in the icy stupor preceding death . . .

Huston crouched down behind a window facing the street, thinking. Somewhere there had to be a key, a device to use . . .

Suddenly he had a thought. Feeble to be sure; but he knew of nothing else.

"Gall!" he shouted. "Bart Gall!"

"Yes."

"Something you should know."

"What is it?"

"There's a posse forming in Sierra. I rode out ahead of them. They'll be up here before daybreak.

We can hold out that long, and when they get here, you're all through."

Silence for a moment, punctuated by the howl of the wind down the mountain. "You're lying," Gall cried back, his voice distorted. "There's no damn posse coming—you're lying!"

"Wait and see."

Gall yelled wordlessly, enraged, and pumped three shots at the hotel.

Huston flattened himself on the floor, allowing himself a little grin. The echoes of the firing died. Huston crouched on his haunches, wishing he could light the cigar in his pocket.

He watched the street. Give Gall enough time, an hour, two maybe, and he might get panicky and run. He wouldn't dare wait and face a whole posse. It was a bluff, but if by some crazy chance it should happen to work—

Huston didn't hear the footsteps behind him until it was too late. He felt his Colt leave the holster and then the barrel jabbed hard into his back. "Stand still," Lil Carney whispered. "Stand still or I'll shoot you, marshal."

Desperation washed over Huston. He hadn't figured on this, hadn't even thought of it. He'd been a fool.

Lil Carney jerked the front door open. "Gall! I've got a gun on the marshal."

"Who's that?" Gall replied over the shriek of the storm.

"Lil Carney. My father's shot. I need a horse. I want to get Pop to a doctor in Sierra. I'll trade you Huston for a horse."

"How do I know this ain't a trick?"

The gun jabbed deeper into Huston's back. "Tell him."

"She's got me, all right," Huston called. He hoped that Gall's natural suspicion would prevent him from even considering the bargain. But then he remembered his own words of a while ago. *A posse on the way.* Gall would be weighing Huston's bluff against that of Lil Carney, with his life depending on the outcome.

"Gall!" the woman called again. "If you come, bring the horse with you. You can be gone by the time I reach Sierra." Bitterly, Huston admitted the girl had a shrewd head on her.

"Gall!" once more, questioningly. The wind howled.

"I'm comin'," came the answer.

### 3

## *The Test*

Huston stood in the hotel doorway for several long minutes, his own pistol still pressed into his spine. He caught a flurry of movement in the street: Bart Gall slipping out of concealment in the store across the way and ghosting through the snow up toward the saloon. When Gall returned, he was leading one of the horses.

He halted in the center of the street. "This is as far as I'm comin'," he called. "Bring Huston out."

Huston's stomach tightened. He felt calm; surprisingly so since he expected that death was only moments away . . .

The woman interrupted his somber thoughts. "Look, marshal." She seemed to be apologizing. "I can't pretend I feel good about this, but—"

"No sense explaining," Huston broke in. "Gall's waiting."

"You've got to let me say this first. Pop's *dying*. I couldn't stand by and let him die, I couldn't—" She stopped. It was obvious from her choked speech that some realization of her guilt was beginning to break through the hard shell of practicality. Before she could speak again, Huston whirled and grabbed for his gun.

Lil Carney gasped, struggling. Before Huston could get the Colt away from her, Bart Gall came charging across the porch. Hands seized Huston's collar, tried to swing him around. With a savage slap, Huston knocked the Colt from the woman's hand. Gall grunted, and Huston knew that only the darkness and the attendant confusion had saved him from a bullet . . .

He whipped his arms out behind him. Bart Gall cursed. Huston lunged out of his coat and dove forward to where the gun had fallen. He seized it as it hit the floor, rolling his shoulder under and snapping a shot at the ceiling. Couldn't risk killing the woman. The shot sent Gall dodging back out of the hotel.

Huston scrambled to his feet. He kicked a table and some chairs out of the way, coming to a stop in the darkness just inside the rear door. The night air cut into his flesh now that he was without a coat. But he had to get out of the hotel, into the open . . .

He threw the door open. The convict named Cody immediately blazed away, chipping splinters from the door's frame while Huston pulled up a window and jumped through. Cody's rifle banged again. Huston hit the snow and lay flat, squinting into the brush behind the line of buildings. He waited.

From behind one of the big pine trees a shadowy

figure hesitantly stepped forth. Huston brought his gun up, took careful aim and pressured the trigger.

The gun bucked in his hand, spitting red flame until the hammer clicked down and kept clicking. Huston was breathing harder. Cody was sprawled face down, not moving.

Huston scrambled to his feet and started forward. Something heavy and hot caught him in the shoulder, hurling him forward. He turned as he fell, bringing the Colt up. The hammer clicked down.

Huston pulled himself to his feet a second time. He stumbled back toward the buildings, aware that Bart Gall was coming rapidly toward him. Huston bent down and scrabbled in the snow until his hand closed on a small rock. He heaved it at the shadow-shape of Gall with all of his strength.

Gall cried out, staggered, then dropped to his knees. Huston plunged down an alley, not looking back.

He ran and kept running, out into the street again and down toward the saloon. His arm throbbed; felt wet. The howling wind muffled the sound of his feet. He reeled dizzily once, almost falling. The snow swirled around him, and the wind screamed banshee-sharp down off the mountain crags. *Get away, get away*, something cried inside him.

He was dimly aware that the buildings had vanished; that he ran among the great black towers of the pines. His mind began to function a little more smoothly, catching hold of the wild fear; wrestling with it. He staggered under pine branches and leaned against the trunk, resting his cheek on the rough bark and sucking the night air in starved gulps. He felt flakes of snow cold on his tongue.

Weak, he closed his eyes a moment. What kind of a nightmare was he living? Only hours before—this same evening, in fact—he had been eating a peaceful meal in the hotel. Then suddenly the world had been torn apart, becoming this nightmare of snow and spurting guns and killer shapes slipping through the gloom.

He felt the gummy wetness of his left arm. He was bleeding, all right. And Elihu Carney was dying and Andy McNulty had a smashed leg and Lil Carney had turned on him. Bart Gall was still alive, unhurt, doggedly hunting him. He had a wild impulse to run again, keep running up into the mountains until he fell frozen in the snow, all terror and all cowardice wiped away by the healing nothingness of death . . .

Once more he fought the panic away. He realized with a deep guilt that his flight from Gall a few minutes before had been just another example of fear's mastery of his life. And yet, he told himself, if he hadn't run, he would be dead. The important thing was—what was he going to do now?

He knew with certainty that he would have to go back and face Gall. Until one of them died, neither would have any peace—Huston because of his need to prove his own capability to resist fear, Gall because of his determination to eliminate any man who could block his passage to freedom. He was sure the bluff about the posse was a failure. Gall would hang on until Huston was finished. So in spite of his fear, Huston had to go back to the main street of Moon Hollow and get Gall before Gall got him.

His teeth began to chatter. It reminded him that he'd lost his coat in the struggle with Lil Carney and Gall. His ammunition had been stashed in the pocket of that coat. With a discouraged feeling he pulled the Colt from his belt. He spun the cylinder; thumbed back the hammer and let it fall. He shoved the Colt back in place and began his trudge toward the main street.

He circled around back of the buildings, hunched in the shadows until he made sure Gall was not still lingering near Cody's lifeless body. He ran forward and knelt down and searched the corpse. He couldn't find Cody's revolvers or rifle. Gall must have taken them.

Huston made his way to the rear of the hotel and quietly went in. A slit of light showed under the office door. His arm throbbed as he pressed his ear to the panel and listened. He was surprised to hear Lil Carney's voice, murmuring low: "Pop, can you hear me?" He couldn't bring himself to hate the woman. In her position he might have done what she did.

He breathed deeply. Gall might be in there.

Well, now was the time to face him, no matter what the outcome. For Pink Fisher . . . to clean the slate dirtied when the young deputy died thinking Huston was yellow. Huston put his hand on the doorknob and pulled.

Lil Carney looked around, startled. Huston closed the door and made sure Gall wasn't anywhere in the room. Elihu Carney's eyes were still closed but his chest moved faintly, fitfully, with life. Lil Carney flushed, looking away as Huston stood slapping his sides to restore circulation.

"Holy hollerin' moses," McNulty breathed. "I thought sure you was done for, Trow, with all them shots out there."

"I was gone, almost." Huston looked at Lil Carney as he tossed his gun onto the table. "That's empty. I don't have any way of fighting Gall, unless my coat's outside."

Lil Carney shook her head. "Gall searched it and took it. Along with all the ammunition in the pockets."

Huston rubbed his hand across his eyes. Lord, he was worn out. He indicated pale-cheeked Elihu Carney. "How is he?"

"Just making it," she answered. "But without a doctor he can't last longer than a few hours." She sucked in her breath sharply. "Why do you keep looking at me like that, marshal?"

"I was wondering why you weren't gone a long time ago. That was part of the bargain."

"Gall canceled the bargain as soon as you broke loose."

"Where is he?"

She lifted her hand in the general direction of the street. "Right where he was before I snuck up on you. In the store across from the hotel." She sighed. "Honestly, marshal, I'm so tired I could go to sleep right now and never wake up. That killer waiting out there—" She shivered.

"Changed your tune a little, did you?" Huston saw the thrust register on her face. She bit her lower lip for a moment.

"Yes. He—he acted like a crazy man after you got away. He hit me, cursed and waved his gun and threatened to kill all three of us. He's afraid a posse's coming, yet he doesn't want to leave you alive—" She choked back a sob. "I tell you, he's out of his mind."

Huston replied with a thoughtful nod. "I'll try once more." He looked at his Colt on the table. "I wish I had something to use against him . . ."

He looked down dully at his bare hands. Lil Carney had been gazing at Huston's bloody shirt. She took a step forward, touching it gingerly.

"Was it Gall?"

He nodded. She seemed lost in thought for a moment. Then she turned, hiked up her skirt and lifted one muddy red slipper and rested it on a chair. A tiny knife winked free of a leg sheath. She handed it to Houston with a wan smile.

"A souvenir of my profession. I thought about using it on myself if Pop died and Gall caught me. But you take it. Maybe it'll help."

Houston's hand closed around hers for a moment. Their eyes met, and he thought that he understood her suddenly; her bitter life; her desire to protect her father; her swift and anguishing repentance. He smiled at her and she smiled back.

Houston left the room then. He circled from the rear of the hotel and crossed the main street where it dwindled into the rocky trail leading down the mountain toward Sierra. The knife felt light but reassuring in his clenched fist. He was sure that Gall couldn't see him through the curtain of falling snow.

The great trees swayed and moaned in the wind. Houston clamped his teeth together to stop the chattering. He slid along the wall of the building in which Gall was supposedly hiding, rounded the corner and came up to the back door. He breathed deeply again, ice in his belly, and a more deadly chill creeping over his whole body. Yet the hand grasping the knife seemed warm.

The door opened inward. Houston eased the knob to the left until the lock was free, still holding the door shut. Going down into a crouch, he leaped forward and to the side as he let go.

The wind smacked the door open with a hollow bang and tore into the room. Still crouching, Houston dove into the room on his chest. He saw a vaguely human shape against the pale rectangle of a window.

"Who is it?" Gall's voice . . . sounding frightened for a change.

Huston drew himself up on his knees. Groped forward with his free hand and bumped a chair. Gall's gun blazed and Huston flung himself out again, deafened by the series of rolling explosions.

All the shots missed; Gall was firing at a man he presumed to be standing. Finally Huston heard the sound he'd been waiting for . . . the click of a hammer coming down on an empty cylinder. He jumped up and ran forward.

All at once, against the window, he could see Gall quite clearly. The killer's arm flew back; he flung his pistol at Huston's head. Huston ducked. Then he dropped his knife. It clattered on the floor.

Maybe he'd gone crazy, he thought. Snow-crazy; storm-crazy; death-crazy. But he wanted to finish Bart Gall with his bare hands . . . to cancel Pink Fisher's judgment.

Gall seized a chair, raised it to smash Huston's head. Huston dodged in, shot his right fist forward and jolted Gall in the belly. Gall *oofed* loudly. His hands opened and the chair fell. The tip of one leg struck a window, shattering it. Pieces of glass clinked and tinkled on the floor; other shards stayed in the frame. Wind whipped snow through the opening, and through the door. It swirled around the two men as they faced each other.

They fought close in, pummeling each other with vicious chopping blows. Huston blocked Gall's punches with his left arm as best he could, grinding his teeth together each time a blow landed near the wound and started fresh throbs of pain. He punched with his right hand. Gall soon sensed what was happening, spun away quickly and held his hand up before his face, near the window.

"By damn, Huston. I got blood on my hand. And it's yours!" He chuckled softly.

Huston brought his right hand clubbing down, but Gall danced away, then rained brutal blows on the other, injured arm. Huston gritted his teeth against the pain. Gall's boot lashed out, tangling Huston's feet and throwing him off balance. He caught Gall with his free hand. Gall jerked back instinctively, pulling Huston upright again. This time it was Gall who teetered. Huston's smashing last-ditch punch to the jaw tipped the scales. Gall fell, uttering a filthy oath. The back of his head struck the window frame and he let out a shriek. Almost instantly, he stiffened, then went limp.

Gall's weight dragged him to the floor. A narrow dagger of glass protruded from the base of his neck. Huston turned away into the darkness and was sick.

After a few minutes of sitting on a chair, letting his strength flow back, he summoned enough energy to move again. He went out through the front door, crossed the street and entered the hotel. He pulled the office door open and leaned weakly against the frame. Lil Carney and Andy McNulty watched him with tense expressions, eyes throwing back yellow pinpoints from the coach lamps.

"Gall's dead."

Lil Carney's face loosened then, lost its stiffness as she began to cry. But Huston realized that their problem was far from solved. He turned to McNulty.

"Andy, I want to try to take Mr. Carney back to Sierra. Can you ride with your leg like that?"

"Hell—" McNulty grunted, attempting to rise. "Sure I can, Trow. You just watch me—*ugh*." He couldn't get up by himself.

Huston gnawed his lip. He couldn't rely on Andy McNulty for any help at all.

He went back across the street. Gall's body smelled bad. Huston held his breath as he pulled the man out of his heavy coat. He climbed into the coat slowly, favoring his bloody arm. The coat kept out the chill wind, although Huston felt that he was now so frozen, it would take him an eternity to thaw out.

It took him nearly twenty minutes to locate the four horses. He found them tethered in the ruins of an old livery stable. He led them back to the hotel and tied them at the rack, rubbing their necks to warm them a little.

Then he began arranging transportation for his strange crew of pilgrims. He worked almost mechanically. He bundled a horse blanket around Lil Carney and helped her climb up on one of the mounts. He bundled Elihu Carney similarly and put him on a second horse, then helped boost Andy McNulty up behind him to keep the wounded man from falling. McNulty's mouth was drawn into a line of pain.

On the third horse, the biggest and strongest, he put the stiffening bodies of Gall and Cody; Elwood he left behind. He mounted the fourth horse and turned to the small cavalcade.

"If you never prayed before, folks, do it now. Pray we get down this mountain."

He clucked to his horse and they started off through the storm.

The hours seemed endless as the horses picked their way down the treacherous snowy trail. Every once in a while Huston would catch himself dozing in the saddle, shake himself awake. His wound tended to dull his senses. But his was the job of guiding them.

The snowfall slacked off after a while. Then the sky seemed to lighten in the east, turn a slate gray color. The nightmare ride ended at dawn, when they moved out of the last clump of trees and saw sleeping Sierra less than a mile below them, half hidden behind wispy veils of blowing snow.

Huston turned to speak to Lil Carney, but her eyes were shut. She was asleep, or close to it, clutching the saddle horn.

Huston rode back to her, touched her arm. Her eyes flew open. She peered at him blankly for a moment.

"We're coming into town," he said. After another moment, her eyes focused, and she nodded.

Huston led them up the deserted main street to Ma Erickson's rooming house. There he got them rooms and went to fetch Doc Pfeffer. The doc complained about being awakened so early, but he came anyway. After a quick but thorough examination of Elihu Carney he stood up and wiped his spectacles.

"Well, we'll patch up that hole and he should be good as new after some food, and plenty of warm blankets and a lot of rest. Now let's fix up that arm of yours."

Before long, Huston was on his way out of the rooming house. Lil Carney ran after him.

"Marshal!"

He turned back. "Yes?"

"Did you mean what you said about letting Pop and me stay here?"

Huston nodded. She smiled tiredly.

"You're a kind man."

Their eyes held for an instant. Huston couldn't hate her. Far from it. The snow had scrubbed some of the dance hall paint from her cheeks, leaving a fresh glow. He saw the clear prettiness that had only been hinted at before.

"I'll call on you in a day or two, ma'am, to see how you and your father are getting along."

She pressed his hand a trifle longer than necessary. "Do that, marshal. Please." He liked her forthright way; liked the honesty in her eyes. She tended to be a reckless young woman, but she had a streak of fierce courage, and he felt drawn to her.

Yes, he would definitely call again.

The town had begun to stir. The wind still keened but only a few random snowflakes blew through the sparkling air. The street was drifted high.

Huston ate a huge breakfast in the empty hotel dining room, topping it off with several cups of scalding coffee. His bandaged arm felt better. It still hurt but it would knit and heal. All he needed was what Elihu Carney needed most, rest.

But he had one score yet to settle. With the town.

When eight o'clock came and the stores opened, Huston mounted up. The two corpses lay on the horse he was leading. He rode down the center of the main street. Men who knew him called out but he ignored them. He pulled up in front of the Mercantile. "Amos!" he shouted. "Amos, get out here."

Amos Dean appeared in a moment. Huston drew his Colt, pointing it at the merchant's chest. With his other hand he tipped one corpse off the second horse.

"That's Cody."

He tipped the other.

"That's Bart Gall. I left the third body up in Moon Hollow."

Dean's eyes widened as he eyed the pistol.

"You still think I'm a coward, Amos?"

Dean's mouth worked a moment before the words came tumbling forth. "No, Trow, 'course not . . ."

Huston's mouth was a grim slit. "Good. Just remember that. And remember I'm still the marshal here."

A gawking crowd had materialized around Dean. Huston swept his eyes over the men and took a deep breath. He'd won his second battle, the battle with the town. He shoved the Colt back into the holster, turned his horse and slowly led the other horse back up the street.

# Little Phil and the
# Daughter of Joy

"Whoa, that's new," Rolf Greencastle said. He couldn't help sounding alarmed.

"Yes, it is," Jimmy said. She slid an old cloth along the short squat barrel of the .44-caliber Deringer she'd taken from the drawer of her writing desk. It was an old piece. Rolf always thought of it as the Gold Rush gun because his talkative uncle Wallace, one of the failed argonauts, had often mentioned the large number of .44 Deringers carried by men in the diggings. It was an outmoded weapon, but a murderous one.

Spring sunshine through the lace curtains ignited a little white fire at one spot on the metal. Jimmy rubbed and rubbed at the barrel, though it was spotless. Sunshine falling on her flexing wrist illuminated the white scars there. Rolf was silent and a little bug-eyed over the unexpected sight of the piece.

He considered the awkwardness of another remark. Her three-word reply had shut the door on easy continuation of the conversation. After several moments of combing his fingers through his shoulder-length hair, he decided that this was serious enough for him to bull right ahead.

"What is it?"

Jimmy gazed at him with those wide eyes that reminded him of a beautiful gray he'd ridden as a boy in Ohio. Jimmy's eyes were her beautiful feature; she was otherwise a plain young woman, with wrinkles already laid into her face by the ferocious Kansas weather and no doubt by her trade, which required her to deal with all sorts of rough types, from customers to her pimp (she had none at the moment). He had known her a little more than a year, both socially and in the biblical sense, and in that time he'd learned that she had a history of violent behavior, sometimes directed against herself.

"Why, it's a genuine Henry Deringer. I bought it in Dodge last Saturday."

"I mean what's it for, Jimmy? Is somebody bothering you or making threats?"

"Why, no, I'm going to use it when General Phil Sheridan arrives next month to inspect the fort. I'm going to kill him with it."

Rolf Greencastle almost fell off his chair in the process of removing his bare feet from the edge of her table. He crashed them down on top of his fancy boots with the pointed toes and mule ears; Rolf was of the opinion that a cavalry scout had to project a special aura—one so strong and awe-inspiring that the officers who signed his pay authorization would think he knew exactly what he was doing even when he didn't.

"I beg your pardon?"

"You heard me," Jimmy said. She kept her eyes on him. It was a disconcerting habit. She kept them open even when she was bare naked on her back, taking care of him.

"That's a pretty damn strange thing to admit to me or anybody, Jemima Taylor."

"I wish you wouldn't use that name. My daddy gave it to me and it's the only thing he ever did that I hate."

"Let's get back to the subject of Little Phil Sheridan. I believe you said you figure on killing him."

"I do." Jimmy saw he wanted further explanation. She shrugged. "Once a Virginian, always a Virginian."

"What does that mean?"

"That foul-talking Yankee rooster and his murdering hordes of mounted shopkeepers and factory hands just completely tore up my daddy's farm in Shenandoah County in September of eighteen and sixty-four."

"You never told me that."

"Hadn't any occasion," she answered with another shrug. She polished some more.

"Jimmy, come on. What's the rest?"

"Simple enough. The day after Sheridan's brutes drove General Jubal Early off Fisher's Hill and sent him scooting down around Masanutten Mountain to hide and lick his wounds, the Yankees came south along the Valley Turnpike, where my daddy's farm was situated. They were chasing stragglers but they ripped up everything belonging to the local people. They trampled our vegetables and torched our fruit trees . . ." She closed her eyes briefly. Her voice grew much quieter. "Just terrible." A moment passed. "Next thing, Phil Sheridan himself showed up, with a lot of his officers. My daddy was mad and het up and he took a shot at Sheridan. Sheridan's men wrestled him down and carried him off and beat him. Then they sent him to prison in Detroit, Michigan. As if he was an enemy soldier. He was sixty-two years old! It ruined his health and gave him the glooms. Same ones that devil me sometimes. But his never left, and they ground him away to nothing. He died two years after they let him out."

"You saw your pa fire off a round at Phil Sheridan?"

Her eyes drifted to the windblown lace. A bugle pealed somewhere on the prairie. Out past the fence that neatly circumscribed her little house, called the Overton Place after a former owner, a troop of shiny-brown Negro cavalrymen cantered by.

"No, I never laid eyes on the little fiend. I was in the smokehouse with some of his men who ripped my dress and—took liberties."

Rolf Greencastle whistled. All of a sudden he was chilly in the spring air. He'd had a perfectly fine time with Jimmy, as per usual when he paid his weekly visit, but this new twist was disturbing; terrifying. Rolf reached for his fringed deerhide shirt. He pulled it on and smoothed it, then reached beneath to free the necklace of big bear claws he never removed. Rolf was a tall, skinny young man with eight knife and bullet scars at various points on his body.

"You absolutely sure it was Little Phil?"

"Yes, it was him. People described him later. Black horse . . . that funny flat black hat he always wore. It was him, and I'm going to kill him."

"Jimmy, I don't think I'm making myself too clear. Don't you see that what you said is pretty—well—unusual? You don't just go tell somebody that you're going to do a murder."

She didn't say a word; apparently she didn't agree.

"Why did you do that, Jimmy?"

She was tight-lipped and silent a while. Then it kind of erupted in a burst. "Because you're my friend. You're not just a customer. After I kill General Sheridan they're going to lock me up—hang me, probably. I'm going to need a friend to straighten things out. Sell this house and send the money to my sisters in Front Royal."

"Well, I appreciate your confidence," Rolf admitted, touched by her unexpected words. "What I'd rather do, though, is talk you out of it."

"You can't. Sheridan's villains raped and pillaged the whole Shenandoah, and they wrecked my daddy's health by throwing him in that Yankee prison, and a Virginian never forgets."

"I think I ought to remind you that the war's been over for three years now."

"Not mine, Mr. Greencastle. Mine isn't over by a damn sight. One more battle to go."

And she snapped the cloth so that it popped. Then she wrapped it around the .44-caliber Deringer. He tried to undermine her determination with scorn:

"If you're going to kill Sheridan, you bought the wrong gun. That little toy only gives you one shot."

She slid out the drawer. "That's why I bought a pair." The drawer clicked shut, hiding both Deringers.

She rose and smoothed her old black bombazine skirt. Rolf Greencastle fleetingly wished that he was just a customer again, not a friend, and didn't have to concern himself with Jimmy's mad pronouncement. Which he knew wasn't so mad. She was a determined thing. Whores had to be to survive.

"You'll have to excuse me, Rolf. Lieutenant Peebles is due any minute."

"All right, but I wish you'd think it over." In the door he turned back to gaze at her in a pleading fashion. "Please."

She gave a little shake of her head.

"Once a Virginian, always a Virginian."

Rolf Greencastle put on his cream-colored Texas hat with its decorative star and red band and left. If

General Phil Sheridan did arrive at Fort Dodge as part of his scheduled inspection of the Arkansas River posts now under his command, he was certainly a dead man unless the scout did something about it. But what?

Rolf lay in his bunk in his underwear with a copy of the *Police Gazette* in front of his nose. One of those inscrutable turns of fate seemingly designed to torment a man had brought this tattered copy of the paper into the barber shop in Dodge where he went for a semimonthly trim of his luxuriant hair and mustachios. Who should be pictured in an heroic pose on the front page? None other than Jimmy's announced victim.

It was four days after his visit to the Overton Place, which Jimmy's husband and pimp, Nimrod Taylor, had bought and occupied for about three years before he up and disappeared. Jimmy once explained with a sad, resigned look that Nimrod had warned her on their wedding day that he was a restless man. He was also something else, because that day Jimmy had a large yellowing bruise around her left eye. She refused to talk about it. After Nimrod Taylor left, he never came back. At least Jimmy got the Overton Place.

In the bunk, Major General Philip Sheridan stared at Rolf from within the engraving as if he were infuriated with the scout. The man had a reputation for a temper, and for peppering almost every sentence he spoke with some kind of obscenity, plain or invented. To Rolf, the new commander of the Department of the Missouri looked like an Irish bartender from New York City (Rolf had never seen any of that species, but he had a fair imagination). With his fierce black eyes and squat, bull-like build, and the somehow sinister soap-lock hanging down in the center of his forehead, Phil Sheridan looked like one hard son of a bitch. Rolf Greencastle had seen a few other pictures of the general, and none was any friendlier.

He tossed the paper aside, hiding the face. "She'll never do it," he said.

Then he considered what he knew about Jimmy.

Suppose she really did murder Phil Sheridan; did she have much to lose thereby? No. Mrs. Jemima Sturdevant Taylor had apparently lived a pretty wretched life till now. She'd inherited the same dark moods, the glooms, that she said contributed to her father's death. Officers on the post had informed Rolf that on at least two occasions after her husband left, Jimmy had tried to commit suicide. Those scars on her left wrist were the evidence. When she was up, she was bright as a sunbeam, but at other times, there was no telling what dark, tormented thoughts rolled around in the depths of her soul.

In Dodge they said she had once grabbed a kitchen knife and mortally injured a teamster who had asked for more than he'd paid for and then began to abuse her when she refused. Evidently she thought a wife had to suffer beatings, but not an independent working girl. According to the story, the teamster was not well liked; he died and Jimmy was released after one night in jail and no more was said.

The image of a gleaming knife sliding into some hairy back, with a consequent gout of blood, caused Rolf to cover his eyes there in the bunk, and change his tune.

"She'll do it."

He fidgeted for half an hour, trying to think of some scheme to forestall the assassination. He was not a bright fellow, and he knew it, so he didn't have much confidence in the scheme he finally concocted.

But he could come up with no other right then. He found a tack and slipped it in the pocket of his buckskin coat, together with the engraving of Sheridan ripped from the *Gazette*.

He saddled Kid, his swift-running little piebald, and set out from his cabin at the edge of town to ride the five miles along the Arkansas to the fort. It was a mean, gusty late-winter day, but you could smell April primping just around the corner. General Sheridan was scheduled to arrive at Fort Dodge the first week in April.

On the post, he nonchalantly tied Kid outside the adobe barracks that housed B Troop, waited until no one was paying attention, then stole inside. Luckily the dayroom was empty. He tacked Sheridan's picture to the notice board, slipped his sheath knife from under his jacket and proceeded to stab holes all over Little Phil's face.

"To what do I owe the pleasure of this visit?" asked Captain Tipton.

"Oh, I was just in the neighborhood," Rolf said.

Captain Tipton's face proclaimed his skepticism. "I never knew you to be so social, Rolf." The captain, whose behind-the-back nickname was Moon Face, was a pale, pudgy young man with a flaxen mustache and small oval spectacles. He'd once been a professor of geography at a young ladies' academy in Kentucky, a land of divided loyalties during the war. Rolf didn't know which flag Moon Face Tipton had followed, and Moon Face didn't say. That he was wearing Army blue meant nothing.

"Well, the fact is, Captain, I'm worried about this here visit of Phil Sheridan's next month."

"It's just a routine inspection of all the posts in the

department. Hancock before him made the same tour. Every new commander does it."

"Yes, but it might be dangerous for him to stop at Fort Dodge."

Now he had Moon Face Tipton's full attention. "What the devil are you talking about?"

"Well, sir, I was just in the dayroom of B Troop, looking for a fellow that owes me a ten spot. On the notice board I saw this newspaper picture of Sheridan. Somebody cut it up pretty bad with a knife."

"You're jesting."

"Sir, I am not."

"But that's ridiculous. Why—?"

"Captain, there aren't more'n one or two other generals hated more than Phil Sheridan. Uncle Billy Sherman, for sure, and maybe that cavalry commander of his, Kil-what's-his-name."

"Patrick. Kilpatrick."

"Yes, sure. Sir, you know as well as I do, this Plains army contains a lot of men who enlisted under different names than their real ones. A lot of former *Rebs*," he added with breathy melodrama, in case Tipton didn't get it the first time.

"I'll grant you that's true," Moon Face said. "What am I supposed to do about it?"

"Well, sir, I thought you might go up the line to your boss, the adjutant, and have him tell General Sheridan that he ought to stay away. Tell him that he ought to bypass this fort."

"*Tell* him not to visit a post he commands? *Tell* one of the toughest, most determined soldiers who ever served in the United States Army that he shouldn't come here because someone cut up his picture?" Rolf sank into his rickety chair. Of course he'd failed; he just wasn't a smart enough fellow. "I think you might as well try to stop one of Mr. Shake-

speare's hurricanoes." It was all Tipton could do to
keep from sounding supercilious. "Now, if you'll excuse me, I've been studying Pliny again, and I'd like
to return to him."

"Yes, sir. Thank you, sir."

Rolf slouched out, humiliated.

Humiliated but not whipped.

He wasn't going to let the murder take place. He
must use force on Jimmy. Restrain her physically
from going anywhere near Fort Dodge while Sheridan was there inspecting it. He knew he wasn't glib
enough to talk Jimmy out of her plan, so physical
force was the only answer. He needn't hurt her—
wouldn't ever do that—but he could lock her up and
sit with her. For days, if necessary.

He stole into the B Troop dayroom again, to remove the picture of Phil Sheridan. Since his last visit,
someone had penciled obscene words on the general's cheeks and forehead. It made him look all the
madder.

During the next few days he blew around and
around like a weathervane. "She'll never do it."
"She'll do it." The two sentences became his litany.

He had never thought about Jimmy much when
he wasn't with her, but now that she was endangered
he thought about her a lot. He was surprised by the
constancy and the urgency of these new feelings.

Riding past the Overton Place one showery afternoon, he saw her out in back, where the chicken yard
sloped away toward the river. Three bottles of different size and color reposed on a log. Ten feet away,
Jimmy extended her right hand. He saw a little squirt
of smoke, then heard the crack as the amber bottle
on the left exploded.

She heard Kid passing. Turned. Recognized him

and raised her hand with the .44-caliber murder
weapon over her head and waved. He snatched off
his hat and waved back. "She'll do it," he said in a
strangled voice. "By God she will."

Another blast from the other Deringer seemed to
verify it.

On the night before General Sheridan's scheduled
arrival, a dismal night of rain that made the Arkansas
rush and roar, Rolf slanted his hat brim over his forehead to drip water and rode Kid to the Overton
Place. He carried no weapons, but his saddlebags
bulged with groceries bought in Dodge that afternoon. He was prepared for a long siege.

As he approached through the rain, opened the
gate in front of the farmhouse, rode in, he heard a
horse nicker. Then he saw the animal tied out in
front. Regulation Army saddle. Did Jimmy have a
customer from the fort?

He picketed Kid to the fence by the gate and
walked to the porch. If she was entertaining someone, he'd just have to huddle out by the hen house
until the man left. He'd just check to make sure;
Jimmy never locked her front door even during business hours.

Sheltered by the porch roof, he eased the door
open. Lamplight and the smell of dust drifted out.
Beyond the closed door of the bedroom, bedsprings
squeaked and groaned, and a bullish voice exclaimed. "Oh, that's mighty fucking good, oh my
Lord yes . . ."

Rolf Greencastle would have lit out immediately
for the hen house but for the intrusion of that obscenity into the unseen customer's declaration of pleasure. That word set his hair to crawling under his
hat. An unbelievable premonition gripped him. Held

him rigid on the porch a good five minutes, while similar professions of pleasure, similarly punctuated with all sorts of bad language, convinced him that his suspicion was correct and that, somehow, he was caught in one of those inexplicable apocalyptic disasters that left total carnage and sorrow in their wake.

Blood rushed to his head. His eyes felt bulgy as he flung the door wide and cannoned across the parlor, nearly knocking over a flickering lamp with a pearly globe. He took a deep, hurtful breath—this was worse than the time he'd ridden carelessly over a rise and come upon half a dozen young men of the Southern Cheyenne tribe, each and every one in a bad mood—and prayed for God and Jimmy to forgive him. But he had to know.

He opened the bedroom door.

A fat-bottomed little man rolled over on his back and shouted, "Who the profanity are you? What the obscenity is going on here?"

"Rolf, oh Rolf," Jimmy said, trying to cover herself with the bedding. She sounded more grief-stricken than angry. As for Rolf, his aching eyeballs were fixed on the soap-lock of the enraged chap leaping from the bed and seizing his yellow-striped trousers while throwing all sorts of obscene invective at the stunned intruder trembling in the doorway.

"Will you get the shit out of here, you bugeyed intrusive little son of a bitch?" screamed General Philip Henry Sheridan; for it was the very same.

"General Sheridan, please calm down," Jimmy said. Rolf could not see her just then, the general was in the way. But he distinctly heard the cocking of the Deringer. Sheridan heard it too, and it arrested his angry rush to dress and depart. His little white corporation quivered above the waist of the regulation trousers he was hastily buttoning. Rolf reckoned him to be in his middle thirties, with careworn lines around his black eyes.

"I have a gun pointed at your back, General," Jimmy added.

"You have what?"

The barefoot Sheridan spun around and his disbelief quickly evaporated. Jimmy was sitting up in bed, one hand clasping the sheet over her bosom, the other pointing the hideout pistol at Sheridan's chest, which was white as a bottle of milk.

"General, how did this happen?" Rolf gasped.

"Who the double profanity wants to know? Who the repeated obscenity are you?"

"Just someone who wants to save your life if possible, General."

"Rolf," Jimmy said, "I don't want to shoot you too. My mind's made up. He's going to die. Don't make more bloodshed."

Water dripped from Rolf's chin. At first he thought it was rain but then he realized he was indoors, and it was sweat. The low-trimmed lamp at the bedside, the heavy draperies closed and securely tied that way, gave the room a confined, sultry air. The air of a tomb, he thought, wishing he hadn't.

Sheridan was struggling into his shirt, one moment looking miffed, the next letting his anxiety flicker through; the man was clearly no fool. "General, how the devil did you get over here?" Rolf exclaimed. "You're not supposed to arrive till tomorrow."

"Arrived early," Sheridan barked. "And I found this letter—this charming letter—" He indicated a paper sticking from the pocket of his blouse, which lay over the back of a chair half hidden by his rain-dampened caped overcoat. "From someone who signed herself Daughter of Joy. It was a very fetching missive." He sounded outraged. "It was a special invitation to one of our, ahem, country's heroes to enjoy an hour in the grove of Venus—free of charge." By now Rolf's mind had begun to edit out all of the simple and compound obscenities with which Sheridan filled these and all his other sentences.

"And you fell for it?" Rolf asked. In other circumstances, you might have heard the crash of an idol coming off its pedestal.

"Well, sir, God damn it, I am a bachelor—a man like any other. A man with appetites! A man with feelings!"

"You didn't have any feelings when you burned my daddy's farm on the Valley Pike in Shenandoah County, Virginia, and sent him off to Detroit, Michigan, to catch the glooms and die."

"Shenandoah County?" Sheridan muttered. He turned to the bed. "I remember that place of course, but not your father. What was his name?"

Jimmy whipped her other hand onto the hideout pistol's grip, and the sheet fell, baring her breast. She took no notice. Her beautiful eyes burned. Rolf knew the end was at hand.

"Cosgrove Sturdevant was his name. He took a shot at you because your damned brute soldiers had ruined our farm and carried me off to rape me. For punishment you sent him to prison up north. A poor helpless middle-aged farmer!"

General Phil Sheridan gathered himself and hooked his thumbs in the waist of his trousers, further revealing his potbelly, of which he took no notice. In a hard, strong voice, he said, "I do remember that incident. And you are wrong about it." He stepped toward the bed. "What happened was—"

"Stand back or I'll blow your head off," Jimmy whispered. Both hands, and the Deringer, trembled, and Sheridan's black eyes darted from the gun to Jimmy's face and back again. He clearly saw his death but a finger's twitch away. He didn't advance but he stood fast, and even a little taller. Rolf almost whistled; the man had testicles of steel.

"I ask you not to pull that trigger until I tell you what happened."

"Your men savaged me in the smokehouse, for one."

"I am deeply grieved," Sheridan said, without a single profanity. "I never intentionally made war on women. I do know such things happened."

Jimmy blinked and sat back, expecting, perhaps, something other than this soldier's calm and measured determination in the face of impending death. "I remember your father, and your farm, now that I put my mind to it, because it was there that we lost a young soldier named Birdage, the day after the battle at Fisher's Hill. A white-haired farmer came rushing from his house as we rode into his dooryard, and he fired a shot."

"Did you expect a man like Daddy wouldn't defend his property from filthy Yankee scum invaders?"

"No, I expect that would be any man's natural reaction," Sheridan said, his voice still level. Rolf swayed in the doorway, dizzy, hearing the beat of rain and what sounded in his ear like the rushing winds of black hell and judgment in the sky. Very soon, he expected to see fountains of blood all over the room's rose-pattern wallpaper. "I can understand why I was a target. Unfortunately your father's shot struck a soldier named Asa Birdage."

"Who cares, who cares?" Jimmy screamed. "He was sixty-two years old!"

"Asa Birdage was eleven years old. Asa Birdage was our headquarters drummer boy."

Jimmy's face was curtained by horror. She flung back against the headboard, wanting to deny Sheridan's statement. He simply stood there with his hands hanging easily at his sides—maybe he wasn't so easy inside, but you couldn't tell except for the rise and fall of his potbelly—and Jimmy began to shake her head from side to side. "No, no" she said, and then she burst out crying. "Liar. You're lying to save your hide."

"Young woman, I am an honorable man. I have been accused of many things, but never of deceit. Your father slew one of my soldiers. Who was scarcely more than a child. I felt prison was fair punishment. Perhaps I erred. Perhaps I was unjust. I acted to prevent another death. Others in my command that day wanted to shoot your father on the spot."

"No, oh no," Jimmy wept. Sheridan's eyes took on a pitying look. Rolf leaped by him, giving him a fist in the shoulder—how many times did you get to land a blow on a hero? on a legend?—and with one quick decisive grab, he removed the Deringer from Jimmy's hand.

"I am thankful that you believe me, miss," Phil Sheridan said in a voice oddly humbled.

"I'm not, I'm not," she cried, covering her tearful face. Rolf knelt beside the bed and with both hands delicately lifted the hem of the sheet so as to hide her breasts. His cheeks were scarlet.

General Sheridan quickly donned his singlet and then his blouse. He was once more sounding stern when he said, "If anyone mentions these events, I will deny my presence. I will lie till the throne of Hell freezes."

Rolf Greencastle was trembling inside. But he tried not to let it show when he turned his eyes on the national hero and scorched him. "I think you'd better light out of here, Phil."

Phil lit out.

\*     \*     \*

After about three hours, Jimmy's sobbing wore itself out and she fell asleep. Rolf pulled up a cane-bottomed chair and sat beside the bed, keeping a vigil. The rain fell harder. About four in the morning, Jimmy woke up.

She quickly covered her left breast, which had been peeping over the hem of the sheet as she slept; Rolf had been admiring it for the better part of twenty minutes. Although he knew her body intimately, his admiration was of a different nature than the simple lust he'd satisfied at the Overton Place before.

"Why did you do that?" she said. "Why did you stop me?" She sounded deathly sad. He feared the glooms were coming again. The terrible glooms.

"You tell me something first. How could you take him into your bed, hating him that way?"

"Oh—" A little sniffle. "Part of the trade, that's all. You learn to shut out everything. How bad the customer stinks. How mean he is. With him it was harder. For a while I thought it wouldn't work, I'd go to pieces. Then I remembered my daddy and I made it work. Got him right where I wanted him."

"It was a mighty good trick," he agreed. "You could have blown his head off any time you wanted to."

"Why did you stop me?"

"I didn't want anything to happen to you. I didn't want you to keep on having the glooms the rest of your life."

"Why, why?"

"I don't know, I guess because I love you."

They stared at each other. He was fully as surprised as she was.


The next day he helped her put the Overton Place up for sale and they rode away together and neither one ever saw General Phil Sheridan again.

# The Tinhorn Fills His Hand

Graham Coldfield walked up the plank of the steamer feeling the dizziness again. The lanterns of the *River Queen* had been lit against the lowering dusk, and he paused in the light of one of them, leaning weakly against the wooden wall, his head bowed. The quiet lap of the Blackwater River rose from the hull.

Beyond the wharf sprawled the town of Herrod's Landing, bawling with laughter and the rattle of carriage wheels and occasional shouts. Coldfield paid no attention. Dizziness fogged his brain. A sharp pain in his stomach made him close his eyes and groan. The damp night air brought a cough to his lips.

A couple dismounted from a carriage on the wharf and came up the plank, brushing past him. The woman gave him an odd look and laughed prettily, twirling her ornamental parasol as she passed. Coldfield ignored her. Terrified, he tried to fight the sickening motion of things around him. The world tilted and blurred before his eyes. He was weak, and ill.

Coldfield was a tall man, slender, with a long-jawed somber face. His gray eyes seemed empty in the lamplight. He leaned against the wall, finely dressed in a dark suit, black tie, and brocaded vest, the very model of a fashionable river gambler. But within his mind, he could already see his position slipping away.

The *Queen* was the best vessel on the river, and her gambling saloon attracted the most trade. Coldfield had climbed as far as he could in his kind of work. He dealt faro on the *Queen*, and made a good living at it. He lived quietly, like a gentleman, satisfied that hard times were over for him. He'd nearly forgotten the cheap back-country saloons; the nickel-ante stud games; the long nights spent in the saddle moving from town to town. He had worked long and hard to reach the position of dealer on the *Queen*. And now suddenly, it was all tumbling out from under him.

It's this damned river, he thought. Always damp and foggy and chill, like tonight. It weakened a man; cut down his resistance. Dazedly, Coldfield shook his head. If Tom Chapman, owner of the *Queen*, found out that he was having these spells, he'd be finished. That thought terrified him more than anything. To go back to riding from town to town, living with a half-empty, growling stomach most of the time—he couldn't do it. He wouldn't. But maybe it's not what you think it is at all, he thought. Maybe you just haven't been eating or resting enough.

He straightened up slowly. He was lying to himself. He was a sick man.

Well, he'd have to be careful. Above all he had to keep the secret from Chapman. He started to move along the deck, aware that the carriages were arriving more frequently now, that the crowd was swelling. He bumped into someone in the shadows and hastily drew back, his fingers reaching instinctively toward the derringer in his waistcoat pocket.

The man stepped out of the dark, lamplight falling across his massive, ugly face. Coldfield recognized

Redneck Bates, wearing a cap and high-collared jacket. Coldfield didn't like Bates, whose position on the *River Queen* was obscure. Bates, Coldfield suspected, was aboard to permanently remove anyone Chapman wanted removed. It was that simple. The dislike he felt for the big man sprang mostly from a contempt for the man's thick-skulled ignorance, mirrored now in his piggy eyes as he squinted at Coldfield. Bates had immensely powerful hands and a short temper.

"Hello, Redneck," Coldfield said quietly. "I didn't see you standing there."

"I been here a minute or so," Bates said. "I seen you, tinhorn." Bates always called Coldfield tinhorn, a word which jabbed the gambler like a thorn. Maybe that was another reason for his intense dislike of the man; that and the fact that Bates lived by the strength of his hands, while Coldfield prided himself on living by the quickness of his mind.

"I seen you," Bates repeated. "You was weaving back and forth." His eyes puckered together. "Are you sick or something?"

"No," Coldfield snapped. "I feel fine."

Bates shrugged. "You sure was staggering a powerful lot. This here river can get a feller mighty sick— you know?" A thick-lipped grin spread across the mouth of the bigger man.

"Forget it," Coldfield said. An instant later he had cause to regret the words; the sharpness in them.

"You wouldn't be ordering me around now, would you, tinhorn?" Bates stuck his thumbs into his jacket pockets, looking for a chance to show off his strength.

"If you want to call it that. I told you I'm not sick and to forget about the coughing spell." He had initiated this. Accidentally, to be sure. But he couldn't turn back now.

"I don't cotton to being pushed around, tinhorn." The wicked gleam in Bates's eyes grew brighter. He took a step forward, as if to see what Coldfield would do next.

Coldfield hesitated; slowly lowered his hands. Then he brought his right hand up with a swift motion, palming the derringer and aiming its tiny barrel at a spot between Bates's close-set eyes.

"Look," Coldfield said quietly, "get out of my way and stop jawing."

Sudden hatred showed on the other man's face. That was replaced by a look of craftiness. Coldfield was amazed at the way simple emotions moved over that flat, brutal face. "Sure, tinhorn. I'll step aside. But I ain't forgetting."

He moved back toward the wall. Coldfield pocketed the derringer and walked quickly by. At the next turn in the deck, he spun around and looked back. Redneck Bates still stood under the lantern, staring off across the water toward the lights of Herrod's Landing. He had a knife in his hand. He didn't look at Coldfield. Coldfield realized he'd made a dangerous enemy in his haste to conceal his own sickness.

The pain was duller, but still with him, as he hurried along the deck and into the brilliantly lit saloon. The hearty sound of male voices mingling with higher feminine ones crashed against his ears like the roar of surf. The small string orchestra wheezed away at "Buffalo Gals." The tables were crowded.

Tom Chapman had done an unprecedented thing with the *Queen.* He'd opened the gambling saloon to women as well as men. He attracted wealthy people that way; young bucks and their ladies who had money and position and who could afford to brave public scorn when the ladies lifted their skirts and stepped up the plank to this less-than-respectable world of green baize tables and easy money. Coldfield looked around, but he didn't see Tom Chapman. Coldfield's regular table, number three, was waiting, deserted as yet.

He crossed the big room, glancing at himself in the mirrored walls. Good God, he thought, I do look sick. Thinner, with sunken eyes. With his hat off, his graying hair was obvious. A man of thirty-three shouldn't have gray hair, he told himself. But he had it, a mark of the way he'd driven himself to reach the top, here in the gilded main saloon of the *River Queen.*

He slipped into his place behind the box. One of the waiters appeared instantly with fresh cards. He cut the paper with his fingernail and began an elaborate shuffle. Before he was finished, he had a full table. They know me, he thought proudly. They come to me for a fair game.

He got the high-stake faro game going, turning the cards out of the box with practiced ease. In less than three quarters of an hour he'd cleared a little over eleven hundred dollars for the house. As players left, new ones took their places. The noise and smell of cigar smoke increased. Coldfield himself lit a Cuban cheroot. He was in control now, though the pain in his chest had grown sharp again. His palms were clammy with sweat. That was something new.

A disturbance intruded on the regular noise of the saloon. A young man at the stud table next to Coldfield's got up quickly, shouting a curse. Frankie Topp, the dealer, also rose. Behind the young man stood a girl, her blue eyes wide with anxiety. She clutched her escort's arm. "Jim, let's get out of here." Coldfield studied her, his hand mechanically keeping up with his own game. She was older than the young man but not by very much. She had a fresh-scrubbed look. Her clothes, like her companion's, were obviously homemade. She didn't fit with the gilded ladies who patronized the *Queen*.

"I'm not getting out of here till I get my two thousand back," Jim said.

Coldfield smiled thinly. Frankie Topp was shrewd, but evidently his tricks hadn't worked this time.

"I saw what you did—palm the bottom card of the deck. I want my money."

Frankie Topp smiled gently and said something apologetic. Jim started around the table, fists clenched. The girl screamed as the small nickeled gun popped into Frankie's fist and exploded with a flat sound. A red smear spread on Jim's shirt, just above his heart. Another woman screamed and the hubbub of voices rose.

Then, almost like some genie from a bottle, Redneck Bates appeared behind the boy and clamped his arms around him. The boy fought, struggled, but Bates had no trouble dragging him to the door and out. The girl followed quickly. Coldfield turned back to his own game. Chapman allowed his dealers to play crooked if they could get away with it. The young couple had made a mistake in coming aboard the *Queen;* the company was too fast, and the boy had a hole in his chest, possibly fatal, for his foolishness. If he lived and made a fuss, Bates would look him up and break his neck. Chapman tolerated no interference with a successful operation.

The disturbance remained a topic of conversation for some minutes. Finally, the saloon resumed its usual tone of busy confusion. The hours wore on; the pain in Coldfield's chest became worse. At last he could no longer fight the dizziness. He cursed himself as the faces across the table swam out of focus.

He reached too quickly for the edge of the table, spilling the neat card decks carelessly on the baize. He closed his eyes, gripped the table edge, his head swinging from side to side. He heard a woman's horrified exclamation from the seat across from his. Suddenly he keeled over, his cheek smacking the table top.

A moment later he opened his eyes. The attack had passed. But he remembered what had happened. His stomach hurt.

Someone tapped him on the shoulder. Another of the house gamblers stood there, motioning him away from the table. He got up stiffly.

"I'll take over for you, Coldfield," the man said, and Coldfield knew that word had already traveled to Tom Chapman: *Coldfield's sick. Coldfield passed out at the table.* It was Chapman's business to know things almost as soon as they happened.

The house man stared at him. "You'd better go see Chapman."

Coldfield nodded, aware of the horrified gaze of the woman at his table. He hurried away from her accusing eyes; blindly he pushed through the crowd and up the stairs to the mezzanine. He didn't bother to knock on the intricately inlaid door. He walked straight in through the curtained foyer to the desk where Tom Chapman sat.

Chapman was built like Redneck Bates. But there the resemblance stopped. Intelligence showed in Chapman's wide-spaced brown eyes. His hands were delicate, almost feminine, untouched by dirt, odd contrasts to his long, thick arms. The office shone with the glow of expensive lamps on polished wood. The peaty smell of good whiskey floated in the air.

Chapman gestured to a chair. "Sit down, Graham." There was no cordiality in his eyes.

"I heard you got violently sick at the table," Chapman said after a moment.

Coldfield shook his head. "No, only a little dizzy. Look, Tom—"

"Don't call me Tom. You're a hired hand, nothing else. Now what happened?"

Wearily, Coldfield replied, "I just got a little dizzy and passed out. A few seconds, no more. I'm tired, that's all it is. Otherwise I'm fine."

Chapman shook his head. "I can't have a sick man working for me. I run this place on atmosphere as much as anything. Everything proper and refined. I can't have dealers passing out, that's flat. I'm sorry, but you're done on the *Queen*."

The words struck Coldfield like a sledge. All his years of struggle wiped out that fast. And Chapman had been so cordial when he hired him. "I thought we were friends. Hell, I've been with you three years now—"

"I'm in business," Chapman cut in; Coldfield saw the ruthlessness he'd always known was there. "The river does funny things to a man. Fever, pneumonia, just plain craziness sometimes. Go out to Arizona. Soak up some of the sun, and when you're over whatever it is, come back and see me. Maybe I can do something for you then."

The words burned Coldfield like heated cattle irons. Chapman didn't give a damn about anybody. He kicked people around, like that boy who was cheated, without ever worrying about it; nothing mattered but the *River Queen*.

In moments, Coldfield's life had gone to pieces. He saw himself in the saddle again, riding from town to town in the cold gray winters; shivering in cheap rooming houses; cadging a drink when he couldn't draw any customers into a game.

"Look," Chapman said abruptly, "this would have come sooner or later anyway. Redneck told me he saw you staggering around earlier tonight. You couldn't have kept it quiet for long. Get off the *Queen* without a fuss and I'll give you two weeks' wages."

"The hell with you, Chapman. I'm all right."

"You're lying." Chapman snarled it. "Now get out and get off before I get angry."

Coldfield drew back his arm and smashed Chapman on the point of the jaw. Chapman jerked backward in his chair, smart enough to roll his head with the punch. Rocketing to his feet, he fanned back his coat. A heavy revolver appeared in his fist. He pointed it toward a curtained doorway. "Out, Coldfield. Or do I have to kill you on the spot?"

"You can't get rid of me that easily."

"You make trouble and you'll be a dead man. Now get."

Coldfield turned shakily and walked toward the curtain. He pushed through it without looking back. He stood a moment in the alcove, listening. The side door to Chapman's office opened; he heard someone come in. There were whispers of conversation; then the door closed again. Coldfield opened the door that led from the alcove and stepped out onto the deck.

Damp mist coiled along the shore of the Blackwater. Coldfield moved down the deck, shivering. Someone stood at the gangplank. As Coldfield approached, he recognized another of the men Chapman employed to do his fighting. Coldfield tried to pass him, but the man seized his coat, dug into his waistcoat pocket and found the derringer. He tossed it over the rail; it plopped into the black water. His mouth split in a yellow-toothed grin.

"So long, Coldfield."

Wearily, Coldfield started down the plank. The cards, as the saying went, were stacked against him. There was nothing left.

His boots sounded hollow on the plank. He stopped midway to the street. Down on the wharf, under one of the lamps, a man was standing. Coldfield recognized Redneck Bates, hands deep in his jacket pockets. Coldfield started moving again, a tight feeling in his stomach. Bates started forward to meet him. Coldfield suddenly knew what the hurried conversation had been about, the moment after he left Chapman.

Bates moved with lumbering steps. He blocked the end of the gangplank. Coldfield looked around quickly. The wharf was deserted. The main street of Herrod's Landing, two blocks up along the river, pulsed with noise, but down here there was only shadow and the Blackwater lapping at the pilings and the echoing squeak of violins from the saloon of the *Queen*. This was why the other man had disarmed him. Chapman meant to demonstrate that he didn't dare fight back. Coldfield couldn't see Bates's face, but he knew from his voice that he was grinning:

"Hello, tinhorn. Seems like I'm running into you a lot tonight."

"Move," Coldfield said. "I want to get by."

"Not right yet," Bates said. "I got a little something to do first. Chapman wants to make sure you won't make no stink." A sharp click in the foggy air; a knife blade winked in the light. Far down the river, a mournful whistle sounded.

Coldfield hesitated only a second, then moved. He lunged to the left, seizing Bates's knife wrist with both hands. He jerked the big man toward him and brought his wrist down hard on the plank rail. Bates howled and the knife fell into the water. Coldfield dodged around him. Bates reared up; Coldfield's advantage of surprise had vanished.

Bates seemed to move like a powerful machine, gathering momentum. He slammed into Coldfield, and the rush carried the two men back across the wharf until Coldfield's back struck the wall of a building. Bates brought his fist clubbing down. Bates laughed as the hard blow landed. Red patterns exploded in Coldfield's head.

He pummeled Bates in the belly, but the man had immense strength; could not be stopped. One after another, powerful punches beat Coldfield down to the wet ground. His mind seemed to float in darkness, even as another blow struck him. No ordinary man could stand up against Bates, he told himself. But he tried; he tried, stumbling to his feet as the big man hit him again.

Something hateful took root in Coldfield's brain as his surroundings spun. No longer was this a matter of business. There was open cruelty in Bates's blows. Chapman, too, was responsible for his pain. Chapman had beaten him down to nothing by firing him; there was no need for this attack. And yet Chapman had ordered it. Chapman was responsible for Frankie Topp shooting the young boy, too. Chapman was a disease; a disease of greed.

And now he must be certain he had broken Coldfield. But a broken man could fight back. A broken man couldn't help fighting back, treated like this. Some men weren't built to be humbled. Coldfield would not be humbled.

And so he fought, weakly, ineffectually, until Bates's heavy boot smashed into his jaw and left him limp on the ground. Suddenly he heard a rattle of hoofs in the darkness, and a clatter of carriage wheels. He heard Bates cry out hoarsely; forced his eyes open long enough to see a whip cut the big man's face and spin him around, sending him staggering.

Bates disappeared in the dark. The carriage stopped. Hands seized Coldfield, tugging at him. A voice said, "Can you climb up into the carriage?"

He couldn't speak; he was in too much pain. But he did pull himself upward, then sank again. The carriage rattled into motion. He knew two things. The voice was that of a woman. And Chapman would die.

Then the carriage rolled and the darkness finally claimed him.

Coldfield awoke in a small shanty, lying in a rude bunk. In the center of the room, a candle glowed on a table; beyond that, on a similar bunk, lay a rigid body. Coldfield saw the face of the boy Jim, lifeless above the edge of the white sheet. He sat up quickly. It made the pains from the beating worse. The air in the shanty smelled of the mud of Herrod's Landing; Coldfield was seized with a fit of coughing. He doubled over, waiting for it to spend itself, all the while seeing the terrible face of the boy's corpse. He struggled to remember. The sound of carriage wheels . . . no, not a dream.

A noise came from a shadowed corner. He turned, still coughing, and saw the girl standing there. Her hands were clenched, her face lightly marked with visible stains of her tears. Her lips trembled. Coldfield's coughing passed. He said haltingly, "It was you with the carriage?" She nodded.

"I must thank you, ma'am. That man had me, sure enough. He might have killed me."

She stepped forward; the candle glow cut across finely molded features. Anger blazed in her blue eyes. "They killed Jim. Cheated us, then killed him on that boat, Mr.—"

"Coldfield. Graham Coldfield." Coughing shook him again.

The girl's name, it turned out, was Harriet Masters. Her parents were dead, and she and her brother Jim had jointly owned a barge that carried freight on the Blackwater. A bad storm had wrecked and sunk the barge, leaving them with just a little capital. Jim had rashly decided the *River Queen* was the perfect place to build the small sum into enough money to get back into business.

"He always thought he was so lucky," the girl finished with a soft despair.

Coldfield watched her, interested. "How did you happen to be there on the wharf?"

She picked up a large reticule from the chair; pulled out a heavy Colt. She held it capably. The barrel gleamed in the candlelight. "This was Jim's gun. I wanted to use it on the man who runs the *Queen.* Chapman's his name. He's got a bad reputation on the river. I warned Jim about him. I . . ."

She stopped, overcome. Fresh tears showed at the corners of her solemn eyes. But she controlled herself, shaking her head. Strong stuff, Coldfield thought.

"I don't live in Herrod's Landing," she went on. "The hotels were full, and this was the only place I could borrow to put Jim's body. He died in the carriage a few minutes after we left the boat." She brushed a hand across her forehead. "You'll have to forgive me. I'm not telling this coherently. After I found this place, I took the carriage back there. I wanted to kill Chapman. I sat for the longest time, but I couldn't get up courage to go on board. Not even with knowing what they'd done to Jim. I guess it isn't very—admirable for me to admit that to you."

Coldfield shook his head as he reached inside his coat for a cigar. "You were sensible. You wouldn't have had a chance."

Harriet Masters looked at him, silently thanking him for his words. "I was still sitting there when you came off the *Queen* and got into a fight. I recognized the big man. Then I found the courage to do something. I used the buggy whip on him."

Coldfield grinned slightly. That was fit treatment for Redneck Bates.

Harriet pulled her chair around the table and sat down facing him. Her body hid Jim's, for which he was thankful. The cramped, unclean room with its candle and sheeted corpse and the tendrils of Blackwater fog creeping under the door depressed him.

"Why was he after you?" the girl asked.

"I worked on the *Queen* up until tonight. As a dealer. Didn't you see me in there?"

She shook her head.

He hesitated then. His business was none of hers. Yet they were strangely bound together, he and this girl guarding her brother's body. Both had suffered at Chapman's hands. So he told her his story, curtly and rapidly. At the end he said, "I'm not after your sympathy, Miss Masters. Men get sick easily enough. I'm sorry I lost my job. It was a good one. But I can stand it. People stand a lot worse."

"Then why are you so bitter?"

"The beating. Chapman ordered Bates to beat me so I wouldn't cause any trouble. That I can't and won't take. That I'll pay him for."

She reached out, touched his hand. Her fingers felt delicate, cool. "You should leave this river. Go into the Southwest, where it's dry and there's plenty of sun. You'd be all right then."

"Maybe I will." His eyes bored into hers. "But not until I get Chapman."

She rose and walked to the door, opening it. She stood with her back to him, looking out into the fog-laden darkness where a few lights glimmered on the river like misty cat's eyes. She had a fine back. Young and firm and straight. He watched her as she said softly, "Mr. Coldfield, I have two thousand dollars on the *River Queen*. Perhaps we could work together."

"I was thinking the same thing."

She turned and faced him as he approached. They stood silent a moment. Then she offered her hand and he pressed it. Her skin had a warmth to it; a warmth that somehow brightened the room despite the presence of Jim's body. He held her hand an instant longer than was necessary. She glanced away, disturbed, and he regretted his forwardness; this was no time for such things. Yet knowing he was no longer alone helped renew his strength.

"First," he said, "we ought to take care of your brother."

Her strength seemed to drain away. She collapsed against him, bitter sobs rising in a broken rhythm. He looked down at her tawny hair and slipped his arm around her lightly, just enough to make her aware that it was there if she needed it. Presently her crying subsided again.

"I think I'd better take the gun," Coldfield said. She handed it to him, and he slipped it into his wide belt. It felt good there, heavy and latent with power. He picked up his hat. "You wait here. I'll be back soon."

He scoured Herrod's Landing for a suitable room.

The hotels, as she had reported, were full. But he managed to locate one vacancy: a small attic room in a boarding house on a side street. They took Jim's body there in the carriage and woke the town's funeral director to make arrangements for burial. Then Coldfield rode back to the boarding house in the long black-curtained hearse and helped with removal of the body.

He made sure Harriet Masters was secure for the night, then strolled over to the main street. The air was chilly, but it did not bother him now. A new calm, a new, almost peaceful sense of purpose filled him. Together, he and the girl would make Chapman pay.

He found a back table in one of the smaller saloons and sat up all night with a bottle of redeye, drinking and thinking his black thoughts and staring off hollow-eyed into a grim nowhere.

They buried Jim Masters in the morning. The plot was tiny, but it overlooked the river from a low bluff. No preacher was available, so the funeral director, a small mousy man, read from the New Testament.

Coldfield didn't hear the words. His eyes were on the river. The *Queen* had left her berth and was chugging downriver toward the burial site, paddle wheel turning over with a continuous roaring fall of foamy water, fluted stacks belching smoke into the morning sky.

The rattle of dirt against the wooden coffin brought Coldfield back to the immediate moment. Harriet was crying again, quietly. Coldfield studied her. A certain amount of grief had to be expected, but some women would have become hysterical. She was holding up well. Coldfield respected her for the way she managed herself.

The last of the earth was shoveled into place and the small headstone set. The gravediggers hefted their shovels and moved off through a grove, lighting cigars as they dropped their feigned air of seriousness. The mousy funeral director hurried over to Coldfield to request his fee. Coldfield paid him from what little money he had left. The man tipped his worn beaver hat and went hopping off through the grove after his workers.

Harriet looked at Coldfield. "Shall we go?"

He shook his head, pointing. "I want to watch the *Queen* go by." Hatred etched his face. Harriet stood by his side, understanding his need for fueling the fires inside him.

The *River Queen* plowed through the turgid, mud-yellow waters, her wheel revolving, scooping and flinging a huge volume of water up and over the paddles. The whistle tooted jauntily. Coldfield clearly made out the pilot's face as the steamer passed the bluff. He saw Redneck Bates moving along the deck but the big man didn't notice the observers. Coldfield's hands closed involuntarily. He cursed. Harriet Masters showed no reaction.

The *Queen* slowly grew smaller, showing her stern with its foaming wake as she nosed out beyond a sand bar and cut around a sharp bend. The smoke from her stacks smeared the sky in ugly clouds as she disappeared.

"I've seen enough," Coldfield said, excited now, keenly aware of the hatred feeding him like some kind of drug. "Come on. We've work to do."

He took the girl's arm and piloted her between headstones toward the cemetery gate. She turned once for a brief glance at her brother's grave, then climbed into the carriage. Coldfield climbed up beside her, somehow unexpectedly proud to be riding with her, to have her for a partner in his little game of revenge in which he'd bought chips. She would be a woman for a man to cherish. She was younger than he; much younger. That would be a barrier—He stopped the reverie. They had no time for such things now. Perhaps later, if Chapman died and they retrieved the two thousand dollars . . .

He hawed to the team and the carriage jolted along the ruts, back down the bluff toward the town.

The next weeks brought an endless chain of surprises. In company with Harriet, Coldfield traveled down the Blackwater, following the *Queen* from town to town, talking with men the girl had known when she and her brother ran their barge business. He was astonished by the amount of resentment against the *Queen* and her customers: young dandies, blooded bucks who drank and gambled their lives away, and women who only had their bodies as collateral for their gentlemen friends. They were in a minority, these men who diced and sported gold-headed canes, these flashy women. But they were intensely disliked by nongamblers, common folk.

That aspect of the gambling trade had never struck Coldfield before. Sitting at his faro table, he'd drawn his salary, lived well, and never considered the morality of his work. He hadn't suddenly become a reformer, bent on stopping the trade the *Queen* represented; men would never stop gambling. But the more he listened to men talk, the more stories he heard, the more it soured him. Because more than one had been cheated. More than one had wound up in an alley, beaten in response to a protest. The idea of running a crooked game had never occurred to Coldfield. He'd always lived by reputation, and a reputation for dishonesty ruined a gambler in the long run, even if he profited temporarily. But evidently Chapman felt differently, and he'd been too self-centered to see it. Coldfield felt as if he were emerging from some kind of dream as the miles rolled under the wheels of their carriage, and he talked to more men and to their stout red-knuckled wives.

Then he went by himself to a shack in a river town and talked to a girl, hardly more than eighteen, who was thin and pale and unhealthy looking as she perched on the edge of a cot in her cheap spangled scarlet wrapper. Coldfield kept smelling the sharp aroma of lye as she told him Chapman's crew acted as pimps when the *Queen* was docked in town. They got a percentage of all the trade from the young bloods they directed to this dismal crib-lined street. Coldfield talked with others, sometimes politely referred to as soiled doves; they told the same story.

In the same town he met a man named Acton, a gray-haired, thick-armed man who said, "You tell me when you're going after Chapman, mister. I'll be there. My girl died down on Crib Street. She ran off—I didn't even know where she was until the pox had her and it was too late." His eyes were sullen, bitter.

Acton and the girls were the first to point a new direction. Now Coldfield began following it from town to town as he followed the *Queen*, always with Harriet Masters beside him. He sought a spot to force a conclusion and decided on St. Elmo, a sizable town at the southernmost bend of the river. The *Queen* would dock there a week before proceeding downstream to the confluence of the big river. Coldfield rounded up sixteen men, secured their promise that they would be in St. Elmo, armed, the first week in October. Acton was among them.

Acton's son Tod, a youth of sixteen, offered to

travel with them, to run errands. Coldfield accepted. He felt like a general gathering an army. But it was a good feeling. The chest trouble had grown worse, yet he managed to put it out of his mind for long periods. He was intent on his plan. And growing close to Harriet as each day passed.

One night toward the end of September, he was eating dinner with the girl in the dining room at the Wagon Top Hotel in Pitcher, a town thirty miles north of St. Elmo. He poured brandy•for himself; lit a cigar. Then he reached across the table and took her hand. "You know, if it hadn't been for you, we'd never have come this far."

"What little we had left after the barge went down—the office furniture and my clothes and the rest—it wasn't of any use to me, Graham." She smiled. "I feel foolish sometimes. We've already spent part of the two thousand dollars, traveling like this. But then I remember Jim and I know it's worth it."

"I feel some others have a stake in this, too. Ben Acton, for one. The *Queen*'s not just a place to gamble. She's a disease, poisoning the whole Blackwater river. And I didn't know it."

Harriet smiled again with gentle tolerance. "You didn't know a lot of things. All of us lived walled up behind our own illusions."

He smiled back at her. "Recognize any more of mine?"

"Well—maybe not knowing how good it is to share something with someone. Just living for yourself, grabbing for yourself—that might be one."

He didn't answer, but he knew she understood he'd accepted her words without rancor. He gave her hand a squeeze. Then he said: "But I've still got my stake. I've got the beating to square. Chapman's going to buy it for that."

A frown crossed her face. "Graham, that's no good. The way you hate him so. The way you're willing to kill him in cold blood."

Anger caught him. "Well, that's why I bought into this game. And that's the way it's going to be."

"Well, I'm sorry for you. I wish—"

The door banged open suddenly. Tod Acton ran in, breathless. "Mr. Coldfield—one of the men from the *Queen*'s down in the bar. I just saw him. A big feller. Looks like the one you're always talking about—"

Coldfield's face hardened. "Dressed like one of the crew?" Tod Acton nodded. Coldfield breathed, "Bates." He reached to the back of his chair and strapped on the Colt in its recently-bought holster while Tod added that there was a second crewman with Bates. From the boy's description, Coldfield tagged the other man as Soapy Mullins, a river rat who'd never face up to anybody head on, even a woman.

Coldfield spun the cylinder. "Now's the time to put the fear of God into Tom Chapman." He moved toward the door, watching the strained, regretful face of Harriet Masters. Well, he thought as he padded down the thickly carpeted gas-lit hall, let her worry about my character if she wants. That's a harmless pastime. I'm interested in seeing Tom Chapman dead.

Coldfield passed through the lobby, catching sight through a window of the *Queen* down on the wharf, lanterns glowing in the dusk. He paused at the bat-wings of the hotel bar, looking in. Redneck Bates and Soapy Mullins sat at a center table, slopping up foamy schooners of beer. Coldfield retreated, went out through the lobby, and down the street till he found a gun shop. The proprietor sold him another Colt and shells. Slipping the gun into his coat after he'd loaded it, he returned to the hotel and entered the bar. He wove his way among the tables until he stood before Bates and Mullins. Mullins looked up suddenly and blew his breath, spraying foam. Bates whipped up his head then.

"Hey!" Bates started to get up, his piggy eyes showing surprise and bewilderment. Coldfield felt a cough coming but fought it back. He had his holstered Colt free, aimed at Bates.

"What the hell you doing messing around here, tinhorn?" Bates bluffed loudly. He glanced around, searching for help. None of the other customers moved. Mullins was too frightened to do so; his almost nonexistent chin trembled.

"Looking for you gentlemen." Coldfield smiled. "Bates, you can get up and come outside with me."

Bates did not move. His fingers began drumming on the table top. He licked his lips.

"I said get up," Coldfield said, harsher this time. Bates rose. Coldfield swung to Mullins. "You sit right there or I'll blow you to kingdom come."

"Sure, boss," Mullins said, nodding vigorously. "I won't move. Swear to God."

Coldfield followed Bates out through the front door. A couple of men continued to stare, but most went back to their drinks. Coldfield prodded Bates off the sidewalk into the street.

"What the hell you trying to pull, tinhorn?" Bates snarled.

"Just want to even things up for that beating you gave me." Coldfield took out the spare pistol. "I'm going to hand you this gun and you're going to fight." He raised the new Colt, held it out.

Bates moved suddenly, whipping his coat open. He growled something, lunging forward. Coldfield took a dodging step to one side, but not far enough. A knife winked in Bates's meaty hand. Coldfield felt it slice through his coat, into his shoulder, impaling him against the porch post. He brought the gun up against Bates's belly and fired. The explosion was muffled. Bates stepped backward, mouth dropping open, and slid into the street.

Coldfield breathed heavily, nearly overcome by the pain. He holstered his Colt, dropped the other, and reached up. With one savage twist he freed the knife.

Blood spread warmly under his shirt. Moving with care, he reentered the saloon. Mullins hadn't moved. Men stared with somewhat greater interest now that Coldfield was wounded.

"Go back to the *Queen*," Coldfield said to Mullins. "Tell Chapman that I'm coming for him, to finish him. Go, right now."

"Sure, boss," Mullins exclaimed, fearful. He dashed out the door. Coldfield went to the bar, ordered a shot, and downed it in two swallows. Then he turned and walked slowly outside. Bates lay where he'd fallen; down the street, Soapy Mullins was churning his legs as fast as he could, heading for the wharf.

Harriet didn't ask what had happened. He told her Bates was dead while she dressed the wound. He saw the regret in her eyes. But he reminded himself that he was a fool if he worried about her feelings. He bid her a brusque good-night and left.

He sat all night by the window of his darkened room, watching the street. Men he recognized from the *Queen* prowled outside, and once he heard footsteps pause on the other side of his door. But the door was securely bolted with a chest of drawers shoved in front of it. Coldfield felt safe for the moment. Chapman wouldn't dare make too much overt trouble; his position was precarious enough already. The black night hours passed slowly. Before dawn, the *Queen* made steam and pulled away from the dock, heading downriver.

The October sun lowered toward the river, an immense red-orange globe. The air coming in through the window had a sharp autumnal tang, and above the rooftops of the main street, Coldfield could see smoke rising; the townsfolk burning weeds and leaves.

Below, men rode by wearing heavy coats. But down at the wharf also visible to him, the *River Queen*'s lights were aglow as if it were still full summer. Before long, Chapman's vessel would be steaming down into the lower Mississippi to spend the winter on the stretch of river above New Orleans.

Coldfield let the curtain fall. His mouth set in a grim line. His men would be gathered in the saloon by nine this evening. He'd spied several on the street already. Turning back to the table where a bottle stood beside his holstered Colt, he poured a drink. His hand shook slightly, and he coughed before he downed the shot.

He and Harriet had grown progressively farther apart these past days. At the beginning, they'd been complete strangers, drawn together by their common hatred. Slowly the bond had strengthened until Coldfield felt that something more than friendship or mutual interest existed. But ever since the night he shot Redneck Bates, the gap had widened again. Coldfield understood. Despite, or perhaps because of, her brother's murder, Harriet couldn't accept cold-blooded killing. And though Coldfield intended to give Tom Chapman every chance, his goal was still the man's death.

Well, he told himself, when she gets her two thousand back, she can ride her own trail. It hurt him, but that's the way it had to be. A man couldn't be humbled without retaliating. Quickly, Coldfield poured and downed another drink.

A soft knock sounded at the door. Coldfield tensed. "Who is it?" No answer.

Harriet would be eating supper about now; and he wasn't due to meet his men until later. He slipped the Colt from its holster and stole toward the door. He set himself, then seized the knob and jerked the door open.

A fist rocketed out and caught his jaw. He spun around, seeing the crag-jawed face of one of the *Queen's* roustabouts whirl out of sight. He staggered back, trying to aim the gun. But there were two of them, swarming over him, kicking and pounding him, grunting softly. His head snapped back, striking the door. A face swam toward him through the delirium of pain. Chapman's face, wearing a cold grin. Coldfield struggled wildly, but it was no use. Another fist clubbed the back of his neck and he went down, a sharp pain twisting in his chest. That pain in turn was deadened by the darkness that suddenly enclosed him.

After a while, he heard a whistle hooting in the distance. He shook his head, trying to clear the fog and pain from it. Dampness brushed his face; the kind of dampness that smelled of the river. Coldfield opened his eyes. Except for the absence of Jim Masters's sheeted corpse, the room was almost a duplicate of the earlier one. An oil lantern sputtered on a hook near the ceiling, moving slightly in air currents coming under the ill-fitted door. Coldfield was in one of the many shanties that lined the mud flats along the Blackwater.

Tom Chapman stepped in front of him, thumbs thrust into his vest pockets. He smiled at Coldfield, but there was little mirth in his eyes, only an amused scorn. "You shouldn't have noised it around that you were going to get me, Graham. I've been on the lookout ever since I heard it."

"How—how did you find me?" Coldfield asked, still shaky from the beating.

"One of your friends got too much redeye in him and started mouthing off at the saloon. One of my boys heard the stupid fool mention your hotel." Chapman eased back the flap of his coat; drew his pistol.

A wave of despair washed over Coldfield. He'd come so close only to be betrayed by someone careless and excessively thirsty. Maybe he should have played the hand alone from the start, without Harriet Masters, without any of them. Now, though, it didn't matter. It didn't matter at all.

Chapman made a half turn, called an order. The door opened. The two rough-looking roustabouts came inside. One settled his greasy cap on his head and ground out a cigar beneath his heel. The other rubbed his hands together. Chapman said, "You're going to get another beating, Graham. Only this time, it's going to kill you. I have to protect my business." Again that thin smile. Coldfield again saw the man's ruthless brutality, his unswerving devotion to his own prosperity.

Coldfield thought of the beating he'd gotten from Bates, at Chapman's orders, and it made the anger boil up again. Without warning he leaped at Chapman, lips skinned back over his teeth, almost snarling. His hands reached for Chapman's throat. One of the others jumped forward, lifting a short wooden club. The club smacked Coldfield's head with a pulpy sound. Coldfield spun away, lights sparkling behind his eyes. The second man got behind him, pinioned his arms, while the other drew back his hand, then whipped the club down again. Coldfield's head rocked on his shoulders. The blows came one after another, in regular rhythm. Somewhere Chapman laughed. He seemed to laugh louder with each blow. Time ceased to have meaning for Coldfield. In his delirium, he still knew that time had stopped for him. Stopped forever.

The beating proceeded slowly, methodically. Finally Coldfield could barely feel the separate blows. The excess of it paradoxically lifted some of his pain. His eyes cleared a bit. Chapman was seated on a barrel, smoking. His gun lay on the table beside him. Anger caught hold of Coldfield again. Perhaps, he thought to himself, perhaps with that I can fight them. He knew that he had to make the effort soon or he'd never do it.

He moved his arms. "Hey!" The man jerked him from behind. But his grip wasn't as tight as before. Coldfield leaned back slightly, feeling something stuck in the man's belt. Had the man been carrying a knife there, or a pistol? He couldn't remember. But it felt like a weapon. And the man's grip had relaxed. Coldfield rolled with the blows of the club, biding his time; gathering his hate and the last reserves of strength it generated.

Coldfield saw the club go up once more. This time, as it came lashing down, he wrenched free of his captor. The club slashed past his head and because he dodged, it missed his shoulder. Instead of turning for his captor's weapon, he kept going forward. His hand beat Chapman's to the table by a fraction of a second. He snatched the pistol and flattened himself against the shanty wall.

The man who'd held him was cursing and tugging the pistol from his belt. Coldfield fired a single shot that sent the man staggering on rubbery legs. Then he fell.

The second man, blunt jaw thrust forward, small eyes glinting, threw a knife. Coldfield dodged, feeling the blade near his temple before it buried itself in the plank wall, quivering. Coldfield's hastily snapped shot hit the man's groin. The man let out a yell and went down.

Coldfield raced for the door and clattered down the steps in pursuit of Chapman. The owner of the *Queen*, unarmed now that Coldfield had his pistol, had bolted for the door the instant the first man took a bullet.

Just outside the shanty, Coldfield hesitated. The fog turned the flats into a dim wasteland of deceptive shapes. He thought he saw a running figure; fired at it. A window broke in a hail of broken glass. A man in long underwear flung the shanty door open, cursing.

Coldfield listened for footsteps. He heard none. He thrust the gun into his coat and started walking. He had to stop once for several minutes while a wave of dizziness struck him. Then he moved again, working his way up the flats toward the lights of St. Elmo.

Harriet Masters gasped when she answered his knock at her hotel room door. He stood leaning weakly against the door frame. He didn't smile at her; he couldn't. She searched his face, then rushed forward, her skirts belling around her. One hand went up to touch his cheek, cool and tender. "Graham . . ." She said it softly, her eyes misting just a little.

He closed the door while she poured him a drink. Briefly he explained what had happened. Her face took on a look of numbed horror. When he finished, he paused a moment, then said, "Now do you see why I'm going after Chapman? This time he was going to kill me. The *Queen* means everything to him. There isn't a thing he won't do to protect her."

She nodded. "Yes, I see now. I—I'm sorry."

He stood up and abruptly the dizziness hit him again. His hands groped to a chair for support. When he recovered, his face had an unhealthy mottled look. But his eyes were like pieces of stone. "I'm all right," he said. "What time is it?"

She glanced at the big clock on the fireplace mantel. "Quarter to nine."

Coldfield took out Chapman's gun and examined it. He replaced the spent shells and put it away again. "Time to get the men in the bar." And, he added silently, time for Tom Chapman to cash in.

She touched his arm. Now, he thought, she understands. She's willing for me to do this. "Graham, I want you to be careful."

He leaned forward; touched his lips to her cheek. "I will." He smiled at her with faint bitterness. "You wait right here. If I'm not back by midnight, you'll know Chapman won the hand." He turned and left the room, shoulders straight despite the pain in his chest.

As soon as Coldfield pushed through the saloon batwings, he spotted Acton and the others along the bar. Quiet, plain-looking men who leaned over their drinks and talked among themselves. Coldfield took pleasure in noting that they were heavily armed and that they numbered closer to thirty than sixteen. Moving toward them, he was startled by the sight of a man wearing a peace officer's star. The man was talking with Acton.

Coldfield tapped Acton on the shoulder; the huge sullen man turned. He extended his hand and Coldfield shook it.

"You sure look like you got run through the grinder," Acton said.

Coldfield nodded. "Chapman. He knows we're in town and he tried to finish me. One of your men drank too much and talked."

Acton's face grew grimmer. "By God, let's find out which one." Coldfield put out a restraining hand.

"Waste of time. Chapman's already prepared." Coldfield indicated the extra men. "Where'd they come from?"

The man with the star spoke. "Coldfield, I'm Winters. Marshal here in St. Elmo." He pointed to a small, meek-looking chap slumped forlornly over a schooner of beer at the far end of the bar. The small man kept wiping his silver-rimmed spectacles and sniffing. He didn't look as though he belonged in the war party. "That there is Knute Hoagstrom. Runs the general store. His boy was gut-shot on the *Queen* two nights ago. That's why I'm here. A few of us townspeople have a stake, too."

Coldfield eyed the marshal. "I'm out to kill Tom Chapman. I won't be stopped."

Winters's eyes had a fierce glint. "Understood."

Coldfield hitched at his belt and looked around again. "Well, then, let's get started."

Acton nodded, unlimbering his gun. The men stirred. With Coldfield, Winters, and Acton leading, they moved out of the saloon.

They walked in near-total silence down the middle of the street. Coldfield noticed a man in a buckboard following them. He asked Winters, "What's in the wagon?"

"Buckets of pitch. We aim to burn the *Queen*." Coldfield smiled and kept walking.

People looked out of windows to watch the procession. On the sidewalk, a couple of ladies of the evening tittered with excitement. Coldfield kept his eyes on the wharf ahead. Only a few carriages were tied up there. Something moved among them suddenly, and Coldfield recognized one of the crew. He had spotted them.

The crewman ran wildly up the plank, waving and shouting something that rang unintelligibly down the street of shadows and dim lamps. Coldfield felt the bite of chill of the night air. The winter was on the way. Maybe I'll get to Arizona. Then he laughed, aloud. Men around him stared. Maybe he wouldn't get to Arizona, either. Maybe he'd be dead after this night's work was over.

When they were still a block from the wharf, a rifle snapped. A squirt of flame showed on the *Queen*'s texas deck. The men split up, racing for the sidewalks. But one stayed prone and bleeding in the center of the street.

Coldfield's men opened fire as they crept along the sidewalk, filling the night with the flat racket of answering fire. Other rifles took up the fight from the *Queen*'s decks. Winters was behind Coldfield, Acton on the other side of the street. Coldfield signaled him, then broke into a run across the open wharf.

He heard slugs whine around him. Something plucked his coat sleeve; he kept running. He reached the gangplank just as one of the crew started to raise it.

Coldfield stopped, aimed, and squeezed off a careful shot. The man pitched forward. The plank fell back into place with a thud; Winters and his men swarmed up. Coldfield followed, just ahead of Acton's group.

Coldfield knew the plan of the vessel, and he deployed the men quickly. Half a dozen went to cover the main saloon. Others headed below, to round up the roughnecks who worked the boilers. Coldfield himself hurried toward Chapman's quarters. Occasional shots banged in the night air. A rifleman went sailing down past Coldfield from the deck above, disappearing into the dark water with a loud splash. Just ahead Coldfield saw someone running. He recognized Frankie Topp and yelled his name. The man turned and spit out a snarling curse as he reached for his hideout gun. The stubby barrel had just cleared the edge of his vest pocket when Coldfield's shot caught him chest high, spinning him around. Topp slumped over the rail, done for. Coldfield stepped around him, hurrying again.

He came to the door, stopped, and steadied himself. With his free hand he reached out and grasped the knob. Turning it, he pulled the door open, slipped silently into the curtained foyer, and closed the door without a sound. He stepped to the curtain, swiftly brushing it aside with his Colt barrel to reveal the office.

Tom Chapman knelt in front of the safe, his back to Coldfield, jamming papers and currency into a carpetbag. Coldfield grasped the curtain with a white-knuckled hand. He wanted to pull the trigger; wanted to see the slugs striking Chapman's back one after another, tearing it apart, ripping bone and flesh into shreds of red and gray. He wanted to see Chapman die as recompense for the way he had humbled

Coldfield and tossed him out like a river tramp. He wanted to shoot Chapman in the back, but in a silent, seemingly eternal moment he realized that he couldn't.

Instead, purposely, he coughed.

As Coldfield moved into the office, Chapman whirled around, his eyebrows rising in a ludicrous expression of surprise. "Hello, Tom," Coldfield said. Chapman's hand groped at his holster. Coldfield let him reach, feel the emptiness. "I've got your gun right here, Tom. You should have taken time to get another."

Chapman licked his lips. "You going to shoot me, Graham?"

Coldfield hesitated a second. "No, Tom." He tossed his Colt on a chair. "I'm going to kill you with my bare hands."

Chapman laughed, pleased. "Tinhorn, you're not strong enough. You're a sick man."

"We'll see, Tom." Coldfield's fist caught Chapman on the jaw, spinning him a quarter turn. But Chapman was powerful; he steadied himself and pounded two blows into Coldfield's stomach that sent the gambler reeling away, pain all through his chest.

Chapman moved to press his advantage. Coldfield brought his fist upward clumsily, bashing Chapman's jaw and pitching him back across the desk top. But he quickly regained his feet. Coldfield parried a jab at his head; took another brutal blow in the gut, then one to the head. Coldfield bounced against the wall. His head struck a framed picture and the glass shattered, splinters drawing blood from the back of his neck.

Chapman staggered toward the foyer, ripping the curtain down and kicking the door outward. Coldfield was after him in a second, fighting the renewed pain in his chest brought on by exertion. But he drove himself, out to the deck and the chill air. Chapman was running aft toward the gangplank. In his rush through the door, Coldfield bumped the rail, righted himself and went after him. Only a few shots sounded now, sporadic and distant.

Chapman stumbled suddenly, tripped by Frankie Topp's body. Coldfield pulled up short a foot from Chapman, reaching for his shoulder. Chapman whirled suddenly, Frankie Topp's gun in his fist. Coldfield saw Chapman's finger whitening on the trigger an instant before he kicked out. Coldfield's boot caught Chapman's hand, diverting the bullet upward. Using both hands, Coldfield jerked Chapman to his feet and shoved him against the cabin wall. Coldfield was ready to work on him when a rifle cut loose in the darkness. Shot after shot ripped out, splintering the planks of the wall. Coldfield ducked instinctively. When the firing died and he looked up again, Chapman was sitting on the deck, legs outstretched. His face was red and almost unrecognizable.

Acton appeared. He stepped over the body and rested his rifle on the rail. "Sorry I stole your thunder, Coldfield." His eyes were shadowed, brooding. "But I lost my daughter because of him. I figured it was my right."

Coldfield nodded. "I got my share." He gripped the rail with one hand, reaching for his handkerchief with the other. Moments later, when the fit of coughing subsided, he realized that Marshal Winters had arrived.

"You gents better get off," Winters said. "We got all of Chapman's men rounded up and me and my boys are going to fire this tub."

Coldfield turned quickly and went back to the office. From Chapman's fallen carpetbag he took two thousand dollars in currency, thrusting the bills into his coat. Then he headed back outside, exhausted, drained of the last reserves of energy. The pain in his chest was sharp, almost excruciating.

A man passed him on the plank carrying two buckets of pitch. Coldfield joined the crowd of curious townspeople on the wharf. A pair of urchins played tag around his legs, pulling at his coattails, asking questions. He didn't answer, watching the first flame shoot from a broken window of the main saloon. Soon the air reeked of smoke and burning. The firelight shone in Coldfield's eyes, illuminating a macabre satisfaction. This part of his life was finished. Somehow he felt relieved.

It took three hours for the *Queen* to burn to the waterline and sink, disappearing with much smoke and hissing beneath the Blackwater after the wreckage was towed out to center channel.

Coldfield turned away then, pushing through the now-sparse crowd. The night air was bothering him. His teeth started to chatter and he felt another coughing fit coming on. Then he saw Harriet, sitting stiffly in the carriage. He walked to her and climbed up. Her hand fastened on his arm, her eyes anxious.

He shook his head. "No, I didn't kill him. Acton got there first." He smiled briefly. "But I got in some licks with my fists. I was strong enough to do that." He couldn't keep a certain fierce pride out of his voice. Sick or not, he still had strength left, and some years; years that might heal his weakened body.

"I've got your two thousand," he added.

"Bless you, Graham." She gestured to the horses. "Where to?"

He stared at her. "Why don't we try Arizona?

Plenty of sun. Plenty of time to relax and live. I ought to be able to make some kind of living out there."

Harriet smiled. "I know a man here in St. Elmo who could arrange things." Something danced in her blue eyes. "Sooner or later, Graham, if a man and woman stay together, they'll probably fall in love: And I want it legal."

He laughed. "You're a forward wench."

She laughed too though he could still see strain on her face. "You don't know everything about me, Graham. Not yet."

He reached for a cigar. "It's a long way to Arizona."

She leaned over and kissed him on the mouth. "I know." The carriage leaped under the reins in her hands and went rolling back up the main street, leaving the river behind.

# The Naked Gun

George Bodie sat smoking a cigar in the parlor of Chinese Annie's house on Nebraska Street when the message came.

Bodie had his dusty boots propped on a stool and his heavy woolen coat open to reveal the single holster with the Navy Colt on his hip. He might have been thirty or forty.

His cheeks in the lamplight were shadowy with pox scars. He was ugly, but hard and capable looking. His smile had a crooked, sarcastic quality as the cigar smoke drifted past his face.

Maebelle Tait, owner of the establishment—Chinese Annie had died; her name was kept for reasons of good will—hitched up the bodice of her faded ball gown and poured a drink.

"Lu ought to be down before too long," she said. From somewhere above came a man's laugh.

"Good. I've only been in this town an hour, but I've seen everything there is worth seeing, except Lu. Things don't change much."

Maebelle sat with her drink and lit a black cheroot. "Where you been, George?"

Bodie shrugged. "Hays City, mostly." His smile widened and his hand touched his holster.

"How many is it now?" Maebelle asked with a kind of disgusted curiosity.

"Eleven." Bodie walked over and poured a hooker for himself. "One more and I got me a dozen." He glanced irritably at the ceiling. "What's she doin'? Customer?"

Maebelle shook her head. "Straightening up the second-floor parlor. We got a group of railroad men stopping over around two in the morning." Maebelle's tone lingered halfway between cynicism and satisfaction.

The front door opened and a blast of chill air from the early winter night swept across the floor. Bodie craned his neck as Tad, Maebelle's seven-year-old boy, came in, wiping his nose with his muffler. Maebelle's other child, three, sat quietly in a chair in the corner, fingering a page in an Eastern ladies' magazine, her eyes round and silently curious.

"Where you been, Tad?" Maebelle demanded.

He glanced at Bodie. "Over at Simms' livery stable. I . . . I saw Mr. Wyman there."

Bodie caught the frowning glance Maebelle directed at him. "New law in town?" he asked.

Maebelle nodded. "Lasted six months, so far. Quiet gent. He carries a shotgun."

Bodie touched the oiled Colt's hammer. "This can beat it, anytime."

Maebelle's frown deepened. "George, I don't want you to go hunting for your dozenth while you're on my property. I'm glad for you to come, but I don't want any shooting in this house. I got a reputation to protect."

Bodie poured another drink. The boy Tad drew a square of paper from his pocket and looked at his mother.

"Mr. Wyman gave me this."

He held it out to Bodie, with hesitation.

"He said for me to give it to you right away."

Bodie's brows knotted together. He unfolded the paper, and with effort read the carefully blocked letters. The words formed a delicate bond between two men who nearly did not know how to read. Bodie's mouth thinned as he digested the message:


WE DO NOT WANT A MAN LIKE YOU IN THIS TOWN. YOU HAVE TIL MIDNIGHT TO RIDE OUT. (SIGNED) DALE WYMAN, TOWN MARSHAL


Bodie laughed and crumpled the note and threw it into the crackling fire in the grate.

"I guess the word travels," he said with a trace of pride. "Maybe I will collect my dozenth." He raised one hand. "But not on your property, Maebelle. I'll do it in the street, when this marshal comes to run me out. So's everybody can see." His hand went toward the liquor bottle.

Maebelle pushed Tad in the direction of the hall. "Go to the kitchen and get something to eat. And take sister Emma with you."

Grumbling, the boy took the tiny girl's hand and dragged her toward the darkened, musty-smelling hallway.

The girl disengaged her hand, and stopped. Curious, she lifted Bodie's hat from where it rested on a chair.

Maebelle slapped her hand smartly. "Go along, Tad. You follow him, Emma. Honest to heaven, that child is the picking-up-est thing I ever knew. Born bank robber, I guess, if she was a boy."

"Where the hell's Lu?" Bodie wanted to know.

"Don't get your dander up, George," Maebelle said quickly. "I'll go see."

She went to the bottom of the staircase and bawled the girl's name several times. A girlish "Coming!" echoed from somewhere above. A knock sounded at the door and Maebelle opened it. She talked with the man for a moment, and then his heavy boots clomped up the stairway. As she returned to the parlor Bodie looked at the clock.

"Quarter to eleven, Maebelle. An hour and fifteen minutes before I get me number twelve." He chuckled.

Maebelle busied herself straightening a doily on the sofa, not looking at him.

Bodie helped himself to still another drink, and swallowed it hastily. "Don't worry about the whiskey," he said over his shoulder. "I'm even faster when I got an edge on."

Light footsteps sounded on the stair. Bodie turned as the girl Lu came into the room. She ran to Bodie and kissed him, throwing her arms around his neck. She was young beneath the shiny hardness of her face. Her lips were heavily painted, and her white breast above the gown smelled of dusting powder.

"Oh, George, I'm glad you got here."

"I came just to see you, honey. Two hundred miles." His arm crept around her waist, his hand touched her breast. He kissed her lightly.

"Well, I'm not running this for charity, you know," Maebelle said.

"I'll settle up," Bodie replied. "Don't worry. Right now though . . ."

He and Lu began to walk toward the stairway.

Another knock came at the door. Maebelle went to

open it, and Bodie heard a voice say out of the frosty dark, "Evening, Miz Tait. Lu here?"

Bodie dropped his arm.

Maebelle started to protest, but the man came on into the lighted parlor. The cowboy was thin. His cheeks were red from wind and liquor, and he blinked at Bodie, with suspicion. Lu gaped at the floor, flustered.

"Hello, Lu. Did you forgit I was comin' tonight?"

"Maybe she did forget," Bodie said. "She's busy."

"Come on, Fred," Maebelle said urgently. She pulled the cowboy's arm. "I know Bertha'd be glad to see you."

"Bertha, hell," the cowboy complained. "I rode in sixty miles, like I do every month, just to see Lu. It's all set up." He stepped forward and grabbed Lu's wrist. Bodie's fingers touched leather, like a caress.

"You're out of luck, friend," Bodie said. "I told you Lu's busy tonight."

"Like hell," the cowboy insisted, pulling Lu. "Come on, sweetie. I come sixty miles, and it's mighty cold. . . ."

"Get your hands off her," Bodie said.

Lu jerked away, retreated and stared, round-eyed, like a worn doll, pretty but empty.

"Don't you prod me," the cowboy said, weaving a little. His blue eyes snapped in the lamplight. "Who are you, anyway, acting so big? The governor or somebody?"

"I'm George Bodie. Didn't you hear about me tonight?"

"George Bo . . ."

The cowboy's eyes whipped frantically to the side. He licked his lips and his hand crawled down toward the hem of his jacket.

"Not in here, George, for God's sakes," Maebelle protested.

"Keep out of it," Bodie said softly. His eyes had a hard, predatory shine. "Now, mister cowboy, you got anything more to say about not bein' satisfied with Bertha?"

The cowboy looked at Lu. Bodie and Maebelle could read his face easily: fear clawed, and fought with the idea of what would happen if he backed down before Lu.

His sharp, scrawny-red Adam's apple bobbed.

His hand dropped.

Bodie's eyes glistened as the Navy cleared and roared.

The cowboy's gun slipped out of his fingers unfired. He dropped to his knees, cursed, shut his eyes, bleeding from the chest. Then he pitched forward and lay coughing. In a few seconds the coughing had stopped.

Bodie smiled easily and put the Navy away.

"One dozen," he said, like a man uttering a benediction.

"You damned fool," Maebelle raged. "Abraham! Abraham!" she shouted. "Get yourself in here."

In a moment an old arthritic black man hobbled into the room from the back of the house.

"Get that body out of here. Take the rig and dump him on the edge of town. Jump to it."

Abraham began laboriously dragging the corpse out of the parlor by the rear door. Boots, then feminine titters, sounded on the stairs.

Maebelle held down her rage, whirled and stalked into the hall.

"It's all right, folks," she said, vainly trying to block the view. People craned forward on the steps.

Abraham didn't move fast enough. "Nothing's happened," Maebelle insisted. "The man's just hurt a little. Just a friendly argument."

"He's dead," a reedy male voice said. "Any fool kin see that."

Bodie stood in the doorway, his arm around Lu once more, complacently smirking at the confusion of male and female bodies at the bottom of the stairs. He heard his name whispered.

The thin voice popped up, "I'm getting out of here, Maebelle. This is too much for my blood." A spindly shape darted toward the door.

"Now wait a minute, Hiram," Maebelle protested.

The door slammed on the breath of chill air from the street.

Maebelle walked back toward Bodie, her eyes angry. "Now you've done it for fair. That yellow pipsqueak will spread it all over town that George Bodie just killed a man in my house."

"Let him," Bodie said. He glanced back at the clock. "In an hour I got an engagement with the marshal anyway. But that's in an hour."

Lu snuggled against him as he started up the stairs. The crowd parted respectfully. Maebelle scratched her head desperately, then spoke up in a voice that had a false boom to it:

"Come on into the parlor, folks. I'll pour a drink for those with bad nerves."

Abraham had removed the body, but she still noticed a greasy black stain on the carpet. Her eyes flew to the clock, which ticked steadily.

Bodie awoke suddenly, chilly in the dark room. His hand shot out for the Navy, but drew back when he recognized the boy Tad in the thin line of lamplight falling through the open door. He yawned and rolled over. Lu had gone, and he had dozed.

"What is it, boy?" he asked.

"Mr. Wyman's in the street, asking for you."

Bodie swung his legs off the bed, laughed, and lit the lamp. The holster hung on the bedpost, with the Colt in it.

"What time is it?" Bodie wanted to know.

"Quarter of twelve. Mr. Wyman hasn't got his shotgun. Said he wanted to talk to you about something."

Bodie frowned. "What sort of an hombre is this Mr. Wyman? Would he be hiding a gun on him?"

The boy shook his head. "He belongs to the Methodist Church. Everybody says he's real honest," the boy answered, pronouncing the last word with faint suspicion.

Bodie's eyes slitted down in the lamplight. Then he stood, scratched his belly and laughed. "I imagine it wouldn't do no harm to talk to the marshal. And let him know what's going to happen to him."

Bodie drew on his shirt, pants, and boots. He pointed to the holster on the bedpost. "I'll come back for that, if this marshal still wants to hold me to the midnight deadline. Thanks for telling me, boy."

He went out of the room and down the stairs, a smile of anticipation on his face.

The house was strangely quiet. No one was in the parlor. But Bodie had a good idea that Maebelle, and others, would be watching from half a dozen darkened windows. Bodie put his hand on the doorknob, pulled, and stepped out into the biting air.

Wyman stood three feet from the hitchrack.

He had both hands raised to his face, one holding a flaring match, the other shielding it from the wind as he lit his pipe. Bodie recognized the gesture for what it was: a means of showing that the town marshal kept his word. Wyman flicked the match away and the bowl of the pipe glowed.

Bodie walked forward and leaned on the hitchrack, grinning. The cold air stung his cheeks. Across the way, at Aunt Gert's, a girl in a spangled green dress drank from a whiskey bottle behind a window.

"You Wyman?"

"That's right."

"Well, I'm Bodie. Speak your piece."

Bodie saw a slender man, thirty, with a high-crowned hat, fur-collared coat, and drooping mustache. His face was pale in the starlight.

"I started out to see if I could talk you into leaving town," Wyman said slowly. "I figure I don't want to kill anybody in my job if I don't have to."

"I'll say you got a nerve, marshal," Bodie said, laughter in his words. "Ain't you scared? I got me my dozenth man tonight."

"I know."

"You still want to talk me into riding without a fight?"

Wyman shook his head. "I said that's why I came, why I started out. On the way I heard about the killing. Hiram Riggs ran through the streets yelling his head off about it. I can't let you go now. But I can ask you to come along without a fight. Otherwise you might wind up dead, Bodie."

"I doubt it, marshal. I just purely doubt that."

Bodie scratched the growth of whiskers along the line of his jaw. He lounged easily, but he saw Wyman shift his feet as the rasp-rasp of the scratching sounded loudly in the night street.

"You know, you didn't answer my question about being scared."

"Of course I am, if that makes you feel better," Wyman said, without malice.

"Nobody ever told me that before, marshal. Of course most didn't have time."

"Why should I lie? I'm not a professional."

"Then why are you in the job, marshal? I'm sort of curious."

"I don't know. People figured I'd try, I imagine." Sharply he raised his heel and knocked glimmering sparks from his pipe. "Hell, I'm not here to explain to you why I don't want to fight. I'm telling you I will, if you won't come with me."

Bodie hesitated, tasting the moment like good liquor. "Now, marshal, did you honestly think when you walked over here that you'd get me to give up?"

Starlight shone in Wyman's bleak eyes for a moment.

"No."

"Then why don't you go on home to bed? You haven't got a chance."

In a way Bodie admired the marshal's cheek, fool though he was.

Wyman turned his head slightly, indicating the opposite side of the street. For the first time Bodie noticed a shadowy rider on one of the horses at Aunt Gert's rack.

"When I come, Bodie, I'll have my deputy. He carries a shotgun too."

Bodie scowled into the night, then stepped down off the sidewalk, trembling with anger.

"That's not a very square shake, marshal."

"Don't talk to me about square shakes. I knew that cowboy you shot. He couldn't have matched you with a gun. And there've been others. If you're trying to tell me two against one isn't fair, all I've got to say is, if I had a big cat killing my beef, I wouldn't worry whether I had two or twenty men after him." Hardness edged Wyman's words now. "I don't worry about how I kill an animal, Bodie. If you'd given that cowboy a chance, maybe I'd feel different. But I've got to take you one way or another. You wrecked the square shake, not me."

Bodie's fingers crawled along the hip of his jeans. "Can't do it by yourself?" he said contemptuously.

"I won't do it by myself."

"Why not? You can't trust your own gun?"

"Maybe that's where you made your mistake, Bodie. I'd rather trust another man than a gun."

"I don't need nobody or nothing but my gun. I never have," Bodie said softly. "Where's your shotgun, marshal?"

Wyman nodded toward the silent deputy on the horse.

"He's got it."

"I'll put my gun up against you two," Bodie said with seething savagery. "You just wait."

Bodie started back for the entrance, and from the shadows before Aunt Gert's came a sharp voice calling:

"He might run out the back, Dale."

And Wyman's answer, "No, he won't . . ." was cut off by Bodie's vicious slam of the door.

Maebelle stuck her head out of the parlor as he bounded up the stairs, his teeth tight together and a thick angry knot in his belly. He had murder on his face.

He stomped into the bedroom, was halfway across, when the sight of the bedpost in the lamplight registered on his mind.

His holster—and the Navy—were gone.

Bodie crashed back against the wall, a strangled cry choking up out of his throat, his eyes frantically searching the room.

He lunged forward and ripped away the bed-clothes. He pulled the scarred chest from the wall, threw the empty drawers on the floor, then over-turned the chest with a curse and a crash. He raised the window, and the glass whined faintly.

He stood staring out for a moment at the collection of star-washed shanties stretching down the hill be-hind the house. Then he sat down on the edge of the bed, laced his fingers together. His shoulders began to tremble.

He let out a string of obscenities like whimpers, his eyes wide. He jumped to his feet and began to tear at the mattress cover. Then he stopped again, shaking.

He felt Wyman laughing at him, and he heard Wy-man's words once more. Black unreason boiled up through him, making him tremble all the harder. With an animal growl he ran out of the room, stopped in the hall, and looked frantically up and down.

He kicked in the door across the room. The girl shrieked softly, her hand darting for the coverlet.

"What the hell, amigo . . ." began the man, half-timidly.

Like an animal in a trap, Bodie scanned the room, turned and went racing down the staircase. He breathed hard. His chest hurt. He felt a sick cold in his stomach like he'd never known before. Hearing his heavy tread, Maebelle came out of the parlor. Before she could speak, he threw her against the wall and held her. Words caught in her throat when she saw his face.

"Where is it?" he yelled. "Where's my Navy?" His voice went keening up on a shrill note. "Tell me where it is, Maebelle, or I'll kill you!"

"George, George . . . Lord, I don't know," she protested, frightened, writhing under his hands.

He hit her, slamming her head against the wall, turning her face toward the top of the stairs. She choked. The fingers of one hand twitched feebly against the wall, the nails pecking a signal on the wallpaper.

"Emma . . . ," she said.

She sagged as he released her. He cleared the stairs in threes to where the round-eyed, curious little girl stood at the landing in her nightdress, shuffling slowly forward as if to find the commotion, and holding the Navy in one hand, upside-down, by the grip, while her other finger ran along the barrel, feeling the metal. Bodie tore it away from her and struck her across the face with the barrel.

Then he turned, lunging down the stairs again, muttering and cursing and smiling, past Maebelle. She watched him with a look of madness creeping across her face.

At the top of the staircase, the girl Emma, as if accustomed to such treatment, picked herself up and started down, dragging the leather holster she had picked up near the baseboard. She came down a step at a time, the welt on her cheek angry red but her eyes still childish and round. . . .

Bodie peered through the curtains.

He could see Wyman and his deputy in the center of the street, waiting, their shotguns shiny in the starlight. He had never wanted to . kill any men so badly before.

He snatched the door open, slipped through, and flattened his back against the wall, the Navy rising with its old, smooth feel, and a hot red laugh on his lips as he squeezed.

Wyman stepped forward, feet planted wide, and the shotgun flowered red in the night.

Then the deputy fired. Bodie felt a murderous weight against his chest.

The Navy clattered on the plank sidewalk, unfired.

Bodie fell across the hitchrack, his stomach warm and bleeding, the shape of Wyman coming toward him but growing dimmer each second. Bodie felt for the Navy as he slipped to a prone position, and one short shriek of betrayal came tearing off his lips.

Wyman pushed back his hat and cradled the shotgun in the crook of his arm.

Across the street window blinds flew up, and then the windows themselves, clattering.

Maebelle stuck her head out the front door.

Lu came down the stairs, crying and hugging a shabby dressing gown to her breasts, bumping the girl Emma.

With round, curious eyes, Emma righted herself, drawn by the sound of the shots.

She started down more rapidly, one step at a time, toward the voices there on the wintry porch, and as she hurried, first the holster slipped from her fingers and then the bright shells from the other tiny, white, curious hand. They fell, and Emma worked her way purposefully down to the next step, leaving the playthings forgotten on the garish, somewhat faded carpet.

# Dutchman

"Willi, someone's out there," his wife whispered, in German. "Willi?"

"Nah, nobody," he said, half awake in the dark of the cramped bedroom. "Go back to sleep." He grumbled it, in English, because he resented her clinging to the old ways; he was an American, born and bred.

He pounded the starched bolster to make a better nook for his head. With his back to Elsa he heard her tense raspy breathing, and then he heard their oldest daughter, Annemarie, sixteen, and subject to nervous spells, ask something of her sister Trudi in a high anxious voice.

And then he heard the front gate squeak.

"There, there," Elsa said, pummeling his shoulder, to be sure he was awake and responsive. Willi rolled onto his back with a groan, a sudden dryness coating the inside of his mouth. He heard them, definitely, in the dark outside the open window. Several men; boots grinding on his carefully raked gravel walk.

"Must be somebody got the wrong house," he whispered.

"Wrong house? That many? You know why they're here. Do something, Willi."

He was a peaceful man. What he wanted to do was stay in bed. Of course he couldn't, and for more reasons than the immediate one. When Elsa urged him to do something, a familiar thought flashed into his head. A thought mingling defiance and family loyalty. *My father didn't run. I must not run, ever. . . .*

For years after the great Civil War, when the reputation of the Eleventh Corps was still clouded, his father had insisted, in long harangues in the native tongue, that it was calumny; that only a few of the troops scornfully called Dutchmen by their fellows had run when Stonewall struck his surprise hammer-blow at the Union flank at Chancellorsville. *"They were brave men. They bled like others. The majority did not run. I did not run!"*

"Aalen?" a voice called from the yard. Annemarie heard it and began to cry hysterically; her younger sister calmly comforted her. "Aalen, you got company out here."

Willi bit down on his lower lip. He was almost certain he knew the voice. It belonged to the lout who swamped floors for his biggest customer. So some of the best people in town condoned this. The realization was depressing.

Elsa clutched his arm. He shook her off. He swung his legs out of bed, stood, and tightened the draw-string of his homemade flannel sleeping drawers. He crept barefoot to the window and knelt there.

The bedroom was located on the north side of the house. The window opened on the yard. He saw shadow figures in the yard, against the distant twinkle of lanterns on the oil derricks. Three, four—no, five men. He saw a gun barrel gleam.

"What do you want with me?" he called. "Don't come around here bothering my family at night."

"We'll come anytime we please, you goddamn traitor," another man said, the voice issuing from the blackness under the broad brim of his hat. "You better pack up your brood and haul out. President Wilson declared war day before yesterday, your kind ain't welcome around here any more."

Willi grabbed the sill with both hands and leaned out, and the starlight fell pale on his broad brow and fair hair. He was forty-two, lean from constant hard work, with bright blue eyes and a striking mustache and goatee on an otherwise unremarkable face.

"You get out of here and leave us alone. I'm a good American. *Mein vater*—" In his nervous excitement he erred into German but quickly corrected. "—he fought for the liberty of this land not six months after he stepped off the boat. He was one of the first recruits in Blenker's Eighth New York. He campaigned with General Frémont in western Virginia. He was with fighting Joe Hooker, and General Sigel, in the Army of the Potomac . . ."

"Who the fuck cares about any of that?" the first voice, the familiar one, interrupted. Willi pointed angrily.

"I know you, Moss Eames. I know you."

His customer's swamper, biggest of the shadow-figures, told him to do something filthy. Willi heard the others talking, joshing—and then he heard liquid slosh in a container. Someone was spilling liquid all over the neat picket fence he'd built by hand. They were pouring kerosene on his fence, and his bougainvillea. "Damn you, stop," he shouted, dimly aware of Annemarie wailing in her bedroom. Then came the spurt of a match.

Willi watched it sail in a low arc and ignite the bougainvillea with a noisy explosion. Elsa burrowed in bed and covered her head. Annemarie shrieked like a mad person, and he heard Trudi—"Oh, papa, I can't stop her"—and then the other, younger ones in their rooms, calling out, frightened . . .

*My father did not run. I will not run. . . .* Willi bruised his shins getting out the window. A rock in the lawn gouged his bare sole. He charged them with fists up, cursing them—German again. Moss Eames pushed down a part of the fence and ran and the others followed, scattering to the nearby alleys because some lights were already being turned on by alarmed neighbors.

Bare-chested and sweating, Willi watched his precious vines blaze, and the flames leaping along the fence. In the distance, the bell of the Planet Volunteer Fire Brigade began to ring, but they would be too late. He dashed back into the house. He ignored Elsa, who was asking questions, because Annemarie, big and buxom as a grown woman, was wailing like a lost infant, clutching to the bosom of her nightdress her little volume of Goethe, as though it had some holy power to save her. Willi cradled his poor unnerved daughter in his arms and soothed her with wordless syllables while the other five children crowded around, wide-eyed. He heard the fire engine horses approach at the gallop, and smelled the burning fence. He had not run, but it struck him that standing fast had done little good.

In fact, none.

No one had appetite for breakfast, and usually breakfast in the household of Wilhelm Karl Aalen was a gastronomic event—in quantity if not quality.

This morning the quantity was there, but no heartiness. Elsa looked wan as she served him his usual plate of crisply fried mush, hard fried eggs, homemade wurst, fried potatoes, biscuits, and a tall stein of dark beer. This morning, the pleasures of a solid nourishing breakfast were worlds away from Willi's thoughts.

He fiddled with his fork, pushing a piece of mush back and forth on his plate; back and forth. Elsa shooed the children out—Annemarie's hair was still uncombed and tangly, and she had a vague glassy look in her bright blue eyes. She was a disturbed young woman; very fragile. He could get no useful advice from the family doctor, and he feared for Annemarie's later life.

Elsa sat with her cup of coffee untouched. She clasped her hands, rubbing them together, a papery sound. Willi flung her a look.

"Say it." His English was fine; no trace of accent.

"You know why they came, Willi. It's bound to get worse. Day before yesterday, at the market, I heard people discussing the feeling about Germans. Margaret Polhaus told me she and Heinz will put their house up for sale this week."

"Elsa," he said, straining for patience, "let me explain something. I am American, you are American— this is April, 1917, and not the dark ages. The United States Congress declared war on Germany and Kaiser Bill, not other Americans. Planet is our home. Nobody is going to push us out. Nobody is going to make me ashamed of what I am."

"But feeling is running so high—"

And so it was, all over the country. It was blind emotion, and cruel. Over in Bakersfield, Heini Holstmann's little dachshund, Fritzi, had been stolen out of Heini's side yard by four small boys. The dog was repeatedly cut with pocket knives, then tied to a tree with wire, doused with kerosene, and burned to death.

"*My* feeling is running high," Willi exclaimed, hitting a fist on the table so hard his plate danced. "My father fought almost four years with the Union Army. He fought despite being spat on and joked about as a Dutchman. He fought even though he could speak only a few words of English. He fought to deliver his new homeland from the evil of slavery and the damn wicked Southerners—he survived the revolution of 1848, and he took words like *liberty* and *democracy* very seriously. So did his comrades. They were proud of their uniform. 'I fights mit Sigel!' It was a proud statement . . ."

But there was less pride when O. O. Howard took over the Eleventh Corps after Sigel fell ill. Less pride when Jackson made his surprise thrust, and certain men of the so-called German Corps hacked the straps of their knapsacks in two so they could unburden themselves and run faster. Flying Dutchmen, the public called them.

*"But I did not run!"* his father insisted forever afterward. It imposed a special burden, which Willi felt with increasing heaviness this morning.

He saw Elsa's worried, drawn expression. He cupped his hand over hers, patting and squeezing. "Please understand my feelings. Over two hundred thousand from the homeland fought for the Union. My papa took a wound that nearly claimed his life. That must not be forgotten. I won't allow it to be forgotten. If we pay no attention—go about our business—refuse to be intimidated—we'll be all right."

"But Willi . . ."

"No," he said, doggedly. "No more discussion. Please see if you can do something about Annemarie's state. I'm going to get dressed and go down to the brewery as usual."

The small town of Planet, California, lay in the low hills along the Kern River on the eastern edge of the San Joaquin Valley. In just a few years it had become the center of a thriving region of oil fields. The roughnecks who worked on the rigs were a noisy, rowdy lot, but generally not threatening; at least not to the settled citizens who lived on several residential streets on Planet's west side. Here Willi Aalen and his family lived.

It was a half mile walk to the downtown from his heavily-mortgaged house with its gingerbread porch. He walked to work every morning, straight along to Kern Avenue, and thence around the corner a half block on B Street to the Planet Brewery, home of Planet Beer ("Best in the Universe"). This morning the sun was up in a cloudless sky, the air warm and typically dry. Willi could almost imagine that Moss Eames and the others had not come in the night; had not burned his picket fence and killed his bougainvillea. Of course there was evidence of the war on a number of porches along his route. Flags had been hung out in iron brackets; and when he reached Kern Avenue, he saw that many of the small shops displayed similar signs of patriotism. The entire second floor veranda of the Planet House was swagged with bunting.

Still, reminders of the newly declared war didn't trouble him so much in the sunshine. As a German-American—a hyphenate, the politicians and the papers called them—he believed steadfastly in his own good citizenship. He wasn't one of those men of dubious honor who had promoted neutrality openly—or secretly, like the rich Milwaukee brewers whose clandestine funding of pro-German "peace" groups had caused a scandal and made German-Americans hated all the more.

No. Willi wasn't that kind. And he'd always had faith in the decency of people, especially those of his adopted country, and he wanted very much to be part of and reflect that decent Americanism. So he tried to reflect it this morning, walking with a brisk, confident stride, and calling a greeting to a child of a neighbor. He was neatly turned out, as always, in a proper worsted suit, starched shirt with high collar, fedora, cane with a gold plated knob. His mustache flowed down in luxuriant curves, ending in finely waxed points. His goatee was equally neat. He was the picture of a good citizen. Washing and dressing had restored his spirits from the outside in.

Six mornings a week, it was his habit to stop off at Bloodworthy's Tonsorial for a shave and trim. He did so again this morning. Elmer Bloodworthy had a customer in the chair; his older brother Loy, the police chief.

"Good morning, Loy, Elmer," Willi said, seating himself and reaching for a copy of the Bakersfield paper.

Elmer merely nodded. Loy rolled his head over toward Willi and Elmer withheld the razor from Loy's lathered face while Loy said, "Heard you had some trouble last night. I'll send Newt Parker out to take a look." Willi realized that Loy sounded unenthusiastic.

"No need," Willi said, waving. "Just some hooligans—a little property damage. Minor." He folded the paper open and smiled. "Looks like you won't be too long, Elmer."

Elmer stopped the straight razor. Loy regarded Willi with a straight look, then straightened his head on the headrest and once again considered the pattern in the pressed tin ceiling. Elmer said, "Willi, I can't take care of you this morning. I'm closing up soon as I finish with Loy."

"Oh?" Willi said, coolly. "Why is that?"

"I got some tooth trouble. Got to go over and see Doc Meeley."

"Tooth trouble? You?" Willi said with a half-laugh, closing the paper and folding it along its original creases and using another smile to hide the little cold flutter of his heart.

"Ain't that what I said? Can't you understand English, Willi?"

"Yes, of course," Willi said, affronted; he reddened.

"Then there's no point your hanging around, is there?" Elmer said.

"No, I suppose not. I'll come again tomorrow."

Elmer concentrated on shaving his brother.

Willi clapped his hat on his head. "Good morning, Elmer—Loy." He walked out, noisily, to show his unhappiness. Elmer Bloodworthy hadn't had tooth trouble since he exchanged his regular teeth for a complete false set three years ago; he bragged about how good they were.

Just outside, he remembered something. Loy and Elmer Bloodworthy's cousin March, who lived up in Oakland, had a boy in the merchant marine. The boy had been aboard the English freighter *Wessex* when a German submarine torpedoed her in a neutral zone. Several bodies had never been recovered, including that of March Bloodworthy's boy.

Willi straightened his hat brim and studied all the red, white and blue decorations along the avenue. He supposed he shouldn't be too angry with Loy and Elmer over *their* anger just now. But he was.

At the corner of Kern and B, as a creaking wagon loaded with driller's pipe passed by, and then a puttering Oldsmobile runabout, Willi looked back at the barber shop. He saw Elmer and Loy regarding him from the doorway like a pair of cigar store Indians. Elmer showed no signs of closing up.

Willi swore under his breath, took a tight grip on his stick, and went on.

He said to himself that he mustn't blow things out of proportion. What had happened at the Tonsorial was an annoyance, but only that. The Bloodworthy brothers and all the rest of the hot heads would get over their new war fervor and life would settle down again. No doubt everyone in Planet was still in shock over the news; he was, after Mr. Wilson's many and frequent declarations that the U.S. shouldn't intervene in the foreign war.

All that had changed two days ago—April 6, 1917—when Congress passed the president's war resolution. The German militarists had refused to behave in a civilized manner. They'd allowed their submarines to continue raiding neutral ships, and now the Yanks were going over. As a good American, Willi intended to support Wilson's decision, and the war effort, one hundred percent.

An ambrosial scent wafted to him as he walked along B Street. The scent was in his bones, and had been since he was a boy, and he tagged after his father in the small Cincinnati brewery where ex-Corporal Aalen had found a job after the war. Willi had grown up with beer-lovers and brewers. He knew the brewing process intimately by the time he was twelve.

In '93, Willi had buried his father beside two cousins in the midst of many friends in the German cemetery in Cincinnati. Eighteen years old, Willi then launched out for the West with his new wife Elsa, who was not as smitten as he was with the glowing phrases and promises in Willi's second-hand copy of a Charles Nordhoff book promoting life and residence in California.

With savings and a bank loan, Willi had opened the Planet Brewery in 1908. The brewery occupied an entire half a block behind a board fence with a wooden gate in it, and a gaudy sign above. *PLANET BREWERY of California.* On the sign, various painted planets enshrouded in gas or flame revolved around a large foaming stein floating in starry space. Willi had designed the sign personally.

His young apprentice, Reinhard, was feeding his caged canary when Willi walked in the office and deposited his hat and stick. The smell of the fermenting beer in the vats out in the brewhouse was thick and delicious. Reinhard seemed nervous. He shot his employer a peculiar, almost apologetic look.

"My young friend," Willi said, lapsing into German, "has someone died, perhaps?"

"Very nearly, Mr. Aalen," Reinhard said. "Mr. Finnerman telephoned twenty minutes ago. He doesn't want me to deliver anything today."

"But it's his regular day," Willi said, puzzled. The Derrick was Planet's largest and most profitable saloon-cum-restaurant, over on Kern. "He wants to reschedule for tomorrow for some reason?"

"Not tomorrow either." Reinhard's canary cocked its head on its perch. Usually obnoxiously fervent about singing, this morning the bird was silent. "What he said, Mr. Aalen—he said he'd get his beer elsewhere from now on."

Willi paled, then sank down on the squeaky swivel chair at his desk. Sadly, the new development didn't surprise him. Nevertheless, his emotional reaction was strong.

"He didn't offer any reason for his decision, I suppose?"

"Well, yes he did," said the ingenuous Reinhard, who had huge muscles but little subtlety. "He said that we were at war now, and the drillers and tool-dressers at his place wouldn't want to drink kraut beer, or give one cent to krauts for making it."

"Damn him," Willi said, his cheeks bright pink suddenly. The points of his mustache quivered. "Damn them all. My father fought for America. He took a Minié ball and shed his blood—we are just as good citizens as James Finnerman and his crowd of oil-soaked hooligans. Wait here. I will set this right before it goes any farther."

"Why, Jim? My beer is superior, how many times have you told me that? It's always delivered on time, fresh. The price is better than the brewery in Bakersfield can give you—"

"You read newspapers, don't you?" James Finnerman responded with an exhausted sigh. He was a bald horse-jawed man who inexplicably reminded Willi of a mortician, a very sad mortician. "You're a Dutchman, Willi—"

"No! Nonsense! Dutchmen come from the Netherlands, not Germany."

"I don't care, to folks around here you're a Dutchman. Buying beer from a Dutchman when there's a war on could be bad for my business. Hell, being a Dutchman could be bad for your own health in a town this small." He paused. "I hear you got some fence and flowers to replace."

"*Ja*, plenty," Willi retorted, standing stiff as a Prussian drill sergeant. He was overwhelmed by the sudden, stupid, seemingly unstoppable tide of antagonism. When the *Lusitania* went down, someone had painted *KRAUT SHIT* on his galvanized mailbox, but he'd painted it over that same morning and figured it was merely a single incident, never to be repeated.

Two hundred thousand Germans or more had mustered for the Union Army—immigrants, mostly—and the roster of their commanders were enshrined in communal memory. Alexander Schimmelfennig and von Steinwehr . . . von Gilsa and the honorable Carl Schurz. Many of those who fought—a few, even, on the damned Rebel side—left children who had grown up as decent, loyal citizens. How many of those were facing this kind of hostility? Thousands? Hundreds of thousands? *Gröss Gott*, it was unbearably depressing.

Finnerman covered his embarrassment by flipping open a cigar box. Willi caught his attention by saying, "Finnerman," sharply. "You are telling me you're cutting off my business, like that?" He snapped his fingers.

"Look, I regret it, don't think I don't. You're an honest man, Willi, and a fine brewer. But I've got to think of my own situation. I don't want a flood of red ink because I'm doing business with a Dutchman."

"Will you please stop saying—?" But Finnerman ignored the interruption:

"I don't want a mob breaking in here some night and smashing up all my furniture and fixtures. I can't afford it."

"But you can afford to treat me dishonorably," Willi exclaimed. "You can afford to insult me." For the first time, Finnerman's eyes flickered unpleasantly.

"I wish you wouldn't yell like that, Willi. I try to be fair in business, and a Christian—" Finnerman headed the local Knights of Columbus chapter, and took pride in it. "—but once I explain how things are, I expect you to honor the explanation and not cause me trouble."

"How can I do that when you're simply giving in to blind fear and stupidity?" The last word brought high color to Finnerman's pasty face. Willi heard the office door open behind him. He had an uneasy sense of who was there. "Of all people, Jim, you should not—you're Irish. Don't you remember what they did to Irish in America not so long ago? 'No dogs or Irish.' 'No Irish need apply.' 'Irish will be arrested for vagrancy.' The Irish were scum, dirt, treated like beasts—your people were just the same as me, only wanting to be good Americans—"

"Spare me all the speechifying, Willi," Finnerman sighed. "Maybe there's something in it, but there's war on, and I've got to pay attention to that, and to this." He slapped the open page on an account book. "Three customers told me last night they wouldn't keep coming to the Derrick if I served your beer. I do business with you, I'll be drowning in red ink."

Willi Aalen had not been entirely Americanized. There was still in him a Germanic side that doted on dry pot roast and boiled potatoes and *hasenpfeffer* in season; on work correctly, not to say fussily done; and there was an extra stubbornness that lingered because of Chancellorsville. *My father did not run. I will not . . .*

Willi's spine stiffened. He put on his fedora and glared at Finnerman. "Jim, I will not be dismissed like this."

"Sorry, I've got no more time to argue with—"

Willi leaped to the side of the desk. "Jim, I demand that you treat me fairly." Finnerman started to struggle. "Fairly and decently, like any other—"

"Let go of my arm," Finnerman cried, writhing in his chair. "Moss, make him let go of my arm."

"Sure, Mr. Finnerman," said young Moss Eames, the swamper and sometime bouncer of the Derrick. It was Eames whom Willi had heard entering a few moments ago. Eames, who couldn't read or write, but who didn't need those skills because his shoulders were half as wide as an ox yoke, and whose hands resembled cantaloupes when he fisted them. He and Willi had never gotten along—and now there was last night between them . . .

"Take your damn hands off him," Moss Eames said, grabbing Willi from behind.

The grip of those hands broke Willi's composure altogether. He wrenched free of Moss Eames, dodged by and snatched his gold-knobbed cane from the chair where he'd left it. With a smarmy smile of pleasure, Moss Eames shambled at him but Willi quickly reversed the cane and jabbed Moss Eames's stained lumberjack shirt with the big knob. The jabs were quick, and hard, three of them. Moss Eames dropped his cantaloupe fists to his sides, unable to believe that this hot-eyed man half his size would dare stand up to him.

Willi's chin came up and he snarled at Moss Eames as if the swamper were a new army recruit. "You witless idiot. I heard you outside my house in the dark, you and your gorilla friends. You come near my house again, I'll horsewhip you, or worse. Now stand aside."

Moss Eames lowered his head, blinking and trying to decide how best to dismember the visitor. Willi's lips puffed out in a tight, determined way and he slashed Moss Eames across the face with the cane's ferrule.

"Get out of my way."

"Do as he says," Finnerman ordered.

The stick had left a red mark. Moss Eames rubbed

it as he stepped back, watching with malevolent eyes while Willi marched out.

"I'll get him," Moss Eames muttered.

"No you won't," Finnerman snapped. "Go downstairs and get to work."

Two evenings later, under a mellow sky full of long thin lavender clouds, Annemarie Aalen came home from school the back way. It was late, with shadows lengthening; she'd stayed an extra hour for glee club practice. They were rehearsing a beautifully sweet war song, "A Long Way to Tipperary." One of the girls in the alto section had asked her, rather nastily, whether she could suggest any songs in German.

Annemarie had almost burst out crying, but walking home in the soft pleasant shadows of twilight rescued her spirits. She had three books tied in a leather strap, and she was anxious to slip out of her tight dress and bathe her face.

She was walking along about a block from the house, paying little attention, when a big-shouldered young man stepped out from behind a shed. He had a mass of curly hair and wore a filthy lumberjack shirt. Annemarie shrieked softly as he jumped in front of her and gripped her wrist.

"Hello, frowline. Out by yourself?"

"Let go, please . . ." She started to struggle.

"Now wait, I just want to show you something." His free hand dropped; fly buttons popped open. Annemarie's eyes grew huge, reflecting the cool orange light of the sky. "You krauts like weenie-wursts, don't you? Here's a weenie-wurst you can bite." He pulled it all the way out and shook it, touching her skirt.

Annemarie screamed and flung herself back, incapable of rational thought. She screamed and kept on screaming, hitting him with her books, kicking him— "Hey, hey, for Christ's sake, you kraut bitch!"—and in order to escape, he had to form a huge fist and bash her twice in the side of the head.

Annemarie sprawled in the alley. A woman stepped onto her back porch, hidden by the shed, and called out, "What is going on out there?" The burly young man turned and fled, stuffing his member back in his pants and struggling with the buttons as he dashed out of sight.

On the ground, lying half in a puddle of mud, Annemarie screamed uncontrollably. The woman ran out, identified her, and telephoned the Aalen house. Annemarie was still sobbing and wailing when Elsa arrived, running and out of breath. Annemarie was still moaning and crying when the family doctor drove up at half past six and forced two teaspoons of an opiate syrup into her mouth; she spit out most of it.

Willi didn't sleep at all that night. He held Annemarie in his arms for a long period, rocking back and forth, or he sat beside her bed, crying harder than she did. He was ashamed of his tears, and unable to stop them.

It was morning before she was calm enough to give her father a description of the molester. As soon as she did, Willi took his cane and went downtown.

"Where is he? Where is the lout?" Willi demanded.

Finnerman laughed nervously; he couldn't believe his red-faced caller was serious. "Willi, what the hell's going on? You don't want to butt heads with Moss, he's twice your size . . ."

Willi rapped the desk with his cane. "Tell me, Jim.

Where do I find him? *Verfluchene Abfall* . . . he's going
to pay."

"For what?" Finnerman asked with false in-
nocence.

"For molesting my daughter Annemarie," Willi
shouted. "For surprising her in the alley near my
house and exposing his most private parts to her.
She is a nervous high-strung girl. Weeping . . . half
crazy because of what he did. Christ knows she may
never get over it." Willi was unconsciously slapping
the cane into his free hand. "He won't, either."

"Jesus and Mary," Finnerman whispered, crossing
himself. "Moss works late in the saloon, I let him
sleep late, I expect he's still snoring out in the shed.
Rear of the yard," he added with a thumb hooked
at the window. But Willi was already thundering
down the rear stairs.

He crossed the trash-strewn yard and kicked at a
grimy mongrel dancing around his pant legs. He was
almost totally unaware of his surroundings, seeing
instead an image of a soldier in Union blue charging
through a smoking wood with a flashing bayonet
upraised. The soldier was his father . . .

"What 'n hell—?" Moss Eames muttered a moment
after Willi kicked open the slatted door. The burly
young man lay on a pallet of old smelly blankets,
and now he struggled up on his elbows, squinting
until he identified the person within the shadow in
the doorway. A smarmy smile oozed over his mouth.
"You dumb heine, what are you doing in here? You
made a big mist—"

Willi slashed the cane down, holding it tight by the
ferrule. This time the knob broke the skin on Moss
Eames's brow. Blood ran. Moss cursed and thrashed,
trying for a hold on Willi's leg. Willi stamped his

crotch, and from then on Moss, despite his size and power, never had a chance.

Cries from the shed brought Finnerman and his morning barkeep on the run. They pounded and shouted at the shed door.

"Keep out, I'm not finished with him," Willi said in an iron voice. Left hand stretched behind him, he held the door shut while, with his right, he struck down again at the cringing bloody heap on the red blankets.

In a fresh collar and cravat, with his hair and mustaches combed, Willi stood stiff-legged in front of the desk. Chief Loy Bloodworthy looked uncomfortable and uncertain; Jim Finnerman, in the side chair, looked miserable.

"Moss is gone," the chief said. "Lit out sometime this afternoon. Guess he was sound enough to walk." Under shrubby brows, his eyes looked Willi up and down with a distinctly new respect. "Guess you didn't kill him . . ."

"It was my right to do that if I wanted," Willi said. "My daughter's mind is unhinged."

"Ah, she'll get over it—"

"Some girls might," Willi said stiffly. "Not Annemarie, I fear. Annemarie is frail in a way her mama and I have never understood." Like a soldier being inspected, he braced his back and clasped his hands behind him. "I had every right to take the life of that trash."

"We won't argue it," Bloodworthy muttered.

"He's got no relatives that I know about," Finnerman said. "To press charges, I mean."

"Then it's settled," Willi announced. "Except for one thing. I would like an apology from someone for all the things I have been called because I am German. I am patriotic, a citizen—I love this land as much as either of you. I am not a *Dutchman*."

Finnerman slouched deeper in the chair; Loy Bloodworthy looked sullenly at the saloon owner. Then, with an equally sullen glare at Willi, he shrugged and hauled his paunchy body up from the chair.

"Guess somebody does owe you that much." Without enthusiasm, he offered his hand. Willi took it crisply, shook it up and down twice, like a pump handle.

"Thank you," Willi said with a bow, and pivoted and left. The door closed.

"Stinking kraut," Loy Bloodworthy muttered as he sank back in his chair. The men stared at one another like lovers suddenly aware of their mutual ardor for the first time.

Two nights later, in shirt sleeves, Willi left the house after supper with some new pickets in hand, plus a hammer and nails. It was a balmy evening, not quite dark yet; he could effect some repairs for perhaps ten or fifteen minutes.

He set his pickets, hammer and nails in the dirt by one of the burned bougainvillea vines twisting out of the ground. He pulled up his old patched work pants and knelt, then pried two blackened pickets from a section of the fence not completely destroyed.

He felt a quiet pride as he set about his work. He had won; been vindicated; there had been no more slurs, no more incidents, since his meeting with the police chief. Annemarie was no better, however; the doctor was thinking of sending her to a Los Angeles physician who specialized in nervous disorders of females. That was a tragic cross for Elsa to bear, but Willi dealt with it by reminding himself that every victory had its price. In the cool, windy evening, he could kneel there in the lowering dark, amid the smells of burned wood and sun-warmed earth, and feel that he had been vindicated.

The Eleventh Corps had been vindicated.

*I did not run . . .*

At the corner of the next house—the Johanssens were gone to a family reunion in Hanford—someone slipped into sight, an indistinct shadowy figure in the dusk, and raised a small pistol and fired one round into Willi's back. He died during his slow awkward fall on the charred picket fence, which collapsed under the weight of his body.

"The wages of a hotel parlormaid are not all that high . . ." said the assistant manager of the Southern Hotel in Bakersfield.

Elsa twisted a black silk kerchief in her black-gloved hands. "I need the job, sir. We have just moved here. I have children to care for." The brewery was shuttered, with no customers; it was up for sale, with no buyers.

The manager wrote in pencil on a small card. "All right. Now you said your first name was—"

"Elsie. It's Elsie."

"Your husband's name?"

"He's deceased. But it was Bill Allen," she said, avoiding his eye. "Bill."

# Carolina Warpath

*In those days, Nick Bray, though hardly a person of consequence, was decidedly a subject for conversation.*

*Often it took the form of a hushed, thrilled recitation of something that Nick had done. Or, if the speaker was an older gentleman, it might be a surly recitation which failed to hide the speaker's envy of Nick's youth and nerve. But whatever the style or substance, you always heard the same thing said in conclusion. "What a waste," they said of Nick Bray, "what a damned, abominable waste."*

*There was about Nick an air of someone doomed, though he was yet a young man in his twenties. But it seemed that he must have lived many more years than that because of all the scars he bore, and all the devils that never quite stayed bottled up inside him.*

*Nicholas Bray. Second of three sons of Solomon Nicholas Chadbourne Bray, merchant of Charles Town. Nick's older brother was Solomon, his younger was Chadbourne. Nick was deemed too frivolous and reckless to be the equal of the thoughtful Solomon, too somber and bitter to be the match of the zestful and carefree Chad. He had fallen out with the family even before he reached his majority. No one knew all the divisive issues, but his father's black bondsmen were surely one of the heaviest. For Nick would argue, "The natural or happiest state of man is freedom.*

*From want, from debt, from servitude. Why should it be
any different with an African?"*

"Nick Bray," they said, in an envious tone if the speaker
was a waddling townsman who wished he could put Nick's
considerable talents to his service. "Nick Bray," they said,
with bosomy sighs that fluttered the candles if the speaker
was a proper young wife of Charles Town already bored
with her lot.

Nick Bray—what was he really? A rover and a rogue,
with his hair to his shoulders, bright with some hideous
Indian grease; his leggings all marked with ungodly stains
of blood, ardent spirits, and other substances best banished
from the Christian imagination; his great slung-jawed
monster of a bulldog, Worthless, who was neither worthless nor comical, having torn out the throats of at least
three who had failed to take serious measure of his master;
his knife half as long as his forearm, and generously nicked
from gouging into the bones of men he'd killed—that was
Nick Bray.

He had a rotund partner, a ne'er-do-well of Huguenot
blood named Huger Noggins (whose first name you must
say correctly—You-gee). Noggins was a tough little fellow
who worshipped Nick Bray with a mixture of mystification
and exasperation. They complemented each other, and they
made a deal of money together.

Nick was, sometimes, a cattle minder on the sea islands
(they said he rustled his herds from Spaniards down in
Florida); and he was, sometimes, a trader to the up-
country tribes. And sometimes he just retreated to a hidden place on the wild shore of Winyah Bay, without his
partner or his dog or any other companionship, there to
carouse and let his demons out.

You saw Nick Bray striding in the sunshine on a Saturday in Charles Town, or riding fast through woodland
shadows on one of his strong ponies, or wagering over a
pit full of blood and feathers where metal-spurred cocks

*fought to the death at twilight, far out in the country near
the salt marsh, away from the constables.*

*Nick Bray of Carolina. A phantom you might glimpse
on the horizon of a sand hill in the fall, swift as smoke to
fly away. A rascal you'd find with a happy tavern slattern
on each knee, but only for the night.*

*Nick Bray of Carolina. A rascal who was present, un-
seen, at many a table where safe, sober people dined and
talked. Nick Bray was very real, even to those to whom
he was no more than a legend. . . .*

The empty coach arrived at the Jacksonborough
trading post on the Edisto on a hazy yellow afternoon in 1722. Twice a year the post held a fair for
traders and neighbors, and on this day the autumn
fair was in progress. The shooting matches and the
contest with cudgels were over. The day's most antic-
ipated events, a raffle for a pair of silver-chased flintlock pistols, was yet to come. The game of the
moment was the pole climb.

About sixty people crowded around the greased
pole, shouting and chaffering as first one local boy
and then another tried to climb to the top. Nick Bray
and his partner, Huger Noggins, were among the en-
thusiasts. Nick waved an ale pot as he shouted a
wager across the crowd. "Taken," a man shouted
back, and Noggins, who resembled a fat keg with
legs on the bottom and a curly mop of hair on top,
groaned at the extravagance. Noggins was flushed to
a dark red from the last contest, bare-handed
straightening of a horse's shoe. He'd won it in half
the time of his nearest competitor.

Nick's forehead glowed with sweat. His fine white
blouse hung open on his chest. Over the rim of the
ale pot at his lips he saw the coach settling on its
leathern springs in the middle of a swirling dust

cloud. He saw the postilion motioning and realized the signal was for him.

"Hold this, Huger." He handed away the pewter pot and loosened his knife in the hip sheath as he walked over. Tan dust was settling like wig powder on the fine horses, the coachmen, the lacquered wood. Nick stopped to look closely at the escutcheon on the dusty door. No mistaking it.

He talked for a bit with the driver, then walked back to his partner. Nick's bulldog lay in the shade of the palmetto-log store, asleep in the heat. The crowd cheered as the favorite slithered to within a foot of the top of the pole before sliding back down with a cry.

"Sir Pierce Cottloe sent his coach for me."

"I don't believe it," Noggins said after he got over his surprise.

"Nor do I. But there it sits. Why do you suppose a man who hates me suddenly wants to give me a comfortable ride up to his house in Charles Town?"

"No explanation from his lackeys?"

"I asked, but they refused. Reckon I'll just have to take the ride to find out." Nick's dark eyes held a look both thoughtful and wary.

Noggins started to protest, but Nick was all energy, rousing Worthless with his dusty calf-high boot. "Mind my horse, and if I'm not here by this time tomorrow, better start a search in the marshes."

His old cloak over one arm, he clapped Noggins on the shoulder and whistled to the bulldog. Worthless jumped into the carriage, and Nick right after him. The carriage bore off on the northern road in a cloud of sunlit dust.

Late that night, in the large house of the landgrave Pierce Cottloe, Nick stood before a tall oil painting of a statuesque young woman with a fall of yellow hair and a cornflower gown that complemented her dark blue eyes. The exquisite portrait, by Ruthven of London, had been done on Barbara's grand tour, a year after she and Nick met and fell in love. The painting was her father's pride. It occupied a place of honor in the main hall. Nick ran the tip of his tongue back and forth over his upper lip; back and forth. His face drained of color as he stared at the picture.

"Nicholas."

He turned to the reedy voice. Sir Pierce Cottloe, owner of substantial estates in the Carolina colony, was a man who physically did not quite fit his status. He was short, bony, with a chin which fell back weakly from his mouth. His frailness was counterbalanced by large, round eyes that seldom blinked; by blinking a man might miss a penny he was owed.

"Sir Pierce."

"I thought you might not come into this house."

"Curiosity lured me."

"How is your father? I've not seen him lately."

"I don't call on him when I come to Charles Town. He cares for me about as much as you do."

Sir Pierce blinked once, to acknowledge the barb. Gesturing politely, he stood aside. Nick went through the door into a comfortable, well-furnished room lit by several sconces of tapers. He didn't miss the fierce, angry gleam in his host's eyes when he passed him.

But the landgrave observed the courtesies. A servant brought mugs of toddy. Out on the stoop, Worthless could be heard snarling at some nocturnal disturbance.

"You still keep that beastly animal?" Sir Pierce asked.

Nick tossed off his toddy. "A man without a wife must have some sort of companionship." Again their eyes locked, without friendship or even civility now.

"Please be seated. You'll sleep here the night, of course. I've prepared a room—"

"I'll sleep at the Ram's Gate. What is this about?"

"The Yamassee and Creeks are sending around the red stick of war."

"That I know."

"Two nights past, in the small hours, a red stick was thrown on the piazza of the royal governor's house."

"That I didn't know," Nick said, with a new and grave air.

The Carolina colony had a long and bloody history of difficulty with the local tribes, especially the Yamassee. Nick and some of like mind blamed the avarice of the English colonists as much as or more than they blamed the Indians. White traders sold rum in the Indian towns despite laws against it. They abducted Indian men for slaves, and Indian women for concubines. They rustled cattle, and the cleverest of them forced trade goods on the Indians, thus creating a "legal debt" which the baffled Indians were forced to settle by ceding their land.

In the year 1715 all of this had come to a head. A delegation of white Indian commissioners went to a powwow with the Yamassee at Pocataligo, there to discuss and redress grievances. On Good Friday morning, after a night of convivial feasting, the Yamassee suddenly appeared with faces painted red and black. The horrified commissioners understood instantly. The color red signified war. Black meant death. The paint meant, "Expect both."

The Yamassee massacred every member of the white delegation. Thus began the Yamassee War, drawing in at its height as many as fifteen thousand Indians of various tribes from Alabama to the sea. It was in this war that Nick Bray had been blooded.

The northern Cheraws ran a brisk trade supplying weapons to the Yamassee. Only when the Cherokee threw in with the colonists, helping them to choke off the trade, did considerable numbers of Yamassee give up the fight and retreat southward. The Lower Creeks negotiated peace with the Carolinians in 1717, but it was an unstable peace; ever since, the Creeks had from time to time attacked the southernmost parishes of the colony. The hand of England's enemy, Spain, reached out from St. Augustine to incite them, it was said. Similarly incited, the Yamassee returned at intervals to burn and kill.

The official policies of the colony hadn't helped matters. The Carolinians had pursued a dangerous and, in Nick's view, wrongful scheme of pretending to be a friend of both the Creeks and the Cherokees, while doing some inciting of their own: pitting each tribe against the other to keep them busy and preserve the white man's precarious minority position. Now, if the evidence of a red stick on Governor Charles Craven's porch could be believed, the sham had ended, and guerrilla war had erupted once again.

Sir Pierce resumed, "The Conjurer says this time he'll drive every white man into the sea to drown." The Conjurer of the Talaboosa was a combination religious and war leader of a tribe that held large pieces of land between the coast and the sand hills up-country. There were similar small tribes throughout the colony, some consisting of no more than one or two towns. Almost all were allied with the Yamassee, overtly or otherwise.

"I always take him seriously," Nick replied. "For

a leader of a small tribe, the Conjurer has a large influence."

He put one boot on the landgrave's fine polished writing desk. The insolence visibly excited the older man's anger.

"This goes back such a long way, Sir Pierce. The Indians have never understood how other men, by reason of their white skins and royal patents, can graze their cattle on Indian lands at will, and kill any red man who objects. I am never surprised when the red stick's passed. It will pass until the tribes are gone, or we are. Now I repeat. What is this about?"

Sir Pierce made a phlegmy sound in his throat. He scraped his buckled shoes on the pegged floor.

"My good wife lies upstairs, most grievously ill."

"I wondered why I hadn't seen her tonight."

"As for Barbara—she is gone too." His cheeks showed spots of color. "To Wyndham's Barony. She has been visiting Jelks Wyndham and his mother the past fortnight."

Nick sat very stiffly now. He was pale again. The barony of Jelks Wyndham, who was betrothed to Barbara Cottloe, lay up-country. To reach it required a journey of two days. It was in the heart of the sparsely populated region freely roamed by the hostile Indians. There, Nick knew very well, Jelks Wyndham had pursued his own selfish policy, which resembled that of the colony itself: setting Indian against Indian whenever possible, to preserve his domain and keep it free of molestation.

"I will pay you twenty pounds, sterling, to ride to Wyndham's and bring my daughter safely back to Charles Town so that she can attend her mother. I need a capable man, because it's dangerous up-country just now."

Nick's lip twisted. "I was not good enough to wed

Barbara, but I'm good enough to shed blood for her, is that it?"

"I want the best man, Nicholas."

"Wouldn't that be her intended? Wyndham?"

"Wyndham's a gentleman—no disrespect meant to you, please understand. What I mean to say is, Wyndham's smart, but he's also soft. He came to Carolina from Bristol but five years ago. He doesn't know the country as you do. He doesn't know the red men, nor woodcraft, nor how to defend himself well in the open." Nick began to shake his head. "If twenty pounds isn't enough—"

"Goddamn you, Cottloe"—Nick sounded like his own dog growling—"you wouldn't have me for your son-in-law, you shipped Barbara away to separate us, and now you have the effrontery to ask me to rescue her." His cheeks were even redder than Cottloe's had been a while before. "And you know I'll do it. That's the galling part."

The landgrave unconsciously pursed his lips; a smug touch. Nick stood up so hastily he knocked over his toddy mug, spilling a few drops on the elegant floor.

"Fifty pounds," he said.

"That's a fortune."

"Your daughter is worth a fortune. Isn't she?"

There was a long, heavy, vicious silence. At last Sir Pierce said, "Done. You are as much a bastard as you always were."

Nick laughed at him and walked out. Over his shoulder he gave one swift look at the Ruthven portrait, wishing the beautiful girl would release him. She never would.

At Jacksonborough, Noggins fairly danced when he heard of the planned journey. "Go up-country? The Conjurer is killing and burning there!"

"That's why the landgrave wants his daughter safely back on the seacoast."

"But we could die up there, Nick."

"We could die right here, any day, any moment, of any of a thousand causes. I've made my way in Carolina without capturing any Yamassee for the slave pens, or running cattle over their land as that fool Wyndham's been doing. When you and I talk to the tribes, it's straightforward. Our iron goods for their deerskins, even and fair. We have that much to protect us. If we go quickly it may be enough."

Noggins popped his tongue between his lips to express his lack of confidence. And indeed, Nick wasn't feeling as confident as he sounded.

. . . With considerable justification, he discovered the next day as they jogged upriver on a dusty path: the old Indian path to the Cherokee villages. It ran from Charles Town to Moncks Corner and up the west side of the Santee to the Eutaws and the country beyond. Nick and Noggins had ridden the path many times.

The two men traveled with four horses. Worthless panted and barked in his constant struggle to keep pace on his stubby legs. About an hour after their departure from Charles Town, a rattling disturbed the palmettos to one side of the trail. Riding in the lead, Nick reined up, left hand in the air, right hand dropping to one of his saddle holsters. Each held an eighteen-inch horse pistol. Nick drew the pistol. From the brush stepped a strapping warrior with a lance raised over his head in both hands, a sign of nonhostility. Blue dragons with red eyes coiled on the muscles of his upper arms.

Nick lowered the flintlock pistol, recognizing him. he was the chief of a small tribe with ties to the Yamassee. "What brings King Coweto back from the

Floridas after many years?" He spoke fluently; he'd learned most of the tribal dialects in boyhood.

King Coweto answered, "There is much to be done."

"At whose insistence? Spain's royal governor at St. Augustine?"

King Coweto didn't answer.

"All right, another question. What are you doing this close to Charles Town?"

"I search for you," said the Indian. "I am the one who knows you best." That was true. Five years before, Nick had conducted the chief to a Charles Town tattoo artist because Coweto wanted dragons on his arms. At that time the Creeks were signing their peace treaty, and Indians could venture freely into Charles Town.

"We heard you would be traveling to our country," King Coweto went on. "I believed you would take this path as always."

Long steamy bars of sunlight fell between the great live and water oaks. Looks flashed between Nick and his partner; that of Noggins was anxious. Nick swatted an insect deviling his damp neck. He was constantly amazed at the way the tribes knew of developments on the coast almost as they happened. But then, in the slave pens and slave quarters, black and red men were allies against the whites who gave them their shackles.

"The Conjurer sends you this message," Coweto said to Nick. "You have never treated the people badly. But your skin is white, and the Conjurer swears to banish all white skins from the people's land forever. Do not continue this journey. We say it to you in friendship."

Nick scraped the muzzle of his pistol over his darkly stubbled chin. "I mean no harm to the people,

Coweto. But I ride where I please. It's always been so. Tell the Conjurer I am only taking this journey to return a young woman to her father. There is no other purpose—nothing that will endanger the people."

"Even so, you are warned not to go. In the up-country there will be much blood flowing. Much carnage."

With an almost insolent expression Nick said, "I could reduce the carnage if I killed you on the spot, couldn't I? The men of your town who must have come up from Florida wouldn't follow the warpath with their chief fallen."

"Do not make evil jokes. You would not do what you say. You are an honorable man. We are not enemies." Nick's smile faded. "I tell you once again. If you go up this path your life is at risk."

Nick straightened on his horse. "Then so be it. I haven't any choice but to go on."

King Coweto looked at him steadily for a moment, large, dark eyes full of sadness, pity. He shook his lance, turned, and faded away into the forest.

As they rode they saw portents. In a small river tributary, half a dozen poles planted at intervals to mark the channel had been broken off near the water. Whitened cattle skulls that once crowned the poles were gone.

By a gleaming marsh they came upon the cabin of a French trader foolish enough to live away from the settlements. Fire had razed the cabin. Two bodies, broiled black, hung from the crooked bough of a live oak. This curtailed conversation between the two men, and left them weighted with melancholy.

A little after dawn on the second full day, they observed a party of Indians striding from south to north through tall savanna grass. The shoulders and headdresses of the Indians stood out above the waving stalks. Behind the marchers the rising line of the sand hills showed as gray blurs.

"Bad luck," Noggins said. "I count forty."

Nick had his hand clamped around the bulldog's muzzle. Worthless growled and struggled, wanting to bark. With his free hand Nick pointed to the warrior with the tallest headdress. "And the Conjurer himself, I think."

They remained crouched until the war party passed out of sight and hearing. Then Noggins said, "Nick, what help can we expect? How many bondsmen?"

"Wyndham has not exactly treated me as an invited guest, you know. I've never set foot on his place, only passed by. So it's all supposition. He may have six, possibly eight. Probably not a white man among them."

The little man spat between his teeth. "So they might run away in hopes the Indians would let them go, not enslave them a second time."

Slowly Nick rose out of his crouch. He released the grumbling bulldog and dusted his hands. The stillness, the flat hot glare of the hazy sun, the immensity and loneliness of the country did not inspire good feelings.

"That is a possibility," he said.

But it was more than that.

The finest feature of Wyndham's Barony was the name. The estate consisted of hilly grazing land and a single dirt track leading away in the direction of the great house. At the border of Wyndham's land, where the dirt track forked from the traders' path, a shanty sheltered two black men. Each had a blunderbuss. The trumpet-shaped muzzles were dented, the brass tarnished. But that wouldn't keep the weapons from tearing a man open with several ounces of sheet lead chopped into irregularly shaped pieces.

The blacks looked at the white men apprehensively. Nick identified himself; they were waved on.

A small pain began to devil his belly as they jogged up the road between scraggly pines. The pain showed how tightly his nerves were drawn. He was a fool to be here, but it was too late to go back. He must concentrate first on keeping his temper in what would be, at best, a tindery situation.

"Where are his cows?" Noggins wondered aloud. Nick shrugged. He, too, was puzzled by the emptiness of the fields roundabout. But as they approached the last hill before the main house, they heard lowing. They exchanged looks. This grew stranger every moment.

At the summit of the low hill Nick reined his horse. Wyndham's home, a rambling log structure surrounded by a palisade and shaded by old oaks, sprawled on the summit of the next rise. Behind it were the cow pens, full. Nick surmised that Wyndham had his entire herd of about two hundred there. His black cattle minders were going about their tasks slowly in the heat.

The palisade gate was open. On a platform inside, a large, rusty swivel gun was mounted so it projected over the wall. Nick recognized it as a punt gun, removed from the boat of some waterman downcountry who made his living slaughtering ducks and geese. Such guns fired two or three pounds of chopped lead or small nails. They were not especially accurate, but at close hand they were deadly. They were also illegal, but that would hardly concern the owner of Wyndham's Barony.

They passed through the open gate in the palisade

and reached the house without interference. The yard smelled of dust and cow dung. A white-haired black man in a cast-off gentleman's vest of brocade bowed them into the lower hall.

"Master Wyndham been waiting for you, sars."

"I expected he might be at the door to greet us."

"Master Wyndham hurt himself, sar. Can't walk."

Nick's belly felt heavy. The pain was sharper. What was going on here?

The dark old hall, brightened only by light from open doors at front and rear, smelled of some kind of broiled meat. Flies buzzed around Nick's head. The cattle lowed.

In the great room he confronted Jelks Wyndham, who sat in a fine gilt chair with his right hand on a silver-knobbed cane and a bandaged left leg resting on a stool.

"My apologies, Bray. Some kind of half-breed nigger devil ambushed me at the creek last Thursday. Struck me with an iron hatchet. Probably one you sold him." He smiled sourly. "Before I disarmed him he succeeded in crippling me temporarily. I hung him up for the turkey buzzards, but it's small consolation."

Nick Bray despised Jelks Wyndham more than he despised any man he knew. In moments of candor he admitted this was because he envied him. First, Wyndham was handsome: fair-haired, with a perfect nose, delicate mouth, soft, hairless hands. Almost a beautiful man, in the Grecian sense; no one should be so perfect.

Second, he had taken Barbara.

Nick waited to see where the talk would lead. He heard a ticking behind him. Worthless sauntered in. Wyndham gave the bulldog a look. Worthless began to growl, a low, ugly sound.

"Kindly take that animal out of here before he soils the house."

"He won't." But as a concession Nick said, "Hold him, will you, Huger?"

Nick's partner crouched beside the bulldog. Wyndham rapped his cane on the floor twice, perhaps to show displeasure. "What difficulties did you encounter coming from Charles Town?"

"None, because we did our best to avoid them. But there's a deal of trouble between here and there." He briefly described what they'd seen. "If you're packed up, we should start for the coast as soon as possible. How many men do you have?"

"Six niggers."

"How many can we depend on?"

"In the event of an attack? Two. The ones presently guarding the road. I allow the others no weapons."

"It's my understanding that Barbara will be going back with us. Is your mother here?"

"Yes, she'll go with us also. You'll see them both at supper. We've cleared out one of the tabby slave pens for you and your partner."

"I think we should leave this afternoon."

"First thing tomorrow," Wyndham said with a shake of his head. It was a clear challenge. But not worth pushing to a fight.

Wyndham shifted uncomfortably. He poked at his bandaged ankle with the cane. Nick saw an ooze of blood on Wyndham's white stocking. "The cattle travel best before it's too hot," Wyndham said.

"Cattle?" Nick repeated.

"Why yes, didn't Sir Pierce explain? The contents of those pens are movable property. Extremely valuable. We're taking them with us to Charles Town so they won't be slaughtered."

Blood rushed into Nick's face. "So that's why I'm

here. To be a damn cattle minder. To take your damn *property* to safety. Is Barbara included?"

Wyndham fought to rise, fingers white on the cane head. "Curb your mouth, you greasy guttersnipe. You're being well paid."

"But I'd never have agreed if Sir Pierce had told me the truth. The real nature of the scheme." He felt gulled; hopelessly stupid. Open windows, their weathered gray shutters folded back, showed vistas of empty hills under hot white sky. Nick's feeling of dread sharpened again.

"And I wouldn't need you to lead us out if I could walk," Wyndham snarled at him. "But I can't, and you certainly won't abandon us. That is, you certainly won't abandon Barbara and my helpless mother. Will you, now?"

Worthless growled. Noggins muttered something to calm him. Nick wanted to wheel and ride out, but Wyndham had him.

"You bastard," he said. "What time do the condemned eat their supper around here?"

Nick didn't set eyes on Barbara until the aforementioned supper. She was almost completely silent throughout. The same couldn't be said for Wyndham's mother, Mrs. Thring, a widow who had acquired her last name from her late second husband, a planter on Barbados. Mrs. Thring was a great whale of a woman with knuckles the size of hailstones. Wyndham informed Nick and Noggins that she would have to be borne to Charles Town in a shaded ox cart.

"Won't be very quick going, then," Noggins muttered.

"But it's necessary; any man with half a brain can see that."

The reproof silenced Noggins, and would do so for the rest of the meal, Nick assumed. Noggins was always shy in the presence of those he deemed his betters. Of course, he had it the wrong way around: Wyndham was inferior to Noggins in so many matters of character, Nick couldn't begin to count them. No good trying to convince Noggins, though.

He shot a look at Barbara. She was as slender and beautiful as memory always painted her. Yet her face lacked the outdoor color he remembered, and her blue eyes danced nervously away from his every time he glanced at her.

When they finished their pewter plates of rice and overcooked pork, and two jugs of excellent claret, Nick pushed his chair back without ceremony. "Barbara, come for a stroll. We've a bit of talking to do."

He took her wrist gently and lifted it, to show he'd brook no argument. She looked relieved that the strained meal was over. Wyndham said, "Walking in the dark is dangerous."

"I believe I can deal with that, sir," Nick said, not a little sarcastic.

"Then stay within the palisade, hear?"

"I am your guide, Wyndham, but I'm not under your orders. Remember that."

He bowed Barbara ahead of him to the hall.

"This is a damned rotten trick, you know," he said once they were safely out of the house. A black man on watch at the gate tried to stop them from going on. Nick brushed him aside.

Barbara walked a safe distance to his left as they climbed a hill. "Oh, Nick, I know. Jelks never said a word about the cattle until just before supper tonight. I knew he sent a runner to Charles Town to appeal for help, but I thought it was to protect his mother and me."

Nick made a scoffing sound. "It's all been very artful, Barbara. Your father enlisted me by saying your mother's ill. 'Grievously ill'—I believe those were his words. Is it so?"

Barbara's voice sounded small. "I don't think so. She was perfectly well when I left last week."

"Then Wyndham's cattle are the reason I'm here, and they set it up between them. Jelks is injured"— *a nice curtain for cowardice, that*—"so I'm to take care of his property. But he had to deceive me, with your father's assistance, to bring it about."

"You paint him very dark, Nick. Don't you think Jelks cares about his own mother? Or the woman he's supposed to marry?"

"Barbara, I wouldn't hazard a guess out loud. I fear if I did, it would offend your feminine sensibilities. The language as well as the content."

"My God, you are bitter." She rubbed her arms.

"With cause. Throwing away my own life is one thing, but gulling someone good and harmless like Noggins into doing it is another."

He hooked his thumbs in his broad belt and leaned against a live oak on the hilltop. Lamps in the main house shone through windows and the open gate of the palisade. The dark land roundabout still exuded a damp heat, and a curious menace under a sky full of stars all smeary and wan.

"There are scores aplenty mounting up here," Nick said. "But we'd best not think too deeply about them. Not with half the parishes besieged by the Indians."

"Nick."

"What?"

"I truly didn't know about any of this, except for the messenger."

After a space he said, "I believe you."

"Will we be attacked on the journey?"

"That will be a matter of chance and luck. The Conjurer and his allies are roaming far and wide. We'll be traveling much too slowly, thanks to the cattle and the cart. Christ, Barbara. You ought to hate that man for dragging you into this."

There was a silence. "I'm pledged to marry him. Perhaps there was a time . . . a time after we parted—"

"*Were* parted. By others."

"I meant to say there may have been a time when I saw qualities in Jelks that really aren't there. Good qualities. It's too late to reconsider, I'm afraid. A lady can't break her vow."

"Oh, Barbara. What nonsense. With sufficient courage—"

He stopped. He knew very well the kind of society in which Barbara lived. Knew she'd been raised to be an honorable member of it. "Never mind. Let's say a proper good-bye now. There may not be another chance."

The pale oval of her face shone before him. She kept her hands at her sides, not trying to bar his hands as he put them on her shoulders and kissed her, long and ardently.

They separated, their faces close together. He could taste a sweet clove on her breath. He touched her cheek and felt tears. She gripped the back of his neck with both hands.

"I'll marry him, Nick. But I'll always love you."

"You'll marry him if we get to Charles Town, which is by no means certain."

They kissed again. At one point, still with his mouth on hers, something made him nervous and he opened his right eye. In the gate of the palisade he saw two figures, one leaning on the other. The leaning man's left hand was propped up by a cane.

What could he see in the dark? It didn't matter. In his wrathful and jealous mind he'd see pictures far worse than the real ones.

Still clinging to Barbara, Nick was cold.

Nick slept badly. For long periods he lay rigid, with all the night sounds of the hilly country rising outside the little tabby slave house. In the dark of his imagination he saw Barbara. He felt and tasted her kisses again and again. He didn't dare hope there could be a chance for the two of them, after the long separation. But he did hope, wildly, exultantly, in spite of the danger waiting in the morning. The excited state kept him wakeful almost until first light. Noggins had no such problem. He snored all night.

Jelks Wyndham chose his strongest horse for himself. Two of his bondsmen helped hoist him into the saddle, with much groaning and cursing on his part. One of the blacks lengthened the left stirrup and in so doing accidentally bumped the injured leg. Wyndham caned him, five hard blows. The slave kept his head bowed. Nick saw blood on the collar of the man's ragged shirt.

And he saw Barbara watching her father's choice with a look of distaste on her drawn, perspiring face.

Noggins supervised the three mounted slaves who would help him drive the herd. The old man from the house, whose name was Poll, was responsible for attending Mrs. Thring once she was seated in the ox cart with the awning on four bamboo poles adjusted above her.

The line of march began with Nick; Wyndham generously allowed him to be the first target for an arrow or a lead ball. Next came Wyndham and Barbara, riding side by side. Then the cart and lastly the lowing cattle. Noggins and his black helpers would eat the dust raised by the caravan.

It was another stifling morning. White sky; no air stirring. Grouchy from lack of sleep and no longer imagining a glorious new future, Nick pointed toward the coast and rode away. He left it to the others to follow.

Worthless struggled along on stumpy legs, sometimes next to Nick's horse, sometimes under him. By the middle of the morning Mrs. Thring was exclaiming constantly and weeping intermittently. The traders' path was rutted and rough, hard on the old lady despite the cushioning of every pillow from Wyndham's house, nine in all. She was flung back and forth, and each collision with the side rails of the cart produced a cry. It made the slaves nervous; silent, where they had been quietly talkative at the start of the journey.

Mrs. Thring called her son to the cart and demanded that they turn back and await cooler weather. He leaned down from his horse and patted her ringed hand to soothe her. She complained all the louder. His face went blank and he trotted away to rejoin Barbara. Mrs. Thring looked furious, then destitute, as if finally coming to realize that her son put his own wishes above hers.

About noon they stopped to rest and water the herd in a little stream the dry weather had reduced to a trickle in the mud. Noggins pulled off his tall wool hat and swabbed his forehead with his arm. He looked southward, to a great waving expanse of grass.

"See that, Nicky? 'Tisn't all the wind." He kept his voice low.

Nick gave a slow nod. "I noticed it a while ago." Behind them the slaves were shouting at the cows and whacking them with sticks. There was a pronounced ripple in the middle of the savanna, distinct from the movement of the surrounding grass. The ripple worked its way southeast in front of them, like a sea wave. Beyond, some distance on, a smudgy line of trees hooked to the right. Continuing to move in that direction, the ripple seemed to smooth out, fade away.

"Well, they spied us," Nick said. "They're in front of us now. They'll wait till they find a suitable place and a suitable moment."

Noggins scratched his unshaven stubble. "Want me to tell the others?"

"No."

"This is a cursed journey, Nicky."

"That, we and they already know."

He checked the powder in his pistols before they rode on.

The march continued through the afternoon, without incident. Dusk brought little relief from the heat. They camped in the woods, a dark cathedral of old, gnarled oaks with smaller volunteer pines between them. The air smelled of wet earth and pinesap.

Barbara supervised the fire. Poll and another slave heated the mixture of rice and black beans and served it with some soggy corn bread. Mrs. Thring loudly declined any food and remained in her cart, moaning at regular intervals as if she feared she'd be forgotten.

Nick slid his tinware plate under the bulldog's snout. Worthless lapped it clean in a trice. Nick smiled, his first smile all day, but rather empty for all that.

Barbara and Poll moved off together to talk. Jelks
Wyndham circled the fire, whose heat improved no
one's disposition. Wyndham braced his left side with
his cane. He was well armed, a beautiful silver-
chased pistol and a fine English knife thrust into the
sash of his doublet. He seemed less assured than previously. He quirked his pale eyebrows at the darken-
ing treetops.

"A lot of owls and mockingbirds abroad tonight."

"Mockingbirds without wings." Nick drank from
a bottle of claret Noggins had provided. Noggins was
off walking the perimeter of the rope pens strung for
the cattle.

"Will we be attacked?"

"It's almost a certainty."

"Any idea as to when?"

"That's the part that makes for strain. It could be
any moment, when we're awake or when we're resting. They won't rest till it's over. They've prepared
themselves, you see. Worked themselves up over several days—danced, sung, fasted. I'm sure they've
swallowed the black drink."

"What the devil is the black drink?"

"A powerful emetic. It must be mixed by a conjurer. They drink it in preparation for war."

"I've never heard of such a thing."

"Nor have most white men in the colony. That's
why the Indians are stronger than we are. War to
them is more than it is to us. To us it's defense of
our thievery. To them it's defense, and sport, and a
holy cause in one."

"Fortunately, Barbara has no idea of the seriousness of our situation."

"God, you give her no credit for brains. Of course
she does. Your poor mother, too, I expect. They all
know you're willing to sacrifice them for your pre-

cious cattle. Well, you aren't going to sacrifice my partner, or me."

"Explain the meaning of that, if you please."

Nick took pleasure in turning his back without answering.

Wyndham spread his blanket near Barbara, who was resting against a wheel of the cart, then laid his pistol on his stomach, his right hand curled around it. He fell asleep almost at once, which only reinforced Nick's feeling that the man was a worthless fool.

Nick had another bad night. He spelled Noggins on guard duty, walking his tour around the pens for three hours and then collapsing near the remains of the fire, which still cast faint, ruddy light over their clearing. By that dim glow Nick saw eyes shining.

Barbara's. She was awake.

When their eyes met, she gave him a weary, despairing smile. He tried to grin back in a cocky way, but it was too late for bravado, and the smile was wan; false.

Out in the woods, the owls and mockingbirds conversed.

An hour after they got under way, the skies opened and poured down one of those hot rains typical of Carolina. The roaring shower lasted but a few minutes. In its wake came worse heat, and insects from nowhere, and clouds of steam from the earth. They were following the hooking curve of the forest, running roughly southeast. The dark rampart of woods to their left smelled wet and rank. Little could be seen there except heavy palmetto growth between the taller trees near the perimeter.

Nick crossed a stream the rain had temporarily replenished. He felt the mud of the streambed under his horse but gave it little thought, all his attention fixed on the path ahead. It snaked through tall grass along the edge of the forest.

Suddenly, behind, Jelks Wyndham yelled, "Whip the ox. Make him move."

Nick looked back; cursed. Mrs. Thring's cart had rolled into the stream and its off wheel was sunk to the hub. The ox, already on the near bank, strained against the yoke. The steeply tilted cart rose slightly but wouldn't pull free. Mrs. Thring, thrown against the side of the tilted cart, wailed and thrashed about. Wyndham rode into the stream and began to beat the ox with his fancy stick. Nick turned his horse around, shouting, "Huger, lend me a hand."

In a moment his sweating partner rode up from the other side of the stream. Nick was already dismounted. Noggins jumped down and, behind the screen of his wool hat, whispered, "They're coming. They're close. Behind us now, I think. Following in the woods."

"Help me push the wheel."

"There isn't room for two to work. Let me try by myself."

Nick didn't argue. The round little man walked into the stream, backed against the mired wheel, lowered his body just a little, then reached behind with both hands to seize the wheel's rim. "When I give the word, Wyndham, hit the ox. Not before."

Wyndham slapped his cheek. The crushed insect left a bloody spot. He glared at Noggins, then at Nick, as if the bite, and all his problems, were somehow their fault.

Short hairs on Nick's forearms itched unmercifully. Something was about to happen; every sensibility cried the alarm. He twisted around to look at the cattle but saw no problems there. The herd had stopped short of the stream, some animals cropping grass while the slaves fearfully eyed the woods or the empty savanna stretching away. A hot, airless vista, but nothing dangerous to be seen.

Yet Nick's nerves were screaming.

Noggins clenched his jaws. His face turned dark as a ripe apple. He shuddered. He shut his eyes. Vessels in his neck thickened under his skin. His forehead seemed to bulge. His lips peeled back from his teeth as the sunken side of the cart rose a little, pulled up out of the mud by his immense strength and will.

"Now, Wyndham. Hit!"

Wyndham was a trifle slow, but he beat the ox as instructed. The ox lunged against the yoke. Noggins made a noise, or Nick thought he did, but it was peculiar—shrill, like a cry of fright. The mired wheel rose and the ox hauled the cart onto the bank, where Nick was now remounting.

"Nick!" He saw Barbara, wildly waving. He understood then. He had heard someone other than Noggins. He wheeled his horse around. It was a slave who'd cried out. The man was vainly trying to keep his seat on his horse while clutching one hand around the shaft of the arrow that was sunk deep in his shirt bosom, where a red flower of blood had bloomed. Nick pulled a pistol from its holster.

Wyndham was paying no attention. He was dismounted, reaching through the cart rails to comfort his distraught mother. The cattle were moving, the leaders starting to run south, over the savanna, away from the trees. Painted Indians were pouring out of the forest behind them. Perhaps twenty of them. Worthless began to bark and snarl and run in circles in the grass.

The slave struck by the arrow slid slowly out of sight. The Indians ran among the other slaves with arrows nocked, lances poised, hatchets raised. They stabbed and lanced the slave horses indiscriminately. A few of the Indians had firearms. An old snaphaunce boomed. Nick ducked low; heard the lead whisper by.

The cattle began to stampede with mad bellowing. Nick charged his horse toward Barbara. "Into the trees. The trees! We need cover." He rammed his horse against hers to get her going. She responded quickly, booting her mount ahead and plunging into the woods. Noggins caught his horse, but the rope bridle broke and the animal ran off. Holding the pistol barrel in his teeth, Nick dragged Noggins up behind him as the Indians split into two groups, the nearer flowing toward the whites while the others chased cows on foot and brought the slower ones down with lance or hatchet.

Wyndham couldn't prise his mother out of the cart. She was wailing and hanging on to the rails. He abandoned her and rode for the woods. "Blessed Jesus," Noggins exclaimed.

He jumped off Nick's horse and loped back to the cart. With fisted hands he hammered Mrs. Thring's fingers until she let go of the rails. Then he pulled her out, lifted her not inconsiderable bulk to his shoulder, and staggered toward the trees.

Nick quickly positioned his horse between Noggins, who was faltering under his load, and the Indians charging toward them from the other side of the stream. He laid his pistol across his left elbow, aimed, and drew the hammer back. He compensated as best he could for the dancing of his horse. The pistol fired, spewing smoke into his face. One of the feathered

Indians fell, a great chunk missing from his right shoulder.

Noggins reached the cover of the gloomy woods. Nick was riding right behind, with Worthless practically underneath. He could no longer see Barbara, or Wyndham. The palmettos grew high and thick in here, concealing whoever might be moving behind their cover. Riding was difficult; Nick jumped down off his horse.

"Barbara?"

"Here." She was some distance away, and the noise of Indians moving back into the forest, rattling the underbrush, made it hard to fix her location precisely.

Noggins was already out of sight. There was noise in the tall palmettos directly in front of Nick. His heart was beating hard. A sickening sense of doom enveloped him. "Huger? Where are you? We must stay together."

The palmettos parted and an Indian leaped out: a Yamassee wearing feathers, with yellow and ocher slashes on his cheeks and his sweating breast. While Nick grabbed his second pistol, the Yamassee raised his blunderbuss and aimed at Nick's face. A shattering explosion followed.

For an instant Nick wondered why he felt no pain; no impact from the ball. The Yamassee's mouth opened wide. His eyes grew round and he swayed forward. As Nick started to leap back the Indian fell on him; the Indian's blunderbuss fetched him a hard blow on the temple.

The Yamassee fell into his arms like a lover. On the Indian's bare back blood flowed over the yellow paint slashes. A step away, shaky, Noggins blew out the muzzle of his empty pistol.

"Him or you," Noggins said as his justification for a shot in the back.

Nick lowered the dying Indian to the ground. A welter of sounds filled the woods. Mrs. Thring crying out; the attackers thrashing among the palmettos and yipping like dogs; Worthless snarling back; a sustained shrieking which Nick took for one of the blacks being tortured. In the distance, the cattle lowed; the sound was receding. Wyndham's property was in flight.

"Where are the others, Huger?"

"Nearby, but scattered."

"Let's find Barbara first, then we—"

Two Yamassee leaped out of the brush to their left. Noggins dived for the fallen blunderbuss, an action which saved him from a lance through the chest. The lance sailed over his head. Noggins seized the blunderbuss by the bell muzzle and swung it against the head of the lance thrower, stunning him.

The other Yamassee leaped at Nick with his scalp knife swinging. Nick rammed his left elbow under the Indian's jaw, pushing upward. Worthless shot into view and began to savage the Indian's leg like a joint of meat.

Face to face, the adversaries struggled. The Indian shot his knife hand up to strike. Nick shifted his left hand and caught the wrist in the air. The Yamassee's bare belly was exposed. Nick snatched his own long knife from his belt; buried it halfway to the hilt.

Spurting blood hit him. The Indian crumpled. Worthless continued to worry his leg until Nick called him off.

Noggins gestured urgently. Nick lurched after him into the palmettos. The shrieking was nearer. Through a break in the brush Nick saw old Poll on his knees, running blood making his face a red-brown mask. He was being scalped alive, from behind, by two Indians.

Nick ran to try to save the old man. The Indians saw him coming. One plunged the bloody scalp knife into Poll's back and grinned. Old Poll toppled forward, dead before he sprawled onto the ground. Nick screamed and lunged at the Indians, his long knife raised. They fled.

Noggins grabbed Nick's sleeve and dragged him ahead to a small open area carpeted with damp, decaying leaves. There, two of their party had abandoned themselves to their fate: Jelks Wyndham, leaning against a live oak with another, smaller pistol in hand; and Barbara, behind the tree, for what scant cover it afforded. One pale hand hugged the bark; only half her face was visible.

When she saw Nick her eyes grew as round as the eyes of the Indian Noggins had shot. Her mouth opened in an *O* of horror. Nick glanced down. She was staring at his blood-soaked leggings.

"Wyndham, where's your mother?" It had come to Nick that Mrs. Thring's cries had stopped.

Wyndham's fine, fair hair straggled in his face. His linen blouse was torn and soaked with sweat. Waving, he said, "Out there somewhere, I don't know."

"Look sharp, Nicky," Noggins yelled. Nick spun as an Indian with an old fowling piece ran into the clearing. Nick's eyes flew wide. So did the Indian's. Tattooed dragons raged on the Indian's muscular arms.

"Nick Bray, I warned you." There was a note of despair in King Coweto's cry. Nick and the chief stared at each other for what seemed a very long time, as if neither man could decide what to do to the other.

King Coweto was faster to recover. He shouldered

the fowling piece, but shifted his aim to Wyndham.
Wyndham fired his pistol and missed.

Two other Yamassee leaped from the palmettos to corner Noggins between jabbing lances. Wyndham caught
Nick's waist from behind and dragged him backward, as
a shield. "Jelks," Barbara cried out in outrage.

Wyndham's arms were strong. Nick lunged one
way, then another, unsuccessfully. In desperation he
cut Wyndham's right hand with his knife. King Coweto was hovering near them, trying for a clear shot
with the fowling piece. Wyndham spat like some
viper and Nick tore free and dropped on his face as
King Coweto fired. Jelks Wyndham flew back against
the tree and then slid down. Blood streamed from
his right eye socket.

Nose mashing into rotted leaves, Nick fought a
fierce stab of conscience. He knew their only chance
lay in a deed he abominated. But he had no choice
if they hoped to live. His left hand caught King Coweto's ankle and yanked on it.

The chief fought for his balance, regained it, and
tried to brain Nick with the fowling piece. As he
leaned over, Nick's right hand flew upward. King
Coweto was very nearly lifted from the ground when
the knife tore into his belly, to the hilt.

The Indian doubled, falling. Nick's trembling arm
couldn't sustain the weight. He rolled and King Coweto toppled to one side. Coweto crashed to earth,
still fighting with the knife in his gut. His hands
closed on Nick's windpipe.

Coweto's long nails tore Nick's skin; blood reddened
the Indian's fingers. Nick and Coweto lay on their
sides, united by that death grip. Nick's cheeks purpled.
His eyes seemed to bulge from his head. Noggins had
taken one more Yamassee out of the fray, rearming
himself with the fallen man's lance. He was *clack-*

*clack*ing lances with another Yamassee like some modern Friar Tuck. But there were earnest, murderous
looks on Noggins's face and that of his foe.

Nick freed the bloody knife from Coweto's belly.
King Coweto felt it and strangled the harder. Nick
looked into Coweto's eyes for some sign of human-
ity, but there was none. The eyes were demonic, as
if in his pain Coweto no longer recognized his victim,
only knew he must claim his life before he died himself. Nick steeled himself. Dark veils were obscuring
his sight. There was no other way. . . .

By sheer muscular force he lifted his right forearm
high enough to position the knife. He cut King Coweto's throat. He couldn't roll away from the torrent
of blood fast enough.

A short while later he regained his feet. His memories of the moments that had passed were two. The
Indian dueling with Noggins had turned and fled—
which is exactly what Nick had hoped for once he'd
steeled himself to slay the chief, a man for whom he
bore no great grudge, understanding as he did why
Coweto took to the path of war.

Secondly, there was Barbara's face. Turned to him
in horror . . . disbelief . . .

Revulsion.

From hairline to breastbone, he was as red as if
he'd dyed himself for war. Sadly, he knew what her
expression meant.

He knelt by Jelks Wyndham, who had tried to sacrifice
Nick to save himself. Wyndham was dead; Nick could
feel no sense of loss. The thought that occurred to him
was shameful: Wyndham's cattle, if they had not all run
off, belonged to any man who would take them.

"Nicky?"

He swung his head around, saw Noggins motioning with a terrified look. Nick reeled to his feet. He felt the sudden exhaustion always produced by hard physical combat. He listened, thought he heard sounds that signified a general Indian retreat in the wake of the death of their leader.

Noggins led him a short way to a crumpled heap of cloth, which on inspection turned out to be the skirts of Mrs. Thring. Nick fell to his knees a second time and gently rolled her onto her back. He examined her dirty gown and what expanses of freckled old skin he could find.

"Not a mark. Not a cut, nor any bullet wound, Huger."

"She was breathing just fine when I laid her there, I swear."

"Poor old woman must have died of fright. Wyndham didn't care who, or how many, he sacrificed for his goddamned property. What a sorry mess."

Nick stood up. Mrs. Thring seemed to be gazing past him through the treetops at the Carolina sky, which was clearing now, turning a pale blue, like the edging on a fine plate. Mrs. Thring's cheeks were a darker blue, her lips purplish.

Worthless limped out of the underbrush. Some knife or lance had gashed the shank of his left rear leg. He was making piteous sounds and snapping his head around, trying to lick the wound. Nick supposed he'd be all right. The dog had half a dozen scars already. Only steel through the heart would kill him.

Nick and Noggins found two of the slaves alive. They expressed gratitude to Nick and his partner, then willingly ran into the savanna while Nick and Noggins found their horses and remounted.

Barbara said she would remain with Mrs. Thring's

body. "I need some time by myself. I need some time to reckon all this. To cry over Jelks's poor mother."

At evening, a brilliant red-gold sky overhung the savannas and the bloody woodland. Wind was rising. The two white men and the two blacks had recovered about one hundred head of cattle, a profitable afternoon's work. Nick ceremoniously thanked the blacks, then said:

"Take your leave. There are hundreds of miles of safe forest between here and the next man who wants to enslave you. You'll never meet that man if you're cagey. Avoid the Spaniards in Florida—they'll chain you up. Make for the Gulf. The islands of the Antilles. Find a place to live free."

One slave's eyes brimmed with tears; they shone like red gems in the sundown. He started to kiss Nick's hand.

"No, don't do that. Don't do that to any man, ever."

Without a word the two ragged black men faded away into the waving grass.

"I'll take every pound you promised me," Nick Bray said to Sir Pierce Cottloe in Charles Town. "Though I do think thirty silver pieces would be more appropriate to the business."

Sir Pierce counted it out. "Nicholas, I had no idea that you would encounter such terrible—"

"You're lying, you damned fraud. But don't worry about me, sir. Not at all. Worry about yourself. Your peace of mind. Reflect on what you did. For the rest of your life, when you can't sleep—if I were a devout man I would pray for your sleeplessness—think about the mother of your fellow conspirator. Think of Sophie Thring. If you'd never tricked me and sent me up there, if we'd never made the journey back down the trading path, that harmless old lady would be alive now. So would an old black man named Poll who didn't have the strength to harm a child. So would a couple of Wyndham's black chattels. The kind of men you brush aside or kill like summer flies. How much Sunday holiness will it take to wash all that off your conscience?"

He walked out of the house, leaving Cottloe gasping like a beached fish.

On the east-facing piazza he met Barbara, for what he had already decided would have to be a quick farewell. The memory of what he'd done to King Coweto was gall; a heart wound that would never heal. There was a temptation to parcel out the blame to others, but only one hand had driven the steel.

He clasped Barbara's hands in his and looked earnestly into her blue eyes. "Your father was wrong about Jelks, but he was right about me: I'm not the sort of man you could display in London town."

He showed her his hands. Dried blood still clung under his thick fingernails. He'd washed and scrubbed repeatedly, but it would not come out.

"I won't argue with you," she whispered, beginning to cry. "I know your mind is set."

"And yours. I saw it when I killed King Coweto. I saw it when you looked at me."

She didn't say he was wrong.

He leaned in to her, grasping her arm as he kissed her. It was a warm afternoon. The air smelled of the ocean. Her hair smelled lightly of lavender.

"Will I see you?"

"If you stay in Carolina. If you look quick, somewhere between the wind and the clouds and the shadows."

"Nick, you saved my life. . . ."

"I'd have done that even if I didn't love you. Good-bye, Barbara."

He vaulted down the high steps two at a time, crossed the rectangular garden, and went out the street gate without a backward look.

Noggins and Worthless were waiting in the garden wall's cool shadow, the one leaning, the other sleeping with his drooly underjaw stuck out. The dog's injured leg was oozing; he tore off every bandage Nick or Noggins tied on him.

Sounding tired, Nick said, "We'll take the cattle down to one of the sea islands to fatten them. We'll have plenty of time to drink. I need to drink for a week. For a month . . ."

"Listen, Nicky, are you sure about this? At the Ram's Gate I heard there are pirates on the coast again. Ralph Rowland and his rotten crew."

"But there are sharks here in Charles Town—much harder to recognize and avoid than those that hide in the sea. I'll take my chances with Roaring Ralph and his mates."

With a resigned sigh Noggins said, "Then I guess I will also."

Worthless snorted in some kind of agreement, and wobbled to his feet as the two friends set out. The men and the dog passed through a patch of shade at the next corner. They turned the corner and disappeared. Over the cream and ivory walls of the street, sound fell lightly. The closing of a shutter; then a woman weeping. The pastel light danced with motes of dust. It was as if Nick Bray had never been there at all.

# Snakehead

Lamar Tisdale left the Ohio Christian Orphan's Home on September 1, 1883. His twelfth birthday. All inmates of the home graduated into the hard world at age twelve.

The managers of the home presented Lamar with a rail ticket to Council Bluffs and a letter of introduction to the supervisor of passenger services, Union Pacific Railroad. Lamar was hired as a peanut butcher, making regular trips between Omaha and Cheyenne.

On this run he traveled with the line's legendary conductor, C. O. ("Redbird") Seelbinder. Redbird Seelbinder was famous for defying management by wearing a red bandanna with his uniform. His nose was as red as the bandanna. He was magnificent at his job, but seldom sober doing it.

Redbird was also famous for his stories, recitations, jokes, and aphorisms, some comprehensible, some not.

Lamar was a stout boy with shrewd brown eyes and a disposition not yet shaped by the world. On his first trip, Redbird took a shine to him, and helped excuse and smooth over the beginner's mistakes. In the baggage car, Redbird took a hearty swig from the bottle of spirits always present in a capacious

318

pocket and insisted that Lamar sit on his knee. Lamar was too large for this, but since the conductor was famous, he obliged. Seelbinder held forth for an hour. He said such things as:

"If you meet a Chinaman, try to think like a Chinaman. If you meet a mountain lion, try to think like a mountain lion. Might save your skin."

And:

"The evil of this world doesn't come like a smart fox, it comes like a drunk ox."

And:

"When I was serving on the old Callawassie & Charleston, our rails were strap iron on top but wood below, spiked down. Now sometimes spikes worked loose and a rail would curl up and ram through the floor of a passing car. It happened to me. This snakehead, as it was called, ripped through the carpet and its coating of tobacco juice—passengers spit right on the floor in those days, don't y'know—and caught me just here, clean through the leg, and pinned me to the car like a butterfly. I bled like a scarlet Niagara Falls for a while. But I was determined not to die, although in hellish pain. A lady loaned me her parasol and I bit down on the handle of it for one and a half hours, until a doctor arrived and saved me. Every man meets a snakehead at least once, Lamar. Prepare to meet yours."

Lamar Tisdale never forgot that admonition.

A year later, the summer of '84, a Nebraska farmer named Carl Lukendorf went crazy. Lukendorf had been accumulating anger for fifteen years, and one morning he just snapped.

Lamar hadn't yet made Lukendorf's acquaintance on the day he left Omaha on another run. It was hot weather. White skies, muttering thunder, no wind, nearly a month gone by without rain. Lamar, by now a cynical veteran of the cars, was feeling uneasy as he filled his tray with his stock of apples, tin whistles, nausea pills, Beadle novels, hard candies, and playing cards depicting famous Indians chiefs as the kings and knaves.

The westbound express consisted of the locomotive, a thirty-five-ton Baldwin 4-4-2 named *Pride of Cheyenne*, a tender, a combination mail-baggage car, and three passenger cars. One of these was a second-class day coach, the other two first-class through cars to California (no smoking). Of these, one was a Pullman Palace Reclining Chair Car. The other featured Mr. Pullman's ingenious upper and lower berths that appeared miraculously at night.

Lamar's procedure was the same for every trip, and for either class of car. He slipped the cord of his tray over his head and worked his way through the train, intuitively matching passengers to items in the tray. He would throw an item into a passenger's lap uninvited and move on. When finished, he'd work the train in the other direction. Some passengers returned his items, but the majority didn't. By the time Lamar made his second trip, they had cracked the seal on the cards, or started reading, or spit on the apple to polish it. So they paid him. In a good week, at twenty percent commission on each sale, he made a hundred dollars.

On this day, Redbird stood swigging and swaying on the platform between the first-class cars. He never held on; he never fell off. They were rattling west by the sludgy Platte, the only river water in America that you had to chew, as the saying went. Everywhere the sky was the same bright, oppressive white. Air fanning over the platform blew from some unseen furnace.

"This weather makes men and livestock crazy," Redbird remarked between drinks. The conductor always had a firm grip on his bottle. He would weep, rave, or fight if accidentally parted from it for more than a few seconds.

"Yes, I've noticed that some of the passengers are pretty cross," Lamar said.

"Got a celebrity in the next car, by the way."

"Who's that?"

"Bart Stopper."

"The Pinkerton detective? You don't mean it."

"I do. He's in there with his wife and little girl, all of them preening like peacocks. They're going on vacation in the Rockies."

"I can't wait to get a look at him," Lamar exclaimed. Bart Stopper, who caught outlaws and broke up strikes by trade-union members, had a national reputation.

"When you do, you won't see much," Redbird said. But Lamar had already gone into the car.

Lamar spotted the Stopper family right off. They occupied a facing double seat, with a table latched to the wall between seats. At night the colored porter, Xerxes Johnson, a former slave, removed the table, converted the seats into the lower berth, and dropped the upper berth on chains from its storage space above. The great detective was riding backward, lounging and fanning himself with his derby, and occasionally stroking his handlebar mustache. He was a young man with a bullying expression. It was evident that he wore a shoulder gun, much too large, under his coat.

The detective's wife was severe-looking, and his daughter, about Lamar's age, had the same baleful, ax-nosed face as her mother. Both ladies were dressed to the maximum, in frills and hoop skirts right out of the latest issue of *Godey's*.

Already in a state, Lamar worked his way toward them. He was nervous about selecting something for the Stopper girl because of her father's occupation and fame. He chose the reddest, ripest apple in his tray. He put a deck of cards with it. Instead of flinging the items into her lap, his usual technique, he placed them with great care. In the process, his hand accidentally came in contact with her skirt.

"How dare you touch me?" the girl cried. "Papa, he touched me!"

Mortified, Lamar began, "Miss, I only meant to offer—"

"Be off," Bart Stopper said, smacking the deck and the apple back into Lamar's tray. Miss Stopper covered her face with her lace mitts and choked and gagged as though she'd encountered something unspeakable.

"Now, now, Lucy, that's all right," Mrs. Stopper said to the inconsolable girl. Is it my skin? Lamar wondered. He was going through the usual adolescent eruptions.

"You can't expect anything else," Stopper said with a dismissive glance at Lamar, who was standing in the aisle with color mounting in his cheeks and his mortification rapidly changing to anger. "You've got to remember, this part of America still isn't civilized. You can't trust Westerners to behave intelligently in any situation."

Oh, yes? thought Lamar, by now a proud Westerner. I'll show you. He had no notion of how to do it.

"Papa, he's still staring at me!" Miss Stopper shrieked.

"Son, you'd better move along or I'll report you."

I sure-God hope I never get famous if that's what it does to a person, Lamar thought, moving along.

A few passengers snickered at his humiliation. Most paid no attention. The express swayed and rattled. Several windows were open in the car, blowing in that hell's breath, and bits of cinder and specks of soot besides. Lamar glanced out the window to the north. Saw the Platte veering off from the right-of-way out there beyond the flat, tilled fields. They'd left North Platte twenty minutes ago, on their way to Paxton.

"Young man, may we see your wares?" said a kindly looking gentleman in the next seat. He'd witnessed Detective Stopper's display of arrogance and provincialism and felt bad for the boy who was its victim. The gentleman, in clerical black, was the Reverend Bannis Beechley, a widower, a Unitarian minister from Boston. He too was on a sight-seeing journey with his daughter. Their destination was California.

Unlike Miss Stopper, this girl beamed at Lamar. She was his age, with yellow hair and eyes as pretty as a bluejay's crest. She blushed when she made eye contact with Lamar. Reverend Beechley scrutinized Lamar's tray.

"Do you have any uplifting reading material that my daughter, Belle, might enjoy?"

Flustered, Lamar grabbed the first thing he could. "This is a dandy." A five-cent novel: *Jesse James The Valiant!—or—Fighting the Desperadoes in the Valley of Whistling Death.* The bright-colored cover illustrated Jesse bravely ventilating some stereotypical evil Mexicans with bullets from his blazing revolvers.

"Well . . ." Reverend Beechley began, then hesitated.

"It looks perfect," his daughter sighed, taking it

from the peanut butcher and accidentally brushing his tanned hand with her soft white one.

Lamar was electrified. He fell in love instantly.

Reality intruded as the train stopped suddenly, nearly hurling Lamar on his face. "What in blue hell?" he said. Belle Beechley gasped at his worldly vocabulary.

"Is this a regular stop?" a passenger asked.

"No, sir, absolutely not," said Lamar. "I'll go see what's wrong." He rushed down the aisle toward the nearest door. This took him past the Stoppers. The girl stuck out her tongue at him. He caught a glimpse of Bart Stopper's silver-plated revolver, revealed in its shoulder rig when the detective stood up. Stopper patted his wife. "If there's trouble, I'm prepared."

Lamar dashed past a worried Xerxes Johnson to the platform. Redbird was already on the ground. In a farmer's field directly north of the right-of-way—a large field of unusual triangular shape—a motionless man in a straw hat stood with one hand on the flank of his plow horse. The man was a stark, black shape against the white sky. Like the Reaper himself, he frightened Lamar somehow.

Redbird and Lamar rushed to the head of the train, where Swanny, the engineer, and Weathers, the fireman, were already down from the cab, scratching their heads. Spikes had been pried up. A rail dislodged and pulled sideways. It was bent out and away from the next rail for a foot or more.

"Old Injun trick," the engineer said, mystified.

"The Indians are pacified," Redbird said ominously.

Lamar pointed to the disturbed earth near the roadbed. "Look, there was a shod horse there."

"Sure, had to be a horse, and a damn strong one," Redbird said. "A man couldn't do this by himself."

"But who would?" asked Lamar.

Weathers grabbed Redbird's braided sleeve and pointed. In the triangular field, the man was moving with slow deliberate steps away from his massive plow horse, toward a farm wagon parked at the edge of the field. It was a stark, somehow sinister image: that solitary black figure walking across the land. The only thing moving in the immensity of prairie and sky.

"What a fix," Weathers groaned.

"Any trains due?" asked Lamar.

Redbird consulted his big silver turnip. "Not for an hour and nine minutes."

The engineer said, "Weathers, you'll have to ride shank's mare into Paxton, inform the dispatcher of our predicament so he can alert the other traffic on the line, and then bring a handcar crew to repair this. Going to put us a good three, four hours behind schedule, but it can't be helped."

"I don't like this," Redbird muttered. "Why don't I like this?"

Nobody answered him. Lamar didn't like it either. He heard the sound of passengers clattering off the train, anxiously asking questions and complaining. Xerxes manfully did his best to placate and console them. Lamar watched the distant figure continue its slow-paced walk to the wagon. His youthful scalp began to crawl. Why, why with the farmer so far away that he was a mere toy figure, did Lamar have the feeling the man was watching them?

The farmer reached his wagon and took something long and stick-like from the seat. He put it to his shoulder. "That sucker's got a gun," Redbird cried, spewing spirits from the bottle still at his mouth.

The rifle's boom was followed by the cry of Weathers, who clutched his breast and fell face down, dead.

*        *        *

Carl Lukendorf's hands trembled, reveling in the feel of the avenging weapon. It was his pride: a .44-40 Winchester, '73 model, with a fifteen-round magazine. He said a prayer in German, asking that his next shot fly as true as the first. This time he intended to fire from a much closer range.

He began to walk toward the stalled train. The passengers were scrambling back aboard.

Lukendorf was short, with an old man's paunch and a cast in one blue eye. He and his wife had come over to America and homesteaded in Nebraska, full of hope for a fine new life with a large, joy-filled family. After several years the couple reluctantly decided that Nathalie would never bear children, for whatever cruel and capricious reason they could not fathom. All right, at least they had each other.

In addition to their farm, the Lukendorfs operated a prosperous little inn and way station on the Platte River coach road. They were industrious people, working eighteen or twenty hours a day, first to tend the farm, then to cook and clean for their guests of the night.

When the Union Pacific—the unfeeling, uncaring, monster corporation—built west in the late 1860s, the line surveyors—terrible, heartless men—swung the route south of the river, starting at North Platte. The old stage and wagon road was quickly rendered obsolete. Business dropped off, and instead of making a tiny amount of money from their inn, the Lukendorfs rapidly lost money. They'd closed the inn three years ago.

Further, the U.P. surveyors, armed with legal documents establishing their land grants, had run their route diagonally across a large portion of Lukendorf's farm. This created triangular parcels, with

short furrows that were ungodly hard to plow because of the need to make frequent turns. Lukendorf
could do nothing about it, except to perform the gru-
eling work year after year.

Yesterday, at nightfall, Doc Viquesny had drawn
Carl Lukendorf into the doorway and struck the
final, back-breaking blow.

"Carl, this is bitter to say, but I can't help Nathalie.
No one can reverse a cancer of the mouth and
tongue. The same disease is killing President Grant
back East. You'll have to resign yourself to losing
your wife, probably within a year."

Lukendorf, not a soft man, wept openly. The doctor was attempting to console him when Lukendorf's
tears abruptly dried up, and the farmer turned on
him with his good eye rolling madly.

"I know who did this to me."

"Carl, no one's responsible for—"

"God did this to me. God and the railroad."

After Nathalie fell into a restless sleep, he took the
oiled cloth wrapping off of his Winchester Model '73.

They dragged Weathers' body behind the locomotive. The engineer looked undone. Redbird kept
swigging from his bottle. Five minutes passed. Lamar
was a helpless observer.

"Who is that crazy man out there?" Swanny asked
rhetorically.

"I don't know," Redbird said. "But he's sure as
hell intent on hurting somebody."

Lamar and the others swung around at the sound
of shoes crunching along the roadbed. Here came
Stopper, natty derby tilted down over his snapping
eyes at a challenging angle. His shoe tips shone like
black mirrors. As he walked, he twirled the cylinder
of his revolver, an ostentatious .44 American from

S&W, silver-plated, elaborately engraved with scrolls and whirls, and fitted with custom ivory grips. Truly a deluxe piece.

Stopper confronted them. "I demand to know what's going on."

"If we knew, we'd tell you," Swanny said in a miserable tone.

"Somebody tore up a piece of track. We can't get by," Redbird said.

"We could back up," Lamar said.

Redbird and the engineer looked at Lamar as if he were Jehovah and had just handed down a surprising new commandment. "Let me relieve myself, and we'll go," Swanny exclaimed, breaking out in smiles.

Stopper nudged Weathers' body with a black-mirrored toe. "This man's dead."

"That's about right," Redbird agreed, untying his bandanna and wiping his face, which was now darker than the cloth.

"It's my duty to arrest the murderer."

"Oh, why take any chances?" Redbird said. "We've got women and children to think about." Lamar heard water trickling behind him, but he was mesmerized by the hot-eyed detective.

"Because I'm a lawman. You let me handle this."

With a swaggering air of confidence, Stopper flipped up his S&W and gave the cylinder another ominous, clicking twirl. Then he stepped past the cowcatcher, raising the pistol chest high. He crossed the track, staring intently at the field. He halted suddenly.

"Where the hell is he?" Stopper asked, his eyes searching the prairie. Lamar peeked around and saw the plow, the plow horse, the wagon, all in silhouette against the white sky. The man was gone. Heat lightning flickered up Canada way.

Lamar screwed up his nerve and walked around the cowcatcher. Someone in one of the cars exclaimed in alarm. Lamar whirled and saw a hunched-over figure near the train, moving in a crab-like run. The farmer. He flung up his rifle.

Stopper struck a pose and whipped his silver-plated .44 forward at arm's length, shoulder high.

"You're under arrest."

Lukendorf dropped to one knee and shot him.

Stopper squealed, blown back onto the tracks when the bullet found his shoulder. His derby flew off and he lay supine, his pistol resting on his chest like a silver lily.

Lukendorf whipped the rifle around and fired a shot at the train, and another, and another. Glass shattered. Fat splinters of wood flew every which way. Women shrieked. Men yelled. Kneeling there on the prairie, a clear target, unharmed, Lukendorf kept on firing. Petrified, Lamar ran back across the track to the others.

Swanny, no longer smiling, relieved himself again, this time unintentionally. Even Redbird, always the master of situations, looked peaked. "Jesus Christ, he is crazy," he said.

And then, from nowhere, it fell into Lamar Tisdale's thoughts: *This is my snakehead!*

He didn't want the burden. But everyone else seemed totally confused and helpless, exhibiting none of the courage or quick wits of the heroes in the Beadle novels he hawked in the cars. The sight of Stopper prodded him too. Stopper had insulted Westerners. Stopper had said they didn't know how to behave intelligently in any situation.

A hoarse voice called from the train. "There's a man down in here!"

"If that madman has enough bullets, we'll all die," Swanny cried. "Somebody stop him!"

"Who?" Redbird shouted. "Who?"

"Mr. Seelbinder." Lamar yanked the braided sleeve. "Mr. Seelbinder, I'm going to try something."

"What, run for help?" Redbird belched, weaving on his feet. He clutched one of the great engine drivers for support. He'd fortified himself too liberally.

"No, sir, something else. I've got a scheme."

"Why, that's the silliest, maddest—"

"Mr. Seelbinder, you're drunk," Lamar exclaimed, prodded to anger by his despair. "Nobody else is doing anything—"

"Because we're whipped," Swanny said.

"We are if we say we are," Lamar protested. Redbird paid no attention. He tilted his bottle and guzzled. "Oh, hell," Lamar cried. He snatched the bottle, leaped on the cowcatcher, and jumped down on the other side.

It took Redbird a moment to realize that his hand no longer contained a bottle. The terror of deprivation infused him with courage. "Come here, you give me that!" He lunged past the cowcatcher in pursuit of Lamar, who now stood in the open, all watery in the knees.

"Give that back, you crazy rapscallion," cried Redbird in quavering tones.

Lamar didn't dare look toward the farmer. If he did, he'd fall apart with fright. He commenced dancing around, kicking up his heels and rolling his head from side to side in a lunatic way. He uttered nonsense words, roughly approximating *yiii-yiii-yiii,* with maximum lung power.

Redbird was agog, staring at the caterwauling youngster dancing around beside the cowcatcher.

Suddenly Lamar flung the bottle away into the

field and hopped backwards, thumbing his nose. "Yah, yah!" he cried, windmilling his arms and then turning a somersault. As he flipped over, he had a weird, upside-down view of the farmer standing near the train, the faintly smoking rifle in his hands.

The farmer observed Lamar and the conductor, and raised the rifle. With a cry, Redbird loped for cover. "Dern boy's lost his mind. Must be scared. Thought he was made solider than that. . . ."

His heart hammering like a sinner's before the Judgment Throne, Lamar went skipping through the weeds toward the farmer.

He'd never been so frightened in all his days. He flapped his arms and lolled his tongue and rolled his eyes around. He jiggled his head back and forth like a scarecrow in a cyclone, and soon he came within thirty feet of the terrible stout man with the wild blue eye.

Lukendorf brought the rifle up and levered another shell into the chamber.

"You, boy, stop right there."

Twenty feet away, Lamar danced and chanted madly. He spun like a dervish. He spit out everything in his mouth, hoping it bore some resemblance to foam.

Ten feet—

"Boy, you keep coming at me, I'll shoot you."

Lamar kept coming. He gnashed his teeth and yanked his hair.

"What's happening, Papa?" That was Belle Beechley, inside the train.

"I don't know, Belle. The poor lad's apparently having some kind of fit."

Five feet—

Lukendorf stepped back a pace, uncertain. He shouldered the Winchester and aimed at Lamar.

Lamar sprang in the air, fell back, landed hard and painfully on his spine, knocked nearly dizzy. *Don't pass out, don't pass out,* he said to himself. He thrashed wildly on the ground, moaning, beating his head from side to side.

Suddenly he arched his back. He beat his heels on the ground and bit his lips and uttered a long, piercing wail. He flopped down again and shut his eyes and lay motionless, his chest heaving.

He listened.

Silence. Absolute silence.

Then crunching footsteps. *Oh God, he's going to put a shell in my head.*

The footsteps stopped. Lamar squinted his eyes open. Saw the farmer towering over him, a queer expression on his face. He no longer looked wrathful, merely old and worn out.

"Boy?" Carl Lukendorf said. "What's the matter with you?"

The rifle hung at the farmer's side. Lamar let out a light, fluttery moan.

"Are you sick? You need a sawbones?"

Lamar rolled over and slapped both hands on the hot metal barrel. Lukendorf swore in German and kicked at Lamar's head. But the farmer didn't have a tight grasp on the piece, and Lamar got it away with one stout yank. He dodged the German's dung-caked plow shoe, panting, and whirled around and around and sailed the rifle high up into the air, away on the other side of the steaming, hissing locomotive.

"Mr. Seelbinder! Pick up Stopper's gun and get him," Lamar yelled.

Lukendorf turned and ran across the triangular field. But it was a lumbering, shambling, tired old run, as if he knew it was all up.

They had him behind bars in Paxton two hours

later. The sentencing judge gave him life imprisonment by reason of insanity.

The exciting, not to say blood-freezing, events of that morning in Nebraska changed Lamar Tisdale's life forever. He decided that he was cut out for bolder things than peanut butchering. Although he had instantly conceived a dislike of Bart Stopper, the man's profession intrigued him. Many years later, in San Francisco, Lamar was the highly successful and affluent operator of the Golden Gate Police Detective Agency, which employed one hundred nineteen operatives throughout California and the Southwest. He paid for C. O. Seelbinder's care at a decent old folks' home in Berkeley until the old conductor died at ninety-three.

One day Lamar had a rare opportunity for revenge. Stopper, now an aging derelict discharged by Pinkerton's for insobriety and general ineptitude, turned up in Lamar's office begging for work. Stopper didn't recognize the agency's owner. Lamar wanted to rebuff him by saying something like, "Sorry, Stopper, we hire only Westerners; they can deal intelligently with any situation."

But he felt sorry for the stumbling wreck of a once-renowned detective and hired him as a messenger and general handyman. Stopper lasted for two weeks, then disappeared.

Each evening Lamar went home to his mansion in South Park, where he resided with his wife and their eleven children. Seldom did a week go by without a parental discussion with one or the other of the children to the effect that each of them, in his or her own good time, and the Lord's, would meet a snakehead. "When you do, remember this advice passed on to me by Redbird Seelbinder. He was an inebriate, which wasn't to his credit, but he was a wise man. 'If you meet a Chinaman,' he said, 'try to act like a Chinaman. If you meet a mountain lion, try to act like a mountain lion.' That time in Nebraska, we met a poor crazy man. I decided that the only way out of our predicament was for someone else to act like a crazy man too. It confused him. That's how I got his gun. I was full of fear, but Redbird's advice saved the day. Keep it in mind."

"Yes, Father," chorused several children.

His beautiful, adoring wife, the former Belle Beechley, beamed and squeezed the hand of Lamar Tisdale.

# Manitow and Ironhand
## A Tale of the Stony Mountains

*Dedicated to the memory of Karl May*

The free trapper, a strapping shaggy white man of indeterminate age, waded into his secret stream about a quarter mile above the wide beaver dam. His darting glance revealed no dangers; nor did he truly expect any, this far into the wilderness.

His buckskin shirt was wet, and soiled by many hasty meals. His buckskin leggings were stagged at the knees, where he'd sewn on pieces of fine English blanket, which wouldn't shrink. Leggings and his wool-lined moccasins were last year's tipi of a Crow chief of his acquaintance.

Shadows of quaking aspens and bending willows were growing longer. It was nearing the twilight hour, the ideal time for setting out traps. He would set this one, his fifth of the afternoon, then one more before returning to his campsite, there to rest until he rose before daybreak to clear the traps. He shifted his campsite nightly; a professional precaution of those who worked alone. Also, he now had eighty plews to protect—a valuable mixed bale of beaver, marten, and otter, weighing nearly a hundred pounds. So far the spring trapping season had been bountiful.

The late afternoon air was light and warm, but the water was still icy from the melted snows. The soft-burbling stream froze his bones and set his hands to aching, the good right one and the mangled left one he concealed with a filthy mitten except when he was at his trade, as now. He went by the name "Old Ironhand," though he really wasn't old, except in spirit. The snowy white streaks in his long hair were premature. There was a bitter cynicism in his eyes, the oldest part of him.

Once his name had been Ewing. Ewing Something. It was a name he no longer used, and struggled to remember. Ever since he'd split with the Four Flags outfit, and Mr. Alexander Jaggers—ever since they'd crippled his left hand, causing him to compensate with exercises that strengthened the other one, welding five digits into a weapon—to the free trappers and those who still gave allegiance to the large outfits, he was Old Ironhand.

He waded along, carrying the seven-pound trap and chain in his left hand, the pin pole in his right. He moved carefully, the small sounds of his passage undetectable because of the water's purl. This was a fine stream; he'd been working it for a year. It yielded fat mature beaver, fifty to sixty pounds each, with choice tails he charred, skinned, then boiled as a mealtime delicacy. Hip deep in his secret stream, he felt good as he approached a natural beaver slide worn into the bank at the water's edge. The shadowed air was sweet. The trees were a-bud, the mountain peaks pristine as a new wedding dress, the sky a pale pink, like a scene from a book about fairyland. He saw a mockingbird singing alertly on a bush. It was 1833, in the Stony Mountains, far from the civilized perfidy of other white men.

He laid the pin pole on the bank. He crouched in

the water and lowered the trap to the bottom, drawing out the chain with its ring at the end. By now he was bent like a bow, half his beard immersed. The water smelled icy and clean.

He pushed the pin pole through the ring on the chain. Then he grasped the pole with both hands and began to twist it into the marly bottom. He leaned and pushed and twisted with his great right hand bloodless-white around the pole. If the trapped beaver didn't gnaw his paw off and escape—if he died as he should, by drowning—the pole would site his carcass.

In order to leave as little man-scent as possible, Ironhand worked obliquely backward toward the bank, to a willowy branch he'd already selected for its pronounced droop. He unstoppered his horn of medicine, which he compounded from secret ingredients added to the musky secretions of beaver glands, and with this he coated the end of the drooping branch. The strongly scented end of the branch hung near the pin pole.

Hands on his hips, he inspected his work. Though by now his teeth were chattering—the spring warmth was leaching from the plum-colored shadows—he was satisfied. Felt better than he had in a long spell. One more trap to place, then he'd have his supper, and a pipe.

He was turning to move on to the next location when the rifle shot rang out. The bullet hit him high in the back. Toppling, he thought not of the awful hot pain but instead of his failure to hear the rifleman stealing up for the cowardly ambush. *Careless damn fool! Should've kept your eyes skinned!* He was reasonably sure of his attacker's identity, but that wasn't much damn satisfaction as the muddy bank hurled up to strike him.

And that was all there was.

*    *    *

Someone had dragged him to level ground.

Someone had rolled him on his back.

Someone had built a fire whose comforting heat played along the left side of his seamed face, and the back of his ruined hand. The fire was vivid, shooting off sparks as brilliant as the mountain stars. A curtain of smoke blew away on a puff of breeze.

He elbowed himself to a raised position, clenching his teeth against the pain. The Samaritan was squatting on the other side of the fire. A young Indian, with a well-sculpted nose, firm mouth, light brown skin that shimmered bronze in the firelight. His glowing dark eyes were not unfriendly, only carefully, unemotionally observant.

Bluish-black hair hung like a veil down his back, to his waist. His costume consisted of moccasins ornamented with porcupine quills and bright trade beads, fringed leggings, a hunting coat of elk leather. Around his neck hung a small medicine bag that nestled inside his coat against his bare chest. Outside the coat, ornamentation was a three-strand necklace of bear claws. A double-barrel rifle rested within his reach.

"I put medicine on you. The ball is still there. It must come out. Do you understand?"

"Delaware," Ironhand grunted, not as a question. He understood perfectly.

"Yes." The Indian nodded. "I am Manitow."

"My pardner, the one they killed at the rendezvous two year ago, he was Delaware. Named after the great old chief Tammany. Fine man." So were most of the members of the tribe who roved the Stony Mountains. The Delaware had been driven from Eastern hunting grounds eighty to ninety years ago; had migrated over the Mississippi and successfully taken up farming on the plains. A few, more restless and independent, had pushed farther on to the mountains. Enemies of the Delaware, including ignorant whites, sneered at them as Petticoat Indians. That was not only stupid but dangerous. Ironhand knew the Delaware to be keen shots, excellent horsemen, superb trackers and readers of sign. They were honest, quick to learn, resourceful in the wilderness. You could depend on them unless for some reason they hated you.

The Delaware could find the remotest beaver streams as handily as a magnet snapped bits of iron to itself. Thus they were prized pardners of the free trappers, or prized employees of the outfits such as Four Flags.

The white man licked his dry lips, then said, "I'm called Old Ironhand."

"I have heard of you. Who shot you?"

"I think it was the Frenchman, *Petit Josep. Petit Josep Clair de Lune.* Little Joe Moonlight."

"Works for Jaggers."

"I worked for Jaggers . . ."

"I know that. Don't talk anymore. The ball must come out." In a calm, almost stately way, Manitow rose from his crouch. His hair shimmered, black as the seepage of one of the oil springs that produced the tar trappers like Ironhand rubbed on their arthritic joints.

Without being told, Ironhand rolled over to his belly. It hurt hellishly. In the firelight a long rustfree knife sparkled in Manitow's hand; an authentic Green River—Ironhand glimpsed the GR, *George Rex,* stamped into the blade in England. It was a knife as good as Ironhand's own, which he'd left with his possibles bag, his bale of plews, and his carbine, in what he'd presumed was a safe clearing upstream.

Manitow laid the knife on the ground. From a pocket in his coat he took the all-purpose awl most Delaware carried. He placed this beside the knife. One or the other, or maybe both, would mine for lead in Ironhand's back. The trapper stared at the implements with bleary eyes and made a heavy swallowing sound.

Manitow knelt beside him. With a gentle touch he lifted Ironhand's bloody shirt high enough to expose the wound glistening with smelly salve. With the fingers of his left hand Manitow spread the dark brown edges of the wound. A swift, sharp inhale from Ironhand was the only sound.

"Be sure you get it out," he said. "I don't want to go down with the sun. That bastard Jaggers has to pay. Little Joe Moonlight will pay. Go ahead, dig."

"I don't have whiskey," Manitow said.

"I don't need any whiskey," Ironhand said. "Dig."

A night bird trilled in the darkness. Old Ironhand listened drowsily. He was coming awake; hadn't died under Manitow's ministrations, which had hurt infernally. He had, however, fainted at the moment the Indian worked the rifle ball out of the wound with bloody fingers, ending the ordeal.

Ironhand's eyes fluttered open. Against a morning sky the color of lemons, Manitow crouched by the fire as he had the night before; a small dented pot, blue enamelware, sat in the embers.

A white mist floated on the high peaks. The air nipped; Manitow had found a colorful trade blanket as a coverlet for the trapper. Ironhand heard a nickering; tried to rise up.

"Your horses are safe, with mine," Manitow said. "Your gun and plews also." Small comfort, now that Ironhand realized the outfit was still after him.

Manitow stretched out his hand, offering a strip of *charqui*, the smoked buffalo meat that was a staple of frontiersmen. The trapper caught the meat between his teeth. He lay back, gazing at the sky, and chewed.

The enamel pot lid clinked when Manitow lifted it. "Coffee is boiling. Ready soon."

Ironhand grunted and kept chewing. A hawk sailed in heaven, then plunged and vanished in the mists. The cold ground smelled of damp and made him think of death, not springtime. On his back under his shirt, where the Indian had prospected for lead, a thick pad of some kind told him Manitow had improvised a dressing.

"You have been a trapper for many years," the Indian said in a reflective way.

Old Ironhand pushed the jerky into his cheek, like a cud, while he answered. "Twenty years next summer."

"All that time. And a man stalks you and you don't see any sign?"

"I wasn't looking for none."

"You didn't hear him?"

His anger was sudden, overriding his pain. "I was in the stream. It makes noise. I was thinking about my traps. I thought the outfit was done with me. Christ, they did me enough damage—why not?"

Manitow's grunt seemed to scorn that naive conclusion. The damn Indian made Ironhand uneasy with his quiet, unruffled manner. His air of wisdom annoyed and puzzled the trapper, because of Manitow's relative youth.

"Done with you?" Manitow repeated. "Not when the fur trade is sickly and you steal profits from the company by working for yourself and selling to others."

"You sure"—a gasp of pain punctuated the sentence—"seem to know a devil of a lot about me. How come?"

Ironhand's head was rolled to the side now; his old reddened eyes stared. Almost shyly, Manitow dropped his own gaze to the smoldering fire, from which he pulled the dented pot. He poured steaming coffee into Ironhand's own drinking cup.

"Help me sit up. Then answer my damn question."

There followed a slow and elaborate ritual of raising him, Manitow gently pulling on his forearms rather than pushing at his back. Resting on his elbows worsened Ironhand's pain again, but his position enabled him to suck some of the bitter hot coffee out of the cup Manitow held to his lips. At length the Indian said, "The people in the Stony Mountains know Old Ironhand. They know the evil ways of Four Flags, too. For five winters and summers I have been north, Canada, hunting and trapping. Even so far away, we heard of the crimes of Four Flags. No more talk. Rest awhile now."

"I've got to go," the trapper protested, wriggling on his elbows and accidentally falling back, a terrific jolt that made him cry out. "Got to go," he repeated in a hoarse voice. "Catch that Little Joe . . ."

"In a day or two. No sooner."

The Indian's flat declaration angered the trapper again. Then a bolt of guilt struck him; he was being an ungrateful bastard. After licking a drop of coffee from his droopy mustache, he said, "I didn't thank you proper yet. For taking care of my wound and all. For coming along when you did. That was a piece of luck."

Manitow silently watched the ethereal mist drifting over the hidden peaks.

"Anyway—it's a debt I owe."

Manitow's eyes, black and opaque, met his again.

"I am sorry I did not come in time to stop the assassin. Fortunately he was a bad shot."

"Little Joe has a big opinion of himself. I 'spect he thought he couldn't miss."

"And I was coming close, so he couldn't wait to find out. I was not far behind him, though approaching from a different direction. That's why I didn't see his sign, only heard his rifle. Until then I did not know there were two hunting you."

Confusion was followed by a stab of fear. "Two? Who else . . . ?"

Manitow stared.

"You? Why?"

"To see what kind of man you were. Are. I hold you responsible."

"For what?"

"The death of my brother. The one who was your pardner."

*Ah, Christ, Christ,* Ironhand cried silently, stunned harder than he was when the rifle ball struck him. *He's no friend. He saved me for the pleasure of killing me himself.*

But there was no apparent hostility in the Indian's speech or demeanor. He merely asked the trapper to give him a brief history of the quarrel that had led to his brother's death, and the cowardly attack by the lackey of Four Flags.

"I'd have to go back a few years," Old Ironhand said. "The summer rendezvous of '28. I had quit as a brigade leader for the outfit a year before, but on good terms with Jaggers—we had an agreement that Four Flags would take all my plews and I'd work for no other." Four Flags was a fur company as big and powerful as Astor's. English, French, Russian, and American interests had pooled money to estab-

lish it. The boss west of St. Louis was Alexander
Jaggers, who headquartered at Kirk's Fort.

The annual summer rendezvous was a combination trade mart and revel, a great gathering where
spring plews were sold, and trappers bought new
equipment pack-trained out from St. Louis, all in the
midst of much drinking and horse racing and woman
swapping and other familiar entertainments of the
frontier. Manitow said that before he went to Canada
he had come down from the Wind Rivers several
times, to the barren and unlovely Upper Valley of the
Green, there to take part in the rendezvous himself.
Ironhand didn't remember meeting him, or hearing
his name.

Speaking slowly, taking occasional sips of the cool-
ing coffee, the trapper explained that it was at the
summer rendezvous of '28 that he saw his first black
silk topper. A disreputable German merchant of
traps, cutlery, and other metalware was wearing it.
The hat was already hard-used, soiled by filthy
stains, and pierced by a bullet front and back. Ironhand had quickly understood it was the enemy when
the peddler said, "These they are wearing on the
Continent now. Gents in the East are taking up the
fashion. It's the modern style, beaver hats will go
out, you mark me. Also my cousin in Köln writes
me to say inventors are perfecting machines to manu-
facture fine felting cheaply from all kinds of materials, even paper. This trade will die. Is dying now."

The following two years confirmed it. In the great
days, the high days of the trade, when Ironhand was
still a brigade leader, the company paid as much as
$9 a plew to certain free trappers to keep them work-
ing exclusively for Four Flags. By 1830 all was
changed; average plews selling for $4 at St. Louis
slipped to $3.75, no matter who trapped the animals.

Then buyers at the summer rendezvous refused to go above $3.50. Ironhand was haunted by memories of the silk topper.

Alexander Jaggers was a short, prim Scot; a Glaswegian. A bachelor, his two passions were Four Flags and his religion. When he first came out to Kirk's Fort in 1822, he had transported a compact gleaming Philadelphia-made pump organ on which he played and sang Christian hymns in a stentorian voice.

In 1831 Jaggers spoke to Ironhand about the price of plews. They were still dropping. Every free trapper working for Four Flags would have to accept $3, St. Louis, or further business was impossible. Ironhand refused.

Alexander Jaggers showed no visible anger, merely turned his back, swished up his coattails, sat at the organ, and began to play and sing "Saviour, Like a Shepherd Lead Us." But to bring Ironhand in line, discipline him, show him his error, Jaggers's henchman, Little Joe Moonlight, set on Ironhand's pardner at the summer rendezvous.

Little Joe, a mustachioed weasel-chinned fellow, turned up with a couple of the bravos who frequently backed his most brutal plays. They cornered Ironhand's pardner while the trapper was occupied with a comely Snake woman, the Snake women being universally conceded as the most attractive, and the most generous with their favors, of all the women of the many tribes.

Little Joe and his cronies pretended they were merely sporting with Tammany, hazing him, before the accident happened. As Ironhand learned afterward, Little Joe and his bravos seized the Indian's wrist and swung him round and round in circles, cracking his arm like a whip. Tammany tried to fight them but the odds were wrong; he was soon reeling.

One of the bravos knocked the bung from a small whiskey keg and poured the contents over the Delaware. The bravos and Little Joe roared. But they swore ever afterward that the dousing was supposed to be the end of it. How the stray ember from a nearby cook fire accidentally fell on Tammany, igniting the spirits, was a mystery. Damn shame, but a mystery. Little Joe and his bravos fled the rendezvous before Ironhand could catch up to them. Ironhand's pardner lived a day and a night, in broiled black agony, before the mercy of death.

Ironhand, who at the time went by his old name, left the encampment at once. He rode night and day for Kirk's Fort, there to confront Alexander Jaggers, who never personally went to the rendezvous. Little Joe Moonlight had beaten Ironhand to the fort and was hovering in Jaggers's quarters when Ironhand, full of drink, kicked the door down and leaped on the Scot to strangle him.

"Little Joe whistled up his bravos," Ironhand said to Manitow. "They swarmed on me. Looking pious as a deacon, Mr. Jaggers said that in a spirit of Christian forgiveness, Little Joe would only break the hand I used least."

He held up the twisted crooked fingers; Manitow had removed the dirty mitten while he slept.

The misshapen claw was sufficient to suggest the scene: Little Joe's helpers knocking Ironhand to the floor, stomping him into a stupor. Little Joe slapping Ironhand's outstretched arm over a table while the bravos held fast to the groggy trapper's shoulders; the bravos had flung him to a kneeling position.

Gleefully, Little Joe raised a trade hatchet and smashed the blunt end of the blade on the outstretched hand. At the organ, his back turned to the mayhem, Mr. Jaggers pumped and sang:

> *We've a story to tell to the nations*
> *That shall turn their hearts to the right!*
> *A story of truth and mercy!*
> *A story of peace and light!*

Little Joe Moonlight grasped Ironhand's index finger, bent it, and broke it. Then he broke the middle finger. Next the ring finger. After a few more blows with the now-bloody hatchet, he broke the little finger. To Ironhand's everlasting disgust, when Little Joe bent the thumb backward and that snapped, he screamed. More than once. Sweaty-cheeked, Mr. Jaggers pumped faster, and sang to drown the noise:

> *We've a song to be sung to the nations*
> *That shall lift their hearts to the Lord!*
> *A song that shall conquer evil*
> *And shatter the spear and sword!*
> *For the darkness shall turn to dawning . . .*

He remembered his hand lying on the table like a bloody red piece of buffalo hump. He remembered starting to swoon.

> *And the dawning to noonday bright!*
> *And Christ's great kingdom shall come on earth,*
> *The kingdom of Love and Light!*

Then Ironhand heard Little Joe, his voice very distant, as though he were shouting in a windy cave. "You don't need to play no more, Mr. Jaggers, he's all done screaming."

Little Joe lifted his head by the hair and let it fall, *thump* . . .

Out of some perverse piety that governed him, Mr. Jaggers rushed Ironhand to a comfortable bunk in the fort barracks, and saw to it that he was given excellent treatment until he recovered his senses.

His hand, of course, was permanently maimed. This Mr. Jaggers totally ignored when he and Ironhand parted. Jaggers shook the trapper's right hand— the left was already concealed by the first of many mittens. "The account book is closed, laddie." It was not, but Ironhand was too enraged to do anything except glare. "We part as competitors, but eternal friends. Christ counsels forgiveness above all."

"Forgiveness," Ironhand muttered, waving his mitten in an obvious way. Mr. Jaggers merely beamed and pumped the other hand . . .

"That was two years back," Ironhand explained to Manitow in a weary voice. "After awhile I came to believe his crazy cant about forgiving and forgetting. I wanted to mend my life, so I didn't take after him as I could have. I sold my plews to Astor, though they say he's tired of falling prices too and will get out. . . . What a fool I was, wouldn't you say? Trying to get on with keeping alive, forgetting Jaggers?"

The spring sun had burned off the spectral mist; the snow peaks were brilliant against hazy lavender sky. Ironhand was exhausted from speaking. Manitow chewed on a strip of *charqui* and considered what he'd heard. At last he said, "Many traps are set in this wilderness. You were caught in the cruelest of all. Trust."

*And do I dare trust you, you ring-tailed savage? Not so far's as I could throw you. I daren't turn my back.*

Still, there were necessities.

"Will you help me up? I have to pee."

"Clasp my arm with both hands."

Ironhand braced his boot heels and was slowly, painfully raised to standing position. His eyes were close to Manitow's a moment but he could read nothing there, except what he imagined was there—an intent to murder. The trap of trust, was it? Well, not a second time . . .

As he hobbled toward a grove of white birch trees, he bit out, "This time I won't turn my cheek. I'm going after that pissant who does the dirty work for Jaggers."

"I will go with you."

Ironhand twisted around, causing a hell-hot pain in his bandaged back. "Why? So's you can pass judgment?"

His face a smooth bronze mask, Manitow said, "It may be so."

*I won't turn my back, you red devil . . .*

But he hobbled on, grasping Manitow's arm for support; for the present he was at the mercy of the unavoidable necessities.

They rode southeast, the direction of Kirk's Fort. The fort stood sixty miles beyond the foothills of the Stony Mountains, at the confluence of two shallow muddy streams. It was the jumping-off place for St. Louis. Ironhand presumed it was also the destination of the quarry whose sign they were following. He was in constant pain, but it was bearable. Hate was a stronger painkiller than opium.

He trailed his three pack mules behind his old roan. Manitow could have sped ahead because he had a better horse, which he rode with only a scrap of blanket and his moccasined heels. The Indian's horse was small, with spots like swollen inkblots on his white rump. The trapper enviously compared his

faithful but sorry saddle animal, Brownie, with the
other horse, which the Cayuse tribe had bred and
sold to the Indian. Cayuse and Nez Perce horses
were the best a man could find. Ironhand had evidence of it the first morning. He woke in his odorous
blankets to find Manitow gone. A distant drumming
stilled sudden alarm. Somewhere in the foothills Manitow was galloping his spotted horse.

Another thing bred envy, in the same dark inner
place as Ironhand's suspicion of murder being
planned: Manitow's skill with sign. The second noon,
examining horse dung, Ironhand said, "He's near a
day in front of us."

Manitow shook his head. "Less than half a day.
Moving slowly. Not fearful he will be caught."

Ironhand's cheeks turned red above his beard that
still held crumbs of ship's biscuit from breakfast.
"Why 'n hell not? He knows he didn't put me down
for good."

"That may be so, it may not. I will show you why
he doesn't worry." Manitow led him to a clump of
stunted shrubbery, stepped around it, pointed. Ironhand saw more droppings. "There are three now.
Your assassin and two more."

"Since when in hell—?"

"Sunset, yesterday."

"You damn well should've told me."

Manitow smiled. "It would have spoiled our supper. If I had told you then, would you have stopped
this chase?"

"Not likely."

The Indian bobbed his head, vindicated.

They talked intermittently as they tracked Little Joe
Moonlight and his companions moving southeast
ahead of them. Manitow expressed no surprise at the
treatment the trapper had received from Four Flags.

"Theft, ambush, murder—it is the way of the strong companies against the single weak rebel. It is the way of those white men who are evil."

Which should have soothed Ironhand's suspicion a little, since it was clear from Manitow's voice and expression which side he favored. But Ironhand wasn't soothed. He continued to insist that Manitow ride ahead of him; they had sorted that out before they started. Ironhand still believed Manitow would try to murder him at the first opportunity.

They exchanged stories of their trials in the wilderness. Manitow pushed up the sleeve of his hunting coat to reveal a snakelike scar on his left forearm. Ironhand, who had seen plenty of horrors in his time, was nevertheless a little sick at the sight of the healed tissue, because of what had made it. Manitow had survived the bites of a rabid wolf, in the land of the Apaches, far south. He didn't explain why he had been in the land of the Apaches.

Ironhand told of nearly starving to death several times during his career. "I slew my mules and drank their blood once. I ate my moccasins twice. Another time, all I could find to feed on after five days were ants from an anthill." Manitow seemed to find these exploits unremarkable; almost to be expected.

He did express admiration for Ironhand's carbine. The trapper explained that it was a custom creation from the armory of the legendary Wyatt Henry of St. Louis. The revolving magazine, Henry's unique design, held five rounds.

Manitow asked to handle the piece. Ironhand said no. Manitow looked at him, and seemed to sneer just before he trotted his spotted horse ahead again.

As the mountains fell behind, the twisted gullies straightened; the shale ridges sank; the spring prairie rose up to greet them. They saw a migratory herd of buffalo passing southward in a dust cloud that boiled nearly to the apex of the sky. "Thousands upon thousands of shaggy brothers," Manitow said. Ironhand growled something under his breath; he already knew the herd was huge; they had been watching it the best part of an hour. The upstart savage was beginning to anger as well as worry him.

Or was it the sign they'd read—two unknown bravos and a third smug killer lolling their way toward Kirk's Fort without concern? Manitow insisted the trio was only a couple of hours ahead now.

A sunlit dust seemed to float above the silent plain surrounding them. The sky was tawny, like the earth, only a few cottonwoods with twisted shapes breaking the horizon. The vista had the serene quality of a landscape painting, but the diffuse light and dust gave it a touch of the unreal, like a picture from one of those fables of old Greek gods Ironhand dimly remembered reading from a hornbook when he was a child, in a civilized place somewhere.

At sunset they stopped to camp and eat. The trapper took some kindling from a parfleche strapped to a mule. Manitow watched him build a small pyramid of sticks, then said, "If you cook they will see the smoke."

"Hardly matters, does it? We'll find each other one way or another. That's the idea."

Late next day they approached a wide turgid stream Ironhand identified as Paint River, though the only artist's color represented in its flow was dirty brown. Natural features surrounding Kirk's Fort had been named by the fur men passing through.

While they watered and rested their animals, Ironhand advised the Indian that one more day would bring them to the headquarters of Four Flags. "I have to speed. Leave the mules. Catch them before they're safe inside the fort."

"Even with three against you?"

Ironhand answered with a nod.

Manitow sighted ahead. "I will go on a little way."

He didn't ask permission, hitting his spotted horse with his heels and splashing on across Paint River. Ironhand hunkered down on the long narrow hump of an island in the middle of the water, where they'd pulled up. What the hell was the upstart savage about?

Manitow galloped away till he was a speck, then galloped back. He threw himself off his spotted horse, looking unhappy.

"One has gone on ahead, leaving two. Their tracks turn north. I think they saw the smoke and are circling back."

Ironhand's gaze crawled to stunted trees on the northern horizon. Nothing moved there, nor anyplace. Manitow said, "We should camp. I do not think you need to chase your enemy anymore. He will find you. He knows you are hurt. But he will think you are alone."

Ironhand scowled, gripping his Henry rifle with his powerful right hand. "I am. Isn't your fight."

"I am here, so it will be. There is no reason not to cook again. Have you any sticks left in the saddlebag?"

Ironhand slept badly, rolling around with his carbine clutched against his middle, the way he'd slept with it nightly since he met the prowling Indian. A new moon shed pale light on the plain, which was flat for miles in every direction save north, where a pronounced tilt raised the horizon. Along that horizon the crooked trees stood out. If there were a fight on this barren hump of island, would he have to look out for Manitow and Little Joe Moonlight at the same time? A threat of death from two directions?

He wished he could sleep but it was impossible. Manitow lay to his left, hands crossed on his shirt bosom, profile sharp in the pale moonshine. The Indian breathed softly, steadily, like a small boy sleeping without care.

He must have dozed. He woke to Manitow barking his name. Ironhand floundered to his knees, saw Manitow standing beyond the mules and pointing to the stunted trees. Two riders were pounding down the inclined plain, riding with their knees and reins in their teeth. Each held a brace of revolvers. Four guns against his one.

"Protect yourself," Manitow cried, diving under the belly of a snorting, bucking mule. Seizing Ironhand, he tried to throw him to the ground. Little Joe Moonlight and his burly pardner were riding hellbent for the hump island, but Ironhand refused to cower. He shook off the Indian and took his fighting stance with his carbine at his shoulder. His blood was up; he didn't care that he presented a perfect target.

The riders were closer. He distinctly saw Little Joe's mean white triangular face, his long Chinese-style mustaches, his leering smirk. Still short of the river bank, Little Joe and his pardner opened up with all four barrels. Ironhand stood his ground and squeezed his trigger. Manitow tackled him. Yelling, Ironhand toppled. Only the fall prevented one of the flying bullets from finding him.

He didn't realize this; all his anger was directed against the damned Indian. He screamed oaths, trying to get up as Little Joe Moonlight galloped into the stream, closely followed by his henchman. Manitow snatched his double-barrel rifle from its saddle loop. The blued metal flashed.

The charging horses tossed up fans of moonlit water. Little Joe passed to the left of Ironhand and the Indian, the henchman to the right. They were firing continuously. One of their bullets hit Manitow's rifle, a lucky shot that blew apart the breech. Manitow leaped back, momentarily blinded. A bullet hit Ironhand's left thigh just as he stood up. With a cry he fell a second time. The back of his head struck the earth. Stars danced.

The mules bucked and bellowed. Two of them tore their picket pins out and ran into the stream, braying. Ironhand heard the attackers splash to the bank of Paint River behind him and there wheel for another charge. His back wound, cruelly bruised by his fall, hurt nearly as much as the thigh wound bleeding into the leg of his hide trousers. He had to get up . . . *had* to. Tried it and, with a howl of despair and fury, fell back again. He heard the attacking horses coming on, in the river.

Standing over the wounded trapper, Manitow said, "Give me the rifle."

*He'll use it to kill me . . .*

"The rifle!"

*Don't dare, I can't trust . . .*

"White man, if you don't, we'll die."

There was a halo of hoof-driven dust around Manitow's head. He looked like some ghost of one of his primitive ancestors. His outstretched brown hand opened, demanding. "White man—*obey me!*"

The hooves were thunderous. Risking all, the supreme act of trust, Ironhand flung the carbine upward and Manitow snatched it and put it to his shoulder. Bullets were flying again but Manitow stood firm and fired and kept firing. As the horse of

Little Joe's henchman passed within Ironhand's field of vision, the trapper saw the nameless bravo lift in his saddle as if being jerked to heaven. The bravo's horse ran out from under him and he crashed and rolled into the brown water, staining it with blood from his open belly.

Ironhand was shouting without realizing it. "Stop firing, there are only five—"

Too late; some part of his brain had already counted five shots. Manitow had exhausted the magazine in one volley.

And Little Joe Moonlight, his long thin mustaches whipping against his cheeks, was unhurt.

He wheeled his horse in the water, making him dance to the island, then stand still while Little Joe raised his revolver with his shooting hand, clasped it with his other hand and pointed it at Manitow's head at close range.

It all happened quickly. Ironhand acted from instinct, coming upright, dizzy and tortured by pain but willing it not to matter. He leaped at Little Joe Moonlight and his prancing horse. Little Joe was angrily heeling the animal while trying to steady himself for the shot. Manitow crouched and pulled his knife to throw it but Little Joe would fire first. There was no cover to keep the Indian from death.

The horse sidestepped again; Little Joe screamed a filthy oath. He realized too late that his mount had sidestepped *toward* Ironhand. . . .

Ironhand's face contorted into a bestial parody of a grin. His filthy mitten closed on Little Joe's right arm. Little Joe understood his peril and shrieked girlishly. Ironhand brought his huge right hand upward from his hip at great speed while pulling his enemy out of the saddle. The angle was right; the edge of the trapper's hand struck Little Joe's windpipe with speed and force.

Paralyzed, Little Joe dropped his revolver. Two streams of blood spurted from his nostrils. Ironhand threw Little Joe on the sere ground and knelt on his chest with one knee. He snatched his knife from the thong at his waist. Poised to cut Little Joe's throat, Ironhand started at a touch on his shoulder.

"Wait. Look at him. His spirit is gone. It flew before he touched the earth."

Ironhand changed position so that he could press an ear to his enemy's chest. He hunched that way for a long space, then raised his head, starting to shake from shock. Manitow was right again. The heart of Little Joe Moonlight had stopped.

Ironhand lurched up. His wounded leg would barely support him. His back was screaming with pain. He poked his knife at the thong loop on his belt and missed. He missed a second time. Manitow took the knife from him and put it in place, giving the thong an extra twist to secure the hilt.

Ironhand raked a trembling hand through his dirty beard. "I—didn't want to give you the rifle."

"Why?"

"I knew you'd kill me after you saved yourself."

"Why?"

"Your brother—"

"The white man's mind," Manitow said with enormous disgust. "Don't you think I had a hundred opportunities to kill you before this?"

"But you said I was responsible—"

"That was before I met you. I wanted to learn what sort you are. I learned. You learned nothing, you were full of poison bile of fear. You're like all the rest of the whites, even though not as bad as some.

It's lucky you broke down and gave me the rifle or
the story would end differently."

He stepped forward suddenly—it seemed menac-
ing until Ironhand realized the true import. Then he
felt a fool. Manitow supported his back and forearm
gently. "Now you had better lie down before you fall
down, white man." He no longer sounded scornful.

Stiff and sore in heavy bandages, Ironhand rode
alone up the dirt track to the gate of Kirk's Fort.
Draped in a U over the neck of his horse Brownie
was the smelly corpse of Little Joe Moonlight.

Kirk's Fort was old and famous on the plains. It
was a large rectangular stockade with a blockhouse
at every corner. Cabins and warehouse buildings
formed two of its walls. Ironhand passed through the
palisade by the main gate, which opened on a long
dirt corridor of sheds and shops. A second inner gate
led to the quadrangle, where Indians were never admitted; all trading was done in the corridor, though
even here there were precautions. Bars on the shop
windows; iron shutters on the windows of the store-
house that held trade goods.

A toothless fort Indian sat against the wall, looking
sadly displaced in a white man's knitted cap and a
white soldier's discarded blouse. He popped his eyes
at Ironhand, whom he recognized. The trapper rode
on through the second gate and straight across the
trampled soil of the quadrangle to the Four Flags
headquarters building. Company employees appeared around corners or from doorways of the ac-
counting office, the strongbox room, the powder
house, staring at Ironhand in a bewildered way.
Someone called a greeting he didn't acknowledge.
No one stopped him as he kicked the office door
open and lumbered through, Little Joe's stiffening

body folded over his shoulder, his Henry carbine tucked under his arm.

Alexander Jaggers was occupied with familiar things: his quill, his account books. Seeing the looming figure, he exclaimed, "Ewing! Laddie—what's this? Ye dinna hae the courtesy to knock or announce yersel—"

He was stopped by Ironhand slipping the Henry onto the seat of a chair, then laying the body of Little Joe Moonlight on top of the wide wooden desk. It disarranged the account books and overturned the ink pot, which dripped its contents on the old floor.

"He met with an accident. It happens often in the mountains," Ironhand said with a meaningful look at the master of Four Flags.

Jaggers reddened, puffing out his cheeks. He darted a hand to a drawer of the desk but Ironhand was quicker. He leaped on the desk, over Little Joe's corpse, and pushed Jaggers, toppling him and his chair at the same time. Jaggers flailed, kicking his legs in the air and yelling decidedly unchristian oaths.

Ironhand jumped down and retrieved his Henry rifle from the chair. He took aim and emptied the revolving magazine, five rounds, into Mr. Jaggers's pump organ in the corner. After the roar of the volley, the organ exhaled once, loudly, like a man with pierced lungs gasping his last.

The trapper stepped to the pump organ and attacked its wood cabinet with his right hand. The hand beat and smashed like a hammer; a mace; a sledge. Thin veneers cracked and snapped. Jaggers was screaming and vainly trying to rise, but his fall had sprung some leg muscle, and each attempt was more futile than the last; he continued to wail on his back, heels in the air.

Ironhand locked his two hands together, the good

with the ruined, and brought this huge hammerhead of flesh and bone down on the frame of the organ, breaking it in two as if it were a man's spine.

Jaggers screamed misery and rage.

Ironhand picked up his Henry and walked out without a backward look.

The daylight was waning too soon. Sunset was many hours away. But the sky and the prairie were dark, and the air was damp. Away in the north, thunder was bumping.

The dew and damp produced a ground mist that congealed and spread rapidly. As Ironhand rode to the cottonwood grove two miles west of the fort, he craned around in his saddle—at no small cost in pain—and saw the corner blockhouses floating above murky gray mist-clouds, like ogres' castles in the sky in a fairytale.

When he reached the grove, Manitow woke up, scratched his back, stood, asked, "Where for you now?"

"Back to the mountains. Back to the beaver. It's the only trade I know. They aren't all wearing silk toppers in New York town yet, I wager."

Manitow paused before saying, "I know secret streams, Old Ironhand. Three or four, locked so far in the Stony Mountains you would never find them alone."

"Hmm. Well. Let's see. I'd like a pardner again. A free trapper needs a pardner. But I never paid your brother any sort of fee, like many do. We split what the plews brought in."

"That would be agreeable."

"If you think you can trust me not to cost you your life?" Ironhand asked, a sudden flash of sourness.

Manitow took it calmly, seriously. "The old Scot

will trouble you no more, I think. But can you trust me?"

Ironhand's wreck of a face seemed to relax. "We crossed that river awhile back."

Slowly, with graceful ceremonious moves, Manitow the Delaware drew from his waist his splendid long Green River knife. He held it out, handle first.

With equal ceremony, Ironhand took his equally fine knife from its thong. He held it out the same way. Among the men of the mountains, white and red, there was no more significant gesture of trust.

"Pardner."

"Pardner."

They exchanged knives. Manitow kissed the fingers of his right hand and raised them over his head in a mystical gesture. Ironhand laughed, deep and rumbling. They mounted up and rode away together into the storm.

## Afterword

The Western writer Karl May probably did more to promote the splendor and excitement of the West to non-Americans than anyone except Buffalo Bill Cody, king of the scouts, the arena show, and the dime novel. Yet not many fans of the genre, perhaps excluding specialist scholars, know of him.

Surely it is because Karl May was born in Saxony in 1842, wrote only in German, and visited America just once—four years before his death in 1912. By that time he had written seventy-four volumes, forty of them set in "the American Wild West."

May was decidedly an odd bird for this sort of missionary work. He knew about the West only through reading—some of which was done in prison. May was jailed four times in his early life, for assorted thefts and swindles. During his longest sentence, four years, he ran a prison library.

May's youth was hard. He was afflicted with spells of near-blindness. He came from what we would call a dysfunctional family. Of thirteen brothers and sisters, nine died.

When old enough, he entered a preparatory school for teachers. He was expelled for stealing. It didn't seem to teach him a lesson; other crimes—other incarcerations—followed.

But reading somehow turned him around, much as it turns around quite a few convict-writers. In 1875 Karl May published the first of his Westerns.

His white hero had different names in different stories: Old Surehand; Old Firehand; Old Shatterhand. He was a *Westmänner* (Westman)—not a native frontiersman but a strong, suave, cultured European who quickly adapted to the rigors and perils of the West by means of intelligence and physical strength. Old Shatterhand possessed a "mighty fist" useful for dispatch of villains. But he also carried firepower, in the form of a fantastic repeating rifle customcrafted by the "legendary" gunsmith, Mr. Henry of St. Louis. This *Henrystutzen* (Henry carbine) with its revolving chamber holding twenty-five rounds is not to be confused with the more familiar Henrys; there is no connection beyond the name.

Partnered with May's Surehand/Shatterhand character was a young Indian, first introduced to readers around 1892. Winnetou is a consistently brave and brainy Apache chief educated by a Christian tutor, hence receptive to the "civilized" ways of Europe, and the white man with whom he adventures.

The two heroes wandered all over the map of the

West, meeting again and again by remarkable coinci-
dence, and removing an untold number of malefac-
tors. In one historical quarterly, a scholar did a body
count of four representative May novels totaling 2,300
pages. The number of persons going to their rewards
was 2,012. They were dispatched by shooting, scalping,
knifing, drowning, poisoning—and sixty-one were
put down by the "mighty fist" previously cited.

May had a fair grasp of Western geography, except
in one respect. In addition to familiar settings of
mountains and deserts, he repeatedly used "an im-
penetrable cactus forest"—exact location unspecified.

May's works have been translated into many languages but seldom, if at all, into English. Yet they've
sold upwards of fifty million copies, and continue to
sell. You find long shelves of May in almost every
bookshop in Germany, just as you find long shelves
of L'Amour throughout the United States.[1]

At least thirty films have been made from May's
novels. An entire publishing house devoted to them
was founded in 1913. At summer encampments similar to those of American Civil War reenactors, mild-
mannered fans gather in costume to act out the exploits of their two heroes. Now doctoral dissertations
are being written about Karl May.

So it seemed fitting, and an enjoyable challenge, to
pay respects to him with a story about a couple of
Westerners who battle a decidedly rotten crew from

---

[1] A recent (2000) book about Hitler's early days in Vienna states
that Hitler was a lifelong May enthusiast (hardly a recommenda-
tion), even though May's West was, as the *New York Times* observed, "scarcely a hymn to the Aryan." Somehow May's writing
convinced the dictator that you didn't need to know the territory,
you just needed a good imagination—a notion that defeats of his
generals often proved wrong.

a fur trust. The story takes place in what May sometimes called the Stony Mountains.

I have used variations of the names of his two leading characters, and kept the marvelous repeating Henry (reduced to an arbitrary five shots). Those are the only resemblances. Ironhand is not a "blond Teutonic superman who speaks a dozen languages fluently and lards his conversations with little sermons about God and Christianity." Manitow is neither a chief nor an Apache. My intent was to create *un hommage* to an important figure in the literature of the West, not to write a pastiche of May's work, which I can't translate very well anyway with my rudimentary German. I wanted a story bathed in a diffuse pastel-colored mist, like a legend. A story not overly realistic. In short, the kind of Western story someone might have written from afar.

One other note: The hymn Mr. Jaggers sings is reverse anachronism; it was composed years after the period of the story. But in context, the lyrics proved irresistible.

# Mercy at Gettysburg

War came to our home in July of 18 and 63.

Our house and the remains of the smithy stood on the Hagerstown Road, southwest of the sleepy little town of Gettysburg, in the hills of Pennsylvania. General Bob Lee had invaded the North. It was a desperate throw of the dice for the Rebs, who were fighting for black bondage and something called secession, which at age eleven I didn't understand.

Rumors of great armies just over the horizon reached us almost daily during the last week of June. I am sure there was fear in every heart in Adams County. Except my father's.

On Tuesday, June 30, a terrified family passed by from the west, saying the Rebs were advancing behind them. My father, a huge, strong man hurt by his blindness, threw his cane aside and fumbled his rifle down from over the hearth.

"If they do come, Daniel, I'll kill a Reb for your brother," he said to me. "You will help."

He raised the rifle over his head and exulted. "God be praised."

My father and mother, Jenny, were Bible people. My mother lived by moral principles without any thought of the cost. Once, right after Pa's accident, when we had almost no money, a grocery clerk making change returned an extra dime. That dime would have bought a lot. My mother courteously pointed out the error and handed him the dime. My mother read the New Testament gospels mostly. For Pa, she read aloud those books that he preferred—the Old Testament, all full of holy anger and vengeance. I suppose he cherished them because of what happened to my older brother Toby, who marched away with General McClellan on the Peninsula and never came back. . . .

Sure enough, before noon on July 1, Reb horsemen came storming down upon us. Wil Sharp, who had the next farm west, galloped through, yelling that the Reb dust cloud was visible from his place.

"Help me, Daniel," my father exclaimed. "Carry my rifle, and set me up on the rail fence where I can shoot at them. You'll tell me when to fire."

"And they'll shoot back, and you'll both be dead," my mother said. My little sister Lisbeth covered her eyes and bawled. Mother told her to hush.

Pa wouldn't be put off. Leaning on my shoulder, he walked out of the house and I set him up with his elbows resting on the top rail and his rifle pointing down the pike. The July day was hot and humming with insects.

We waited perhaps ten minutes, Pa with his rifle, me with my heart thumping in my breast, certain I was enjoying my last summer on earth. Then a dust cloud rose above the next hill. My mouth was so dry I could barely croak.

"There they are."

"How close?"

"Other side of the ridge."

"God strengthen my arm and steady my hand." He could have put on a robe and grown his beard long and passed for one of those Old Testament prophets full of rage for justice. My brother had taken a Confederate ball in his vitals at some little Virginia creek, and then—I learned this later, when my mother thought I could bear hearing it—Reb scouts had outraged his body with bayonets. Or so his commanding officer wrote.

"I've got to kill at least one for Toby," Pa said as the tan cloud rolled down the hill like a cyclone. I remember his voice gentling then. "Scared?"

"Oh, Lord, yes, Pa." He must have believed me, since he didn't reprove me for speaking the Lord's name in an irreverent way. He found my head and ruffled my hair, then appeared to gaze down the road, squinting his pale blind eyes. Lightning had set fire to the smithy one spring night in '59. Pa rushed inside to save his tools and two horses he was shoeing, and a blazing beam fell on top of him, right across his eyes—one bright glory and then perpetual dark. If not for Ma tutoring the children of some families in town, we'd have starved.

I saw the horsemen then; I have always supposed they were mounted scouts on the right wing of Heth's division. Swords flashed like lightning inside the cloud. "I hear them," Pa cried, for their hoofbeats sounded like drums. He laughed loudly.

A moment later, the Reb riders veered north and swept away, behind our property, out of sight.

"They're gone," I said, thinking we were saved. I guided Pa back to the house, joyful that I might live another summer.

Ma tried to take the rifle from him. He was mad with disappointment and wouldn't let go. Lisbeth tugged at my sleeve.

"There's a sojer out back. I think he fell off his horse, he's all bloody."

Little fool, she didn't whisper softly enough. Pa heard. "What's that? A soldier?"

My mother seldom showed anger, but she gave Lisbeth an eyeful of it then. "Jenny," my father said, "take me to the soldier. This instant."

She was a dutiful wife, my mother. She led Pa out past the jumbled black timbers of the smithy. He walked with his shoulders back, steel and death in his blind eyes again. Mother walked with her head bowed. I was a ways behind, with Lisbeth hanging onto my waist and mewing in an annoying way.

Then we heard him. Not a loud cry, but heart-wrenching all the same. Like an animal holed up with a broken paw.

I saw him sprawled in the tall weeds at the ruined corner of the smithy, a soldier in Confederate butternut, all covered with dirt and blood. The bloodiest was his left leg, where someone had shot him. He must have lost his horse, right enough, and maybe in all the dust and noise no comrade had seen him fall. You could hear him breathing.

"Aim the muzzle for me, Jenny," Pa said, hoisting his rifle. "Aim at his head."

The Reb was dazed but awake; he saw what my father intended. He tried to thrash backward into the tall weeds, but he was too weak. His eyes fixed on my father. They were big brown eyes, almost girlish. I don't suppose he was eighteen yet.

"Damnation, woman, hurry up. I'm going to kill the bastard." Behind me, Lisbeth was gasping; she was little but she knew that when Pa stooped to bad language, the sky was falling.

"Jerusha Lamb, you can't," Mother said with a keen look at me, then one at Lisbeth, which was wasted. "I must take care of this boy, he's a Union boy. You can't see him but I can, he's wearing Union blue. He must have been chasing those others."

Bees were buzzing. Up toward the Chambersburg Pike, cannon began to bang away, a big battle. I thought I'd wash away, so much fearful sweat was rolling down inside my shirt.

"Woman—woman, if—if you—" Pa was shaking. He loved my mother too much to accuse her of lying. But he knew how to discover the truth:

"Lisbeth? Daughter?"

Lisbeth's eyes got huge with tears; she couldn't lie to Pa. Knowing I might go to hell for it, I put my hand over her mouth and clamped her to my side and said, "She went back to the house, Pa, she's a scairdy cat."

My father held still a minute, then put his head back and gazed at the unseen sun and cried out, "Toby . . . Toby."

He walked away into the weeds with his rifle, weeping; ashamed of being unmanned.

I never saw the Reb again. My mother insisted on tending him by herself, keeping him warm and well fed in a little lean-to she made from a blanket and sticks. In the morning he was gone.

"Oddest thing," my mother said to me then. "His last name was Tobin. Toby—Tobin—isn't that odd?"

The battle of Gettysburg ravaged the town and the land roundabout for three days. We mostly hid in the root cellar. After General Pickett's doomed charge, thousands of men and boys mowed down as they marched through an open field, right into the Union guns, General Bob Lee retreated south and never came back. Many said he lost the war that July in Pennsylvania.

My father died two years later, never having received the payment he thought he was owed.

In 18 and 66, my mother got a letter from a Leverett Tobin of Wytheville, Virginia. He had survived the war, married his sweetheart after the surrender, and recently opened a hardware store. He praised my mother's compassion that July day.

My mother gazed at the letter laid in her lap. Her face showed no joy; there isn't any in war, or memories of war.

"Daniel," she said, "I pray that when I come to judgment, God can forgive my untruths."

"Mine too, Mama. But I think He will." I put my hand over hers in a clumsy way. "Yes, I'm sure He will."

# Credits